Judy Nunn's career in has been a long and illustrious one. She is currently best known to television viewers in Australia and the UK as Ailsa Stewart in the internationally successful series 'Home and Away'. Much of her acting life has, however, been spent 'treading the boards' and she has played leading roles in countless stage plays, both in the English and the Australian theatre.

Judy began her writing career in television and radio, from there branching into children's literature. She is the author of a number of best-selling adventure novels for young people and is published in Australia and Europe. Her first venture into adult fiction was the best-selling novel *The Glitter Game* which is to be released in the UK in 1993. *Centre Stage* is her second novel and a third is due for publication in Australia, also in 1993.

Also by Judy Nunn in Pan

The Glitter Game

JUDY NUNN

CENTRE STAGE

PAN
AUSTRALIA

First published 1992 by Pan Macmillan Publishers Australia
a division of Pan Macmillan Australia Pty Limited
63-71 Balfour Street, Chippendale, Sydney

National Library of Australia
cataloguing-in-publication data:

Nunn, Judy.
Centre stage.

ISBN 0 330 27348 5.

I. Title.

A823.3

Typeset in 10½/12pt Plantin by Midland Typesetters, Maryborough.
Printed in Australia by The Book Printer

Thanks go to Captain Robert
Lawrence, MC, and Robyn Gurney
for their invaluable assistance
in researching this book.

For my husband Bruce Venables,
who never saw me play Hedda Gabler.

The Swan and the Globe and the Mermaid Tavern
All rang with the song of the golden age
And all the words in the world were woven
And roared into history from centre stage.

A poem by Harold Beauchamp
from *Beauchamp: A Life in the Theatre*
(Julian Oldfellow, 1999)

PROLOGUE

Lexie watched fascinated as the desk drawer slid silently open. He was transfixed as his brother carefully took out the revolver they were forbidden to touch. As Tim opened the cardboard box, removed six bullets and put them in the pocket of his denim shirt, Lexie thought, 'He's going to be in deep shit', but still he couldn't tear his eyes away.

It was Lexie's fascination which urged Tim on. It always did. Even though Tim felt the vast superiority of his ten years, and even though he considered the adventures he and Lexie shared to be of his own invention, it was inevitably his little brother who was the catalyst.

Lexie never got the blame. And it never

occurred to Tim to wonder why. By the time Tim had received the full measure of Lexie's admiration and approval, he'd forgotten that his deed had evolved from a veiled suggestion from Lexie and he was fully prepared to accept the responsibility.

Today was no exception. As they closed the back flywire door and set off for the woodshed, Tim could feel eight year old Lexie's eyes shining with love and respect.

'You're going to be in deep shit, Tim,' Lexie whispered. And Tim thought it was worth it.

The woodshed was down the back of the block next to the chicken coop. There was nothing but bush stretching to the river behind. To the right was a vacant block and the Delaneys to the left had taken their brood away for the school holidays.

It was one of those rare days when their father was off duty and one of those even rarer days when their parents had accepted an invitation which didn't include the kids. They were out on a riverboat cruise celebrating a friend's thirtieth birthday and wouldn't be back for at least three hours.

Tim had everything worked out. He even intended to fire the revolver into one of the big chaff bags of chicken feed to deaden the sound.

He carefully loaded a bullet into each of the six chambers. 'See,' he boasted as he snapped the cylinder closed, 'told you I knew how.'

Holding the revolver in both hands, he pressed the muzzle firmly against the chaff bag and, with both index fingers, he eased back the trigger.

There was a muffled crack, not unlike the sound his cap gun made, but Tim was far from disappointed. The weapon kicked thrillingly in his hand, the air was filled with the acrid smell of gunpowder and there was a neat hole in the chaff bag.

It had worked. Tim's heart was thumping with excitement and adrenalin pounded through his body, but he looked to Lexie for his ultimate reward. He wasn't disappointed.

'Wow!' Lexie breathed out a long, gentle sigh as he stared down at the chaff bag. He squatted beside it and tentatively poked at the hole. 'Wow!' he marvelled again.

'Want a go?'

His eyes as big as saucers, Lexie looked up at Tim and nodded.

'Use both hands,' Tim instructed. 'And ease the trigger back,' he said. 'Don't jerk it.'

Lexie did exactly as he was told. He pressed the revolver against the bag and, with both index fingers, he pulled on the trigger. It was harder than he thought. Far from 'easing' it back, Lexie had to muster every ounce of strength he had before he felt the trigger move at all. But finally it did and he too felt the power of the recoil as the gun kicked like a living thing in his hands. Lexie was overwhelmed. It was awesome! It was thrilling! To feel such power . . .

He stared down at the second hole and again knelt to examine it. Then he lifted the side of the bag to peer at the damage underneath.

'Watch it, Lexie,' his brother warned, taking the weapon from him. 'You've got to be careful with guns.'

Lexie wasn't listening. 'Look, it's gone right through the other side.' Chaff started to pour out of the hole. 'It's making a mess.'

'Doesn't matter. The feed bin needs filling. We'll empty the whole bag in when we've finished.' Tim grinned. 'Dad'll be pleased with us.'

But Lexie wasn't listening. He was thinking about the chicken he'd watched his father kill for Christmas dinner two months before. 'I wonder what it'd be like to shoot something real.'

'What do you mean?' Tim asked.

'Remember when Dad killed the chook?' Lexie did. He remembered vividly the suddenness of it all. One minute a squawking bird, then nothing but a carcass. Imagine having that power! He shivered at the thought.

'Kill one of the chooks? You're joking.'

Lexie stared back at Tim for several seconds. Then he shrugged. 'OK,' he said flatly, 'we'll stick to the feed bag'.

Tim wondered why the idea was so shocking to him. He'd seen his father kill several chickens over the years and it had meant nothing. With the exception of Ted the rooster and several layers, the rest of the brood was destined for the table anyway. They didn't even have pet names. No, it was the idea of killing one *himself* that was so shocking. Shocking enough to be thrilling.

'That hole in the chookyard where Ted got out isn't fixed up too good,' he said thoughtfully. He could feel Lexie's eyes on him again, the younger boy looked as if he was holding his breath. 'We could say they got out and we couldn't catch them all.'

Lexie nodded, still hardly daring to breathe.

'OK.' Tim made the decision. 'We'll shoot one of the chooks.'

'Agatha's bigger.'

It was a breathless suggestion and Tim wasn't sure if he'd heard correctly. 'Agatha? Kill Agatha?'

'She's bigger.' The bigger the victim the greater the power, calculated Lexie.

But the idea of slaughtering the pet goose they'd fed by hand was repugnant to Tim. 'We'll do one of the chooks, OK.' It was a command rather than a question.

'OK,' Lexie grudgingly agreed.

It took them ten minutes to catch the right bird. Lexie insisted on the fattest one.

'That'll make Dad even madder—she's just about ready for eating,' Tim grumbled, but he clasped the bird's wings against its back and told Lexie to latch the gate behind him. 'We better not forget to rip that hole in the fence,' he said as they returned to the woodshed.

Tim had decided that they should shoot the bird against the chaff bag. 'There'll be blood,' he said.

'Yes,' Lexie nodded. 'There'll be blood.'

Between them they dragged the feed bag to the corner of the shed and propped it up. Tim made sure he had the chicken firmly pinioned against it with one hand, then he gestured to Lexie.

'Give us the gun. Watch it,' he said as Lexie fumbled the exchange.

As Tim turned the gun upon the bird, he must have loosened the grip of his left hand. Or some instinct might have warned the bird of its fate. Whatever the cause, the chicken let out a demented shriek, twisted between Tim's fingers and had escaped out of the woodshed door in an instant.

Tim whirled to clutch it, there was an explosion,

a thump and then nothing but the squawking of the chicken as it headed for the river.

Lexie stared down at Tim. He was sprawled against the chaff bag, his fingers still curled around the gun. His head was flung back, his eyes were closed and his mouth was slightly open.

'Tim?' Lexie knelt beside his brother and examined him closely. He was still breathing and he appeared unmarked. Except for the powder burns and the bullet hole in the chest pocket of his denim shirt. Lexie wondered if it had gone right through the other side. Maybe even through the chaff bag as well and into the floor.

He leaned forward on his hands and knees and peered at Tim's mouth. His breathing had a funny rasping sound to it and Lexie wondered whether he was dying. But if he was dying, why wasn't there more blood?

Then he saw the pool of red seeping from beneath the chaff bag and he watched as it grew and grew until it became a bright red river channelling its way to the door. Yes, Tim's dying, he thought. And he stared at his brother with the utmost respect. It was Tim's ultimate feat and Lexie was lost in admiration.

He had no idea how long he knelt there. Tim's face grew whiter and the rasping turned to a gurgle. With each gurgle blood bubbled from his mouth. And still Lexie didn't move.

It was near the very end, when the gurgles were barely audible that he heard his father's voice. 'Tim! Lexie! You there, boys?'

Silence. Then the slap of the flywire door as it swung closed.

Not long after that the gurgles stopped. Tim's

face was white as white and everything about him was so wonderfully still that Lexie hardly dared move for fear he'd lose the moment. It had happened. Death. He savoured it for a full five minutes.

Then he rose to his feet. That was it. It was over. He crossed to the door, carefully avoiding the blood, and started up towards the house.

'Dad,' he called.

ACT I

1969–1971

ACT I

SCENE 1: 1969

As she crossed her legs she felt his eyes linger on the expanse of thigh exposed by her miniskirt. She had a horrible feeling she knew what he was thinking.

'You're very young,' he said.

Oh hell. She'd been right.

'I'm eighteen.' Maddy wasn't lying. People always took her to be around fifteen. Because she was blonde and petite she looked very young and delicate and she constantly had to show her driver's licence at hotels and discos.

Maddy had come to the conclusion that there were two basic categories of middle-aged men: the paternal sort with kids her age at home, and the lechers who lusted after schoolgirl flesh. The fact that a lot of the lechers also had kids her age at home had come as a shock to her. Despite the last hard, fast few months of growing up, her protective boarding school background had left her prone to disillusionment.

'I see that you only just scraped through your final exams.'

'Yes,' Maddy nodded, 'I wasn't happy in my last year at Loreto.' She tried to look contrite.

Jonathan Thomas wasn't watching. He cleared his throat and fixed his attention on the papers before him. Oh God, he thought, she saw me. He couldn't fail to notice Maddy's response to him. It was the same response he received from every teenage girl he was confronted with and, as one of the directors of the most prestigious drama school in the country, he was confronted with many teenage girls. They all thought he was a creep, he knew that.

He tried desperately to check his reactions but it was impossible. How could he fail to notice that glorious expanse of youthful flesh as the girl crossed her legs? And those firm, ripe breasts beneath the flimsy silk shirt? Without a bra, of course. His eyes were drawn to them like a magnet and try as he might to avoid them, he found it physically impossible not to flicker a glance now and then.

He meant no harm. He never touched the girls. God forbid, he'd be too frightened. Jonathan's sex life was non-existent. He wasn't a paedophile or a defiler of young women. At worst he was a lonely middle-aged fetishist who occasionally masturbated cleanly over the toilet bowl with a copy of *Dolly* magazine or *Teen Vogue* in his other hand.

It had, therefore, come as a terrible shock when

two years before he'd been suspended pending investigations into a claim from a seventeen year old student that he'd interfered with her.

Questioning revealed that many of his female students accused him of perving on them. Jonathan was shocked. He was sure they hadn't noticed.

Things were not looking good for Jonathan Thomas until it was discovered that the student who had claimed 'interference' worked three nights a week in an up-market brothel in Surry Hills. The investigation took a different turn and, shortly after, when it was also discovered that Jonathan had recommended she be dropped at the end of first year, he was reinstated.

But it had undermined what little confidence he possessed. He had lost standing with the other directors and members of the teaching staff and he now knew the students considered him to be a joke. Try as he might to concentrate on his work—and he was a good teacher—Jonathan was not a happy man.

He cleared his throat again and looked up from the desk, willing his eyes to go directly to Maddy's and not to linger over her breasts. He failed.

'And why do you feel you want to be an actress?' he asked.

A perve on the board of NADA, Maddy thought, a lecturer and director of the National Academy of Dramatic Art, no less! Tough as she'd tried to make herself over the past months, Maddy was deeply shocked. Oh well, she supposed they were in every walk of life, and she certainly didn't want to jeopardise her chances of getting into NADA.

She smiled and took a deep breath, which

Jonathan couldn't fail to notice. 'I've wanted to act since I was ten.'

Nobody took her seriously when Maddy made the announcement shortly after her tenth birthday. 'I'm going to be an actress. In the theatre.'

'Of course you are, darling.' Her mother was pleased. It was so beautifully normal. Every little girl who didn't want to be a ballet dancer wanted to be an actress.

'I'm going to act at the Theatre Royal,' Maddy declared. Her mother was a subscriber to the Elizabethan Theatre Trust seasons and Maddy had been to the Theatre Royal many times. 'And then I'm going to act in London.'

Helena smiled at her husband. 'I think we've got a star on our hands, Robert.'

Robert McLaughlan smiled back and returned to his paper. He was very fond of Maddy, just as he was very fond of Helena. They both conformed happily to the lifestyle he provided for them. Which couldn't have been too difficult—after all Robert was a generous provider.

The only son of Scottish immigrants, Robert had been the pride and joy of his hardworking parents: worth every penny they poured into his education.

Even as a child he had the uncanny ability to decide upon his course and apply himself to it with a tunnel vision amazing in one so young. It was therefore no surprise when Robert became one of the youngest orthodontists ever to set up practice in Sydney. Certainly it was no surprise to Robert; he'd planned on becoming an orthodontist since he was fourteen. There weren't too many of them around then and there was big money in dentistry, especially orthodontics.

Robert hadn't been wrong. Orthodontics had provided a harbourside home, the latest model Mercedes and most of the things that money could buy.

It was exactly the life that Helena's parents had wished for her and, indeed, that Helena had wished for herself. She'd merely switched harbourside homes, really: from Mummy and Daddy's to Robert's. And Daddy was an orthopaedic surgeon with consulting rooms two blocks from Robert's practice in Macquarie Street, so they had a lot in common.

Like her mother, Helena worked tirelessly for charities and was one of the most featured faces in the magazine society pages. Occasionally Robert would accompany her to the special race days, award nights or gala premieres but he was more than happy to contribute generously to the cause while she attended with a 'celebrity' escort.

The one issue in their marriage which could have become a bone of contention was fairly easily resolved. Helena's parents, being Protestants in name only, weren't too upset about Robert's insistence that any children be brought up strictly under the guidance of the Catholic Church. Robert didn't even insist that Helena convert, which was surprising, really, given his devout beliefs.

It was an exceedingly comfortable marriage and far from disrupting it, Maddy fitted in perfectly. She arrived on the due date at the convenient hour of four pm, Helena suffering only minimal discomfort during the birth. And when she was taken home from the hospital Maddy slept at the right times and cried only when Nanny was around to tend to her. In all, she was the perfect baby and grew into the petite, devastatingly pretty child Helena had always wanted.

Robert was content with his life and his 'two favourite girls', Helena was content with her social life and her good works, Maddy was content with her dolls, her secret harbourside cubby house and the fantasy world her parents didn't know about. So when did it all start to go wrong?

For Maddy it was when they sent her to boarding school. It wasn't the nuns, although there was one strict disciplinarian she could have done without. It wasn't the heavy-handed religious instruction which pervaded every waking hour at the convent. It wasn't her dormitory mates or fellow students. It was plainly and simply the lack of privacy.

At the age of twelve, having been left to invent and explore her endless realms of fantasy, Maddy was totally unprepared for the lack of space allowed her at the convent. And she rebelled. For five years she rebelled.

Finally, at seventeen, when she'd just managed to scrape through her final exams, she looked back on the whole ordeal and saw it as nothing but a blur. What a waste of five years, she thought, and decided then and there to make up for lost time.

'I want to go to drama school,' she announced to her father.

For once Robert was unforthcoming. Apart from their bewilderment at Maddy's low school marks, and the frustratingly repetitive report card comments—'could do better if she concentrated'—he and Helena were unaware of just how unhappy

Maddy had been at the convent. 'It's puberty, dear. She's restless,' Helena had said time and again and it seemed a satisfactory explanation.

Now, try as she might, Maddy couldn't get through to her father. He refused to discuss it. If she wanted to go to university and study something sensible like Law or Medicine, of course he was right behind her. Why not orthodontistry? With his help she'd be assured of a bright future there. But acting? The theatre? It was a foolish profession for which one certainly didn't need training.

'I don't mind if she dabbles in some amateur stuff for fun,' he confided to Helena. 'But it's ludicrous to treat this acting business as if it's a profession. Just a lot of silly people dressing up and making fools of themselves.'

Much as she loved the theatre, the opera, the ballet, the splendid opening nights and the glamour of it all, Helena didn't defend the performing arts. She liked to think of herself as a serene woman and she never made waves.

That was it. The die was cast: no drama school. So Maddy ran away to share a flat with two art students in Kings Cross.

The very expensive private detective Robert hired found her within a week but it didn't do any good. Maddy was adamant. She was going to make it on her own. She had enough money in her personal account to see her through for a while, she said. Then she was going to get a job and she was going to audition for NADA, she said. And then she was going to drama school the following year, and that was that.

'But what if you don't pass?' Robert asked as he squirmed uncomfortably in the beanbag. There wasn't a chair in sight and he was beginning to wish he'd opted for the camp bed in the corner.

'Then I'll keep auditioning till I do.'

'Your mother's very upset.' Robert looked around at the room which, although large, seemed unnecessarily cluttered. Posters covered every inch of wall space, a fringed shawl hung from the central lamp and beanbags and cushions were strewn about the floor.

A kitchenette arrangement of sink, stove and cupboards ran along one wall and two tattered bamboo screens stood at the far end of the room.

'Where do you sleep?' he asked.

'There.' Maddy pointed to the camp bed.

'And the others?'

'Behind the screens.'

Robert nodded. The room smelled of mould and he was beginning to feel a little queasy. 'I might just pop to the bathroom, dear,' he said. But the beanbag was a very sloppy one and the more he tried to get a purchase on the floor, the more horizontal he seemed to become.

'Do you want a hand?' Maddy offered, jumping out of her own beanbag.

'No. No, thank you. I'm fine.' Robert eventually had to roll over onto his stomach and struggle up from his hands and knees. He took a deep breath of the damp air before he could trust himself to speak. 'Where is it, dear?' he asked.

'Down the end of the hall and up one flight of stairs.'

He stared at her, aghast. 'You don't have a bathroom.'

'Of course not, Dad.' Maddy smiled condescendingly. 'It's called a flatette. Some of them

18

don't even have a proper kitchen set-up. We're lucky, we—'

'That's it, Maddy.' Robert couldn't take any more. 'You're coming with me right now.'

'I'm not, and you can't make me.'

Robert stared at his daughter. Where had he gone wrong?

'I'd only run away again.' Maddy's voice was gentler.

She had everything money could buy, he thought. A comfortable home where her friends were always welcome, successful parents she could be proud of—what more did the girl want?

'I'm seventeen, Dad, I'll be eighteen in a few months.' She took her father's hand. She knew what he was thinking and she felt sorry for him. 'I want to do things my own way. I'll be OK. Honest.'

Robert felt helpless. She was his daughter, there must be something he could do for her. But his hand felt trapped in hers and he wanted to leave. Prolonged physical contact always made him selfconscious.

'I'm going to write you a cheque,' he said, disengaging his hand to reach for his breast pocket.

'I'll only tear it up.'

Robert conceded the battle. Three months, he thought, as he climbed into his Mercedes, she'll last all of three months.

Robert was wrong. Maddy lasted much longer than three months.

One night Maddy came home four hours early from the Indian restaurant where she washed up three nights a week.

There'd been no bookings, the one family of

regulars had eaten and gone and Mrs Predan, the chef-owner, wasn't feeling well so she decided to close up for the night. 'Do not be worrying, my dear, I will not be docking your wages,' she'd said. She was a nice woman. 'Go home now.'

So Maddy had gone home, thankful that this was one Thursday night she wouldn't have to stand over the kitchen sink for an hour scrubbing the turmeric stains out of her fingernails.

What would she do, she wondered, as she fumbled for her front door key. She could give herself a facial; she had enough Clarins left for one more treatment. No, she decided, remembering her budget, she'd better save that for the NADA audition in six weeks.

She'd spent her entertainment allowance in one hit when she'd gone to the opening night of *Othello* at the Old Tote Theatre on Tuesday. The theatre should really be listed under study allowance, she thought, not entertainment. But then study allowance went on voice classes, books, plays and trade magazines.

It was times like this she regretted not having accepted her father's offer of a television set. No, bugger it, she told herself proudly as she pushed the door open, she'd made her statement and—

The room was filled with convulsive animal sounds. Maddy instantly broke into a cold sweat.

'Oh God, help me!' It was a tortured scream. It was Sal! Sal was having an epileptic fit or a heart attack or . . .

Maddy dropped her bag, raced to the bamboo screens and threw them aside.

Sal was naked, her head lolling over the side of the bed, her eyes rolling in their sockets and her mouth wide open. She was clutching fistfuls of bedding in each hand. Her knees were spread wide, her back was painfully arched and there was a head between her legs.

The bamboo screens crashed to the floor. There was a split-second pause, then they both looked up at Maddy.

'Shit,' Sal said and lay back, exhausted.

Maddy was in a state of shock. She'd never seen a couple making love before. And certainly not two women.

Jane got up and crossed to the sink. 'Serves you right, Sal.' She poured herself a large glass of water. 'How many times did I say it? You should have told the kid.'

Strangely enough, Maddy's relationship with her flatmates improved from then on. The fact that she didn't gather her belongings together and move out in high dudgeon immediately endeared her to Sal.

Soon Maddy found herself being whisked out to all the lesbian night spots, bars and private parties, Sal protectively warding off any would-be contenders with a 'naughty, naughty, hands off, pet, she's mine'. And to Maddy's astonishment the hulking, leather-jacketed bull-dyke with the crew cut would shrug and skulk away to search elsewhere for fresh meat.

It was all very novel to Maddy whose only experience of lesbianism had been one dark night at the convent when a classmate had slid into her bed and placed a hand between her legs.

'What are you doing?' Maddy had asked, not even aware who it was.

'Open up and I'll show you a good time,' the voice urged.

Oh no! Eunice! 'Piss off, Eunice,' Maddy said as she kicked the girl out of bed.

Eunice was a grubby little creature who boasted about getting off on a bicycle seat and, although Maddy hadn't quite understood what that meant, it sounded decidedly tacky. If Eunice was what lesbianism had to offer then Maddy wasn't interested.

For a short, disturbing while she wondered how she might have reacted if Eunice had been Megan, the Firsts hockey captain she idolised. But not long after the Eunice episode, one of the final year girls was caught with the assistant handyman in the gym equipment storage room. Rumour reported that both of them were stark naked and heavily 'at it' and Maddy found the mental image of them so erotic that she supposed she must be heterosexual and she paid no further attention to lesbianism. Now here it was, thrust at her in the form of Sal and Jane.

After one inoffensive pass, Sal good-naturedly accepted the fact that Maddy didn't want to convert and even the surly Jane was persuaded to join forces in protecting Maddy's virginity.

'What do you mean she's a virgin?' Jane had exclaimed in astonishment. 'The kid's eighteen in a minute.'

'We're not all sluts who lost it to our cousins at ten, pet.'

'Oh fuck off, Sal.'

But Jane was impressed nevertheless and decided that she quite liked the kid. She also decided that the kid needed some general all-round survival lessons. The first was to be a crash course in shoplifting.

It suddenly became clear to Maddy why the kitchen cupboards were always full of luxury items. She'd wondered how the girls, who never had any cash, existed on smoked salmon, pates and imported cheeses. As far as Maddy had been able to ascertain, the sales of their paintings were few and far between. Both girls were in the final year of their art course at Tech and they augmented their income by hiring themselves out as kitchen hands whenever things got too desperate. Indeed, it was Sal who had introduced Maddy to Mrs Predan.

Flattered as she was that Jane should go to the trouble of teaching her, Maddy didn't take well to shoplifting. As she lined up at the checkout counter with a loaf of bread, a carton of milk and a bag of sugar in her basket, she felt herself break into a sweat that she was sure the shopgirl must notice. Just as the girl must notice the bulges in Maddy's sleeves and pockets where the packets of bacon and cheeses were stuffed.

Jane had it down to a fine art, with concealed pockets sewn into several special shoplifting garments. Winter was the best season for shoplifting, she told Maddy—all those heavy clothes. She always stocked up on tins and jars in winter.

Although Jane, like Sal, was only three years older than Maddy, she was a tough, streetwise young woman. Maddy was totally in awe of her and, after three consecutive Saturdays of feeling sick with nerves, she didn't quite know how to approach Jane with the news that she didn't want to be included in the shoplifting roster.

'Wimping out, are we?' It was more or less the reaction Maddy had expected. 'Chicken, eh?'

23

'Leave her alone, Jano.' Sal came to the rescue.

'Well, the kid's got to pull her weight.'

'She does, you cow. She's better with her rent than you are. And who the hell brings home the curries every fortnight?'

It was true. Mrs Predan's curries were served to her patrons for two weeks and then the remnants were scraped from the massive pots into a series of plastic bags which Maddy brought home. For several days a fortnight the girls pigged out on lamb, beef or chicken and a choice of korma, kofta, or vindaloo.

'Yeah.' Jane looked thoughtful. 'I'd forgotten about the curries. Fair enough.' And Maddy was let off the shoplifting.

All in all, it was a good time for Maddy. A learning experience. She adjusted astonishingly quickly to the cockroaches, the mouse droppings and the coin-operated gas meter in the upstairs shared bathroom.

She was finally growing up, she told herself. No more cotton wool. This was life and she was living it. She'd soon be a struggling young actress and struggling young actresses needed to know about life. She worked hard at her voice classes, she devoured a half a dozen books a week—some from the library and some purchased with her study allowance—and she never once questioned whether or not she would pass her NADA audition. She was on the road to becoming an actress and that was that.

Besides the expanse of thigh and the ripe young breasts, it was Maddy's commitment that Jonathan Thomas noticed during the interview and it impressed him. He was further impressed by Maddy's audition. It was a raw talent, one that needed shaping but it was most certainly talent and her attitude was perfect. Maddy was one of the first selected for admission to The National Academy of Dramatic Art for the year of 1970.

1970 was indeed the year that shaped Maddy's destiny. It was the year she went to NADA, and it was the year she met Alex.

ACT I

SCENE 2: 1970

Alex Rainford was a typical Australian: sandy-haired, tanned, healthy white teeth, a smattering of youthful freckles about his shoulders. But he wasn't handsome. Certainly not by Australian standards. For starters, he wasn't the mandatory six feet tall. He was a good two inches short of the mark, his body was too thin and his face was too bony.

So why was Alex fascinating? Why was he devastatingly attractive to men and women alike?

The too-bony face was intelligent, certainly. And the blue eyes focused on the object of their attention with a flattering intensity. And the women Alex bedded found that his skinny body was far from unattractive when naked. It was lean, wiry, well-endowed and knew exactly what it was doing.

On examination, Alex's charisma might have been a mixture of all these things. But it wasn't. It was something far more simple. The reason Alex Rainford was so fascinating was because others were so fascinating to him. And the intensity of Alex's fascination reflected itself accordingly: the more fascinating he found others, the more attractive he became to them.

All in all, Alex had a lot going for him, so it wasn't surprising that he was one of the five per cent of auditionees accepted into NADA for 1970.

His examiner, Jonathan Thomas, wasn't altogether sure of the boy's talent but his sex appeal was undeniable and that was a useful commodity in the profession, particularly in film, and the Australian film industry was on the move. If his talent proved insufficient and Alex wasn't coming up to scratch towards the end of first year, Jonathan decided, then the boy could always be one of the thirty to forty per cent of students who didn't make it to second year.

Jonathan Thomas always hated the seedings that took place during first year but he knew it was a necessary process. So many young people wanted to be actors and it would be unfair to release all of them into an already overcrowded industry. A few too many got by as it was, in Jonathan's opinion, and it was heartbreaking. There they were, proudly waving their diplomas, deluded in the belief they had a talent and a tenacity that the profession was going to recognise. Jonathan would have preferred to be more ruthless—it was kinder in the long run— but some of his colleagues didn't agree with him. Some of his colleagues were more concerned with the need to push the correct ratio of 'full fee' students through to second year in order to augment government funding and compensate for the allowances made for scholarship students.

Alex was a scholarship student. Although Jonathan thought his talent borderline, the means test proved Alex fully qualified. The boy came from a deprived background. He'd left home at seventeen, having gained excellent marks in his exams, and had lived alone and supported himself for the following two years. He was currently working two jobs, stacking supermarket shelves on Saturday mornings and operating a petrol pump two nights a week, in order to put himself through the first term of drama school. The NADA directors were all in agreement: that sort of commitment deserved full encouragement.

'Well done! Good lad!' Harold Beauchamp's fruity baritone was warm and genuine as he engulfed Alex's hand in his two huge paws and pumped effusively. 'A full scholarship too, by God, not one of those puny little half-measure things. Well done!'

Harold was an actor and lived up to the image he felt an actor should have. He was larger than life. Well, he believed he was and he certainly appeared to be. He was a big man physically, fat, but not obscenely so, and his build suited him. He dressed flamboyantly, his gestures were grandiose and his manner of speech highly theatrical.

Naturally Harold came in for his share of criticism, mostly from fringe theatre devotees who were equally pretentious in their own way and from failed actors who were jealous of his success. The fact was that Harold was a good actor and a successful one. His appearance as well as his talent made him extremely useful and for years he'd had the pick of the leading roles for character actors: Big Daddy, Sheridan Whiteside, Cardinal Wolsey, the lot.

Now in his mid-sixties, Harold could easily have passed for fifty-five, but no one believed him when he said he was, because they all knew how long he'd been around.

When Alex first met him two years before, Harold had been playing Captain Shotover in *Heartbreak House*. Alex, who had never been to the legitimate theatre, was overawed. His girlfriend's parents had given her their subscription tickets because they didn't like George Bernard Shaw's plays and Alex had let himself be dragged along purely so that he could have Lenice's body on the mouldy carpet of his Darlinghurst bedsit afterwards. They always made love on the floor—Lenice liked it that way.

But they didn't go back to his bedsit that night. In fact they didn't go anywhere together that night. Alex insisted Lenice take him backstage and introduce him to Harold Beauchamp. Lenice was a twenty-four year old socialite and any connections she didn't have Mummy and Daddy certainly did, so it was an easy introduction for her to effect.

An hour and a half later she wished she hadn't. She sat totally ignored, as Alex became immersed in Harold's theatricality and Harold became a victim of Alex's fascination.

She was shocked. Tears welled up in her eyes. Then she scolded herself. She was above this sort of treatment—what on earth had she been doing with a nineteen year old boy from the gutter anyway?

If Lenice had known that Alex was only seventeen she wouldn't have minded at all. To the contrary, she would have been delighted: she liked rough trade and she liked it young.

Lenice was shocked because this wretched old ham was obviously a queen and did that mean that Alex was possibly bisexual and if he was, how dare he make love to her! What the hell, she thought, and walked out of the dressing room with great dignity, closing the door only a little too firmly behind her.

Neither Alex nor Harold heard the door and it was half an hour later before Harold gestured to the empty chair.

'Your woman,' he said.

'What?' Alex looked around.

'She's gone,' Harold announced.

'Oh.' Alex was momentarily disconcerted. He supposed it was because he'd been talking too exclusively to Harold, but she could have interrupted, surely. 'Oh, well.' He stood up. 'That means I'll have to walk home. I'd better be off.'

But Harold had a better idea. 'Coffee and cognac at my place,' he said. 'And we can talk into the wee hours.'

They hailed a cab—'I don't drive,' Harold explained, 'never have'—and arrived at his Double Bay apartment at one-thirty in the morning.

At five o'clock it was Harold who finally called it a night. '"And so to bed", dear boy, "and so to bed".'

Alex hadn't understood any of Harold's weird turns of phrase but he loved the theatricality of the man.

'You're here,' Harold said as he threw open the door to the spare room. 'Don't wake me before midday.' And he went to bed.

It crossed Alex's mind that Harold was a singularly trusting man. Even to a seventeen-year-old it was evident that there was money strewn all about the elegant Double Bay apartment. Harold's taste in objets d'art was impeccable.

Alex helped himself to one final tiny slug of Bisquit cognac, quietly opened the balcony door and stepped outside to admire the view. The first glimmers of dawn flecked the sky and Sydney Harbour was still and unspoiled, yet to be churned over by the water traffic that would shortly start its daily grind. Nestling comfortably in the marina below were millions of dollars' worth of luxury boats. Alex wondered if Harold had a boat. Probably not, he decided, he wasn't really the type.

What a life, Alex thought. An apartment like this, a view like this, nightly acclaim from appreciative audiences, respect, fame and fortune. Then and there Alex decided he'd become an actor. He drained the Bisquit and went to bed.

By the time Harold had dragged himself out of bed shortly after midday, Alex had been out for the morning papers, washed up the glasses and coffee cups from the previous night, brewed a fresh jug of espresso and was waiting to pick up the conversation where they'd left off. Despite a rather seedy hangover, Harold was touched and flattered.

From that moment on a bizarre but comfortable friendship developed.

Alex maintained his Darlo bedsit, despite Harold's offers to move in to the Double Bay apartment. As most of their evenings were spent together, though, he more often than not stayed at Harold's. And their evenings together were invariably spent at the theatre. Alex watched Harold from the wings or, if Harold was not performing, they went to one of the other productions around town.

Harold was flattered that his example had inspired Alex to a life on the stage and he proceeded to teach the boy all he knew. After several lessons he came to the regretful conclusion that the spark of instinctive talent wasn't in Alex. Not that it mattered particularly, Harold thought. Many actors achieved great success without a shred of talent, let alone the divine spark. But he would have wished his protege to be that one in a million. What the hell, with Alex's looks and charisma the world of film could be his oyster. It would be a safer bet than the stage and wasn't such hard work, anyway.

He suggested as much to Alex one evening over an after-theatre supper. 'Treading the boards can be such a wearisome business. Six nights and two matinees a week; week in, week out. I think perhaps, my dear Alexei Alexeivitch, we should look to the world of film for your future.'

But Alex was adamant. He wanted to act in the theatre. He wanted to be a part of that world. It fascinated him.

But he wanted to go about it the right way. He didn't want any favours, he didn't want Harold pulling a few strings to get him a bit part or an understudy job. Alex knew only too well where that would land him. He could hear them now: 'The kid only got the job because he's fucking old Harold Beauchamp'.

Already many actors thought he was Harold's 'boy'. It didn't seem to offend Harold. 'Oh, let them talk,' he said dismissively. 'We have set the catamite among the pigeons.' He laughed, delighted with himself. 'It bothers me not one whit.'

Alex decided it wasn't going to bother him either. In fact he considered it the least he could offer. Although Harold swore to his friends their relationship was platonic, Alex knew the actor was secretly flattered when nobody believed him, and flattery was a fair exchange for Harold's patronage. But gossip would turn to jealousy if Alex were to allow Harold to pull special strings for him and jealousy could seriously jeopardise his career.

He was, therefore, grateful when Harold stopped trying to grant favours and sat him down and mapped out a strategy for him.

'NADA, dear boy, NADA to start with, and a scholarship at that.'

'Really?' Alex was surprised. He'd been expecting a rundown on which agent to tackle first, which casting director to crack a meeting with, which audition to try and crash. NADA hadn't occurred to him. 'You think I need drama school?'

'Unfortunately, yes, my dear Alexei. Not necessarily for the tuition, of course, but it's the old school tie.' Harold puffed on his cigar and leaned forward conspiratorially. 'You want to make it the legitimate way in the legitimate theatre? Well, I tell you, dear boy, the legitimate theatre is going to become more and more elitist, mark my words. These trendy little graduates are already in positions of power, particularly in subsidised theatre, and it's a case of jobs for the boys, including the new boys, so long as they wear the old school tie.' Harold

33

leaned back and drained his cognac. 'So I fear NADA it must be, my boy. NADA ventured, NADA gained.' And he laughed uproariously.

Alex took Harold's advice and NADA it was. He took Harold's further advice and lined up two dead-end jobs to prove to the assessors how keen he was and how eligible for a scholarship. Although Harold would have been quite happy to pay Alex's fees, he was aware that applicants were judged as much by their attitude and commitment as they were by their talent, and of course he was right.

On the Saturday before Alex was to start at NADA, he and Harold had a celebratory night out. They went to a performance of *The Caucasian Chalk Circle* and then on to Harold's favourite supper haunt in Kings Cross. Alex had wanted to go backstage and talk to the actors, all of whom Harold knew well, but for once the old actor was reluctant.

Harold's strangely introverted mood lasted till halfway through supper when the second bottle of Bollinger seemed to take effect and he made the sudden decision to let it all out.

'It's going to change, my dear Alexei. It's all going to change.' There was a slight break in his voice and the hint of a tear in his eye.

'What is?' Alex wasn't sure whether Harold's sentiment was genuine or affected but it was very touching nevertheless.

Harold was aware of the pathos of the moment and he played it to its fullest, as he always did. But his feelings were utterly genuine—his theatrical presentation of them covered even deeper emotions that would always remain unsaid.

'Your world, dear boy. Our friendship.' Harold's heart ached with love for Alex. He turned his head slightly and set his gaze just above the boy's head. It was a good angle and the lighting was excellent. 'In just a very little while you'll be immersed in your exciting new world with your exciting new friends. You'll be a "student actor"'— the term had a very bad taste to it and Harold spat it out—'and you'll think of me as that dated, boring old fart who doesn't understand the new wave.'

'I will not, Harold, and you know it.'

'Ah, but your friends will and they'll convince you. No matter, no matter.' He waved his hand dismissively, lowered his gaze and looked at Alex. His voice was as untheatrical as he could possibly make it. 'It's been a fine friendship.'

Alex took the actor's hand in both of his. 'And it will continue to be . . . now stop queening it up.'

Harold smiled back at him. Shortly after, he excused himself and went to the lavatory where he had a good cry and repaired the damage unnoticed.

'Julian Oldfellow.' He waited for a titter to follow. It did. 'And I'm used to that.' There was another titter and Julian smiled. 'It's a bastard of a name but I've learned to live with it.'

Alex leaned forward in his seat and studied the young man intently. What an interesting person he seemed to be. He was physically unattractive by normal standards—angular, bony, his nose just a little too big, his straight, lank hair just a little too long—but there was something about him . . . An intelligence and a confidence that was disarming. His homosexuality was obvious but unaffected and somehow added to his confident demeanour. Most of the other homosexuals at NADA, Alex had noted, were either poseurs or closets. Julian was a young man quite at home with his sexuality.

'Born in Wagga Wagga,' Julian continued. 'Father district health inspector, mother president of the CWA, a big sister with three year old twins and a very straight husband. All living in Wagga, hence my coming to Sydney as soon as I could get the train fare.'

There was an appreciative laugh from the rest of the class. 'No, that's not very fair of me, really; they're a nice bunch.'

Julian's eyes were drawn to the young man at the end of the second row who was staring at him so intently. He'd noticed him earlier—what was his name? Alex Rainford. God, he was attractive.

'They're very fond of me and I'm very fond of them,' he continued after flashing a smile at Alex, 'but ever since I discovered my sordid secret I thought it would be best if I left Wagga. Probably as much for their sake as mine.'

It was the first day of the first term for the 1970 NADA recruits and this was their first improvisation class. Norah Hogarth, the rather intense English improvisation teacher, always believed in having her class introduce themselves to each other.

'I want you, one by one, to tell us *all* about yourself,' she'd say. It was an unnerving experience for some of the shyer students but, over a full term, Norah invariably managed to weaken the barriers of even the most reserved—probably because of her own readiness to bare her soul and to even, at times, make such an utter idiot of herself that it was difficult not to warm to her. She was certainly one of the more popular tutors.

'Well, I guess that's about it.' Julian smiled once

more at Alex. He could have sworn the bloke was straight when he'd noticed him that morning but . . . Christ, I've never had such a come-on, Julian thought. 'I reckon that just about sums up Julian Oldfellow,' he announced to the class and sat down.

Norah nodded to the girl sitting next to Julian.

Maddy stood up and faced the class. 'Maddy McLaughlan,' she said. Her heart was pounding but she felt good. This was the beginning of it all, she told herself. This was the birth of her career, the first day of her life, in a way, and she could barely contain her excitement.

And her excitement was contagious. The interest Julian had held for Alex was forgotten in an instant as he studied the tiny pulse throbbing in Maddy's left temple. Funny how more pronounced it was on the left side; the right was barely noticeable.

He's straight, Julian thought, with a wry smile to himself. He's definitely straight.

'Born and bred in Sydney, father an orthodontist, mother . . . um . . .' Maddy fumbled for the correct description. Helena certainly wouldn't want to be labelled 'housewife', but what exactly was she? Charity worker sounded a little too noble. '. . . um . . . orthodontist's wife.'

The laugh she got was bigger than any of the appreciative chuckles accorded Julian, and Maddy, although momentarily startled, learned her first lesson: in this new world she was about to embrace, anyone and anything was fair game—if the timing was right and it was a good laugh line, nothing was sacred. She realised at the same time that it wasn't only her mother they were laughing at but

37

the image she herself was presenting. Despite the fact that she'd been slumming it in a Kings Cross flatette for several months she looked like a rich man's daughter and she knew it.

Maddy didn't know whether to be offended or hurt. She felt her cheeks slowly start to burn. 'And I don't think my mother's any more to blame for being the way she is than Julian's parents are to blame for being the way they are.' She glared back at the class, not sure whether she was defending her mother or herself.

Julian, who had been staring spellbound at Alex who had been staring spellbound at Maddy, was jolted out of his trance by the mention of his name and suddenly realised what the girl had just said. She's dead bloody right, he thought, and started clapping loudly.

Norah Hogarth also approved. 'Well done, Maddy, well done. We're here to express exactly how we feel. That's what this class is all about.' She also started clapping and several members of the class joined in. But there was a faction who decided then and there that Maddy was spoilt, arrogant and self-opinionated.

If he'd attempted to analyse her, Alex probably would have agreed with them but it wouldn't have mattered anyway. Maddy was fascinating and he had to know her. He had to know everything about her.

'Alex Rainford. Hi.' He was waiting beside the main gates.

'Hello,' she said, as she started walking down High Street.

'Loved your intro,' Alex said, falling into step

beside her.

'You weren't one of the ones who clapped though, were you?'

Alex was pleased. He thought Maddy hadn't noticed him. 'So?'

'So, half the class think I'm up myself, I could sense it.'

'Fuck them.'

Maddy stopped and looked at him.

'Fuck the lot of them,' he repeated.

Alex had been wrong. Maddy had noticed him, all right. She'd felt him staring at her so intently that she hadn't dared to look at him. He'd been sitting there in the corner of her vision ever since she'd stood up to address the class and when he hadn't clapped she'd felt more than disappointed. She'd felt betrayed in some strange way.

When it had been Alex's turn to stand up before the class she'd feigned disinterest. She'd doodled in her notepad or stared out the window.

Now finally their eyes locked and she found she had to force herself to break away.

'You're right,' she laughed. 'Fuck the lot of them.'

They walked down to Anzac Parade and caught the bus together, talking nineteen to the dozen about their first day at NADA, the teachers, the other students and what had made them want to become actors in the first place. Finally, as they got off the bus, Alex turned the conversation to the coincidental fact that Maddy's flatette and his bedsit were only four blocks apart—so whose place should they go to for coffee and more talk?

There was no innuendo to his suggestion at all but something told Maddy to go slowly. She had a definite feeling she was getting out of her depth. How could anyone be so attractive, so instantly?

'Why don't we have a coffee in The Village? There's a place that does great espresso.'

'OK.' Alex grinned. Whatever she wanted was fine by him. So long as he could be with her.

For the first two hours and three cappuccinos they continued to discuss acting, NADA and their fellow students, particularly Julian Oldfellow. They came to the mutual decision that they liked Julian.

Then, over plates of toasted cheese, ham and tomato—temptingly titled 'toasty tasty cheese melts' in the menu—they got down to the more intimate details of their lives. Well, Maddy did. She found herself discussing her parents, the convent, Mrs Predan and the Indian restaurant, her flatmates and the shoplifting lessons. To her utter amazement she even heard herself recounting the time she sprang Sal and Jane in the throes of passion.

Alex did a fair amount of talking too but, a further two hours and another cappuccino later when they were informed the coffee shop was closing, Maddy realised that he hadn't told her anything intimate, nothing about his family. She mentioned it as he started to walk her home but he shrugged and said, 'Harold's my family now'.

Maddy recalled that when it had been Alex's turn to introduce himself during the improvisation class, his manner had been equally indifferent. He'd said his father was a security guard with a hefty drink problem and his mother was a housewife who put up with it. It appeared not to bother him but maybe his disinterest was a cover.

Maddy decided not to pursue it. 'Goodnight, Alex. I'll see you tomorrow.'

They were outside Maddy's block of flats and she felt strangely gauche as she wondered whether or not she should ask him up. She could hardly offer him coffee when they'd had four cappuccinos each. It was nearly ten o'clock at night, the girls would probably be home and . . .

'Sure, see you tomorrow.' Alex could sense her indecision and made it easy for her. He smiled disarmingly, squeezed her hand and gave her a peck on the cheek.

When Alex got home he found a telephone message had been slipped under his door: *Harold phoned to say where are you?* Damn, he'd completely forgotten that he'd agreed to have dinner with Harold. 'I want a blow-by-blow account of your first day, dear boy,' Harold had insisted. 'Down to the merest detail, mind.'

Poor old Harold, he'd be feeling wounded, Alex thought, as he ferreted about for some change. The one and only telephone was in the hall. It was frequently out of order and the relaying of messages was entirely dependent upon which of the tenants chose to take the call.

'I met this stunning girl, Harold. We've been sitting in a coffee lounge for hours.' It didn't occur to Alex to lie and Harold liked him for it.

'Of course you did, my dear Alexei, of course you did. And when am I going to meet her?'

'Hey, that'd be great!' Alex was genuinely delighted at the prospect. 'Can I ask her over on the weekend? She'd love your place: her Dad's filthy rich and she's got real style.'

Harold's roar of laughter was so deafening that Alex winced and held the receiver away from his ear.

'Make it Saturday lunch and I'll get one of those huge and magnificent lobster quiches from the corner patisserie,' Harold said when he'd recovered.

He didn't feel remotely piqued as he hung up the receiver. Of course the boy had forgotten all about him—he'd been confronted with a beautiful young woman and that's exactly the way it should be.

The wonderful thing was that Alex wanted to include Harold. He wanted Harold to meet his girl and Harold was overjoyed. He glowed with a parent's love as he drained the bottle of Bollinger he'd bought especially for Alex.

'Hey, Julian, come and join us,' Alex called as he saw the gangling figure appear in the doorway. Julian smiled, waved back and started weaving his way towards them through the noisy, crowded cafe.

Maddy shifted her chair closer to Alex's, making way for a third chair. She didn't mind Julian joining them—she didn't mind anyone joining them. The peremptory way Alex always took her hand as soon as lunch break was called assured her that she need fear no competition. The thought thrilled her. Maddy was falling in love.

'My God, what an honour.' Julian swept back his lank forelock as he sat. 'An invitation to join the Scott and Zelda of NADA 1970,' he continued in answer to Alex's raised eyebrow. 'Pretty elitist stuff.'

He was sending them up, but not viciously. Although it was only the end of the first week, Julian was not alone in recognising Alex's and Maddy's attraction—not only to each other but for the rest of the students.

Yes, they're definitely going to be the leaders of the class of 1970, Julian thought. Which wasn't why he was about to accept their friendship. Julian was happy to go his own way. But he liked Maddy and he found Alex fatally attractive.

'Don't tell anyone,' Julian whispered conspiratorially, 'but I'm faking this acting shit.'

It was an hour later and they knew they were going to be late back for the voice class but as it was one of Jonathan Thomas's they didn't worry unduly. Maddy thought him a perve and the boys thought him a wimp.

'What do you mean, "faking"?' Maddy asked, confused.

'I'm *pretending*, my darling. I'm *pretending* to train as an actor.' Julian's cheeky smile to Maddy assured her that he was sending himself up, not her. 'I have no intention of becoming one. It's a ridiculous career.'

'Bullshit. Why are you taking the course then?' Alex's tone was slightly belligerent.

'Don't get bolshie, Alex.' Julian dropped the banter. 'Look at me! I'm twenty-two years old, juvenile lead age, and look at me. Would you cast me opposite Maddy?' Julian put a bony arm around Maddy and pressed his cheek next to hers. They looked utterly incongruous.

'So? You're a character actor. So what?'

'And how long will it be before I come into my own or even earn a decent living?' Julian gave Maddy's arm a squeeze before releasing it. 'This one is talented.' Then he pointed at Alex. 'You are charismatic. You both have every chance of making it.'

'OK, OK. So why the bloody hell are you doing the course then?'

'Know any other director who's done the NADA first year acting course?' He smiled confidently at them. 'Too many directors in this country don't know enough about acting, in my opinion. I'm going to do my acting groundwork and then change courses.'

'Will they let you?' Maddy asked. 'It hasn't been done before, has it?'

'Not to the best of my knowledge, which is another reason I want to do it.' He winked at her. 'I like being the first. And yes, I think they will let me. Our Jon Thomas advised me to take the directors' course, actually.'

'Why? Was your audition that bad?' Alex laughed.

Julian wasn't offended. 'No, but I have an Arts degree and they like their fledgling directors to have some academic background.' He rose from his chair. 'And when we've left NADA we'll form our own company. We have everything it takes,' he said, then looked at Maddy. 'Talent', then turned to Alex, 'Charisma', then put a hand on his own chest. 'Genius.'

'Bit of money wouldn't go astray,' Alex muttered as they prepared to leave.

'Maddy can bring her Dad in on the deal.' Julian was out the door before Maddy could make her retort.

Harold and Maddy took to each other immediately as Alex knew they would. Lunch was a resounding success.

Maddy got to the Double Bay apartment twenty

minutes before Alex who came straight from his Saturday morning supermarket stint. As he opened the door, he heard her shriek of laughter. Harold was onto his second anecdote. Like Alex, Maddy loved the man's theatricality.

Harold in turn was bewitched by Maddy's childlike beauty. So young, he thought, she didn't look any more than fifteen. But he very quickly recognised the strength of will that lay beneath the fragile appearance. My God, he thought, if she's got talent as well there'll be no stopping her.

Lunch with Harold became a regular weekend event. When it was on a Sunday neither Maddy nor Alex had to work so the two of them would catch a bus back to Darlinghurst and sit for a further couple of hours in his bedsit. They'd talk over endless cups of coffee or glasses of flagon 'plonk' which tasted terrible after Harold's cellar wines but neither of them really noticed.

When it finally came time for Alex to walk her home, they would kiss, deeply and fondly, and occasionally Alex's hand would stray to her breast. Each time Maddy froze. This is it she'd tell herself, now it's going to happen. And each time Alex would break the embrace. 'Home time,' he'd say. 'Classes tomorrow.' Maddy was confused. She was aching for him—didn't he know that?

Four tantalising Sundays in a row were too much for Maddy. On the fifth one she decided to take the initiative.

She deliberately wore a shirt that unbuttoned easily down the front, and didn't wear a bra. As soon as they started kissing, Alex found his hand firmly guided to a small, perfectly formed breast and rock-hard nipple.

45

Maddy expected some change in pace at this point. She expected him to pause and ask if she was sure, did she really mean it, or words to that effect. He knew she was a virgin, after all. But Alex didn't hesitate for one second. His hand gently cupped her breast, his forefinger playing subtly over her nipple, sending tiny tremors through her body as his tongue started exploring her mouth with greater urgency.

There was an ache between Maddy's legs she'd never felt before. She'd never known she was capable of such feelings and, as he unzipped her skirt and eased it down over her hips, she moaned and thrust her pelvis forward. Alex had adroitly managed to pull off his shorts and her skirt without breaking the moment or the kiss, and as Maddy felt his erection hard against her groin, it was all she could do to stop screaming. She ripped at his underpants and then at her own and it was Alex who finally drew breath.

He took her face in both hands and slowly eased their mouths apart. Her eyes were shut, her head was tilted back and she was moaning gently. 'Shall we take our shoes off?' he whispered.

ACT I

SCENE 3: 1970

Maddy and Alex were in love. Maddy in a way she'd never dreamed possible: desperately, passionately, obsessively. Her sexual awakening had been unlike anything she'd ever imagined. Liberated magazines for intelligent women had informed her that most females lost their virginity by rape or mistake and her friends had told her that the first time was painful and forgettable. Not for Maddy.

Despite his youth, Alex was an incredible lover. And despite her inexperience, Maddy recognised it. She recognised it with every fibre of her being that first night as she clung to him tightly, trying to draw him deeper and deeper inside her. But he held back, eluding her, teasing, keeping her at the very brink, until Maddy's final moment was so overwhelming that she cried out in ecstasy.

It wasn't difficult for Alex. Sex had never been difficult for Alex. The effect his control had on women was such a fascination and a pleasure to him that he was never tempted to let go. Ejaculation, although pleasurable, was simply a physical release. His true sexual excitement was the response he drew from the woman as she gave herself to him. And Maddy's response was the most fascinating and fulfilling he'd ever experienced.

They had spent that first night curled up in Alex's narrow bed and Maddy couldn't resist asking him why he'd waited for her to make the first move.

'I wasn't sure you wanted to,' he answered. 'You always froze up whenever I touched you. Besides,' he kissed her lightly, 'the sex wasn't all that important.'

'How can you say that?' Maddy pulled away and looked at him, astonished. It was the most important thing that had ever happened to her.

'I wanted more than the sex and I didn't mind waiting.' It was a simple statement. 'I wanted all of you, Maddy.'

That was when Maddy fell hopelessly in love.

Six months later they moved into the tiny studio flat Harold had helped them find and were blissfully happy.

It was only two blocks away from Harold's apartment, but without his water views. A large bed-sitting room affair with doors leading to a tiny kitchen one end and a bathroom the other, it was nevertheless more expensive than either of them could afford and Alex had finally persuaded Maddy to accept some financial assistance from her father.

He wasn't chasing any gain for himself. He quite honestly could not understand how Maddy's pride could allow her to forgo the comforts that her father was only too keen to provide.

'But he's rich, for God's sake, and he wants to help you.'

'I know, I know.'

'Christ, he deliberately stopped your chances of getting a scholarship so that he could support you—why the hell won't you let him?' It didn't make sense to Alex.

It was true that when Maddy had been accepted to NADA Robert had paid a visit to the Academy and assured Jonathan Thomas that all fees and living expenses would be met by him.

'Scholarships are for the underprivileged students, surely, Mr Thomas,' Robert had said in reply to Jonathan's assurances that Maddy's talent had put her on the selection list for partial assistance.

Certainly Robert McLaughlan was appalled at the thought of his daughter receiving government funding—good grief, she might as well go on the dole. But it was more than that. He was sure that when Maddy found she needed his money, she'd come home, and Robert desperately wanted her back. For some unknown reason, things were not going well with Helena; Robert's comfortable existence seemed to be slowly disintegrating around him.

Unfortunately his interference had pushed Maddy in the opposite direction altogether. She wrote him a scathing letter, his cheques she returned shredded, and whenever he phoned she hung up on him. Then she left the Indian restaurant and found herself a full-time waitressing job, six till midnight, in a sleazy Hungarian restaurant in Taylor Square. Robert was a very unhappy man.

'So why don't you accept money from Harold?' Maddy had countered when Alex insisted she accept her father's help. 'You say he's your family and he's got plenty of money.'

'That's totally different, Maddy, and you know it.'

'It bloody well is not!'

'It bloody well is too!'

Then they laughed, made love and resumed the argument the following day.

Finally Alex agreed to let Harold provide them with some furniture if Maddy accepted a modest weekly allowance from Robert. 'Then you can leave that shonky restaurant,' he said. 'It's the pits.'

So it was settled. Except that Maddy insisted on working Fridays and Saturdays at the shonky restaurant. The tips were fantastic, she said, but Alex knew it was really a statement. She wasn't giving in on all sides.

And Maddy laid down one further condition to Alex. Robert was not to know that they were living together.

'I told you! Daddy's a devout Catholic and he'd be livid, and I just don't want the hassle.'

Alex gave in and left the flat the day Robert came around for an inspection.

'But it's only one room! Couldn't you find somewhere a bit bigger?'

'It's a studio flat, Dad, and I like it.' Thank goodness her mother hadn't come, Maddy thought. They would have had to move all Alex's stuff. Helena would have been into every drawer and cupboard. Maddy knew her father would never intrude upon another's privacy. If he only knew the top drawer of the dresser he was leaning on was stuffed with Alex's socks and underpants.

'I do hope you'll pop home and see us from time to time, dear,' Robert said. 'Your mother's been a bit strange lately, a bit irritable, you know, jumpy. Probably just some woman's thing but I'm sure seeing you would help.'

'I will, Dad, I promise.' And she meant it. Not only because it would help prevent any unexpected calls to the flat, but she felt sorry for her father. Poor Daddy, she thought. He looks so tired. 'I'm sorry for being such a . . .' she just stopped herself from saying 'shit'. The NADA vernacular had certainly made its stamp on her. '. . . Such a pain.' And she gave him a hug.

Robert held her to him for a second, grateful to have his little girl back. Then he broke the clinch before it became uncomfortable.

'You know the birthday cheque you sent back several months ago?' he asked. Maddy nodded, hoping that he wasn't going to give her another lecture. 'Well, would you accept a belated present?' Then he added hurriedly, 'So long as it wasn't money.'

Maddy smiled. He was trying so hard. 'Sure. That'd be great.'

The present turned out to be a bright red MGB which Alex made her accept even though they both knew the disapproving faction at NADA would think Maddy had gone even further up herself.

'Fuck them,' said Alex, and once again Maddy had to agree.

The bond between Maddy, Alex and Julian

continued to grow. Not only did they enjoy each other's company but they nurtured each other's egos and fed each other's ambitions. They even produced their own pub revue and managed to score a regular gig every second Sunday at a Woolloomooloo dockside alehouse. For fifteen years the pub had specialised in weekend jazz but a new wave management had decided to branch out and vary the programme.

It was an exciting existence. NADA continued to be stimulating and there was the heady knowledge that, at the end of it all, they would be fully equipped to launch themselves upon the outside world and make their impact on the Australian theatre.

It was the end of second term and Julian had finally decided to set into action phase B of his plan. He had learned a great deal about acting in eight months of full-time study. Indeed it was a far more complicated and interesting craft than he had originally assumed. But he hadn't been tempted to change his strategy.

'I'd like to transfer to the directors' course, Mr Thomas.'

Jonathan Thomas was surprisingly obliging. It appeared that Julian was a borderline case in the selection lists for second year anyway.

Julian stared at the man in amazement. 'You're not serious,' he said disbelievingly.

Jonathan read the young man's reaction perfectly and smiled as he opened a folder on the desk in front of him. 'You'd be surprised, Julian,' he said. 'We have to let many clever and talented young people go. The only way we can handle the numbers is to be extremely selective.'

He ran his finger down a list of names with comments beside them. 'Some people who don't complete the NADA course prove us wrong and go on to achieve great success but we can't take that risk. Our directors have to assess as they see fit at the time.'

'And I was going to be kicked out?' Julian still couldn't believe it possible.

'No,' Jonathan's finger stopped halfway down the list and his eye scanned the comments on the right-hand side. 'As I said, you were borderline. Your theory and improvisation would have got you through.' He flashed a quick smile at Julian. 'Augurs well for the directors' course, doesn't it?' Then he returned to the comments. 'My report goes before the Board in a fortnight—you would have been advised to work harder on your voice and movement and . . .'

Julian didn't hear the rest. He was trying his utmost to read the list upside down. It was in alphabetical order and he could see Maddy's name above his. Beside it he could distinctly read the word 'excellent' a number of times, and her comment section was brief.

He skipped down to the Rs. The comment section beside Alex Rainford was twice as long. He'd deciphered the terms 'too remote' and 'not enough' when Jonathan Thomas closed the folder and looked up at him.

'So, all in all, I think it's an excellent decision for us to transfer you, Julian. Of course you'll have to wait till first term next year to start the directors' course but I'd strongly recommend you finish this year. A first year acting course can only stand you in good stead.'

'Yes, that's what I thought,' Julian agreed, but he couldn't wait to get out.

'No, I'm not joking!'

Maddy and Alex stared at Julian in horror. It was lunchtime and they were about to pile into Maddy's car. Although it was only mid-August, spring was definitely in the air and they'd recently made a habit of zooming down to Bondi Beach during their break.

'His report goes to the Board in a fortnight. I couldn't read it properly, but my guess is they're going to kick you out,' Julian continued.

'Only one way to find out.' Alex nodded for them to get into the car. 'You go on without me; I'll see you when you get back. And grab me a pie or something, will you, I'm starving,' he added as he walked back to the main gates.

The folder wasn't on top of Jonathan Thomas's desk when Alex stole into the deserted office several minutes later. There was nothing on top of the desk except a telephone, a notepad, a tray of pencils and pens and a large, leather-framed blotter. Jonathan was a compulsively tidy man.

Damn, he must have hidden it, thought Alex. But as he slid open the top left-hand drawer, there it was. He ran his finger down the page to 'Alex Rainford' and started scanning the comments opposite. They appeared to be a compilation of quotes selected by Jonathan Thomas from the various tutors' end-of-term reports and there was a summation in Jonathan's own hand at the end.

'*Improvisation lacks involvement, too remote*'. Bloody Norah Hogarth, Alex thought, he'd been sure she liked him. Then from the acting tutor: '*Approach clinical, short on passion, but intelligent, nothing that can't be worked on*'. Theory and voice classes were both conducted by Jonathan Thomas himself and the comments were not good: '*Voice average quality, vocal range not improving with tuition*'; '*no applied application to theory; appears more interested in other class members than study of classics, poetic metre and history of theatre*'. The comments on film and television technique both concluded that his looks and personal presence were good enough to maintain a pass so Alex skipped through to the summation. '*Borderline case but recommend letting him go. There is a lack of commitment and he seems to rely too much upon his personal charm to get him by which, in my opinion, is not enough.*'

Julian had been right. They were going to kick him out. No, not 'they'. It was that bastard Jonathan Thomas. Where did they get off letting a wimp like him have the casting vote?

It was true that the final decision did, in the main, rest with Jonathan. The other members of the Board had voted it Jonathan's duty to draw up the final report and summation and he considered it a personal honour. The other board members were only too happy to allow Jonathan his personal honour as it saved them all extra work and the only time his recommendations met with any disagreement was when a board member's relative or 'favourite' was involved.

Alex returned the folder to the drawer and slipped quietly out of the office. He almost ran into Jonathan Thomas, who was crossing the courtyard with an orange juice in one hand and his customary salad sandwich in its white paper bag in the other. Alex smiled warmly at him and Jonathan replied with his tight smile before disappearing into his office. Bastard, Alex thought, his mind seething with plans and ideas. There had to be a way, there had to.

'Yeah, you were right,' he said to Julian as he took another bite of his Sargent's meat pie. 'Shit!'

They were sitting on the bench underneath the giant Moreton Bay fig tree in the centre of the courtyard.

'What are you going to do?' Maddy asked.

'I'm working on it, Mad, don't you worry.' He winked and kissed her. 'Everything's going to be fine.'

Maddy could taste the spicy, peppery pie on Alex's mouth and she smiled back at him. God, how she loved him.

'Everything's going to be just fine,' he repeated as he took another huge bite. And he meant it. Alex had a plan.

Later that night a weary Maddy let herself into the flat. Friday was always busy in the restaurant and Alex was usually fast asleep by the time she got home. Invariably he'd wake and they'd make love, languidly, tenderly. Not tonight.

'Hello, girlie, fancy a bit of rough trade?'

Maddy gasped as the lights came on and Alex stood before her, his hand caressing the bulge in his tight blue jeans. He hadn't showered or changed from his night's work and the battered singlet he wore smelt of petrol and sweat. His hair was wet and his arms and hands were covered with black

56

grease stains. As he slowly started unzipping his fly, he held his other hand out to her.

'It's all yours, baby. Come and get it.'

And Maddy did. As she sucked and licked and straddled and bucked, somewhere in the vague recesses of her mind was the image of Helena. What would her mother think? And the threads of that song from *Sweet Charity*: 'If they could see me now' . . . It added to her excitement. Then she heard her voice. Good God, was that really her? 'Fuck me, Alex, fuck me, fuck me,' over and over again. And then the flickering images of her mother disappeared as Maddy abandoned herself completely.

When they awoke in the morning, the sheets were covered with black grease stains.

'Oh, hell,' Maddy nudged Alex awake. 'Look.'

'Well, you will go in for rough trade,' Alex shook his head disapprovingly. 'I mean, you lie down with pigs . . .'

'It'll never come out.'

''Course it will. It's only a mixture of black pancake and glycerine.'

Maddy looked at him incredulously. 'But I thought . . .'

'That I'd come straight from work? Christ, Mad, I'd get the sack if I served customers like that. I ran all the way home to get up a sweat, then I threw a bit of petrol on the singlet, grimed up with the pancake, head under the shower and, bingo, instant rough trade.' He kissed her and jumped out of bed. 'Come on, let's take all this to the laundry.'

'Why, Alex?' Maddy looked a little bewildered.

'Why did you do it?'

It was Alex's turn to look confused. 'Why does there have to be a reason? You enjoyed it, didn't you?' Maddy nodded. 'So, why not?' She shared his smile, then he heaved her off the bed, smacked her on the rump and started stripping back the linen. 'Now give me a hand with this and we'll go on to the next stage of your sexual development.'

'Which is?'

'Erotic photographs in public places.'

Maddy laughed until she caught sight of the blouse she'd been wearing the previous night. It was ripped to pieces. 'Oh no,' she said, picking it up. 'It was one of my favourites.'

'Doesn't matter. We'll buy you a new one. Now we need plenty of film for dirty pictures.' Alex started rummaging around in a drawer.

'You can't be—'

'Bring some changes of clothes and wear a skirt to start with.'

'You can't be serious.'

But Alex was.

'Where the hell am I going to wear it?' Maddy pirouetted in front of the mirror while Alex looked on admiringly. The blouse was the sheerest, flimsiest silk and, because it wasn't in any way tarty, utterly erotic. Soft, pink folds of material caressed the delicate shape of Maddy's nipples and, from the side, with the light shining through the folds, the contour of a perfectly shaped young breast was faintly and tantalisingly revealed.

'It's a bit see-through. Maybe I should wear a bra with it.' Maddy was not in any way a vain girl. She wasn't stupid, of course, she knew she was pretty. And she was glad she was slim and relatively small-breasted because it was the fashion of the day. But she would never have used words like 'beautiful' or 'sexy' to describe herself.

'You bloody well will not wear a bra with it,' Alex insisted. 'You'd look like a tart or an idiot or both.'

The attractive young shop assistant nodded her agreement. A guy with taste, she thought. And sexy too! But she didn't attempt to flirt with him, it was not only bad business, but how could you compete with his stunning girlfriend? Pity.

'Where to now?' Alex asked as they left the boutique. 'Watsons Bay?'

Maddy nodded happily and got into the passenger seat carefully nursing her new blouse. Saturday was her favourite day. Alex had long since given up his supermarket job and Harold's lunches, lovely as they were, had recently been exchanged for midweek dinners so that Maddy and Alex could have Saturday to themselves. They'd go to Paddy's Market together or hop in the MGB and burn up to Watsons Bay where they'd sit in the beer garden and watch the yachts on the harbour. Saturday night saw them working petrol pumps and waiting tables again but the day was theirs alone and Maddy loved it.

On Sundays Julian came around and the three of them worked on their NADA assignments together, learning lines, rehearsing, reading plays and essays and, every second Sunday, performing at the Woolloomooloo pub.

It was a sparkling spring day and the beer garden was quite crowded. A couple of tables in the centre were free but Alex insisted they wait for one down by the fence to become available. They were onto their second beer when the family at the corner table gathered their belongings together and got up to leave. Alex dived for the table immediately. It directly overlooked the promenade, the narrow beach and the beautiful spread of harbour dotted with sailing boats.

'Perfect,' Alex said.

'Yes, isn't it beautiful?' Maddy agreed.

Alex put his hand between Maddy's thighs. 'Spread them a bit,' he whispered.

'What?' Maddy looked confused.

'Erotic photo time. Open your thighs a little.'

Maddy looked about guiltily and locked her thighs together. 'Don't be ridiculous, Alex. I couldn't.'

'Nobody can see, sweetheart.' Alex's hand caressed Maddy's leg as he slowly edged her miniskirt up even higher. 'Look, there's no one on the beach, no one on the footpath. They're all behind us.' He kissed her ear lobe and she could feel his warm breath on her neck. 'Just for me Maddy, just for me.'

His hand felt wonderful, his breath was caressing and the mere thought that he might be aroused sent a tremor through Maddy's body. She parted her legs several centimetres.

'Good girl,' Alex breathed. 'Stay like that.' And he slung the camera around his neck and was through the gate and out on the footpath in a matter of seconds. He jumped the metre from the promenade to the beach and looked back up at the beer garden. He was the only person privy to the glimpse of Maddy's crotch, encased in white Cottontail panties—with the crowds of carousing weekend drinkers behind her, the view was extremely voyeuristic.

He squatted down on the sand so that he was even further beneath her, gestured for her to drink her beer and gaze out at the harbour, and he started snapping away. He could feel himself becoming aroused and, as he watched Maddy squirm slightly in her seat, he knew she was too.

At one stage an elderly couple walked along the promenade for what seemed an age and Maddy's legs snapped shut. When the couple had finally passed, she once more spread her legs. This time there was a fraction more white Cottontailed crotch—the thighs were now a little further apart.

Alex made himself stop. He mustn't waste all the film; they had a lot of ground to cover that afternoon.

'Oh God, you're turning me on, baby,' he whispered as he rejoined her at the table.

'Me too. Shall we go home?' she asked breathlessly.

'Oh no.' His grin was irresistible. 'You don't get off that easily. Let's try the new shirt.'

He photographed her sitting on the beach looking at the boats. The camera's zoom lens, focused on the blouse, caught to perfection the innocent invitation of her breasts.

Another change of clothes. Maddy lying on the grass of the adjacent park reading a newspaper and eating a sandwich. Leaning on her elbow, one knee raised. The camera again zoomed in on the crotch of her skintight jeans.

Another change. Maddy leaning forward to entice a pigeon to feed from her hand. The camera zoomed in on the gaping neck of the denim shirt to reveal an entire breast unwittingly exposed.

And in between each set-up pose they whispered their desire to each other until, after two hours, they could bear it no longer. They found a niche in the rocks down by the foreshore of the park and made love, frantically, feverishly, aware that at any moment they could be discovered— but it didn't matter, nothing mattered.

It lasted only seconds and, afterwards, Maddy could barely believe that she'd done it. But they'd got away with it and she laughed breathlessly with a mixture of relief and sated desire.

Alex insisted they take the film directly to the all-hours chemist at the Cross for development as soon as possible.

'They'll be ready in a week,' he told her as he got back in the car. 'I can't wait,' he said, grinning, 'it'll be like doing it all over again.'

'Why don't we?' suggested Maddy. Alex looked questioningly at her. 'The photos,' she continued. 'Why don't we do it all over again? We could do it every Saturday.'

Alex burst out laughing. 'Hell, Maddy, it'd cost us a fortune.' He kissed her deeply, his desire mounting once more. 'For a late starter you're sure making up for lost time,' he said fondly.

As Maddy rummaged through her T-shirt drawer on Monday morning, Alex said, 'Wear your new one'.

Maddy was about to protest but he got in first. 'I'd like to see you in it.' He ran a finger along her cheek. 'It'll remind me of Saturday.'

In the cold light of Monday morning Maddy

felt a little self-conscious about her abandoned behaviour. 'It's too dressy, Alex. Besides, I want to wear it somewhere special the first time.'

There wasn't even a second's hesitation. 'We're going to Harold's straight after classes.'

'Great.' Maddy was pleased; she always enjoyed going to Harold's. 'Why so early?'

Alex shrugged. 'I don't know. He's probably got something planned.'

'OK, I'll wear the blouse.'

Harold was thrilled when Alex rang him at lunchtime. He thought it was an excellent idea to have an early meal before the theatre and he was only too happy to collect the tickets.

'What do you want to see, dear boy? There's . . .'

'Don't care, Harold. You decide.'

Poor Jonathan Thomas. The moment Maddy walked through the classroom door in the new silk blouse he knew he was undone. Why did they do it to him? Why? The jangling braless breasts in the T-shirts were bad enough, but this! And Maddy, with her woman's body and her fifteen year old face, had always been the most tempting of his students. He moaned inwardly and did his best to avoid her.

It was impossible from the start. 'Heads to the left, two, three, four. To the right, two, three, four. To the front, two, three, four.' The first three neck exercise commands were as much as Jonathan could manage. 'To the back . . .' And as he counted out the following three seconds all he could see was the beautiful column of Maddy's neck, the delicate collarbone, the porcelain skin, the . . .

Oh God, those breasts! His eyes locked on them.

In the instant that all heads snapped back upright, Jonathan turned his back on the class and fumbled for the ruler on the blackboard ledge. It was a habit of his to tap a trouser leg when he was nervous.

'Hands on ribcage.' He walked to the rear of the class, checking the students' postures and beating his grey flannels remorselessly. 'Breathing in, two, three, four. Out, two, three, four. Feel the diaphragm. In, two, three, four.'

Everyone did as they were told and breathed in as Jonathan circled back to the front of the class. The view of Maddy side-on was even more erotic. The sun's rays pouring through the window clearly framed the perfect breasts rising and falling beneath the soft pink fabric.

Jonathan switched to automatic pilot and made it through the class avoiding Maddy as best he could. But his lust had not gone unnoticed. Alex smiled to himself.

For that entire week Alex's sexual appetite was insatiable and Maddy, in responding to him, felt as if she was 'on heat' the whole time.

He encouraged her to wear revealing clothes to classes, to sit provocatively so that he could catch fleeting glimpses of thigh and breast. And the more Alex encouraged her to tantalise, the more she had eyes only for him and was totally unaware of the effect she was having on Jonathan Thomas.

The following Monday morning, on their way to classes, Maddy and Alex collected the photos.

'Three lots of film,' Alex said as he opened the

first pack. 'Cost the earth.' He started flipping through them. 'Bloody well worth it though.'

Maddy, leaning over his shoulder, couldn't understand what he saw in them. Just pictures of herself showing a flash of crotch, thigh or breast. But the intensity with which he was selecting his favourites must mean that he found them arousing and anything that Alex found arousing never failed to excite Maddy.

She put her hand on his knee but he didn't seem to notice. 'We'll be late,' he said as he pocketed his favourite half-dozen photos and handed the pack to Maddy. 'Let's go.' He revved the engine up and ducked into the stream of traffic wending its way through Kings Cross.

Jonathan Thomas had a mid-morning break between classes and he went to his office with the intention of finalising the end-of-term student assessments. He'd finally received Belinda Bellamy's report.

Belinda Bellamy wasn't a bad singing teacher but, in Jonathan's opinion, she was a bit of a twit and always irritatingly late with her reports. Now at last he'd be able to finish his compilation and assessment, and then it would simply need typing up by the administrative secretary . . .

There was an envelope with his name on it sitting on the centre of his blotter. It was marked 'Personal'.

Jonathan opened it to discover a photograph of Maddy McLaughlan. She was sitting in a beer garden looking distractedly into the distance and sipping a drink, obviously unaware that a photograph was being taken of her and that a flash of white-pantied crotch was visible to the unseen photographer.

There was another photo. Maddy in a park feeding a pigeon, the unseen photographer perfectly capturing an exposed breast. There was another and another. Six in all.

Jonathan felt a slow, steady erection. Someone had obviously followed the girl—over a period of days, it would seem: different locations, different outfits. But why send them to him?

He tried to will his erection away but it was impossible. Oh God, there was a photo of her in that blouse. Focusing on the breasts, obviously taken with a zoom lens.

Jonathan quickly returned the shots to the envelope and put it in the top drawer of his desk. He sat down sweating slightly, his mind racing, his penis rock-hard. What was happening? Why had the photos been sent to him? What should he do about them? But, behind all the questioning, behind all the mystery, was the image of Maddy. He couldn't get the photos out of his mind.

Jonathan had two more classes before lunch and still the image stayed with him. At a quarter past one, as he put his salad sandwich and his orange juice on the desk before him, he fought against his desire to open the top drawer.

It was impossible. He had to see them. Just once, he told himself, and he spread the photographs out on the desk. Just a look, he promised himself, but of course it was useless.

He checked his watch—half past one. The rest of the staff would be at lunch. On Mondays they congregated at the coffee shop and on Fridays the pub. It was only midweek that they hung around the classrooms with their sandwiches.

Jonathan pocketed the photographs and visited the deserted staff lavatory. Just the once, he told himself.

But the end of the day saw him again in his office staring at the photos spread out on his desk and again wondering if there would be anyone in the staff lavatory. He didn't hear the gentle tap on the door. He didn't even hear the door being quietly opened.

'Excuse me, Mr Thomas.' It was Alex Rainford. In one swift movement Jonathan swept the photographs up and dropped them into the top drawer.

'Yes, Alex?' he said, quickly shutting the drawer.

'I'm sorry. I knocked, but you didn't—'

'That's perfectly all right,' Jonathan snapped, telling himself there was no way the boy could have seen. 'What can I do for you?'

Alex had now closed the door behind him and his servile manner disappeared immediately.

'You can leave my girlfriend alone, that's what you can do.'

'I beg your pardon!' Jonathan stared back, dumbfounded.

'You've been following her, haven't you?' Alex hissed. 'Following her and perving and—'

'I have no idea what you're talking about.' Jonathan rose from his chair to calm the young man who seemed to be on the verge of hysteria. 'But I suggest you . . .'

Before Jonathan knew it, Alex had shoved him aside, pulled open the drawer and slammed the photographs on top of the desk beside the blotter.

'Perving and taking photos. Like these. Haven't you? And I bet there's more.' Alex congratulated himself on how easy it all was. He'd anticipated having to tear the room apart in a fit of rage to find the photos. Jonathan's swift, guilty move to the drawer had certainly simplified matters.

Jonathan stared down at his desk, his mind numbed by the speed of it all. How had the boy known he had the photos? How could all this be happening to him? Why?

'I didn't take them,' he heard himself stammering. 'I found them on my desk. They're not mine, I didn't take them.'

'You expect me to believe that, you dirty wanker! You follow my girl, you perve and take pictures and then you expect me to believe they just landed on your desk?'

Flushed with the guilt of his trip to the staff lavatory Jonathan could only nod. 'They did, they did just land on my desk. This morning.'

'You don't have a very good track record, do you, Thomas?' The rage had gone from Alex's voice and the simple statement totally confused Jonathan. 'I don't think you'll find anyone who'll believe you.' Alex paused. 'Of course, if you could see your way clear to changing my assessment, no one need ever know about the photos.'

Jonathan stared at Alex and slowly shook his head in disbelief. 'You took them, didn't you?'

Alex nodded. 'Yes. I want to stay at NADA, Mr Thomas.'

Jonathan felt faint. He sat heavily and put his hands on the desk top, breathing deeply.

Alex stood watching the man, waiting for the admission of defeat.

Finally, Jonathan took his hands from the table and looked directly at Alex. 'Well, you've obviously researched my weakness. Very thorough. Well done.'

Alex nodded his agreement. He felt no triumph but he was pleased. His had been a good, simple plan, born of necessity, not malice.

'However,' Jonathan continued, 'you've most certainly underestimated my strength.'

Strength? Alex waited. What strength? The man was a joke.

'I have never compromised my principles as a teacher and I don't intend to start now.' There was an unexpected edge to Jonathan's voice and he looked at Alex with contempt. 'I suggest you take your photographs to the Board and attempt whatever damage you can.'

Alex was surprised. Who would have thought the man had a backbone? They stared at each other for several seconds, then Alex turned and walked out of the office.

Jonathan's instinctive rush of relief was short-lived. His office door opened again and Alex reappeared. Maddy was at his side.

'I hadn't actually thought of going to the Board, Mr Thomas.' Alex flashed a winning smile, first at Maddy, then back to Jonathan.

As Maddy smiled a greeting at him, Jonathan found himself automatically nodding to her before turning once again to Alex. So this was the boy's trump card, he thought, and he started to feel sick.

How would he ever be able to prove to the girl that Alex had taken those photographs? How could he tell her that her own lover had so compromised her? Then a thought flashed through

69

his brain that perhaps the girl had posed for the photographs, perhaps they were a lovers' game. Either way he was sure she had no idea how Alex was using them.

Was the boy bluffing? he wondered. But, even as he wondered, he knew there was no way he could afford to take the risk. There was one thing Jonathan knew for certain. The thought of Maddy knowing how he had used her image over the toilet bowl in the staff lavatory was beyond endurance.

Under the pretext of tidying his desk, Jonathan gently placed the blotter over the top of the photographs.

'You've made your point, Alex,' he said with deliberation. 'I think we can solve things without involving the Board—or others in general.'

'Oh, thanks, Mr Thomas.' Alex shook Jonathan's hand effusively and grinned to Maddy. 'Did you hear that, Mad! He's giving me another go. Thanks, Mr Thomas, that's great!'

In the corridor outside, Alex picked Maddy up and whirled her about. 'See! I told you there was no need to worry.'

'Oh, Alex, that's wonderful.' She kissed him. 'But why did you want me there? Why did you make me wait outside?'

'Because I knew he was going to give me another chance, sweetheart, and I wanted you to hear him say it yourself. I want to share everything with you, Maddy. Oh God, I love you!' And any other questions Maddy may have had disappeared altogether as he kissed her deeply.

On the other side of the door Jonathan sat unmoving, staring at his blotter. His head ached. Slowly he slid the blotter to one side and looked down at the photographs. And as he did he felt, to his utter humiliation, the familiar stirring in his groin. Not now, he thought, surely not now?

As Jonathan's erection grew, so did his feeling of shame. He knew that it would always be like this. For the rest of his life he was destined to be tormented. He detested himself. He sat staring at the photographs for a long time, then he picked up the phone and dialled.

'Mrs Laney? It's Mr Thomas. I wonder would it be too inconvenient for you to come around tomorrow instead of next Tuesday?' As he spoke he took an envelope from one of the drawers and slid the photographs inside. 'Yes, a special occasion, so I want the house looking nice and tidy. That's excellent, thank you. The usual time.'

The next morning, Mrs Laney opened the letterbox outside Jonathan's apartment with her special key and took out the customary envelope. Mrs Laney had 'done' for Jonathan every second Tuesday for eight years and, along with her cash payment, there was always a letter which contained her special instructions for the day—the oven to be scoured or the refrigerator to be defrosted or the venetians to be cleaned.

She was surprised to find that the envelope contained an extra twenty dollars and she wondered why. It wasn't Christmas, could it be a mistake? But it wasn't like Mr Thomas to make mistakes. She read the note: 'Dear Mrs Laney, I'm so sorry to inflict this upon you'.

When she opened the door she was overwhelmed by the stench of gas. It was a small apartment and every crack in every window was blocked with towels. With the exception of the bedroom, all doors were open, however, to ensure the gas would permeate the two small rooms from kitchen to bathroom.

A practical woman, Mrs Laney turned off the gas, opened the windows and searched the apartment before calling the police.

Jonathan was in the bath up to his neck in water, fully clothed, with the veins of both wrists neatly opened. Apart from the bright red water there wasn't a speck of blood to be seen. He'd been very meticulous.

It hadn't hurt at all. He'd soaked in the hot water for a good ten minutes and the three Valium he'd downed an hour before were well and truly taking effect before he got to work with the razor blade.

When he'd finished, he carefully rinsed the blade and set it on the side of the bath. He then looked through the open door at the clock on the lounge room mantelpiece. Eight o'clock. Twelve hours before Mrs Laney arrived. He'd been very thorough and he'd accomplished it all with the minimum of mess—there'd be very little cleaning up to do. That's good, Jonathan had thought, as he relaxed and let his mind drift.

He recalled the edges of the photographs as they curled and blackened in the washbasin. And he smiled: as he'd watched the flames licking at the image of the girl, he'd felt no sensation in his groin at all.

Jonathan had felt a magnificent contentment as he lay back and watched the water turn pink.

ACT I

SCENE 4: 1970

The whole of NADA was shocked by the news of Jonathan's suicide. It was so unexpected, everyone said, including Alex, and he meant it. Jonathan's death had been the last thing he'd intended and he couldn't understand it. Surely they'd come to an amicable enough understanding? Alex had certainly intended to keep his part of the bargain and not breathe a word to anyone. He would even have been happy for Jonathan to keep the photos of Maddy for his personal use.

Then another thought occurred to Alex. What if Jonathan had handed in his report before he killed himself? Hell, of course he would have: the man would want blood for blood. Alex cursed himself. So the whole exercise had been in vain.

There was only one way to find out. The morning after the news had broken, Alex stole into Jonathan's office.

The folder was where it had always been, sitting in the left-hand desk drawer. How strange, Alex thought, but how fortunate. He slipped the papers under his jacket, checked the corridor and ducked out quietly, closing the door behind him.

The funeral was late Friday afternoon and NADA classes finished an hour earlier than usual so that those students who wished to attend could do so. A surprising number of them did, including Alex, Maddy and Julian.

'Bit hypocritical, isn't it? You didn't even like the bloke,' Julian argued when Alex suggested they pay their respects.

'I'd like to go,' said Maddy, who felt saddened by Jonathan's suicide and even a little guilty. What terrible turmoil the man must have been in without anyone knowing, she thought, regretting the times she'd dismissed him as 'that old perve'. 'Let's go,' she insisted and Julian shrugged and gave in.

Alex was grateful that Maddy had been the deciding factor; he would have had trouble explaining his desire to go. The truth was he didn't really know himself. But as he sat there, his eyes fixed on the casket, trying to imagine Jonathan inside, he was fascinated by the knowledge that he himself had been the catalyst. Of course the man must have been unhinged to have taken such drastic measures, Alex told himself, and someone else and some other set of circumstances could have brought about the same result. But it hadn't been someone else, had it?

Alex felt a surge of power, mingled with respect for Jonathan. That sort of decision took guts and the guy had certainly done the job well according to the stories that were circulating.

He said as much to Julian that night at the Oxford Street pub after Maddy had left for the restaurant. The boys had shared two joints in the men's lavatory and Alex had phoned in sick to the garage, a thing he'd never done before.

'Yeah, it'd take a helluva lot of guts to kill yourself,' he repeated.

Julian looked at him closely. Alex was in such a strange mood tonight. Maybe it was just the mixture of the wine and the grass, Julian thought, aware of his own euphoric glow. But they'd 'mixed' many a time in the past and Alex had never been affected like this.

'There's something I want to tell you, Julian.'

For twenty minutes Julian didn't say a word. He sat frozen as Alex recounted, step by step, the events of the past two weeks.

'It never occurred to me that he'd kill himself,' Alex concluded. Julian remained transfixed.

Julian's mesmeric reaction was goading Alex on. He sensed a growing revulsion and he was curious as to how much truth Julian could stand.

'Just as it never occurred to me that my brother would kill himself.' For a moment Alex wondered why he'd said that. Then he smiled. 'But it was fascinating when he did,' he added. Of course he knew why he'd said it. He wanted to test Julian's love for him. Something inside was telling Alex that he needed to share his power with Julian. 'Did I ever tell you about Tim?' he asked.

It was a rhetorical question and Julian remained

breathlessly still as Alex leaned back in his chair with his hands behind his head.

'It started out as a dare,' he said.

As Alex carefully recounted every detail of that summer's day nine years ago, Julian tried as hard as he could to contain his horror. It was only when the image of Tim's white, drained body was indelibly printed in his mind; when the image of the broken man kneeling in the blood beside the boy was more than he could bear; when little Lexie's voice was ringing in his ears . . . 'he killed himself, Dad' . . . it was only then Julian managed to tear his attention away from Alex.

He concentrated on a squashed cigarette butt beside his right shoe, wishing he'd never heard what Alex had just told him, realising that he'd listened compulsively and now, compulsively, he had to know more.

'Why did you tell your father Tim killed himself?'

During the telling of his story, Alex had wondered whether he'd made an error of judgment, whether he'd chosen the wrong listener. He'd been wanting to tell one of the three people who loved him about Tim for quite a while now. Maddy was out of the question, of course, she'd never have coped, but Alex now thought that maybe he should have chosen Harold.

'Why did you tell your father Tim killed himself?' Julian repeated the question.

'Because he did kill himself,' Alex replied.

Julian didn't pursue it further. He had too many other questions. 'Why didn't you go for help?'

Alex relaxed. No, he hadn't chosen the wrong listener. Julian was riveted. He was shocked and repulsed and he would see Alex through different eyes from this day on, but he was riveted.

Nevertheless Alex decided it was time to soften the blow a little. He frowned slightly as he considered the question. 'I suppose I must have been in a state of shock. That's what everyone said, anyway. And I was sent to psychiatrists for the next couple of years.' Julian waited for him to go on and Alex shrugged obligingly. 'They didn't find any answers.' His smile was deeply apologetic. 'I guess I was a pretty weird kid.'

It was true that psychiatric treatment had been of no use to little Lexie—there had apparently been nothing to treat.

Psychiatric treatment had also been of no use to Brian Rainford who agonised over why his ten year old son would want to take his own life.

Everyone told him it had been an accident but when the inquest report stated that the boy had fired the gun himself and when young Lexie, the only witness to the event, stood firm in his conviction that Tim had killed himself, Brian Rainford was tormented by massive guilt.

The inquest report also revealed that it had taken an hour and a half for Tim to die. The thought that Lexie had sat and watched and the knowledge that the boy might still be alive if he'd received instant medical attention was more than Brian could bear. He'd failed his eldest son who'd suicided and he had to face the fact that his youngest son was a monster.

Two months after the shooting Brian Rainford was retired from the police force on medical grounds. His resilient wife Trish, who at times so wanted to give in as well, had no option but to grit her teeth and fight to preserve what little was left of her family. She convinced herself it had all been a terrible accident and that Lexie was anything but the monster his father believed him to be. Indeed, she told herself, the child was so traumatised that even the psychiatrists couldn't analyse the depth of his shock. She fought with every fibre of her being to preserve her husband's sanity and to create a secure environment in which Lexie could grow up feeling loved. But it was no good. Brian's analysts eventually agreed that he needed to be institutionalised for his own safety as well as that of his son.

When he was released nine months later Brian Rainford got a job as a security guard at one of the large hotels but he only lasted six months. He was dismissed on the spot when he was discovered to be the reason for the hefty increase in theft from the bottle department. It was only the plea from Trish and her revelation of the family tragedy that saved him from prosecution.

There followed a procession of security guard jobs which, together with Brian's police pension, kept the family financially solvent but, as the black moods and the bouts of drunkenness increased, even Trish gave up. She stopped pretending everything was going to be all right some day, and learned to suffer the occasional beating and the pathetic remorse of the following morning. One day, when Alex was seventeen and announced that he was leaving home, she found she had no more feeling left in her except a vague sense of relief. Perhaps, ungoaded by the constant presence of his son, Brian's black moods would abate a fraction. Perhaps, every now and then, there might be just a little peace and quiet. All Trish wanted was a little peace and quiet.

Norah Hogarth's introductory improvisation class flashed through Julian's mind. That first day at NADA when he had been drawn to Alex like a magnet: 'My father's a security guard with a hefty drink problem and my mother's a housewife who puts up with it' . . . Christ, no wonder! The poor bastards!

And now Alex was flashing that devastating smile of his and shrugging off the destruction of his family with an apologetic, 'I guess I must have been a pretty weird kid'.

'So that's my sordid past, Julian.' Alex's contrite smile broadened to a confident grin and Julian knew that there was now a bond between them. An insidious but inescapably magnetic bond.

Later that night Julian started recording the first of many notes on the complexities of Alex Rainford. He wasn't sure why. Whatever the reason though, his study of Alex was to become a lifetime occupation and was destined to have a vast impact on both their lives.

Julian went through a brief agony of indecision as to whether he should tell Maddy about Alex. But one had only to look at Maddy to realise that she was totally in love. Julian couldn't bring himself to shatter her dream. He could only watch, wait and hope that somehow she might escape, that her affair with Alex would not lead to her own destruction.

Surprisingly enough he didn't have to wait long. Maddy's 'escape' came far sooner than he'd anticipated and in a manner he'd least expected.

It was a hot spring afternoon exactly one month before the last day of their first year at NADA. Maddy had dashed off to the Family Planning Association at lunch break to check out why she'd missed a period and to enquire whether she should change her brand of contraceptive pill if it was going to continue giving her these strange side effects. She was understandably stunned to find herself part of the one per cent failure rate attributed to the birth control pill.

'Geez, Mad, that's not fair.' Alex was dutifully sympathetic but didn't appear to be particularly fazed by the news. 'I mean, how unlucky would you have to be?'

'What am I going to do, Alex?' Maddy was holding her tears in check. He was right—it wasn't fair. 'I'm halfway through NADA, I've been working hard and doing well. I can't drop out to have a baby.'

''Course you can't. Here, have a sandwich.' Alex unwrapped the lunch he'd bought her and gently offered her half a chicken and avocado sandwich, her favourite.

Maddy barely heard him. 'What am I going to do?'

'Get rid of it, of course.'

Maddy heard him that time. She ignored the sandwich and stared at him, bewildered. 'Have an abortion?' she whispered after several seconds that seemed like an age.

'Sure.' Alex registered her horror but couldn't for the life of him understand it. 'Oh, come on, Mad, it's the only thing to do and it's no big deal.'

He put the sandwich in her hand and gently wrapped her fingers around it. 'There you go. I got double avocado. God, you've got expensive tastes.'

Maddy stared down at the sandwich, feeling numb. 'Lots of top doctors do abortions on the side these days,' Alex continued. 'Doesn't matter what it costs—we'll get the money from your father.' Maddy's eyes left the sandwich and she looked at him blankly. 'Or I'll get it out of Harold,' he corrected quickly. 'No one needs to know what it's for.'

Maddy wondered for an instant why Alex's easy way so shocked her. Then she realised. It wasn't the influence of her father's devout beliefs, it wasn't her Catholic schooling. It wasn't even the idea of abortion itself. It was the sudden knowledge that Alex couldn't truly love her as she had believed he did. And, in that instant of recognition, the innocence of Maddy's own love died. Her unquestioning belief that her love for Alex was equally reciprocated disappeared.

Over the next few weeks Alex, convinced that Maddy's depressed state was due to the prospect of an abortion, came up with a series of more 'natural' abortive procedures than an illegal visit to a doctor. He got two sets of pills 'bound to bring about a miscarriage'. Both failed. He insisted she try the old housewives' remedy of the hot bath and the bottle of gin. Maddy threw up copiously, just as she had with the pills, but nothing else happened. Heavy exercise and overlong saunas failed to do the trick and eventually there was nothing for it but to make the appointment with the doctor.

Maddy had quietly accepted the rigours Alex put her through and her final acceptance of the inevitability of abortion appeared to be just as placid. She nodded when Alex told her one night that he'd been recommended an excellent GP who conducted abortions from his own practice at night with a nurse in attendance. 'No back street job, Mad. He's the best.'

As Maddy continued to nod, Alex thought it might be advisable to follow through with his suggestion that the money come from Harold rather than her father. Maddy's strangely withdrawn mood had been unsettling and Alex didn't want to do anything to unnecessarily rock the boat. The sooner they got rid of the baby, he thought, the sooner things would get back to normal.

'No,' Maddy said surprisingly. 'I'll get it from Daddy.'

'What will you say it's for?'

Maddy shrugged. 'Doesn't really matter: next year's school fees, new gear—he wants to give me anything I'll accept.'

It was true. Robert McLaughlan had been trying even harder of late to involve himself in Maddy's life. He was desperately unhappy but Maddy hadn't been able to discover why. Whenever she visited the family home her mother was as bright and effervescent as ever and her father was his usual considerate but withdrawn self. It was only when Robert rang to invite himself over to the flat, fortunately allowing time for Maddy to hide Alex's gear, or when he invited his daughter out to dinner that he gave himself away. His eyes looked sad and defeated but when Maddy questioned him he got embarrassed and changed the subject.

'Nothing's wrong, dear. Now tell me about your classes: how are they going?'

When Maddy rang her father to suggest she call around for dinner on Saturday Robert said he'd rather take her out. 'Your mother's off to a charity function so it would only be the two of us anyway.' Maddy was happy enough with the suggestion; her father would be less inquisitive than her mother about why she wanted 700 dollars, anyway.

'Yes, of course, dear, I'm only too glad to be of some help. Is 700 dollars enough?' Robert seemed preoccupied. He pulled his cheque book and his gold Sheaffer pen from his breast pocket and started writing. 'Why don't we make it a round thousand?'

'All right.' Maddy hadn't even given a reason for her request and she watched with interest as her father handed her the cheque, cleared his throat and started poking his dessert spoon at the chocolate mousse he hadn't yet tried.

'I was glad you wanted to meet tonight. There's something I want to tell you.'

Maddy had suspected as much. The comfortable silences that normally existed between father and daughter had been filled with nervous small talk as Robert McLaughlan had picked his way through half a dozen rock oysters and a broiled lobster. But what was he avoiding?

Now he dropped all pretence of interest in his chocolate mousse, pushed it aside and looked directly at her for the first time that evening. 'Your mother and I are separating.'

Maddy stared back at him, dumbfounded.

'I'm selling up the practice and going to England next month.' Now that he'd broken the ice there was no stopping him. 'I'm not granting her a divorce of course, I'd never do that, but she'll be well looked after. The house'll be hers and she won't be short of money.'

Robert didn't even wait for a comment from Maddy. 'I've been offered a partnership in a Harley Street practice. Fellow called Bill Davenport. He's on the board of The Royal College of Orthodontists and we've become rather pally at international conventions over the years so it's working out quite well.'

'Why, Daddy?' Finally Maddy interrupted.

The waiter was hovering nearby and Robert nodded curtly. When the table was cleared and they were waiting for coffee he hesitatingly explained that he hadn't realised how dissatisfied Helena had become with their staid lifestyle and how she craved more excitement than was in his power to give.

'I thought her social life was enough of an outlet, but . . .'

It was only when Robert was towards the end of his second cognac—and he rarely drank—that he admitted Helena had been having an affair for several months now. 'At least that's all she'll admit to,' he said, draining his brandy balloon and nodding to the waiter. 'Graeme Doyle, you'd remember him.'

Maddy did. 'But he's twenty years younger than she is.'

'Fifteen, actually. He's just turned twenty-nine.'

Maddy remembered Graeme Doyle vividly. He'd been one of her mother's regular escorts for the past six years at least and had made a pass at Maddy when she was fourteen. Maddy hadn't bothered telling her mother at the time because Graeme had turned it into a joke when he saw her reaction, and she knew her mother wouldn't believe her anyway.

Graeme was Helena's favourite escort and she treated him like a wayward child, teasing him remorselessly about his penchant for women old enough to be his mother and why didn't he find a nice young girl his own age and settle down. Indeed, Maddy had decided very early on that Graeme preferred the company of older, prominent women because they were far more advantageous to his tenuous actor-model career.

Now the mature Maddy wondered just how long her mother's playful banter had been that of a woman to her lover. Poor Daddy, she thought.

The depth of sympathy she felt must have been instantly readable because, as the fresh brandy balloon was placed on the table, Robert waited only seconds for the waiter to clear the previous glass and turn away before he lifted it to his lips and drained it in one gulp.

'Yes,' he said, the fumes catching at the back of his throat. 'She says it's only been going on for a few months and I suppose I'm to believe her.' It was obvious he didn't. His voice was harsh and rasping, due not only to the brandy fumes but to the bitterness and accusation he was fighting to control.

Maddy put her hand over his and for once he let it remain there. 'Shall we get the bill?' she asked. A fourth cognac and he'd write himself off driving home.

Later that night, Maddy showed Alex the cheque. When he asked if she'd had any trouble she replied, 'No, it was easy'. And when Alex then said, 'You'll have to cash it in, Mad, he wants twenty dollar notes', she made the decision she'd been agonising over for the past fortnight.

'Helena, isn't it? Helena Rainford?' Maddy nodded. She didn't know why she'd chosen her mother's first name and Alex's surname. But then, why not? The doctor's smile was frozen and glassy as he went through the bedside manner motions and Maddy knew that he was just waiting to talk cold hard cash.

Sure enough, after he'd discussed dates, given her a physical examination and ascertained she was six to eight weeks pregnant . . . 'You realise the fee is 700 dollars. Do you have the money with you?'

The glassy smile was gone and it was down to business as the doctor skinned the glove from his hand, threw it in the bin and turned to the sink.

'Yes.' Maddy felt weird, as if she wasn't really there and this was happening to someone else. Everything was strangely remote, even the doctor's hands as he'd felt her womb and pressed her abdomen.

After she dressed she didn't bother sitting down but took the envelope from her pocket and placed it on the desk. 'In cash, as agreed,' she said.

The doctor finished drying his hands, sat at his desk and picked up the envelope. 'Is tomorrow night convenient? Nine o'clock?'

Tomorrow. So soon. 'Fine.' Maddy started to leave. She didn't want to watch him counting the money.

'He told me I have to be on my own,' she explained to Alex later that evening. 'But I guess it's OK if you wait outside.'

'I'll stay in the car.' Alex kissed her tenderly. 'Don't worry, Mad. Everything'll be all right. They say he's the best.'

At five to nine the following night Alex watched Maddy walk under the street lamp and then up the darkened steps to the unlit front door. He felt a sense of relief. Soon it would all be over. Soon Maddy would be his again and they'd be able to get on with their lives. He switched the car radio on to the soft music station and sat back in the MGB to wait.

He was still there an hour later and starting to wonder whether he should do something when the door opened. A shaft of light streamed onto the front porch and Maddy appeared. For a second she swayed, unsteady on her feet, then the door closed and she was in darkness.

Alex raced up the steps. Maddy looked as if she was about to faint. He gathered her in his arms and carried her to the car, ignoring her protestations. 'It's only the anaesthetic, Alex. I can walk, really, I'm just a bit woozy, that's all.' But she slumped in the seat and, when they pulled up outside the flat twenty minutes later, she was almost unconscious.

He carried her inside and laid her on the bed. He took her shoes off but wasn't sure what else he should do. When he tried to unbutton the top of her blouse she mumbled something incoherent which he took to be a protest and so he decided the only thing was to maintain a watch. Her breathing seemed normal and he presumed everything was all right.

Alex sat and watched for an hour before Maddy's eyes flickered open. She looked at him for several very long seconds and her expression was so enigmatic that Alex wondered whether he should worry. Then she smiled. Beneath the weariness of the smile was understanding and forgiveness. 'I'm all right, Alex. Go to sleep. Please.'

He smoothed her hair back, kissed her on the brow and gave a deep sigh of relief. His Maddy was back.

For the next two weeks she wasn't quite the same Maddy—she was a little withdrawn and she didn't want sex but Alex supposed that was under-standable. In an effort to discover exactly what it was she wanted he tried to play the situation several ways: sympathy, bitterness, commiseration, but every approach drew the same response. 'Alex, I'm fine. I don't want you to worry about me. Please.'

She was tender, she was understanding, but she was also remote and it irritated him. If she wanted to play martyr then bugger her, he thought, and he allowed himself to be distracted by Susannah.

Susannah Wright was Maddy's rival in the top female student stakes. Susannah Wright was also one of NADA's 'serious' students. Wraithlike-thin, she wore her 'serious student uniform' of black mini, black tights and black ankle length boots with pride, played Masha in *The Seagull* well and was destined for 'the classics'. There was a sterile sexlessness about Susannah. But she was unaware of this, blissfully convinced that her talent, her passion, her intensity, her very name—'Susannah with an "h"'—made her unattainable and desirable. She fiercely maintained her virginity, pouring all of her considerable energy into her work.

It took Alex exactly one week of concentrated effort to get Susannah into bed. Hers, of course—he didn't want to upset Maddy. After all, it was only a one-night exercise to prove he could do it, just a distraction from the stalemate situation at home.

It therefore came as a bit of a shock to Alex when Maddy disappeared. Surely she couldn't have left because of Susannah. He'd been so discreet! He didn't worry for the first few days. It was the weekend, after all, and he figured Maddy was probably taking a dramatic stand. She was probably staying at Harold's and they were having a great time badmouthing him together, so Alex didn't ring.

But when Maddy didn't turn up for classes on Monday Alex had to think again. Her friends were also mystified. Both Harold and Julian rang the McLaughlan house to discover that nothing had been heard from Maddy and that Robert McLaughlan had left for overseas.

Alex was angry and refused to make any further enquiries. 'She can go to hell,' he said to Harold. 'She obviously doesn't give a shit about me.' And Harold said nothing, his heart bleeding for the agony Alex must be going through.

Julian's visit to the McLaughlan house also failed to shed any light. It was six o'clock in the evening when Helena opened the door to him and, although she wasn't rude, she was very brittle and evasive.

'This is Graeme Doyle,' she waved towards the handsome young man whom Julian had met around the traps on several occasions. 'Would you like a glass of wine?'

She was obviously a little drunk and she dismissed every one of Julian's questions about Maddy. 'I've no idea where she is but I'm sure she'll be in touch at her own convenience. She always was a wilful girl.' Julian felt sorry for the woman; she seemed desperately unhappy.

Enquiries as to Maddy's whereabouts were also made by the directors of NADA but again nothing was forthcoming. With no explanation whatsoever, one of their prize pupils had disappeared. Why? Nobody could come up with any answers. Maddy had gone and that was that.

ACT II

1972–1981

ACT II

SCENE 1: 1972–1973

Alex escaped the Vietnam war. At first he felt vaguely disappointed, but when he thought harder about it he felt positively let down. He'd been conscripted in 1971 but had deferred for a year to finish his NADA training. Three months after he left the Academy there was still not an acting job in sight and Alex decided that going to war would perhaps be more interesting, and certainly more lucrative, than milling around with the other hopefuls at casting session cattle calls.

He waited impatiently to be called up again by the military and was about to make waves and demand attention when suddenly the Australian troops were pulled out of Vietnam and there followed a weary return of soldiers to an ungrateful country. They were quick to discover that it had been a grubby war. Academics informed them that 'we should never have been there in the first place' and advised them to keep quiet about having gone.

Alex, however, was a most rewarding listener. He sought out any Vietnam vet who wished to talk about his experience and sat enthralled by the tales of war. Whether they were stories of action or fraternisation with the Vietnamese women or merely about the boredom and inactivity of war, he was equally attentive.

Because of his sympathy with the bitterness so many felt and his offence at their unheralded homecoming, Alex made a number of new friends. Friends who, much to Julian's disapproval, didn't realise Alex was living a war vicariously through them and their stories.

Alex sensed Julian's disapproval and for a while they drifted apart. He 'raged' with his heavy-drinking soldier mates while Julian continued to serve a further twelve months at NADA completing his directors' course.

Alex's fascination with the war soon waned, however, and he dropped his new mates as quickly as he'd adopted them.

Alex called around to see Harold one afternoon. He hadn't seen him for months and rarely answered his phone messages—so rarely, in fact, that Harold had sadly given up ringing.

To Alex's surprise, Julian was there. It was a late Saturday afternoon and he and Harold were sitting on the balcony drinking gin and tonic with huge wedges of lime—the only way to drink gin, according to Harold.

Julian had socialised with Harold many a time over the past couple of years but only ever in the company of Alex. Now here they were together and apparently great pals. It didn't for a moment cross Alex's mind to be jealous. His two best friends were waiting for him, ready to welcome him back, and he couldn't be happier.

'Bit of a change from triple bourbons with beer chasers,' he winked at Julian as he watched Harold carefully slicing another lime to add to a fresh gin he was making for Alex. 'Haven't I been a silly-billy?' He gave one of his special grins and camped it up for Harold as he took the drink. 'Am I accepted back into the fold?'

Harold and Julian exchanged a look that said it all and then they both laughed. There was no denying it, Alex had them in his pocket, all right. He knew it, they knew it—why bother denying it?

The truth was that the friendship forged between Harold and Julian had been born directly of their love and fascination for Alex. When Harold's pride told him to stop leaving unanswered messages he sought out Julian to discover the reason for Alex's avoidance. It was a relief to find that Julian was being avoided just as assiduously and that he was convinced this was 'one of Alex's fads'.

'Just Alex being a shit, Harold, using people as he always does. He'll come back, don't worry.'

Harold countered Julian's accusation with stories of the early days when Alex had steadfastly refused not only money, but Harold's offer to 'pull strings' to advance his career.

Julian shrugged. 'It simply means that wasn't the way he wanted to go at the time. It wasn't because of any moral sense. He doesn't have one.'

The two men met regularly after that and Alex was invariably the topic of conversation. For a long time Maddy also featured regularly in their talks. Harold couldn't understand how Alex had so quickly come to terms with Maddy's disappearance. He couldn't fathom the fact that Alex no longer talked about her. Indeed, whenever her name was mentioned there seemed to be a fractional delay as if Alex were reminding himself of who she was.

'It's an act, surely,' Harold insisted. 'He's covering the fact that he's hurting.'

'Balls,' Julian scoffed. 'It's nearly two years since Maddy left. Another two years and he'll have forgotten her entirely.'

Harold was a little taken aback by Julian's harsh view of Alex. 'Why the venom, dear boy? You're his best friend. Well, you and I are his best friends,' he hastily corrected.

Julian looked at the aging actor for several moments and his eventual reply was evasively kind. 'No venom, Harold. Just the knowledge that Alex is a bit of a heartbreaker and he can hurt people without realising.' Love is certainly blind, he thought. For a man of perception Harold was blissfully unaware of Alex's barefaced manipulation.

'Oh, don't I know it,' Harold agreed heartily and theatrically. 'He is one for whom people are destined to die, that boy.'

You said it, Julian thought, and he vowed never to tell Harold the tales of Jonathan Thomas and Tim.

And now here was Alex, back in their lives again and surveying them with amused affection. That afternoon on the balcony he dubbed them his 'odd couple' and the term stuck. From then on it was weekly dinners or lunches at Harold's as usual but with Maddy replaced by Julian.

It was towards the end of the year that The Way In Theatre Company held its general auditions for the upcoming 1973 season. The Way In had been formed the previous year with Arts Council funding and a generous and most unusual government grant. Its policy was to produce only the classics, its Board of Directors was comprised solely of NADA lecturers and ex-NADA graduates and the actors and directors employed from the work force were invariably ex-NADA.

Harold had been right. The old school tie did count and Alex knew he stood a more reasonable chance than he'd had of late with the commercial theatres. Julian helped him select his audition pieces—'plenty of colour and movement; don't forget Norah Hogarth's doing choreography for the season'—and Harold's untiring coaching was of tremendous assistance.

Alex arrived at The Way in Theatre at his allotted time, two o'clock on Tuesday afternoon, feeling positive. He refused to allow his confidence to be undermined when he stepped into the foyer to see seven other auditionees all waiting their turn, although there was the customary rush of irritation. Why were special times ever allotted for auditions? he thought. They invariably ran late and they invariably turned into cattle calls. He was also aware that this was only the second day of a planned four-day line-up. How many other hopefuls were there, for God's sake? But he wasn't going to think about that, he was going to . . .

'Alex!' It was Susannah Wright. Even more

wraithlike than ever. How thin can a person get? Alex wondered momentarily, hoping that she was well over their long-ago one-night stand. She'd chased him for months after it, he recollected. Hell, a painful scene now before his audition was something he didn't need.

'How great to see you!' Susannah enthused. 'Good luck with the audition.' She certainly appeared to have got over it, thought Alex with relief. Of course, a successful career would help. She'd been fresh out of NADA and the youngest actor to be contracted by The Way In Theatre Company for its premiere 1972 season. 'I'll be reading opposite you.' She smiled encouragingly.

'How come?'

'They've signed me up for the next season and I'm here to read opposite the male auditionees.' The door to the auditorium opened. The stage manager appeared, consulted his list and called 'Leonard, Peter-John.' Then he nodded to Susannah and disappeared.

'Got to go. Chookas.' She patted him on the arm as she wished him the actors' term for good luck.

'Thanks. Hey,' Alex called after her, 'what time are they finishing up today? Do you want to go for a drink?'

'Around four-thirty. Love to.' And she was gone.

Whatever had happened to the arrogant, self-opinionated Susannah? Alex thought. She was charming. And for such a thin person, devastatingly attractive.

Success did indeed agree with Susannah and her driving ambition had most certainly helped her get over Alex, with whom she'd been besotted. He was her first, after all. In fact, Susannah had only been with two men since and they'd both been so vastly inferior to Alex as lovers that she'd quickly got rid of them. If she couldn't have the best, she didn't want anything at all.

As she did with everything that affected her, Susannah set out to use her experience with Alex. So that's how loss of virginity felt, she told herself. So that's how good sex and infatuation felt. Then the poignant ache of a broken heart, unrequited love. So they felt like that, did they? On and on: Susannah analysed all aspects of every emotional experience and stored them up to apply to her craft whenever they might be called upon.

Susannah looped the feather boa around his neck. 'Doesn't it feel nice and soft, Jack?' Her eyes were full of promise and she twirled about him coquettishly, fluttering her plastic prop fan as if it were the finest Edwardian lace.

Alex was lost in admiration. She was fascinating. Then he dropped his eyes to the script in his hand and they continued with the scene.

They were doing an excerpt from *Man and Superman* which pleased Alex. He had always loved the clinical quality of George Bernard Shaw's plays. His mind flashed back to the first time he'd ever gone to the theatre. That had been a Shaw play. Harold of course, being brilliant in *Heartbreak House*.

And now here *he* was, Alex Rainford, playing Jack Tanner opposite Susannah's tantalising Anne. The audition was going well and he knew it. He'd performed his solo prepared pieces smoothly and, when the impromptu piece set by the directors proved to be a scene from *Man and Superman*, Alex took it as an omen. Surely he was home and hosed now. And Susannah was pushing him along every inch of the way.

'It went well, don't you think?' Alex found himself feeling uncharacteristically nervous as he asked Susannah's opinion. He'd downed a couple of beers in the local pub while he waited the two hours for her to finish the afternoon's readings.

'Great,' she answered. 'You got a car?'

'Sorry.' Alex shook his head apologetically.

'That's good, it's less complicated. We'll go in mine.'

'Go where?'

'My place.'

'Oh! Yes! Yes!' Susannah cried out and shuddered orgasmically for the fourth time. Alex waited for her to calm down before he withdrew and started gently, teasingly, all over again.

'No more, Alex,' Susannah moaned, 'I can't take any more.'

'Oh, yes, you can,' Alex whispered and he smoothed her hair back from her face, kissed her lingeringly and waited for the involuntary shudders to start all over again.

Alex got the job. A six-month contract with The Way In Theatre Company. Two weeks after he signed the contract he gave up his three-nights-a-week and all-day-Sunday garage job, handed back the keys to the Double Bay flat and moved in with Susannah.

The Way In's opening production was Arthur Miller's *The Crucible*. Susannah was perfectly cast as the sensual, scheming teenager Abigail but, to Alex's surprise, his role was very much a minor one.

'What did you expect?' Susannah countered when Alex complained. 'You're far too young for John Proctor.'

'Fair enough.' Alex had to admit she was right. 'So long as they give me Jack Tanner.'

Man and Superman was the second production planned for the season. Susannah personally thought Alex lacked the vocal strength and presence for the role but she didn't say anything. He certainly looked right, so maybe he'd get it.

But he didn't. A week before *The Crucible* opened the company announced the casting for its second production.

'Shit!' Alex had managed to contain his anger until they got home from the dress rehearsal. They had two hours to rest up before their first preview performance that night but resting up was the last thing Alex wanted to do. He tried to pace about the sitting room of Susannah's tiny terrace house but it was impossible. He kicked the large leather pouffe by the open fireplace and it skidded across the polished wood floor to collide with a delicate Chippendale coffee table. 'Octavius! He's a bloody wimp!'

'He is not,' Susannah argued. 'He's a gift of a role and stop taking it out on the furniture.'

Susannah was very proud of her collection of antiques which had been left her by a doting grandmother. Alex loathed them. They cluttered up the already too-small house. He was starting to regret his hasty decision in giving up the Double Bay flat. He scowled at the coffee table and wondered whether he should kick it just to annoy her.

'Oh, who's a sulky sulky sourpuss,' Susannah chanted in her baby voice. 'What can Mummy do to make him feel better?' She sucked his ear lobe into her mouth and ran her fingers through his hair.

Alex didn't allow himself to thaw immediately. He didn't want to—he was too genuinely irritated. But as Susannah progressed through the various roles she chose to play during their lovemaking, Alex finally responded. There was the baby talk, then the slut who wanted to do it dirty, then the plea to 'love me, Alex,' then there was the real Susannah, bucking and moaning and writhing in abandon. It was an added pleasure to Alex that Susannah always believed she was the seducer. She always believed that the power was hers.

That night, as Abigail teased, taunted and sexually provoked John Proctor before a charity preview audience of stolid Rotarians, Alex took great pleasure in witnessing the influence he had had on Susannah.

A week later it was the official opening night of *The Crucible* and the buzz in the air was electric. The cream of Sydney society, the doyens of the theatrical world and the major media critics were all present. The premiere production of The Way In Theatre Company's 1973 repertoire of classics was the theatrical event of the season.

There was a massive opening night party after the show and, while Susannah was being feted, Alex made a point of seeking out Myra Nielson. The

102

leading critic for the country's foremost national newspaper, Myra Nielson's reviews were the most feared and respected in the business.

Myra was a wealthy woman, having received handsome settlements from her two rich ex-husbands, one an industrialist and the other a theatrical entrepreneur. She wrote purely for her love of the theatre. Despite this fact, or possibly because of it, she spared the rod for no one. She was sophisticated, well-travelled and well-read, and her knowledge of theatre was vast. The few envious journalists who tried to dismiss her as a socialite who 'dabbled' were quickly forced to admit their mistake.

'Miss Nielson?' She turned. For an older woman she was extremely attractive, Alex thought. She must be nearly forty.

Myra Nielson was actually forty-eight but had avoided children and direct sunlight. She followed a rigid diet and exercise programme, regularly visited the best beauticians, hair stylists, manicurists and couturiers and wondered how it was that some women could let themselves go the way they did. With the exception of a tiny snip around the eyes two years before, she had never undergone cosmetic surgery and she was proud of that fact.

'We met once before,' Alex continued, 'through Harold Beauchamp. He's a friend of mine.'

'Harold Beauchamp, really? What a marvellous actor.' Myra offered her hand to Alex. Once! Only once, she thought with a touch of outrage. She'd seen Alex around the traps at least a dozen times and, although they had indeed met on only the one official occasion through Harold, she had lost count of the number of times she'd watched Alex across a crowded theatre foyer or late night supper club. She felt intensely irritated, then reminded herself that of course it was never good to appear too keen, especially for a young actor. He's probably pretending he doesn't remember, she thought.

But Alex wasn't.

'Did you enjoy the show?' Myra asked.

It was Alex's turn to burn. 'I played Ezekiel Cheever.'

'Of course.' Myra quite honestly hadn't realised. Not that it embarrassed her in any way. How could such a rivetingly attractive young man so completely disappear on stage? she wondered.

'Very clever make-up,' she smiled. 'You looked so much older with the pince nez and the grey sideburns.'

'Yes, that was the idea.' Alex was warming to her. 'I added a bit of thickening to the nose too. I'm playing Octavius in *Man and Superman*, you see, so I wanted—'

'Oh well, that's a role closer to your own age.' Several people had been queueing up for Myra's attention and she now gracefully eased herself away from Alex. 'I look forward to seeing it and I wish you every success.'

Alex was aware that Myra had found him attractive but he didn't have time to ponder upon the impact he'd made or failed to make as an actor.

Susannah was pushing her way through the throng. 'Alex, this is my brother Michael.' Alex found himself shaking the hand of a tall, sandy-haired man in his late twenties.

'Hi, I've heard a lot about you.' The teeth were pearly white, the carriage was proud and erect and the bones were finely chiselled. Patrician to a tee,

104

Michael was a replica of his sister except he wasn't pencil-thin. He was perfectly in proportion and devastatingly handsome and should have been an actor, Alex thought. But he wasn't. He was a farmer, and a wealthy one at that.

'Hello, Michael. Susannah didn't tell me you were coming down.'

'I didn't know.' Susannah's eyes were sparkling with excitement. It was her night and she knew it. 'Michael flew in this afternoon. He's staying at the Hilton. He was going back in the morning but I've made him stay an extra night so he can come to supper with us tomorrow.'

'You came down just for the opening?' Alex was impressed. He knew Michael flew his own plane and made quite frequent visits to Sydney but a quick trip from a Queensland avocado farm just to catch his sister's opening night was taking sibling love beyond Alex's comprehension.

'Always do. Got to keep the folks posted,' said Michael with a smile. 'Dad can't travel the way he used to and Mum won't go anywhere without him, so that leaves me.' He shrugged and grinned at Susannah, who beamed back.

'Oh.' Alex wasn't sure what to say; it was all rather precious and exclusive. He prepared himself to be bored but was mercifully saved by the arrival of Harold and Julian.

'We thought we'd steer clear while you chatted Myra up.' Julian gave him a nudge and embraced Susannah. 'Great work, Suzie,' he whispered. 'Really good stuff.' Julian had always been the only person to get away with calling Susannah 'Suzie'. It had started at NADA. 'That girl really does need the piss taken out of her,' he'd insisted. And now she liked it.

Harold too was effusive in his praise of Susannah's performance. Alex had brought her to dine several times. Despite Julian's approval of the girl, Harold had always maintained his reservations in deference to the memory of Maddy. But after tonight's performance, he was prepared to rethink his opinion. He was a talent snob, after all, he told himself, and Suzannah certainly had talent.

The quality newspapers took their time publishing their critics' views.

Only two newspapers carried reviews the morning after a major theatre opening and these reviews were invariably written by journalists who had been transferred from the sports section or the social columns and who were not considered to be of much worth within the profession. But awaiting their words of wisdom was still a nerve-racking business. Although they tended to play safe with the classics in order to avoid any possible display of ignorance, if they *did* decide to turn bold and hate the production the general public was quite likely to take note.

It was nearly three o'clock in the morning—still two hours before the delivery of the early editions. The older members of the Company had called it a night and only the hard core remained to sweat it out: Alex, Susannah, the senior leading actors, Hugh Skiffington and Rosie Lee and of course The Way In's artistic director Roger Kingsley.

When the papers finally arrived Roger was the first to pounce. 'Here we are,' he announced, 'the gospel according to Kitty Cusack.' Catherine Cusack doubled as regular columnist in the women's pages and once-a-month theatre critic and was the butt of many a joke.

'Once again Hugh Skiffington as John Proctor proves himself Australia's premiere actor in the truly heroic mould.' Roger looked across at Hugh who was leaning over Rosie's shoulder scanning the other review. 'Christ alive, pet, you really should give this woman your body.'

Hugh grinned back. Rosie nudged Susannah and read, 'After one year of supporting leads, relative newcomer Susannah Wright proves herself a consummate actress in the demanding role of Abigail.' Rosie gave Susannah a generous hug. Although only five years her senior Rosie's attitude to Susannah was very maternal, but then Rosie's attitude to everyone was very maternal. In her first term at NADA seven years before, buxom Rosie Balcock, fresh from the country, had been advised to change her name, was labelled 'character actress' and destined for an early middle age.

Hugh read: 'Roger Kingsley presents us with the definitive production of Arthur Miller's *The Crucible*'. He held his hands out to Roger in mock admiration. 'Ah, my King! My King! You've reached new heights. *Definitive!*'

'Oh good,' Roger grinned. 'Old Bill Foley's found a new word. I wonder how many productions he's seen in between rugby finals.'

But mock as they did, everyone was relieved. Particularly Roger Kingsley. Much as he berated and belittled critics, and much as he pretended such scum meant nothing to him, he secretly hung on their every word.

Kitty Cusack and Old Bill Foley did them proud. Along with unstinted praise for Hugh,

Susannah and the production, Rosie's Elizabeth Proctor abounded with 'a warm human dignity', Alex was a 'talented newcomer to watch with interest' and every other member of the sizeable cast was individually congratulated together with the set, costume and lighting designer. Just for good measure Kitty lavished praise upon the stage management for tight, speedy scene changes.

It was a good night all round and they went off to breakfast at the Bourbon and Beefsteak and didn't go home until nine o'clock in the morning.

The following night the show was a little flat, but then second nights usually were.

Alex found the after-show supper with Michael and Susannah even flatter. At least in the initial phases. All the talk about family: Daddy's heart problem, how he really must take it easy, Mummy's devotion to him. Hell, his heart problem was why Daddy had prematurely handed the avocado farm over to Michael and shifted to the penthouse at Surfers Paradise. Michael was bloody lucky, Alex thought. Daddy wasn't even sixty and if his high blood pressure hadn't been diagnosed Daddy would still be on the farm and Michael would be no more than a glorified labourer.

However, when the filial duty to Mummy and Daddy had been duly paid and Michael and Susannah continued to gaze into each other's eyes and talk fondly about their childhood, this favourite horse and that favourite dog, to the exclusion of all else, Alex started to find it interesting. It was almost incestuous. Michael had a wife and a one year old baby but, apart from courteous enquiries en passant, they formed no part of the conversation.

They're mad about each other, Alex thought. How fascinating! He charmed his way into the conversation and decided to take a great deal more interest in the relationship of Mr and Miss Wright from then on.

Two days later the national weekend newspaper was on the stands. In it was the review everyone was waiting for.

Alex opened the first page of the Arts section to reveal a large photo of Susannah and a veritable rave about her performance. Such a rave, in fact, that the critic considered the production to be a little uneven. However Susannah was not to be held responsible for this—it was a flaw in the play's direction, the critic insisted, and a stronger actor should have been cast as John Proctor. Bloody right there, Alex thought, and he read on approvingly until he got to the end of the review and discovered that his name wasn't mentioned at all. The critic was Myra Nielson.

She might at least have commented on his effective make-up, Alex thought churlishly. He knew he was being childish but he didn't want the woman to ignore him. She was too interesting.

He frowned as he reread Myra's appraisal of Susannah's talent: 'Although I have respected the perception and intelligence of Susannah Wright's previous performances, I have remarked upon a certain remote quality, even a coldness, which in my opinion could limit the progression of her talent. At last Wednesday's opening night performance of *The Crucible* she dropped these barriers completely and unleashed upon us an Abigail of immense passion driven by a sexuality which was positively mesmeric, not only to John Proctor, but to the entire audience . . .'

Alex was irritated. He was responsible for that 'mesmeric sexuality'; he was the one who had unleashed that 'immense passion'. If it wasn't for him . . . He remembered the afternoon of that preview performance when Susannah had played her seduction game and been even more insatiable than ever.

In fact, Alex now recalled, her sexual demands had grown proportionately stronger as the production of *The Crucible* intensified. Then he realised: he'd been used. He'd never been used in his life before. He didn't like it much.

A grudging form of respect started to outweigh his irritation. Myra was right; Susannah was a very talented actress and it was quite likely that she wasn't even conscious she was using him. He decided not to say anything to her but it would be very interesting to observe just how much of their relationship Susannah channelled into her work in the future.

In the meantime there was something far more important to concentrate on. There was a test he must set himself. And that test was Myra Nielson. He wanted to impress her as an actor. He wanted a review like Susannah's. But more than that, he wanted to impress her as a man too. He wanted to arouse in her an 'immense passion'. She could hardly ignore him then, could she?

'The woman's a fucking idiot!' It was Saturday afternoon, half an hour before the two o'clock matinee and Roger Kingsley was stomping around backstage, bursting in and out of the dressing rooms,

110

waving aloft the newspaper containing Myra's review. 'A fucking idiot! Unbalanced production, my arse!' He loomed over Susannah as she added the second layer of mascara. 'Haven't been giving her a bit on the side, have you, pet? It reads like the Susannah fucking Wright show.'

Rosie glanced at Susannah and hoped that she wasn't getting upset by Roger's ranting. Personally Rosie agreed with Myra's review. Magnificent as Hugh's voice was, the big, butch roles like John Proctor were just a little beyond him, but then Roger always cast him because they were an 'item'. She also agreed with Myra that she herself was a little too healthy and buxom for Elizabeth Proctor. Yes, the production was uneven and Susannah shone.

'An ignorant cunt, that's what she is. One who likes a bit of skirt now and then.' Roger really is a bitch, Rosie thought, and she glanced again at Susannah, ready to leap to her defence. But Susannah wasn't taking a blind bit of notice as she started on the third layer of mascara.

'This is your quarter-hour call, ladies,' the assistant stage manager said, tapping on the door. And, frustrated, Roger stormed into the men's dressing room to stir up some support there.

Despite Myra's review, *The Crucible* played to packed houses and rehearsals for *Man and Superman* commenced with a positive zest. It was hard work for the actors who were in both productions, rehearsing one show in the daytime and then reporting back to the theatre at the half-hour call for the evening performance, but nobody minded. The Way In's 1973 season promised to be one to remember.

Sundays were precious: the one day of the week the actors had for themselves. To Harold's delight, Alex and Susannah invariably chose to spend their Sundays with him.

It was a pity Julian wasn't here, Harold thought as he lifted a fresh jar of quail eggs out of the carton. He always bought quail eggs by the carton these days; they were one of the few foods Susannah seemed to genuinely relish. No wonder she stayed so thin, Harold decided.

'So, when does the tour finish?' Susannah asked, sipping the chilled white wine Harold had just poured for her.

'In three weeks.' Harold poured a glass for Alex. They were discussing Julian. 'Pouilly Fuisse, you dear boy. I adore you.' Alex took great pleasure in arriving with one of Harold's favourite wines every time they visited.

'Three weeks? As soon as that?' Alex was surprised. 'Cheers.' He toasted the table.

'Salut.' Harold returned the toast. 'It was only a two-month tour you know. Poor lamb, he's hating every minute of it.'

'Well, they say never work with children.' Susannah toyed with the fragment of smoked salmon and lettuce leaf remaining on her plate, then carefully cut the lettuce leaf in four.

'It's not the children, it's the parents. Apparently they're following the tour around being absolute monsters.'

Although Julian had graduated from NADA with flying colours, his first directing job had been slow in coming and he'd finally accepted a country tour of *The Sound of Music* for the Elizabethan Theatre Trust. Along with his contract as director he also had to accept the position of tour manager, a task which he was sure he'd loathe, but it was that or no job at all. After all, it was not a huge budget show and he was new to the industry. *C'est la vie*, he thought, as he prepared to go on the road.

It wasn't his favourite musical, it wasn't his favourite cast and being stranded in country towns in the company of people with whom he had very little in common was as trying as Julian had anticipated it would be. Harold received regular phone calls and blow-by-blow accounts of just how trying it was.

Every country town reminded Julian of Wagga Wagga. Indeed, one of the tour dates *was* Wagga Wagga and the week he spent there reinforced not only his reasons for leaving in the first place but his determination never to go back.

That very Sunday evening, as Susannah meticulously wrapped her smoked salmon in a piece of lettuce, Julian accepted a third cup of tea from his mother and sat back to watch his father watching television.

'Come on, Mum, sit down and stop waiting on me.'

'All right dear, I'll just finish the last of the washing-up.'

'Why don't you let me do it?' Julian half rose but the look of horror on his mother's face made him hastily sit back again.

'I wouldn't hear of it. You sit and watch the TV with your father and I'll bring us in some nice shortbread.' Gwen Oldfellow disappeared to complete yet another leg of the washing-up marathon.

Two hours before, on the dot of six-thirty, the three of them had sat down to a roast dinner followed by apple crumble with ice cream; intermittently ever since then, his mother had leapt from the table to clatter about the kitchen in a fever of activity.

Julian had managed to persuade her to let him dry the pots. 'And the cutlery, Mum?'

'Yes, all right, dear, if you like. But just the cutlery. The dishes I drain.'

He felt very much an intruder in the kitchen and sensed his mother's relief when he rejoined his father.

'You sure you won't have a port, son?' his father now asked for the third time.

'No thanks, Dad, the tea's fine.'

Norman Oldfellow settled back to watch his favourite current affairs show but he didn't feel totally at ease. Even if the boy did join him in a coffee and a port it probably wouldn't make any difference. They didn't have much in common and they never had. Norman wondered guiltily whether he should turn the telly off and try to make conversation—but then it probably wouldn't work out, he thought, so he decided not to.

Julian was also feeling guilty. He knew his father wasn't really enjoying the port. As he'd watched Norman carefully pour one lone glass Julian had suddenly remembered—oh God, how could he have forgotten?—the crystal decanter which always lived on the lounge room sideboard cabinet was reserved for visitors and special occasions.

It wasn't that the family was poor. Far from it. Norman had always been a good provider and Gwen was an excellent housekeeper. Julian had wanted for nothing in his childhood. But his parents were sticklers for doing the correct thing and, as their knowledge and enjoyment of alcohol was virtually nil, this meant a beer or sherry before dinner and, if there were visitors, a port with coffee after.

Julian felt lost. His parents were both trying to do the correct thing. His mother was turning back the clock and treating him like a child and his father was offering him port, 'man to man'. Julian was stranded somewhere in the middle with the guilty feeling that he was letting them both down, that he never had been, and never could be, what they wanted him to be.

He remembered with gratitude his affair with Leon MacLeod at university when he'd realised exactly why he'd never really fitted. He was homosexual and that explained everything. Dear Leon, Julian thought fondly. I wonder what he's doing now?

Julian, just nineteen and very naive, had been drawn to Leon on first meeting. Everyone was drawn to Leon. His superior intellect and charm demanded it, and no one seemed to mind that he was a raging homosexual—a point which slightly puzzled Julian whose father would certainly have been critical.

Julian was surprised and flattered when Leon chose his company over many of his other admirers and together they stayed up till all hours discussing literature and reading poetry. Leon was such an inspiring friend to have.

It shocked Julian deeply when one day a fellow student remarked that Leon had ulterior motives. 'He's after your body—surely you realise that?' was the bitchy comment.

'How can people be such shits!' he said to Leon that evening after he'd relayed the episode over a bowl of spaghetti at their favourite cheap noshery. 'I mean, why say it, for God's sake?'

'Because it's true.' In the stunned silence that followed Leon ate two more heaped spoonfuls of spaghetti and swilled a glass of cheap chianti. Then he laughed. 'Don't look so shocked, Julian. It's true I'm after your body and you should be flattered. You're not the type I fancy at all normally. It's probably because we have such a cerebral affinity,' he added.

As Julian continued to stare at him in a state of shock he dropped the banter. 'To be quite honest, my friend, I'm merely biding my time until you wake up to the fact that you're homosexual.'

Their affair lasted a whole year, after which Leon got his degree with flying colours, was awarded a scholarship and left to further his studies in Paris.

Since then, with the exception of his family, Julian had never again apologised for, or attempted to disguise, his homosexuality. Who knows, he thought, if Leon were still around maybe he'd even come out of the closet to his parents. But old habits die hard, he told himself. Bad luck, Leon, you can't win them all.

'What a pity Wendy couldn't be here with the kiddies.' It was his mother, sitting beside him on the sofa and placing a cake dish of assorted shortbreads on the centre coffee table.

'Not to worry, Mum, we had a good old natter after the matinee yesterday.' 'Good old natter'— had he really said that? Good, his mother would have liked it. Julian racked his brains to come up with some more homespun colloquialisms.

'Oh that's nice, dear. The kiddies have never been to the theatre, you know. Well, not the real theatre, just the cinema.'

'So Wendy was saying.' Julian dutifully picked up a shortbread. 'They loved the show and she's going to take them regularly from now on.'

Julian had enjoyed the meeting with his sister. Although Wendy had stayed in Wagga, she had somehow escaped the malaise and it had been lovely to see her and the rowdy twins. They'd sat in the park while the children shrieked and the swings squeaked and they'd talked about everything and nothing. When it was time to go they hugged each other warmly and somehow Julian had the feeling that Wendy knew about him. He loved her for that.

'Like a port, Gwen?' Norman needed an ally.

'Oh.' Gwen rarely drank port, even when there were visitors. 'Well, if you're having another one, dear.'

Norman's face lit up. 'I'll get you a glass. Think I might have a beer myself,' he said as he heaved himself out of his armchair.

'I'll join you, Dad, if that's OK.' Julian put down his teacup.

'Sure, son, fine.'

When they were all settled again Norman shook his head at the television set. 'Another hijack. What a terrible business. I don't understand how a human being could do something like that.' He sipped his beer, Julian agreed and sipped his, and the rest of the current affairs programme was spent companionably discussing Baader-Meinhof, the PLO and terrorism in general.

An hour later Julian left for his hotel. From the outset he'd insisted on staying at a hotel—his late nights were bound to disrupt the household, he maintained.

It's nobody's fault, he told himself, as they said their farewells. Not theirs, not mine. A childhood memory flooded back. He was ten years old and he could hear his mother: 'It's Mr Nobody's fault!'

His mother's voice jolted him back to the present. 'You should have worn a jacket, dear. Autumn's colder in Wagga than it is in Sydney.'

He hugged her warmly, then he hugged his father, much to Norman's surprise. And then he left.

It was only ten o'clock but, as he let himself into his hotel room, Julian felt weary. They'd bumped out last night and bump-outs were always the most tiring part of touring, especially weekly touring. It meant that every Saturday night and well into Sunday morning the stage management crew had to laboriously dismantle the sets, pack the mountains of props and costumes into huge wicker skips and load the whole lot into the tour truck.

The actors had it easy. All they had to do was clear out their dressing rooms, put their make-up kits under their arms and take off. Yet still they whinged. Julian wondered which bright spark had coined the phrase, 'a gaggle of geese, a pride of lions and a whinge of actors'. He smiled. It was true, all actors whinged—it was mandatory to the image, apparently. The nice ones, and there were many, managed to do it with an air of self-deprecation. And the others? Well, every profession had its bores, Julian supposed. And, my God, hadn't he copped some beauties on this tour? *The Sound of Music* cast was a whinge of actors at its worst. Only three weeks to go, he thought thankfully, and he vowed never to accept a tour manager job again.

As tired as he was, the family visit had set his brain ticking and he decided to ring Harold. To talk about whingeing actors, he told himself as he dialled. Hell, poor Harold had copped a weekly whinge from the very outset of the tour. He'd certainly been a lifeline, Julian thought gratefully.

'Julian! Dear boy! I had a feeling it would be you. How did the family dinner go?' Harold turned to wink at the others. 'Alex and Susannah are here and we all want a blow-by-blow account.'

Julian bypassed the family dinner but ten minutes later, as the phone was passed from person to person, he had them all in stitches with the latest escapades of the actress playing the eldest of the Von Trapp children. It had become a running gag that Lucy Langley was fifteen years too old to be singing 'I am sixteen going on seventeen'. Besides, she was anything but virginal; it was a well-known fact she was a sexual virago.

'She had a field day in Canberra last week,' Julian said, 'but now it's got out of hand. Two blokes left their jobs with the public service and followed her here to Wagga. They keep trying to fight each other and she can't get rid of them.'

By the time all the news and gossip had been exchanged and it was time to hang up, Julian's spirits were well and truly restored and he felt revitalised to the point where going to bed seemed a pointless exercise. He opened up his briefcase and lifted out the dog-eared file which by now contained hundreds of sheets of paper. Half of them were notes, half of them were taking on the shape of a play and nearly all of them were influenced by his observations of Alex.

Writing was proving to be the best lifeline of all for Julian and, although he knew he must prove himself as a director, he was already aware that his greatest ambition was to see a play of his successfully brought to life in the theatre.

As the *Man and Superman* opening night grew closer and closer Alex felt himself becoming excited at the prospect. Susannah had been right: Octavius was an excellent role. And of course Susannah as Anne was a joy to work with.

At home Susannah's sexuality was less fervent and at times she didn't appear to want sex at all. Paradoxically, Alex found her even more interesting, as he realised that her aloofness was part of her acting process: Anne didn't find the lovelorn Octavius sexually attractive.

It was when he started to respond to Susannah's process that rehearsals became stimulating to Alex and he knew that he was on the road to a fine performance. Hell, who wanted to play Jack Tanner? he told himself. All that rhetoric, all that posturing and posing, speeches that went on for page after page: Hugh Skiffington was bound to bore the pants off the audience while Alex could come in as the naively passionate and humorous Tavy and steal the show.

Newcomer Alex Rainford proves that a scene-stealer of a role can disappear in the hands of an inept actor. Although pleasing in appearance, his presence is minimal. In past productions, this critic has sometimes

*wondered why Anne chose the pompous Tanner over
the romantic Octavius. Last Wednesday night Anne
most certainly made the right decision.*

'Would I be correct in presuming you didn't like
my performance?'

It was Friday, nearly a week since Myra's review
had appeared, and Alex had been doing the after-
show night spots regularly in the hope of seeing
her.

'Yes, you'd be correct,' Myra answered and
was surprised to see Alex smile back disarmingly
at her.

'Oh well, can't win them all.' Then, even more
disarmingly, the smile disappeared and he seemed
in deadly earnest. 'The "pleasing appearance" and
"minimal presence" was a bit confusing though.'

Myra looked closely to see if he was joking but
he didn't appear to be and, within minutes of further
questions and apparent genuine interest in her
answers, she was engaged in a very absorbing
discussion about theatre and the craft of acting.

Even as she asked herself why she was giving
so much attention to a novice actor, Myra found
herself more and more drawn into conversation. She
barely noticed her escort's irritated attempts to
interject or his final admission of defeat as he turned
his attention to the other couple at their supper
table. But then Myra rarely noticed her escorts of
late. Since her divorce from Rudy she had steered
clear of any emotional involvement and the
succession of handsome young men who
accompanied her were chosen strictly for
appearances' sake and regular meaningless sex.

Alex's original plan had gone completely by the

boards. His intention to charm Myra, to hopefully seduce her and prove himself the winner had dissolved within seconds of their conversation. There was so much he could learn from this woman.

And, of course, the more probing his questions and the more spellbound his attention to her answers, the more fascinating Alex became to Myra.

'We should meet again and continue this discussion,' she said when she realised it was three am and they were beginning to appear conspicuous. The other couple had left thirty minutes ago, the place was emptying and Escort was looking daggers.

'When? Tomorrow?' Alex was completely unaware that he could have got Myra to bed that very night if he'd wanted to. He was far more interested in talking.

'Ring me.' In one swift, practised movement Myra flipped a business card out of her bag, leaving it face down on the table in front of Alex, and rose to her feet, smiling brightly at her companion. 'Home time, I think.' There was little that Escort could do. He hated Alex, he hated Myra even more, but he was an actor.

'Four o'clock,' Susannah muttered, checking the clock as Alex slid into bed beside her. 'That's disgraceful, Alex—matinee tomorrow.' And then she went straight back to sleep. Apart from Saturdays, Susannah rarely partied during the run of a show and never before a matinee day.

Alex lay awake thinking till dawn. Myra had unreservedly told him she didn't believe he'd ever make a really good actor. 'Well, not in the theatre,' she qualified. 'Film maybe.' She was looking at him as if he were a piece of meat in a butcher's window. 'You've certainly got a great head.' Then she lowered her gaze, picked up her drink and shrugged diffidently. 'Of course that's only one person's opinion and you should never be led by one person's opinion.' Which was probably the only piece of bullshit she'd spun him all night, Alex now thought. Myra's whole life hung on the fact that thousands of people were constantly led by one person's opinion.

When he finally fell asleep it was with the knowledge that he would give up acting. If he couldn't be the best, or at least one of the best, he'd get out. Stuff film; who wanted to be a pretty face. Besides, the theatre was where he'd set his sights and it was in the theatre that he'd make his mark. Actors were small fry, he told himself. The real power lay in production.

'It's right for me, Myra, it's what I need. The power. I don't know why I didn't realise it earlier. I've always been a manipulator, not an interpreter.'

It was midnight and Alex was pacing about Myra's apartment working himself up to a fever pitch of excitement about his new career.

'A manipulator, eh?' Myra sipped her vodka martini and smiled at him indulgently. He looked like a ten-year-old about to be taken to the circus and she was having trouble controlling the hoot of laughter which threatened to erupt at any moment. 'Well, a producer certainly needs to be able to manipulate, that's for sure. So how do you intend to set about your new-found vocation?'

Alex didn't appear to register the irony at all. 'The Way In Theatre's built up a really strong policy in less than two years,' he said, throwing himself onto the couch beside her and nearly spilling her martini. 'I can make a good study of that for the rest of my contract with them, but my main aim is the commercial theatre—that's where I'll make the killing.' His smile was devastating. 'And I'm sure *you* could give me a few pointers there.'

He was referring to her entrepreneurial ex, Rudy. That was when Myra decided he might be slightly overstepping the mark and it was time to get down to business.

'I'm sure I could,' she said. 'In the morning.' And she led the way to the bedroom.

Alex was genuinely surprised. He was also a little disappointed. He would much rather have continued to talk about his future, he thought as he followed her.

It crossed his mind as he was undressing that this was bound to make for drama with Susannah. When Susannah had suggested they go out to supper he'd refused, saying that he was meeting someone. 'So, I'll come along,' she'd said. 'It's Saturday, Alex, we always go out on Saturday.' Alex never lied unless it was essential. He told her his appointment was with Myra Nielson, that it could be good for his career and he should see her alone. 'OK.' Susannah always understood career moves. 'But watch her, love, she's a ball tearer.'

Now, as he thought of Susannah, Myra's review of *The Crucible* flashed through his mind and his original motives flooded back to him. Alex was suddenly glad of the turn of events. He'd worry about Susannah and any dramas tomorrow. Tonight was the night he would arouse in Myra Nielson an 'immense passion'.

As he'd expected, Myra was an extremely sensual woman and she responded to his lovemaking with a lack of inhibition which Alex found not only rewarding, but exciting. In fact she was so in tune with his thrusts that, as he felt her reaching orgasm, he was aware that it was quite possible he could lose control. That wouldn't do at all.

Running his hand under her arched neck he gently lifted her head and kissed her throat, his tongue exploring the curve of her jaw, the velvet of her ear lobe. While his other hand continued to caress her breast, he buried himself deep inside her and remained very still. In a matter of seconds he would regain control. In a matter of seconds she would orgasm. Then he could take his time. Soon, Myra Nielson, he told himself, soon, your 'immense passion'.

Myra was feeling very horny that night. And she'd lusted after young Alex Rainford for quite a long time now. Wallow a bit, dear, she told herself, you deserve to let yourself go. And she did. She was surprised, and more than a little delighted when Alex proved to be such an accomplished lover but, when she felt him call in the reserves, her pride rebelled immediately. Oh, no you don't, kid. Two can play at that game. And, as she continued to moan, she locked her legs around his back and held him prisoner inside her.

Good, Alex thought, the legs linked at the small of his back meant she was about to come. He'd regained control and he started to gently withdraw only to find that he couldn't. Not only were the legs holding him in a vicelike grip, there was a muscular clamp around his penis which was contracting like a suction pump. He was lost in the embrace of a boa constrictor and he was being devoured alive.

He didn't have time to consider whether or not it was enjoyable. He didn't have time to consider whether his ejaculation was the greatest sexual experience of his life or whether it was merely the most expedient method of escape. And, as they climaxed together, neither did Myra.

Alex Rainford had more than met his match, as had Myra Nielson. Their obsession with each other had only just begun.

ACT II

SCENE 2: 1977

Maddy looked out of the train window at the English countryside flashing by. It was all so amazingly green. And neat. Stone fences and hedgerows dissected the land. The southern villages and farmhouses always seemed particularly tidy, Maddy thought, as if they were only too happy to distance themselves from the sprawling industrial north.

It had been a glorious spring and the early hot June days were promising a scorcher of a summer. Strange how she'd never thought England would be hot. As usual, the heat brought thoughts of home.

Maddy never thought of Australia when she found herself snowbound on a midwinter tour, but a summer tour of small coastal towns where boats nestled in bays and stays clinked against masts brought memories of the cosy coves of Sydney Harbour flooding back. Seven years! She'd been away seven years! It seemed an age.

It had been a good year for her so far but the journey up the ladder was a slow and sometimes painful process and there were regular bouts of 'resting'. She'd long since given up office work as an alternative form of income. Between repertory seasons and tours she reverted instead to the role of waitress or hostess: night-time tips, she'd quickly discovered, far outweighed daytime basic wages.

Each time Maddy found herself waitressing at the Bier Keller in Trafalgar Square or hostessing at Danny's Downstairs Nightclub in Soho, the irony did not escape her. Here she was in the heart of the West End. But doing what?

And that's where she'd be in two weeks, she reflected ruefully. Downstairs at Danny's. Bournemouth was the last date on the *Hayfever* tour—only a fortnight to go.

Maybe Phil would pull off that film job! Mentally Maddy crossed her fingers. Oh God, wouldn't that be wonderful? Surely if anyone could do it, Phil could.

Since she'd changed agents and signed up with funny little Phil Pendlebury who worked out of a tiny room around the corner from the Aldwych, things had certainly taken a turn for the better. Three months before, when she'd done six weeks on the trot at the Bier Keller, she never would have believed it possible that she'd be playing Bessie Buchanan's daughter in *Hayfever*. And yet here she was en route from Bath to Bournemouth on the final leg of a tour with one of the great stars of the forties. Well, it had certainly sounded impressive to Maddy at the time.

The rest of the cast had travelled from Bath the day before but Maddy always liked to spend the Sunday after bump-out on her own, particularly if they'd been playing somewhere pretty.

And Bath was certainly magnificent. Maddy loved the place. She'd played the Theatre Royal there twice before with *Gaslight* and *The Hollow* (good old reliable thrillers—the public loved them) and she never tired of the city.

She looked at her watch. Not much longer to go. When she reached Bournemouth she would have just two hours to dump her gear at the digs she'd lined up, get to the theatre, set up her dressing room, grab something to eat then report back for the half-hour call.

Then, compulsively, her mind went back to the movie. Phil had phoned her at Bath on Friday and promised to send the film script direct to the theatre at Bournemouth. It wouldn't be there for several days yet, Maddy thought impatiently. It was only a test: she must keep telling herself that. Nothing definite. But they were very keen to see her on her return and she seemed perfect for the role.

'Got to be petite, love—boyish, you know what I mean?—and they don't come much petiter than you, do they?' Phil was a fast-talking cockney who never seemed to stop for breath. He was fifty years old, small and beetle-like with suspiciously black hair scraped from one side of his head to the other to hide the central bald spot. Although he was a bit of a villain, he was a good agent—fast, pushy and cunning. And for some reason he seemed particularly fond of Maddy. She had no idea why; he'd certainly never made any advances toward her.

In fact he seemed more paternal than anything, which was ludicrous. It was all very simple: Phil's clients were his meal ticket and that's why he looked after them.

The truth was, Maddy constantly forgot the effect her appearance had on people. Because she knew herself to be strong and determined she forgot that she presented a youthful fragility which brought out the protector in people—even people like Phil Pendlebury. And when Phil, always astute in his character analyses, recognised Maddy's strength, it didn't detract from his paternal affection. It simply made him proud. His Maddy was a fighter—good on her!

'They saw you in that episode of "Z Cars" where you played the sixteen-year-old, remember?' he told her over the phone. 'And they're mad keen to have a squizz at you, but they don't want a blonde, so the first thing you do on the Monday you get back to London is you take yourself off to the hairdresser, you go black and short, and you have your eyelashes and brows done too, the works, because I've set up the test for eleven o'clock Tuesday morning. Got that?'

'Yes, Phil.' That was very often all Maddy said during her phone conversations with Phil.

'And you come in and give me a look at you first thing on the Tuesday, say around half-past eight, and then if you've buggered things up we've got a couple of hours to get you looking good.'

It wasn't a big budget film. As cinéma vérité, it would do the circuit of the art houses only, but that merely served to boost Maddy's confidence. After all, she was an unknown; who on earth would want her for a big budget feature? Certainly, to cut off her shoulder-length fair hair and dye it black was a pretty drastic step for a test, but Phil's enthusiasm was contagious and Maddy would probably have shaved her head if he'd suggested it.

'Boyish, love, that's what they want, you'll understand when you read the script, now you have a lovely time in Bournemouth, the weather's nice for it, and make sure you've got scenes nine and thirty-six off pat, they're the ones they'll be using for the test.'

'Yes, Phil.'

'I'll see you Tuesday, chookas for the Bournemouth run, have fun and keep yourself nice, there's a good girl. Bye.' And he hung up leaving Maddy breathless, excited and frustrated. There were so many more questions she wanted to ask him.

'Hello, Marj.'

'Madeleine! Dearie, you look wonderful!' Maddy's head was clutched between two matronly breasts as Marjorie Brigstock, landlady to the stars, locked her in a vicelike embrace.

'I've put you in the little room at the top with the ocean view, love, I thought you'd like that. You don't mind finding your own way, do you? Wilf can bring your case up later.'

'It's OK, Marj, I can manage.'

It was a constantly observed ritual. Marj never went upstairs—she had bad knees—and the actors never allowed her poor asthmatic husband Wilf to carry their luggage; the pokey little room at the top was always reserved for the younger members of the company and the 'ocean view' could only be glimpsed if one climbed out of the attic window.

Maddy had stayed at Marj's guest house twice before (*Gaslight* and *The Hollow* had played the same circuit) and on each occasion she'd been allocated the little room with the 'ocean view'.

This time, however, she was playing the juvenile lead and her name was on the posters and handbills. In small print and at the bottom, admittedly—and she was fully aware one had to be up near the title to qualify for a ground floor room—but surely she should have scored the second floor, she thought, as she wearily dragged her heavy suitcase up the four flights of stairs.

Although Marj's rates were well below those of the average seaside boarding house, she considered her lodgings and her clientele to be elite. She had no time for the Bel Airs, the Casas del Sol and the Paradises sur la Mer that were frequented by tourists. She catered exclusively for thespians (which was precisely why her rates were low) and she was well qualified to do so.

A one-time trouper herself, Marj knew the tour circuit and the actors' requirements: open house late into the night in case they wanted to sit around discussing the show over supper and cheap wine; quiet in the morning until ten o'clock (Wilf was banned from his vacuum cleaner until eleven); and the right food at the right time. Not necessarily good food, mind, but plentiful. She did a huge late breakfast-brunch, a substantial tea at six o'clock and a light supper at eleven. She didn't do lunch, except on Sundays for those who wanted it. And then, although it was the traditional theatrical digs roast— beef the consistency of wood shavings, soggy brussel sprouts and a Yorkshire pudding that weighed a ton—no one complained. Marj made an excellent trifle to follow, it was their one day off, and the air was thick with the camaraderie of old actors' tales.

When Maddy arrived at the theatre she made her customary inspection of the posters and production stills displayed outside the main entrance, then checked out the foyer display. She feigned nonchalance in front of the middle-aged woman in the box office as her eyes flicked past the portrait shot of herself.

'Hi, Joan. They've come up well, haven't they?' Until *Hayfever* Maddy had never had an exclusive portrait photo of herself in a theatre foyer; she'd always only been in the production stills.

'Miss Frances! Welcome back. Yes, it's a lovely photo, you've come up a treat.' Maddy felt herself blush; Joan had well and truly caught her out. 'I think it's high time too, a lovely actress like you. Next time they'll have your name and photo right up there above the title, I'll be bound.' Joan nodded towards Bessie Buchanan's portrait, which was not only above the title, but also above Noel Coward's name. Just about as high as you could get, Maddy thought, and laughed. Of course Joan had meant no malice. Despite the fact that, in true British front-of-house and stage-door tradition, Joan refused to call any of the actors by their Christian names, she was always very maternal toward the younger company members.

'You're right,' Maddy admitted, 'it gives me a bit of a buzz every time I see it.' And, unashamedly this time, she looked back at the photo and its caption: *Madeleine Frances as Sorel Bliss.*

Maddy had long since adjusted to Frances, even though the choice of her mother's maiden name had angered her father at first. 'For God's sake, Dad,' she'd argued, 'if you don't want my sordid theatrical career to soil the name of McLaughlan then surely the alternative choice can be my own!' It had been just one of the many rows they'd had since coming to England and Maddy heaved an inward sigh at the thought that there was bound to be another one when she saw him on her return to London. He seemed to be becoming more and more unreasonable as the years passed.

'Madeleine, darling! You're so late!' One of the doors to the auditorium was thrown open and Bessie Buchanan made her entrance. She kissed the air on both sides of Maddy's face then leaned back theatrically against one of the foyer pillars.

'You naughty girl,' she scolded. 'I'm starving and I've been waiting for you to have a pre-performance snack with me.'

Bessie Buchanan's pre-performance snacks were invariably three-course meals and to Maddy, who, like most actors, ate sparingly before a show, a total turn-off. She couldn't possibly refuse the woman, though; she never did.

The pillar against which Bessie was draped bore an almost lifesize photograph of the actress which said it all. The photo may have been taken in the fifties but more likely, the late forties. The 1977 real-life item beside it was undoubtedly the same woman and, despite the ravages of time, there was still a prettiness about her, but the sad fact was that Bessie Buchanan had got fat. It had started about twenty years ago, when her star had been well and truly on the wane, and had continued ever since.

Bessie refused to acknowledge her weight problem. She was no longer wealthy, having been bled dry by the many men in her life, so she simply had her designer gowns let out to accommodate her growth. When she reached the point where panels had to be added to the sides of her gowns she still didn't give up and it saddened Maddy greatly when she heard the whispers and sniggers from the gallery during the dinner party scene in Act Two. For the dinner party scene in Act Two, Bessie had opted to wear the very same dress she'd worn when the foyer photograph had been taken over twenty-five years before. Not only were both the woman and the dress now twice their former size, but the added side panels were a distinctly different blue.

On 'B' circuit tours even the stars were requested to supply their own wardrobe should formal wear be required. In this instance however, the management had gently tried to pursuade Bessie that, for a star of her magnitude, they were more than happy to supply a new gown. 'And what would you get me?' Bessie had queried. 'A Schiaparelli? A Dior? A Chanel?' There was a significant pause. 'Exactly,' she acknowledged triumphantly. 'Thank you, but no thank you. I shall supply my own.' And the management had to live with the mismatched panels and the foyer photo.

For some reason unknown to Maddy she had found herself adopted by Bessie Buchanan from the very outset of the *Hayfever* tour. 'Oh, stuff that Miss Buchanan rubbish, you must call me Bessie, dear,' she'd been told. And when the stickler-for-form tour manager rebuked Maddy for being too familiar with the star, Bessie overheard and was quick to dismiss him: 'Go away, little man'. It didn't endear the tour manager to Bessie one bit, but fortunately he was a fair man and didn't hold it against Maddy.

So Maddy found herself living through the saga of each of the lovers who had broken Bessie's heart, the four husbands who hadn't, the three ungrateful children who didn't give a fig for their mother and, the unkindest cut of all, the loss in Bessie's life of the thousands to whom she had once been an idol.

'Of course, there's still my loyal fan club,' Bessie would say, dabbing at the irreparable damage her mascara had caused. 'They send me a copy of their newsletter once a month and that's a comfort.' It was usually well after midnight and well into the second bottle of white wine when the fan club was invoked, and Maddy always knew what to expect next. 'If only Biffy were alive everything would be all right. Oh, why did he have to die?' At the mention of her old song and dance partner and the great love of her life, who had died thirty years before, Bessie gave up all attempt at stemming the flow of mascara-streaked tears and threw herself upon Maddy, weeping uncontrollably.

Bessie Buchanan was a desperately unhappy woman, it was true, but she was also a survivor. If it was necessary that her life take such a tragic turn, then it was only fair she be allowed to wallow in it. She had twice attempted suicide, once with pills and once with gas—and both times with the sure knowledge that she would be discovered well and truly in time. The pills attempt made a short column (no photo) on the entertainments page which was very disappointing. When the gas attempt six months later received no response whatsoever she decided she would have to gain attention and sympathy on more of a one-to-one basis. That was when she took to adopting a female junior member of whichever company she was touring with at the time. (Bessie spent her life touring the 'B' circuit.)

Maddy was one of the most sympathetic listeners she'd ever cultivated and Bessie had grown genuinely fond of the girl.

'Come along now,' she said to Maddy. 'We only have an hour before the half.'

'Can you wait five minutes? I have to set up my dressing room.' Maddy turned to go but Bessie grabbed her by the arm and bustled her towards the auditorium doors. 'It's much quicker if we go through the house. I'll come with you.'

Most stage managers frowned upon actors arriving or leaving via the auditorium. Even when the theatre was deserted the correct approach was through the stage door. The crew was busy setting up for the evening performance and, as Bessie bustled her down the aisle, Maddy shrugged apologetically to the stage manager. He gave her an understanding nod in return. The world-weary stage manager knew that stars, even those well and truly on the wane like Bessie Buchanan, had to be indulged by the lesser members of the company. It was a recognised fact.

But in this instance, the stage manager was wrong. Maddy certainly did indulge Bessie, but not out of a sense of duty; she actually liked the woman. Bessie might have been irritating, but she was protective, generous-spirited and enjoyed teaching Maddy everything she knew about the business, which was considerable. Maddy was not only extremely grateful, she was fully aware that, in the years to come, there would be many a time when she would apply the lessons she'd learned from Bessie Buchanan.

Maddy was sad when the tour came to an end. It had been, without a doubt, her most successful job to date and she would miss Bessie and the gang. But in true actor's style her feelings were mixed—she also couldn't wait to get on to the next job. And the possibility of the film role was awesome.

The script was wonderful—warm and humorous, sad and tragic, threatening and violent, and boldly sexual throughout. So much so that if it wasn't brilliantly directed, it could end up being messy, melodramatic and decidedly tacky. When Maddy voiced this worry to Phil over the phone he immediately placated her.

'Ever seen Viktor Hoff's work?' he demanded.

'Well, of course I have; what actor hasn't, but—'

'Exactly, so he's a master, isn't he, so you trust him, don't you, the man's a genius. Now you come straight round the agency next Tuesday and show me what you've done with the hair . . .'

Maddy was staring at the long blonde curls on the floor of the hairdresser's but she didn't see them. She was going over and over scenes nine and thirty-six in her head. The first scene was the meeting between the boyish fifteen year old Francine and the middle-aged man who was to become her lover. It was a cheeky, humorous scene with only a hint of the sexuality to follow. Scene thirty-six took place three years later and it was harsh and sadistic. As the true femininity of the eighteen year old Francine emerged, the man was forced to question his sexuality. His guilt and turmoil were directed against the girl, creating the path to their destruction.

Androgyne was a brilliant script and Francine was a fascinating and complex character. Like Nabokov's Lolita, there was an ambiguous quality to her sexuality. Just how aware was she of the power she had over the man? Just when did Francine realise that the man's agony over his possible homosexuality was a weapon she could use against him?

'How's that?' Maddy came to with a jolt. The hairdresser was holding a hand mirror behind her head and looking enquiringly at her in the main mirror. But who was the dark-haired youth staring back? It was Francine, that's who it was, Maddy thought with a surge of confidence. Phil was right: she was spot-on for this role, and, by God, she'd get it!

And she did. The test wasn't gruelling at all. The moment she walked into the bare rehearsal studio she knew that Viktor Hoff wanted her for the role. His reaction was exactly the same as Phil's had been when she'd walked into his office two hours earlier to show him the new dark bob. 'Perfect! You look perfect,' Phil had enthused.

'Wonderful! You are wonderful! You are my Francine,' Viktor insisted. 'This is Rodney Baines, your lover.'

As Maddy shook hands with the extremely good-looking Englishman standing beside Viktor she wondered how she could possibly be 'his

139

Francine' when she hadn't even read for the role yet. Little did Maddy know that Viktor's ego was of such proportions that if she were to test badly he would still cast her, confident that his direction could bring a brilliant performance out of even the least talented actor. Even if she were to prove a complete moron it wouldn't matter—he would shoot the film with such expertise that no one would know.

As it turned out, Maddy performed the scenes wonderfully, leaving Rodney Baines far behind her. Did he already have the role, she wondered, or was he auditioning as well? His face looked familiar and he was devastatingly handsome, but his performance was rather wooden.

It was all over very quickly. Viktor took them through each of the scenes only twice. Then he clasped Rodney and Maddy fervently to his breast, saying, 'You are my Christmases, come both at once'.

Viktor was a tall, craggy man with a pterodactyl face, a strange accent which was actually a mixture of Dutch and Polish, and a habit of confusing the cliches he insisted on using. In reality, his command of the English language was masterful and his confusion was probably a deliberate addition to the colourful Continental image he chose to present. His films were immensely successful in the art cinemas of Europe and the UK but he had yet to conquer the American cinéma vérité circuit. That was his main aim, and he was convinced that *Androgyne* was the film that would do it.

As soon as Maddy arrived home at her Kensington bedsit she rang Phil from the share phone on the ground floor to tell him the good news, but he already knew.

'Viktor was on the blower the moment you walked out the door, love. Told you you were a walk-up start for it, didn't I? Now did Viktor mention the nudity clause, not that you need to worry about it, of course, it'll all be very tastefully handled.'

Maddy was fully aware of the erotic nature of many of the scenes but hadn't really contemplated the necessity of working stark naked. She and Phil finally agreed that, if Viktor was prepared to discuss his intent and the angles of his shots before they commenced each of the scenes (naturally in a closed set), she would quell her inhibitions and agree to work nude.

'He'll come at that, love, don't you fret. Now off you go to your Dad's and I'll give you the nod as soon as we've sorted out the money and the dates are set.'

Maddy hung up and bounded up the four flights of stairs to her attic bedsitting room to start packing. She was pleased that she'd been able to agree so readily to the nudity clause. Hell, why not, she convinced herself. Viktor was a genius and a man of great taste. No hint of salacity would be allowed to sully a Viktor Hoff film.

Maddy hugged herself gleefully and smiled as she looked around at the tiny room with its pot of yellow daisies sitting on the window sill. After *Androgyne*, there would be no more attics, she told herself. Attics had become synonymous to her with the bottom rung of the ladder. No more stealing greenery and branches of berries from Kensington Gardens at dusk to augment the daisies and cheer up her room. (She was thoughtful enough never to steal the flowers—what would happen if everyone did?) And, best of all, no more recycling of clothes four times a year. At the start of each season, shortage of hanging space found Maddy swapping the clothes from her tiny cupboard with those bundled away in the three tattered old suitcases stashed under the bed. *Androgyne* would mean built-in wardrobes. What bliss, she thought, as she started to pack her army surplus duffle bag.

It was two o'clock. She had an hour to walk around the corner to Gloucester Road tube station, catch the underground to Paddington Station and be on the three o'clock for Windsor. Maddy felt very happy.

It was Phil Pendlebury who experienced a pang of misgiving as he hung up. He was pleased that Maddy felt confident about the nude scenes and Viktor Hoff's treatment of them, but he wondered whether maybe he should have told her about Rodney Baines. Oh well, he decided, she'd find out for herself soon enough . . .

Maddy tied her sweater around her waist, heaved her duffle bag over her shoulder and started on the one and a half kilometre trek from Windsor railway station to Robert's home.

It was another lovely day. She was hot already and much of the walk was uphill, so she was bound to have worked up a sweat by the time she arrived. She could just hear her father: 'Look at the state you're in, Maddy, you should have let me know what train you were on. I really don't mind picking you up, you know.' There would be that edge to his voice which had become steadily more brittle over the years. And she would say, 'It's a lovely day, Dad, I really felt like a walk,' which they both knew meant nothing. If it had been raining she still would have walked and her reply would have been 'But I like walking in the rain, Dad.'

Maddy rounded the corner at the top of the hill and walked up to the red brick building in the middle of a row of ugly but impressive Victorian terraces. She pressed the bell beside the metal plaque which read, *Robert McLaughlan, Orthodontist BDS., MDS (Ortho)*.

The door was flung open before she'd lifted her finger from the bell.

'Mummy!' And Maddy was nearly bowled over backwards by the six year old dynamo that launched itself at her.

'Jenny!'

'I've been waiting for hours and hours. You're all sweaty.'

'Yes, I know, darling.'

As Jenny, legs wrapped around her mother's waist, continued to chatter away and nuzzle Maddy's neck, another figure appeared in the doorway.

'The child's been waiting all afternoon. You could have let us know which train you were on. I would have been quite happy to—'

'Yes, I know, Dad, but it was such a lovely day . . .' Maddy couldn't be bothered pointing out to her father that she had told him she would be on one of the midafternoon trains. Yet again she was a bad mother but she told herself to let it rest.

'Hello, Alma,' she said to the matronly, once-pretty woman standing quietly in the shadows at the end of the hall. 'Has she been good?'

'A handful, Miss Frances, but on average, yes.' The housekeeper smiled, stepped into the light and deftly disengaged the child so that Maddy could retrieve her fallen duffle bag.

'Want to help me unpack?' Maddy asked Jenny.

'Any presents?'

'What do you think?'

Maddy piggybacked the girl upstairs to the bedrooms, Robert returned to his surgery to tend to his last patient for the day and Alma retired to the kitchen to prepare the evening meal.

Later that night, after one of Alma's excellent hotpots, Maddy tucked the child into bed and started reading *The Gumnut Babies* to her.

'Not again,' she'd said to Jenny's request. 'This'll be the fourth time around.'

But Jenny nodded firmly and there was no getting out of it. *The Water Babies*, *Toad of Toad Hall* and *Peter Pan* were all firm favourites but *The Gumnut Babies* reigned supreme. Jenny was fascinated by her Australian antecedents and was determined to live in Australia one day.

'When you're older we'll go there,' Maddy promised over and over.

'How old? Seven?'

Eventually Maddy gave in to a ceiling age of ten. It seemed a lifetime away to Jenny but it nevertheless satisfied her. 'When I'm ten I'm going to Australia,' she boasted to her school friends.

And to Maddy, Jenny's tenth birthday became a deadline. By then she was determined to have 'made it'. She wanted to be in the position of being able to spend time in both countries. Much as she loved England, she wanted to foster her daughter's affinity with Australia. And most important of all, of course, she wanted Jenny to get to know her grandmother.

Although Maddy hadn't seen Helena for nearly seven years, she and her mother were closer than they had ever been. It hadn't started out well. Six months after Robert took his pregnant daughter with him to England, Helena had a nervous breakdown. The social whirl she'd adopted took its toll and she signed herself into a clinic for repairs. She hadn't let Maddy know and, by the time she left the clinic, there were endless worried phone messages, letters and photos of a brand-new bouncing baby girl. It was all Helena needed to perfect a total recovery. As a concerned grandmother she took stock of her life, realised it was frivolous, and resigned from all social committees except those which benefited handicapped children. Then she met Todd Hall, a fifty-five year old widower with two adored grandchildren of his own, and married him.

Maddy smiled every time she heard her mother's voice over the phone, dripping with maternal concern, or read her mother's letters full of the latest correct diets for infants. It was yet another image Helena had decided to adopt—she hadn't really changed at all. But she would make Mr Todd Hall very happy. She had been a perfect hostess-wife for Robert, now she would be a perfect grandmother-wife for Todd.

Maddy realised that she finally knew her mother. It wasn't Helena's fault that she had no concept of herself as an individual, that she could only be what others wanted her to be. It was sad, really, Maddy thought. So she encouraged the grandparent in Helena and even joked with Jenny about the extra grandpa she'd inherited, Todd of Todd Hall, who looked very nice in the photos.

They never joked about Todd of Todd Hall in front of Robert, of course. Even Jenny knew that was taboo. Robert had allowed Helena to divorce him but he in no way considered himself free of his wife. He never mentioned her name and never intended to see her again but, as far as he was concerned, Robert and Helena McLaughlan were married for life.

After the initial shock when Maddy had announced her pregnancy, Robert had derived a certain pleasure at the thought of an impending grandchild and it was his idea that Maddy accompany him to England and have the baby there. He would employ a full-time nanny and they could all live very comfortably together. Subconsciously, Robert was building yet another cocoon for himself and when Maddy rebelled, demanding she be able to pursue her career, it spelled destruction for their relationship. If she wished to abandon her child for a life of frivolity in the theatre she must do it under another name, he insisted.

Maddy's rebellion was total. She took the baby and left. Then she found a cheap bedsit in Kensington, changed her name and set about trying to find herself some work. It was an impossible situation, Maddy realised, doomed to failure from the outset. Robert was horrified at her absconding with the baby, and begged Maddy to at least accept money, but even that was impossible. If money was all it took, Maddy could have approached Helena. But Jenny needed a home and Maddy finally relinquished the struggle, accepting Robert's total support of the child until she could make a career for herself. She refused to accept Robert's money for her own support though, even between acting jobs. She earned more when she wasn't acting, anyway, particularly at Danny's Downstairs.

The days she could spend with Jenny were precious to the two of them. She kept the child well up to date with the progress of her career. They would read through Maddy's scripts together and Jenny would become as excited as her mother at the prospect of a new role.

'*Andro* . . . How do you say it again?' Jenny asked as she leafed through the script of *Androgyne*.

It was Friday. They'd been for a walk around Windsor Castle and now they were picnicking in the park. The castle and the picnic were regular activities when the weather was fine and Jenny never seemed to tire of the combination.

'*Androgyne*,' Maddy pronounced carefully.

'Can we read the part where they meet and he thinks she's a boy?'

With the exception of some of the more explicit scenes, they had read the entire script through together and Maddy had been very open about the subject matter.

Although puzzled to start with, Jenny had been fascinated. 'I didn't know boys loved boys.'

'Some do.'

'Do they get married and live together and have babies?'

'They can live together sure, but they can't have babies, Jen. You need a boy and a girl to make a baby. I've told you that.'

'But they could in your movie,' Jenny insisted, 'because Francine's not really a boy.'

At which point Maddy had laughed and admitted defeat. 'That's true.'

So the scene where the lovers met at the fancy-dress ball became Jenny's favourite. When Maddy explained that Georges Sand, Francine's choice of character for the Great Figures of Literature theme, was a woman who dressed as a man, Jenny was completely won by the mystery and romance. Francine became yet another role which Jenny was determined to play one day.

'But they might not make any more films of *Androgyne*,' Jenny pointed out. 'They don't keep repeating films the way they do plays.'

'Sometimes they do,' Jenny countered, 'when the films are really good ones.'

'Yes, sometimes.' It was easier to give in when Jenny's obstinate streak showed itself. The girl was already determined to be an actor and Maddy was constantly reminded of her own stubborn determination as a child. She was also reminded of Alex.

God, how like her father she is, thought Maddy as she looked at Jenny. The same sandy hair, the same fine bones, the cheeky, defiant grin and, above all, the same fascination with everything about her. And, like Alex, her fascination was her fatally attractive quality. Although Jenny lacked her mother's fragile beauty, when she turned her full attention upon the object of her interest, the force of her personality was undeniable and her piercing grey-blue eyes were riveting.

Although the child was a constant reminder of Alex, Maddy's pain had long since passed. All she felt now was relief that she had summoned the strength to escape him. She remembered the decision over which she had agonised during the fortnight of abortion pills and hot gin baths. With each sickening experience she felt a deeper guilt at her weakness in allowing Alex to so orchestrate her life. And, each time her body refused to miscarry, a tiny seed of triumph grew. Her body wanted this baby, she told herself. Why should Alex deny it her?

The deep-rooted teachings of her childhood crept more and more into Maddy's consciousness until, finally, the moral belief in her child's right to life gave her the courage to make the decision. The decision to leave Alex.

In doing so, Maddy was convinced that she would never experience such an all-consuming love again but perhaps that was for the best. She would become her own person once more. Giving birth to her child was the first step, building her own career and her own life was the second. Some instinct told Maddy that if she allowed herself to remain so inextricably tied to Alex he would destroy her.

The night of the 'abortion' was her first show of strength and her memory of it was one of the highlights of Maddy's triumph.

'I don't want this abortion,' she'd said.

The doctor had shrugged disdainfully. 'Yes, it's not altogether uncommon for some young women to reconsider their decision to terminate at the last minute. It's entirely your prerogative, of course, but you must realise that, as I have allocated my surgery time and booked my assistant,' he gestured to the crisply starched nurse standing to attention by his desk, 'I can only refund fifty per cent of—'

'I don't want a refund.'

There was a pause. 'I beg your pardon?'

'I want you to keep the money and I want to

stay here for as long as the abortion would take and I want you to tell me what the aftereffects would be.'

That was when the doctor's jaw had dropped and Maddy suddenly knew she'd made the right decision and everything was going to be fine.

The doctor went to dismiss the nurse, but Maddy called her back. 'No, I'd rather you stayed. My friend is outside and he might see you go.'

The nurse looked sulkily at the doctor. Having assumed she'd been granted a last-minute reprieve, she was loath to relinquish a paid night off. 'I can leave through the back garage,' she suggested.

'Sit down,' the doctor said.

So the nurse sat down and remained scowling while the doctor answered Maddy's questions. He was quite happy to list the physical reactions following a termination. Due to the anaesthetic she would possibly be dizzy for ten minutes or so upon leaving the surgery. 'We anaesthetise for the minimum amount of time and we like to get you up and about fairly quickly to reduce the aftereffects.'

I bet, Maddy thought, and to reduce the time I'm lying around in here.

'You would be advised to go home and lie down,' the doctor continued, 'and you would probably sleep quite deeply for a couple of hours.'

Maddy listened attentively while he told her of the cramps and the bleeding she could expect following the fatigue. 'Those are merely the physical effects, of course,' the doctor concluded. He seemed to be enjoying his lecture. 'The emotional reaction differs with every patient, depending on—'

'Thank you. That's all I need to know.'

And the three of them sat in uncomfortable silence for a further fifty minutes until the time was up. Then the doctor bundled Maddy out the front door and turned off the light, wishing she'd been the usual distraught teenager only too grateful to have her problem sorted out for her. What right did she have to make him feel guilty? He was only doing what a number of his colleagues did, cleanly and well, thereby saving the reproductive systems— and sometimes even the lives—of many young women who would otherwise be forced to suffer the butcheries of backyard abortionists. Besides, abortion would be legalised any day now so the whole argument was redundant.

Maddy hadn't intended to make the doctor feel guilty at all. Although she hadn't liked his cold cash approach from their very first meeting, she'd made no moral judgments about him. He was supplying a demand and presumably doing it well. She was, however, aware of his discomfort as she sat in the chair opposite him, serene and confident in her decision. She knew he was faking his sudden interest in his files and, although she felt no vindictiveness, she simply couldn't be bothered attempting to put him at his ease.

It wasn't all downhill after that. Alex's attentiveness was seductive and difficult to resist. But she managed. She had been deeply hurt by his subsequent fling with Susannah—which a fellow student had been only too quick to report to Maddy. But it also helped her make that final break.

And then, of course, it was all worthwhile: then there was Jenny. And Maddy was glad, so glad, that she'd found the strength to resist Alex.

'Goodbye, darling, I'll see you Sunday.' Only a couple of days away, Maddy thought, as she hugged her daughter. She didn't want to leave, but a Friday and Saturday at Danny's were too good to knock back; she could earn a full week's tour wages on those two nights alone.

'Bye, Mummy. Chookas.'

Although she was vague about it, Maddy always allowed Jenny to believe she was performing somewhere, a one-off radio drama or a charity concert. Who needed a Soho nightclub hostess for a mother?

'Goodbye, Miss Frances.' Alma put a protective arm around the child but it wasn't threatening and Maddy didn't mind. The woman was worth her weight in gold.

'Do you know what train you'll be on?' The avenging angel was standing beside Alma.

'No, I don't, Dad. I'll give you a ring.'

She started down the hill, then turned and waved at the three of them standing on the front step. She'd insisted on walking, as she always did when the weather was fine, and her father had protested as he always did. And as always she turned back to see the familiar sight: the three of them, looking like a family. Robert with his proprietorial air. Alma with her arm around Jenny.

Maddy had a sneaking suspicion that, although she was unaware of it, Alma was actually in love with Robert McLaughlan. With the exception of sharing his bed, she certainly fulfilled all other wifely duties. She not only looked after the child and the running of the house, she also cooked, washed and cleaned. And whenever Robert suggested hiring a maid she wouldn't hear of it. 'What on earth for,

Mr McLaughlan?' she'd say in her pleasant, no-nonsense voice with its trace of a Midlands accent, 'A waste of money it'd be.' Alma was fifty years old and childless, and an excellent housekeeper and nanny: firm, capable, and always pleasant. But she belonged to a breed previously unknown to Maddy—in fact, to the best of Maddy's knowledge, a breed unknown to Australians in general. Alma was born a servant. Her parents and her parents' parents had all been servants. They saw no shame in it and they trained their children to follow in their footsteps.

At a quarter to nine Maddy walked out of Leicester Square tube station and started up Wardour Street. Only two nights at Danny's, she thought gratefully.

At nine o'clock she seated herself at the bar along with the other five hostesses in their cocktail dresses. Maddy only owned two cocktail dresses, one black and one red, but she varied them with an array of costume jewellery or home-made corsages.

The bar was lined up with opened bottles of dummy champagne and the hostesses sipped apple cider until a client asked the girl of his choice to join him, at which point the champagne became the real thing. Although it was cheap and nasty bubbly, the management charged the earth for it and the girls were on commission—three pounds for each bottle of champagne a client bought them. Maddy ended up quite drunk the first night she worked at Danny's and it looked as if it could become an occupational hazard until Kath, the thirty-five year old cockney 'den mother' with the silicone breasts and bright red hair, taught her the routine disposal methods.

'You offer it round for starters, dear—the barman, the other girls, the piano player. That gets rid of a bottle and the clients understand it's the done thing. After that you go to the Ladies and tip it down the lav, and of course you always try and get a chair near one of the pot plants. If the worst comes to the worst you sneak it under the tablecloth and tip it onto the carpet.' It certainly explained to Maddy why the pot plants were in such a shabby condition and the carpet always smelled sour.

Surprisingly, the food at Danny's was good. It was just as well. Maddy often had to eat a second meal with a second client if the first one, disappointed at her knock-back, left to chat up one of the girls who 'did'.

It had taken Maddy quite a while to realise that she was the only girl who 'didn't'. She'd been introduced to the job by another struggling actress she'd met during a repertory season at Crewe and it came as quite a shock when the girl, who obviously didn't adhere to the champagne disposal routine, whispered drunkenly to her one night. 'I only do it with them when I'm pissed.'

Maddy had been further shocked to discover that the talented cabaret performer who played piano and sang torch songs on Fridays and Saturdays was also on the game. Strangely enough, when she thought about it, the prostitutes were really being the more honest ones, weren't they? They were selling a commodity while she was just conning people.

Maddy had been on the verge of leaving but Kath, who by that time had well and truly taken her under her maternal wing, dissuaded her. 'Where are you going to make money like this for your

154

little girl, dear?' Kath had two daughters of her own, aged six and eight, who lived with their grandmother in the house Kath had bought in Canterbury. She lived a completely double life, exemplary widow-mother five days a week in the country and hostess-whore two nights a week at Danny's Downstairs. Not that the girls slept with their clients on the premises, of course. Danny's was a legitimate nightclub and no girl was allowed to leave work until the place closed at three, but the assignations were made there and Kath had a very comfortable little flat in Frith Street.

'There's absolutely nothing wrong in what you're doing, dear,' Kath insisted when Maddy told her of her misgivings. 'You don't have to go on the game to provide a service. These are lonely men. You've talked to them, you know that. They're out-of-towners, they want someone pretty to talk to, someone who'll make them feel attractive, wanted. What's wrong with that?'

Maddy was about to interrupt but Kath countered her. 'And everybody knows the nightclub set-up, dear. Everybody knows they have to pay big bucks for cheap champagne. God, you think Danny's is a rip-off, you should try the top spots!' Kath rolled her eyes in mock horror and flicked her mercurochrome hair over one shoulder. 'I started out nine years ago at the Mayfair. The poor buggers who go there are fleeced by everyone from the doorman and barman to the bouncer and lavatory attendant.'

Maddy smiled. Kath's life-preserving ability to justify was either very simple or very clever. It was actually a persuasive mixture of both. Maddy not only stayed on at Danny's but allowed Kath to include her in several lucrative after-hour jobs which, although shady, were harmless enough. She double-dated as a dance partner for a friend of one of Kath's clients when they all went to Tramps; she lunched several times on a private yacht with Kath and friends who looked suspiciously like mafiosi; and she helped make up the female numbers required for a party of Arabs who had centre court tickets at Wimbledon. Kath always accepted the money and paid her the next time they saw each other at Danny's. One time Maddy even agreed to be an 'onlooker'.

'Sure proof of my trust in Kath,' Maddy thought as she watched the man's buttocks pounding up and down and listened to Kath's murmurs of encouragement.

'He's a regular, dear,' Kath had explained. 'He always books two girls and he thinks he's going to get off with them both but he never does. His eyes are bigger than his tummy, silly thing, and there's two hundred quid in it for you.'

Two hundred quid! 'OK,' Maddy had said warily.

But what if this time his eyes aren't bigger than his tummy? she thought, feeling very silly sitting there in a miniskirt and knee-high boots drinking a pretend martini.

Then, as the man's breathing became laboured, Kath started making signs at Maddy over his shoulder. Oh yes, Maddy remembered, now I'm supposed to put the kettle on.

Ten minutes later they were sitting around drinking English Breakfast and eating chocolate digestive biscuits. The main topic of conversation was their respective children and it was all so strangely comfortable that Maddy inwardly chastised herself for not feeling remotely guilty. What on earth was happening to her morals!

'Hello, Madeleine.'

'Oh. Hello, Jack.' She'd been mentally going through her lines for *Androgyne* and hadn't noticed the arrival of one of her several 'regulars'.

Jack was from Manchester and he was a large man. Not tall and not fat, but square. Everything about Jack was square, his build, his face, his hands. And his smile. It was a very nice, broad, square smile. You'd never know to look at Jack that he was rich. He dressed plainly and simply, despite the fact that he was a director of one of the largest haberdashery companies in Manchester. He came to London once a month for conferences with the big city buyers and always sought Maddy's company at Danny's Downstairs.

She joined him at a corner table by the largest pot plant and nodded to the waiter. She was pleased. Jack was always good for three bottles of champagne, a meal and a hefty tip.

'How's the acting business coming along?' Jack asked, sipping his pint of beer and watching the waiter pour Maddy's champagne. 'Thank you.' He slipped the waiter a pound note and settled back to listen as Maddy excitedly recounted the latest turn of events.

Maddy knew that Jack was a little bit in love with her but he never came on heavy and she assumed that it really was only the company he was after. Then, one night, when she'd been returning from a quick visit to the Ladies to tip her third glass of champagne down the lavatory, she'd caught him in a brief exchange with one of the girls. An agreement had obviously been made and he leapt aside guiltily as he saw Maddy approaching. She said nothing but she felt sad that he couldn't quite meet her eyes for the rest of that evening. Why on earth should he feel guilty? He was a lonely, divorced man with a daughter her age and every right to seek female company, sexual as well as emotional, wherever he could find it. Surely she was the one who should feel guilty— for not providing the full service he was obviously seeking.

When she saw Jack coming into the club the following month, she pretended not to notice him and signalled Kath to join her in the loo.

'Send one of the other girls to him, Kath.'

'But he only ever wants you, dear.'

'No. Last time I saw him lining up a trick with one of the girls so it's only fair—'

Kath laughed at Maddy's naiveté. 'He lines up a trick with one of the girls every time, silly, but it's you he wants to talk to. The girls don't mind, they understand.' Which only made Maddy feel worse.

'Very interesting,' Jack was saying. '*Androgyne*. I didn't even know there was such a word.' For once she didn't seem to have his full attention. 'But it sounds like a wonderful opportunity for you,' he added hastily when he saw her querying look.

'Is everything all right, Jack?'

'Sure. Fine, fine.' And, although the champagne bottle was nearly full, he signalled for another one. 'Take that to the girls at the bar,' he told the waiter, 'and I'll have a large Scotch.' Something was definitely wrong, Maddy thought. She'd never seen Jack drink anything but beer.

An hour before closing time, with six double Scotches and six beer chasers under his belt, Jack was very drunk and prepared to tell her. 'Lost my job, didn't I? Retrenched. "No hard feelings", they said. No hard bloody feelings!' He drained the last of his Scotch and signalled the waiter. 'The bastards know bloody well how hard it is to get another job when you're fifty-three.'

'But how could they sack you? You're a director of the company.' Maddy was mystified. Jack never got drunk and never swore and his accent was twice as strong as it normally was.

His laugh was hollow. 'I'm a salesman, love.'

'But—'

'And I'm not divorced and I don't have a daughter your age. I've never even been married.'

'But why—?'

'Oh, who the hell knows? Who the hell cares?'

'Another champagne too, sir?' The waiter held the nearly empty bottle aloft as he took Jack's glass. It was a rhetorical question—the waiter was already turning to go. This would make the third bottle and Jack always bought three. Jack nodded automatically but Maddy called the waiter back.

'No,' she said. 'No, thank you.' The waiter stared at her, astonished. 'I said, we don't want any more champagne, thank you.'

The waiter backed off to the bar and whispered to the barman-manager as Jack continued, apparently oblivious to the exchange.

'So this is a sort of farewell visit. I shan't be working South any more. I'll stick to finding what I can around Manchester.'

'Jack, I'm so sorry. I didn't know . . .' Maddy felt utterly wretched.

'Well, how could you? It only happened last week.'

'No, I mean . . .' How could she tell him she was sorry about everything? She was sorry about the monthly savings she'd conned from him, she was sorry about the fact that she hadn't given him honest value and slept with him, she was sorry that he was a bit in love with her, she was sorry . . .

'Madeleine, can I have a word with you please?' It was Mick, the barman-manager who also happened to be 'Danny's' younger brother.

As soon as they were safely out of earshot, he hissed, 'What the hell do you mean by knocking back the champagne?'

'He's broke—he's lost his job.'

'Well, you want to watch it, love, or you'll go the same way. Now get your butt back to that table and order another bottle.'

Maddy was weary with self-loathing. She couldn't be bothered retaliating. Mick was a spiv, a crook and a con man, which made him pretty much on par with herself, after all. 'No, I'm sick of the stuff,' she said. 'I'm going to talk to my friend.'

As she turned away, Mick snarled, 'Don't bother coming back tomorrow.' Then he returned to the bar. He knew better than to cause a scene with one of the girls when there were clients about. Besides, it was closing time in a few minutes.

'We're in the same boat, Jack,' she said as she joined him. 'I just got the sack.'

Jack was jolted out of his drunken fog and he looked at her for what seemed quite a long time. 'That's good.' He smiled. 'You don't belong in a place like this.'

Maddy felt the prickle of tears but Jack didn't notice as he stared back at his drink and drifted back into his fog.

'Stay there, Jack. I'll only be a few minutes and I'll get you a cab.'

No sooner had she closed the door to the Ladies and started checking her eye make-up than Kath appeared. 'What's going on?' she asked. Maddy told her. 'Oh, shit,' she said sympathetically. 'You want me to have a word with Mick for you?'

'No, thanks.' There was no way Maddy could tell Kath the utter relief she felt at leaving the place. 'I start work on the film next week anyway.'

'Fair enough. I've got a good one for you to go out on, though.' Kath winked. 'Little Tommy Tucker's picking me up at closing.' She looked at her watch. 'Like in a couple of minutes.'

'Oh.' Little Tommy Tucker was the nickname Kath gave to the man with 'eyes too big for his tummy' who always double-booked.

'Yeah,' she continued. 'He's got a porn movie and he wants two girls to look at it with him before he does it. 'Course he'll only end up doing it with one. You want to be in it?'

'I don't think so, Kath, thanks all the same.'

'Oh, come on, dear, don't look so down.' Kath put a comforting arm around Maddy. 'I tell you this bloke's nothing like your Jack. He's as rich as Croesus and he wants a fun night, you'll be doing him a favour, and there's three hundred quid in it for you.'

Maddy couldn't help laughing. She nodded. What the hell, this was her swan song. Everybody had their price, after all. She'd watch the dirty movie with the poor rich bloke, make three hundred quid

161

and tomorrow she'd wake up with a clean slate and forget that she'd ever allowed herself to sink so low. 'Sink so low?' She scolded herself for being a drama queen as she left to gather up Jack and put him in a cab.

A very attractive pair of naked male buttocks filled the screen. The camera panned around to a side angle shot of a groin and the biggest erect penis Maddy had ever seen. Then the camera zoomed in closer and closer, moving slowly up the shaft of the penis to linger lovingly on a close-up of the glistening glans. The titles started to roll in bold black letters: THE ROD in VENUS REVEALED.

The camera eased back to a wide shot of the man, who was standing frozen in a formal mini-Versailles garden alongside several naked women also pretending to be statues. Slowly the man came to life, turning his head towards the camera. Maddy gasped out loud just before the name appeared on the screen: *Starring Rodney Baines*.

'Why didn't you tell me!' Maddy screamed at Phil. It was Sunday morning and Maddy never phoned him at home but this was one time she thought she had ample reason.

'OK, OK. So he does hard porn—but only expensive, quality stuff, and he's the most famous blue movie star in the UK.'

Maddy suddenly remembered where she'd seen Rodney Baines. It was in one of those glossy liberated magazines she'd flicked through somewhere. The kind of magazine that ran articles like 'The men we'd most like to sleep with as long as we didn't have to talk to them'. The in-depth interview with Rodney Baines had quoted him as saying he'd 'like to be taken seriously'.

'He wants to be taken seriously,' Phil was saying. 'This is going to be his first legitimate film.' Phil went from 'Rod'll be great, the camera loves him', to 'It's a Viktor Hoff film, how can you lose', and finished up with 'Well, you're contracted, so you'll have to live with it.'

Maddy finally gave in. She'd just have to hope for the best. What else could she do? Oh God, she thought, what have I let myself in for?

ACT II

SCENE 3: 1978–1979

The marriage of Alex Rainford and Susannah Wright made headline news. Even six months before the event the women's magazines were glorying in the match: 'Australia's Most Popular Television Actor to Wed Leading Classical Actress'. And accompanying the stories were glossy stills of Alex from his hugely successful series 'Outback Force' and portraits of Susannah as Hedda, Nina and Major Barbara from the Ibsen, Chekhov and Shaw she'd performed in that year at the Sydney Opera House.

On the day itself, shots of the happy couple leaving the church made television news footage on every channel, with special coverage of the lavish wedding reception by Channel Five. Channel Five had been granted exclusive rights because they owned 'Outback Force'.

'Congratulations.' Alain King shook Alex's hand then kissed Susannah on both cheeks. 'You look radiant,' he told her. She did for one so thin, he thought. The flowing auburn hair and the translucent skin did it: very much the classical dramatic actress image. No tits, bit short on sex appeal, he thought critically, but then Alex more than compensated as far as sex appeal went. Alex looked devastatingly sexy, the two complemented each other perfectly, and Alain couldn't have been more delighted. Channel Five's cameras were whirring and flashlights were popping and it was all wonderful for the ratings.

Alain King was the producer of 'Outback Force' and the most successful entrepreneur in Australian commercial television. Still in his early thirties, he was sought after by every major production company with their sights set on top-rating drama series.

Ten years before, Alan King had added an 'i' to his name, made the switch from market research to television and quickly become an expert in the field of popular demand. He'd been tempted to start his own production company but, deciding not to risk his capital, he started saving for the million dollar city penthouse he intended to buy and hired himself out to the highest bidder. A columnist who believed Alain's Midas touch was due more to talent than sheer luck had dubbed him The King and the term had stuck.

Alain had 'discovered' Alex. At least he maintained he had. The fact that Alex had successfully graduated from NADA, starred in The Way In

Theatre Company's 1973 season and even received rave reviews in their production of an early Bill Davison play meant nothing as far as Alain King was concerned.

'You'll never reach the masses via the stage,' he told Alex on their first meeting over a bottle of house champagne in the theatre bar after the show. 'In fact, you won't even reach them via the movies, not in this country. Maybe one day, but not yet.

'You star on the small screen in a regular drama series, though, and you're made,' he continued. 'I tell you, this country is finally going mad over its own kind. A home-grown television star gets more recognition than Paul Newman and Steve McQueen doing a tango down George Street on a Saturday night.'

When Alex looked doubtful, Alain came in for the kill. 'Sign up for this new show I'm doing. It's called "Outback Force" and it's going to be a hit. Sign for a year and I'll prove it to you. In a year you'll be a national star.'

Alex was sorely tempted, despite his commitment to the theatre and his rave reviews in the Bill Davison play. And they had certainly been raves. Even Myra Nielson had given him a good wrap: 'Alex Rainford has found his niche. After fumbling with the classics he has now ably demonstrated that his true talent lies in the contemporary Australian theatre. In fact, if producers were a little more adventurous and gave our local playwrights a chance, Rainford could well prove the definitive Australian actor of today.'

Alex had been pleased, of course. Very pleased. Myra had finally recognised his talent and it had nothing to do with their ongoing sexual battles.

However, he had not been deterred from his intention to pursue a career in production. If he signed with Alain now it would mean shelving his plan for a year. But then, he reasoned, surely he would carry more power as a producer and doors would open more readily if he had a high commercial profile.

'And as far as a projected view of the Australian television market's concerned,' Alain continued confidently, 'my bet is we'll be selling internationally within five years. At least, *my* shows will be.' He grinned his engagingly boyish grin, the one he always used when he knew he was home and hosed in clinching a deal. 'Australian actors can finally achieve international stardom without leaving home,' he concluded triumphantly. 'About time, eh?' Alain King couldn't give a stuff about Australian actors. In fact Alain King couldn't give a stuff about actors in general, but he certainly knew how to manipulate them. It was probably one of the reasons he despised them, he supposed. They were too easy. No spine.

'Alex. Good show tonight. Well done.' It was Roger Kingsley, white wine in one hand, other hand drooped over Alex's shoulder. He made no move to acknowledge Alain King. 'The second Act fight's getting a bit sloppy though. How about you and Hugh come in a quarter of an hour before the half tomorrow and we run through it a couple of times?'

'Sure. This is Alain King, Roger Kingsley.'

'Oh. Hi.' Roger pretended to suddenly notice Alain and offered his hand. He read the newspapers: he knew who the man was, and he'd noticed him the moment he'd entered the bar. So this was the king of soap, he thought. Arrogant-looking bastard.

'Congratulations. What an excellent play,' Alain replied, fully aware of the fact that Kingsley, with his well-publicised devotion to the classics, probably hated the play. He returned the handshake and deliberately avoided any compliment on the production. Kingsley was a conceited queen who needed putting down.

'Yes, it is a good play, isn't it?' Roger replied when he'd waited long enough to realise that Alain wasn't going to follow up with praise for his direction. 'I've commissioned Bill's next play and I think we can safely say that Australia's brightest new playwright is about to come into his own.'

'Not before time, don't you think?'

Roger started to bristle. 'The Way In Theatre Company is always searching for material from new playwrights,' he countered. Which wasn't true: dozens of plays ended up in Roger's wastepaper bin unread. He presented one new Australian play a season to meet the demand for local material and he usually relied upon these productions to make a loss in order to justify the whopping government subsidy granted to The Way In Theatre Company. The success of the Bill Davison play had come as a complete surprise to Roger. Not that he would admit it, of course. He was riding the crest of the success, had commissioned the playwright's next work and was quite prepared to wear his losses elsewhere.

'Good.' Alain didn't believe Roger's protestations for a second. 'As producers, it's our duty to promote Australian material, don't you agree?' Alain had never considered it his duty to promote anything but he was on the attack.

Somehow he had allowed this self-opinionated poofter to get under his skin.

Roger gave a derisive snort, sipped his white wine and flared his nostrils at Alain. 'Well, of course, that's much easier to do on television.'

'My King!'

Alain automatically turned, but the words weren't directed at him.

'I'm dying.' Hugh Skiffington gulped from Roger's glass and handed it back to him. 'Ah, bliss.' He put an arm around Susannah who was standing beside him and flashed a friendly smile at Alain. 'On Wednesdays we all die.' Wednesdays were matinee days.

So this was the actor who'd played the big ocker tough, thought Alain. No wonder he hadn't been able to handle the role. No wonder Alex with his heterosexual Aussie charm had walked all over him.

'This is Hugh Skiffington and Susannah Wright.' Alex introduced the two actors.

'Yes, so it is,' Alain said as he shook hands with Hugh. Then to Susannah. 'Congratulations.' Arty little thing, but talented. Obviously anorexic.

He turned again to Roger. 'I disagree. No one medium is easier than any other; it's a matter of talent. Some producers can successfully interpret original material and others need a safe blueprint from which to copy. The latter producer invariably sticks to the classics and pretends they're difficult.' Alain put his untouched glass of house champagne on the bar. Trust the theatre to serve such cheap shit.

He slipped a card into Alex's hand. 'Ring me,' he said and swept out, aware that Roger was fuming behind him and Hugh was making 'what did I say?' gestures. Bloody fairies.

Alex had been very impressed. Four years later he was still impressed; Alain was an impressive person. He was manipulative and powerful, and there was a lot Alex could learn from him—and he did. He learned the technical aspects of production: the product, the market, the investment, the promotion. But more importantly he learned, directly from Alain's example, the seductive art of selling an idea. And he witnessed at first-hand Alain's ability to wield power and manipulate those responsible for artistic input.

'They're writers, Alex,' Alain told him. 'They're writers and actors and designers and composers and they need you. They need the work. Nine times out of ten you don't bother bargaining. It's only the one-off talent that needs to be fêted and there are usually ways of getting around that. Quite often it needn't even affect the budget. It might be something they want done, or someone else they want in the production or . . .' he shrugged vaguely, '. . . a number of other tacks can be taken.' He didn't specifically mention anything underhand, but it was implicit in his tone.

From the outset, Alain realised that Alex was using him. When he challenged Alex about it, he openly admitted it. 'Of course, Alain, that's why I accepted the acting job. I only want to learn from the best.'

It was a simple statement of fact and Alain didn't even feel conned. It was obvious that Alex was genuinely fascinated by him. The flattery was irresistible and Alain agreed to teach the young actor.

His first lesson was to demonstrate that

everything had its price. And the price for Alex's tuition was a two-year option on his twelve-month contract should 'Outback Force' be a runaway success.

Alex learned quickly. Before agreeing to sign up for a possible three years, he countered with a request of his own. His friend, Julian Oldfellow, was to be employed as one of the directors. 'Just give him a trial, Alain. If he's no good then you can get rid of him.'

'You're damn right I can.'

Surprisingly enough it had taken quite a bit of pursuading to get Julian to accept the directorial job.

'I believe the Arts Council's sending out a schools tour of *Little Women*,' Alex said sarcastically at Harold's the Sunday night after the offer had been made. 'I suppose you want to apply for that?' It was a full year since the *Sound of Music* tour but the memories were still vividly unpleasant for Julian. 'You can't exist on play readings and workshops for the Alternate Theatre Space, you know,' Alex continued relentlessly. 'You're not experienced enough for the commercial managements and, face it, Roger Kingsley's never going to give you a go at The Way In.'

'It's true, Julian. You're too avant-garde for him,' Susannah agreed as she peeled her second green grape and avoided the cheese board.

'What's more, he doesn't fancy you, dear boy,' Harold added. No one could reply to that.

Julian finally agreed to direct a maximum of six of the twenty-six episodes made in the first production year ('That is, if Alain likes your first one,' Alex couldn't resist saying) and even then he only acquiesced because it would leave him enough time to continue with his writing. He was sure that within twelve months he would have a play ready for production.

The phenomenal success of 'Outback Force' put paid to both Julian's and Alex's carefully laid plans. They both found themselves well and truly seduced by the trappings of success and it was a full four years before they finally withdrew from the television spotlight. By then 'Outback Force' had more than served its purpose for them both.

Julian had written no less than five plays and the most recent, a black comedy called *I, Me and Us*, was more than ready for production.

Alex had not only applied the lessons he'd learned from Alain King, he had used his commercial profile to its fullest advantage and had aroused more than enough investment interest to embark on his first production. Not surprisingly, his first venture was to be *I, Me and Us*, starring Susannah Wright. Rehearsals were to start a fortnight after the wedding.

Alex had made Susannah read opposite the string of hopefuls testing for the male lead for nearly a fortnight. He and Julian had agreed, however, that it was best not to let the press know that Susannah had always been the walk-up start. Not that they were particularly concerned about accusations of nepotism. The powers that be were generally supportive of new entrepreneurial ventures. Even if the production failed, the critics, scribes and knockers-in-general were happy to patronise elegantly from a great height with comments like 'a worthwhile venture which didn't quite come off', or 'with a little pruning and stronger direction' . . .

'First times are comparatively easy,' Alain assured Alex. Repeating the success was the hard part—that was when the Australian tall poppy syndrome was applied with a vengeance. 'They can't wait to cut you down,' Alain warned. 'You've got to really come up with the goods the second time around.'

Alain had been openly encouraging when Alex's plans to leave 'Outback Force' and return to the theatre had been announced to the press. Everyone had been surprised and warmed by the generosity displayed by The King. It was presumed he would have been possessive about the star he'd created. Such a presumption couldn't have been more incorrect. Not only was Alain only too happy for Alex to go, he used the character's departure as a further lesson for his protégé.

'Never let an actor become more important than a show, Alex, and that applies to the theatre as well as television. Oh, give the public their stars, certainly,' he said expansively. 'They love all that. Make sure they run out and buy their tickets and tune their dials to the biggest or the newest hot favourite. But only to start with! If you want to create an ongoing success and make money, the show has to take over. The actors have to become totally dispensable. Otherwise you might as well go into the superstar concert stakes.' He gave a snort of derision. 'And then you've got to deal with their personal managers and their lawyers. You've got to import their families, their entourage and their Christ-knows-what and, I tell you, it becomes a regular shitfight.'

Alain had ceased to think of Alex as an actor. He was more like an extension of himself, a young

Alain King. Although only ten years older than Alex, Alain couldn't remember when he'd last felt a rush of youthful enthusiasm. And now here was Alex, leaning on his every word and learning every lesson, even when Alain spelled it out the way it was: ruthlessly. In fact, the more ruthless it was, the more Alex seemed to lap it up.

Alex even helped Alain to train the actor who was to take over from him. They tested dozens of hopefuls to find the correct mix which they could market along the same lines that had proved so successful with Alex. 'It doesn't matter if he can't act,' Alain had said and Alex wasn't the least bit offended.

The new leading role in 'Outback Force', the press was informed, had been developed not only by the creative consultant but the executive storyliner, the executive editor and the writer who was responsible for the character's introductory episodes. In reality, the new leading role was an Alex Rainford clone who had been created by Alain and Alex three months before and fed to the executive writers piecemeal at dozens of script conferences until they dreamed it was their own.

Although Alex had left the show two months earlier, his character was still to air at the time of the wedding. It was deliberate. The wedding date had been yet another agreement reached between Alain and Alex, together with the exclusive rights granted to Channel Five to cover the reception.

'You don't mind, do you, Sooz?' Alex had asked beguilingly. 'It's good for Alain's ratings and great publicity for us.'

So long as it was agreed the cameras were not to come anywhere near the church, Susannah hadn't minded in the least. She was fully aware of the value of publicity.

Susannah did, however, consider it poor form when Alain, having told her what a radiant bride she made, saluted her with the Bollinger and said, 'Tonight's episode'll be up at least five points'. She didn't like Alain.

Alain was aware of her dislike and it didn't bother him one bit. He in turn didn't care for Susannah. He wasn't one for actors at the best of times, but committed actors like Susannah were Alain's least favourite. They didn't seem to have any comprehension whatsoever of the value of money, which made them very difficult to manipulate. All they cared about was the role, the director, the cast and artistic integrity. They were the type who held up production while they said 'Let's talk motivation'.

Indulgent bunch of retards, the lot of them, Alain thought, as Susannah excused herself and joined her brother and his wife who were talking to Harold Beauchamp.

Alain headed for another Bollinger. 'Not long to go now, Julian,' he said heartily, flashing his most amiable smile by way of greeting and nodding at a waiter who poured a fresh Bollinger.

'Yep, one more week and it's goodbye Channel Five.' Why is Alain being so jovial? Julian wondered.

'We'll miss you,' Alain said as he shook Julian's hand. Julian looked around and noticed the television camera behind him recording their every action. Oh, that's why. Well, he didn't mind playing the game. He smiled back.

175

'Yes, I think I'll miss Channel Five too. Four years is a long time.' He wouldn't miss it at all. In fact he couldn't wait to complete his final week of post-production, but he was grateful for everything he'd learned at Channel Five.

Julian didn't like Alain and Alain didn't like Julian but they had a healthy regard for each other's talent. Despite himself, Alain had learned to respect Julian's ability to communicate with actors. Usually he had little time for 'actors' directors', as they were termed within the profession ('wankers' was Alain's translation), but the results spoke for themselves in Julian's case. The actors' performances in 'Outback Force' were one of the show's strongest assets.

While quite happy to release Alex, Alain had actually fought hard to keep hold of Julian, particularly now the show had been sold to the UK. Alain had infiltrated the international market a full year before he had predicted and, when Julian knocked back the offer to direct an episode in London, it was a source of great irritation to Alain. The man was turning down international exposure in order to pursue his own puny little career in the Australian theatre! It was an insult. Oh well, he consoled himself, directors were a dime a dozen. There were plenty of other good ones and Julian was a poofter, after all.

Julian was fully aware of Alain's opinion of him, both the good and the bad, and he couldn't care less so long as he was left alone to get on with his job. Much as he respected Alain's vast knowledge of the television medium, he loathed the man.

'Lovely wedding,' he said.

'Yes,' Alain agreed distractedly. And they parted company.

Trust Alex to invite Alain, Julian thought.

Alain had been one of the few business associates invited to the actual wedding. Susannah had been against it from the outset but, despite her protestations, Alex had insisted. 'Fair's fair, Sooz. You've got your whole family coming and I—'

'Don't tell me you consider Alain King *family!*'

But Alex shrugged, smiled and refused to rise to the bait.

Susannah could hardly contest the ratio of numbers. Although her parents were absent due to her father's fragile condition and his inability to travel, her family was very well represented: brother Michael, his wife Priscilla, their six year old daughter Caroline and at least a dozen aunts, uncles and cousins from both sides.

During the service it was easy not to notice the small, rather colourless woman accompanied by a homely, awkward couple who looked out of place. It was Trish Rainford with her sister and brother-in-law.

'It was a lovely wedding, dear.' Trish kissed Susannah. 'I don't think you've met Alex's Auntie Rhonda.'

Rhonda in turn kissed Susannah. 'You look beautiful. This is Terry.' She introduced her husband.

Susannah certainly hadn't met Rhonda. She'd only met Trish on two occasions and then it was at her own insistence, just six months earlier when she and Alex had decided to marry. Alex's father was now permanently institutionalised and Trish kept very much to herself, preferring only the company of her sister. At least that's what Alex said when he explained why he never visited his mother.

Trish Rainford looked as if she wanted to be left alone. On close inspection her face wasn't really colourless at all—it was quite handsome, but it was tired, expended of energy. She looked as though she didn't want to fight any more.

'It's a long drive home, so we won't stay for the reception, dear.' The three of them left gratefully and the vast majority of guests never even knew they'd been there.

Nevertheless, Julian was right. It was a lovely wedding and a lovely reception. The dearth of family on Alex's side was more than made up for by the dozens of industry friends who'd become family to both bride and groom over the years. Harold was Master of Ceremonies and ably compensated for parental absence by playing mother-of-the-bride and father-of-the-groom simultaneously and with great enthusiasm. Julian was best man and Rosie Lee, née Balcock from The Way In Theatre Company, now a happily married woman herself and mother of two, was matron of honour. Brother Michael gave Susannah away, of course, and Caroline was a nauseatingly precocious flower girl bent on stealing centre stage for herself.

'Isn't she a scream?' Priscilla gushed. 'She's going to be an actress just like her famous auntie.' There were mutters of 'Get the kid off,' and 'Kill the kid' from various thespian elements.

Although protective of the wedding ceremony itself, Susannah had taken great pains to invite the upper echelons of the theatre world to the reception. 'It's politic,' she said and Alex naturally agreed.

The vast majority accepted but there was one major critic sadly unable to attend. Myra Nielson was conspicuous by her absence but she sent her abject apologies and a telegram wishing the young couple every future happiness.

'I don't think my coming to the wedding would be a good idea, Alex,' Myra had said one Saturday night as they stripped off in her bedroom. Their sexual bouts were usually reserved for Saturday nights because Alex wasn't filming the following day; and usually for around eight o'clock so that he had plenty of time to join Susannah for drinks at the theatre bar and supper after the show.

Although he told himself it was a convenient and pleasurable way to fill in the time till eleven and the Saturday curtain, it wasn't really as flippant as that for Alex. In fact it wasn't really flippant for either of them.

An ongoing sexual battle was raging between Alex and Myra. It was doubtful whether either of them received much actual pleasure from their coupling but they were evenly matched and the thrill of winning the game far outweighed mere physical pleasure. The game was simple. Whoever held out longest and forced the other to climax first was the winner. And winning had become an obsession to them both.

They had a rapport outside their sexual combat but it was distinctly nonphysical. They never kissed, caressed or showed any signs of affection but they were two of a kind: each had a healthy regard for the other's views and they communicated keenly.

Myra had long since ceased to patronise Alex, having realised that he had a talent and a single-minded purpose which was destined to make its mark. She was quite prepared to invest in Alex's first entrepreneurial venture should she consider it worthwhile and they found it stimulating reading scripts and discussing production projects together. Strangely enough, it was Myra who pushed for Julian's script.

Like everyone else in the industry, Julian knew Myra quite well, although like everyone else in the industry he knew nothing of her affair with Alex. When he told her he was writing and she professed an interest in seeing his work, Julian was naturally delighted.

'Hey Alex,' he said excitedly, 'guess what? Myra Nielson wants to read my play! Isn't that great?'

'Yeah, terrific.'

Alex didn't wait for Saturday. He rang Myra that night. 'Why the hell do you want to see Julian's script? We can't use it.'

'Why not? Have you read it?'

'Yes.'

'And it's no good?'

'It's terrific.'

'So, why can't we use it?'

'Because I need to stick to a safe bet: a West End or a Broadway hit. We've talked about it. I need a show that's been tried and tested; you said yourself that—'

'I've changed my mind. Now listen to me, Alex,' Myra continued before he could interrupt. 'If the script's good, maybe we should think of going bold. "New young producer has the guts to go with new young playwright".' She sensed Alex was about to interrupt again. 'Besides, paying peanuts for the rights to Julian's play would save us a fortune.'

There was a moment's hesitation and Myra again dived in. 'At least wait until I've read it, all right?'

A pause. 'All right,' Alex grudgingly agreed. 'We'll talk about it then.'

Myra loved the script. 'It's the best play since "*The Doll*",' she said. (Myra rarely prefaced a statement with 'In my opinion'.) 'And I tell you something else, Alex, it'll stand the test of time better than Bill Davison's plays. They're topical and they're fake; this is universal and it's real—it might even become a *great* play.' Alex had rarely seen Myra so excited. 'And best of all, it's commercial! It'll make them laugh, it'll make them cry, and you're mad if you don't grab it!'

Myra's enthusiasm was contagious but Alex nevertheless reserved his opinion until he had reread the script. Although he'd realised it was good on first reading, he'd paid scant attention to it, as he was sure it would be of no use to him.

'What's it called?' he'd asked six months before when Julian had suggested he read it.

'*I, Me and Us*. It's a black comedy.'

Julian had spent three months rewriting *I, Me and Us* before he had found the courage to give it to Alex to read. Even then, he fervently hoped the play was well-disguised enough for Alex not to recognise the truth.

Alex didn't. 'It's good, Julian, very good,' he said. 'I won't be able to use it, though. Certainly not first up. I'll have to go with an established success.'

Julian was disappointed but of course he understood. Six months later he could barely believe his ears. 'Myra Nielson phoned me,' Alex was saying. 'She knows I'm looking for a project and

181

she's mad about your script. Maybe we should have another think about it, what do you reckon?' And the die was cast.

The news in financial circles that Myra Nielson was investing in *I, Me and Us* rapidly aroused interest from other investors. Myra kept a low profile, however, as far as her artistic input went. Even Julian had no idea of the extent of her contribution.

'You're spot-on for the lead role, Alex,' Myra said. 'In fact, I think Julian wrote it for you, but you're mad if you do it.' Alex agreed. He'd have enough to do as producer. 'Susannah should definitely play the female lead—she's ideal casting and she's a superb actress.' Alex again agreed. 'But you're insane if you let Julian direct.' And that's where Alex disagreed.

'Playwrights directing their own work?' Myra was aghast. 'Disaster. Every time.'

It was eight-thirty Saturday night and they were drinking coffee in Myra's kitchen. Fifteen minutes earlier they'd been panting and writhing in the bedroom. Myra had won the bout and they'd adjourned to the breakfast nook. They never discussed business in the bedroom.

'Julian was a director way before he was a playwright,' Alex insisted. 'It's what he's trained to do.'

'It makes no difference! He wrote the damn thing, he won't be objective.' Alex wouldn't listen. 'And,' she added conclusively, slamming down her coffee cup, 'they'll tear him to pieces for having the audacity to direct his first play—you can bet on that.'

Still Alex wouldn't listen. 'What do you think

of Harold Beauchamp and Rosie Lee for the mother and the doctor?' he asked.

Myra realised he wasn't going to give in. 'You probably wouldn't get Harold Beauchamp,' she snapped back. 'It's only a cameo.'

'Not only will I get him, he'll do it for a song.' Alex grinned. He felt elated. He didn't even mind the fact that Myra had won the sexual bout. Hell, this was better than sex, anyway. 'And Rosie'll do it for a song too; she'd walk on hot coals for Susannah.'

Myra assumed that Alex's insistence on Julian as director was an uncharacteristic display of misplaced loyalty. But she was wrong. Loyalty had nothing to do with it. Myra was not the only stimulation in Alex's life. His discussions with Julian on the text, the direction and the balance of the play were inspiring and he could think of no one else who could possibly do justice to his production.

Alex worked tirelessly and efficiently and, as time progressed, everything tied together beautifully. His decision to leave 'Outback Force' and the news of his impending wedding to Susannah were announced simultaneously. Then, three months later, the impressive cast which he had signed up for his exciting production of a new Australian play was released to the press. It was also announced that a 'hot new actor' had been signed to play the male lead.

The day the glittering Rainford-Wright wedding saturated the airwaves there wasn't a viewer tuned in who didn't know that the happy couple pointing the knife at the croque en bouche wedding cake were shortly to embark on a thrilling theatrical event called *I, Me and Us*.

Yes, the publicity wheels were perfectly set in motion, Myra thought, as she sat back in front of the television, sipped her Scotch and watched Alain King shake hands with Julian Oldfellow.

It certainly looked as if it had been a lovely wedding. Ah, here were the newlyweds, talking to a handsome man and an effusive woman holding a waving flower girl up to the camera. Mercifully the camera man directed his attention back to the bridal pair. Alex was giving his wife one of his heart-throb smiles. But was it for Susannah or for the camera? Myra wondered.

God, Susannah was looking good. Love the way she's wearing her hair, Myra thought, lots of it, fluffed out, down to the shoulders. And the natural titian colour beautifully set off the chiselled face and the classical bones.

So Alex wouldn't be visiting for the next few Saturdays. Myra didn't really mind. Actually she was quite looking forward to a bit of a rest, she admitted to herself. Maybe it was time she gave the competitive sexual activity a miss—she was fifty-three, after all.

Not that her libido was diminishing. To the contrary, she was feeling very horny right now. She wriggled in her chair. But maybe she needed something a little more laid back, a little more exploratory. She picked up the phone and dialled. Variety was the spice of life, after all. A voice answered from the other end.

'Hello, Anita,' Myra said as she watched Susannah smile radiantly at Alex.

Myra wasn't the only person looking forward to

a break from Alex Rainford. Julian needed some space too. He found Alex draining at the best of times but with all guns blazing, obsessed with his forthcoming production, Alex was exhausting to be around. Stimulating certainly, but exhausting. And, of course, there was the added pressure of Julian's 'secret'. If Alex were ever to guess at the original inspiration behind *I, Me and Us*, he would surely realise the extent of the power he had over Julian.

During an early brain-draining session when they'd been discussing the direction they should take with the production, whether to lean a little more to the comedic or dramatic approach, Julian had dared to venture into the danger zone.

'What exactly do you think this play's about, Alex? You tell me.'

Oh shit, Alex thought, hoping that Julian wasn't getting too precious about his material. 'Sure. I'll tell you,' he fired back. 'It's about a girl who really wants to be a bloke so she turns schizo and spends half her time responding to things as a man. Simple. Come on, Julian,' he argued, 'it's got all the ingredients of a commercial success—an updated *Goodbye Charlie*, for God's sake—so let's keep it simple.' He held up his hand, thinking Julian was about to interrupt. 'OK, OK,' he said. 'If we want to get all fancy we could say it's about dual personality and mental illness, it's about father complex and penis envy, you name it, but we should still lean towards the comedy angle.'

Julian breathed an inward sigh of relief. 'Sure,' he agreed. 'I don't mind if we point up the comedy— that's what it's there for. The funnier it is, the bigger the impact at the end when she goes insane.'

Alex smiled, glad that he'd made his point, and

Julian retreated, grateful that his massive rewrite had worked and that Alex obviously had no idea of the original theme of the play or the inspiration behind it.

The fact was that Julian's obsession with Alex Rainford had not abated over the years—it had become more and more of a driving force in his life and, in one way or another, had formed the basis of every one of his plays.

While he was writing *I, Me and Us* he switched his style and tried desperately not to be influenced by Alex, but the play wasn't working and he knew it. Finally Julian decided that if he wasn't going to write about the man himself, he would write about his obsession for the man himself. And it worked. Except for one thing.

The play's central character, Simon, whose fatal fascination for his friend eventually results in insanity, became suspiciously familiar, despite the black humour Julian injected. And the development of Simon's dual personality as he parodied his hero hinted at a frightening revelation. My God, Julian thought appalled, do I really want to be Alex? Surely not. But he realised with horror, as Simon emerged more and more clearly on the page, that maybe he did. He'd always thought he was happy with his homosexuality, but maybe he wanted to be straight after all. He'd always been quite content with his appearance, but maybe he'd really wanted to be handsome all these years.

Julian felt as though he was going mad himself until suddenly he hit upon the perfect solution. Not only would it alleviate his own agony of self-questioning, it would confuse the issue enough for the real characters to be unrecognisable. His hero,

Simon, would become his heroine, Johanna.

And it worked. The black humour skyrocketed, the issues, if one chose to see them, became far more complex and Julian found he had written a potential hit.

The fortnight after Alex and Susannah left for Fiji on their honeymoon was one of the happiest periods Julian could remember. For the first time in years he put aside any form of work. With the absence of Alex, the driving force in his life, it was surprisingly easy to do.

Julian didn't delude himself. It was borrowed time and he knew it. His own work ethic wouldn't allow him to wallow in books and music and long walks for more than a fortnight, anyway—he needed to write. He also didn't delude himself about the longevity of his other diversion. David wouldn't last either.

They'd been together three months now, ever since the auditions, and naturally they'd had to keep their affair strictly under wraps. Only Harold knew and, even then, Julian hadn't told him. He'd guessed. 'Takes one to know one, dear boy,' he'd said. 'I'm very happy for you.'

David Arncliffe was an up-and-coming young leading man in the theatre. Very few people guessed that he was homosexual. The infamous Roger Kingsley didn't even bother making his customary advances, so convinced was he that David was straight.

'I suppose that's my chance with The Way In Theatre out the window,' David said to Julian. 'I couldn't bear to let him know I was "one of us" though. He's such a terrible old queen.'

187

'I wouldn't worry: poor Roger's a dinosaur well and truly on the way out,' Julian replied. 'There's half a dozen new brooms all lined up ready to do the sweeping—it's only a matter of time.'

What would Alex say if he found out the 'hot new actor' signed to play the male lead in *I, Me and Us* was homosexual? Julian wondered. He smiled to himself. What would Alex say if he knew the leading role was based entirely upon him? What a perfect irony.

Julian hadn't quite been able to believe it himself that first time. He and David had been discussing the play, the characters, then theatre in general. They'd been talking for hours; early dawn was lightening the sky; they were seated comfortably in Julian's lounge room; when David stood up, Julian, disappointed, assumed he was leaving. 'Shall we continue this discussion in bed?' David suggested. They weren't even drunk.

As they undressed each other, a nervous Julian—it had been such a long time—joked, 'If you want to screw your way to the top you should never choose the writer, you know.'

'Damn,' David said. 'I thought you were the producer.' Then he kissed him.

They spent the night together at least once a week after that, but it was when David moved in to Julian's house at Bondi Beach for the halcyon fortnight before production that the affair truly blossomed. With the exception of Harold, they saw no one in the industry, they wined and dined at out-of-the-way restaurants and spent mornings walking along the nearby beachfronts like any other young lovers.

The small Federation-style house Julian had

bought a couple of blocks back from the beachfront was a cosy little nest for two. He had spent much of his hard-earned television money on renovations resulting in a vine-covered courtyard out back with a sundeck above where one could catch glimpses of water views. 'Well, if you risk life and limb by standing on the railing you can,' he laughed to David when he gave him the guided tour. 'It's a perfect suntrap in the winter, though.'

'Great,' David said. 'We'll loll around and sunbake together.'

Julian couldn't help but thrill to the words— he so wanted the relationship to last. Then he chastised himself: Don't be so bloody stupid; it's far too good to last . . . just enjoy it while you can.

David actually did very little 'lolling around'. An avid sportsman, most of his mornings off were spent surfing at Bondi. Even though it was early September he would stay in the water for hours.

'How do you do it!' Julian exclaimed. 'It's bloody freezing!'

'See this?' David laughed, snapping the wrist band of his wetsuit. 'It's called a wetsuit, dummy, you should give it a go.'

But Julian was perversely proud of his lack of ability and interest in any form of sport whatsoever. 'You have to have the exception to prove the rule,' he insisted, 'and I'm it. Five generations Australian and useless at every sport known to man. I can't even hit a dartboard at ten paces.' And he refused to budge.

He enjoyed walking, though, and he always ended his morning walk with the view from the cliffs of the south headland. To his right, further down the coast, he could see Waverley Cemetery sprawled untidily on the side of a hill which spilled out into the ocean. To his left was the magnificent expanse of Bondi Beach with its buildings so evocative of the thirties. And below, at the base of the headland, was the tatty old Icebergs Clubhouse and pool, famous home of the first Winter Swimming Club (Men Only) and bastion of the last of the true-blue Aussie mysogynists who needed to escape from their women.

There were always Council promises to give Bondi a facelift but nothing ever happened. Julian was rather glad. Bondi was as tatty as the Icebergs and equally colourful.

He'd always loved Bondi Beach. He remembered those early days at NADA when he and Alex would pile into Maddy's red MGB and the three of them would race down to Bondi to eat home-made pies from the corner shop and watch the ocean while they made their grandiose plans for the future. The pieshop was still there, the pies were still good, and Alex's and Julian's grandiose plans certainly seemed to be coming to fruition. The only thing missing was Maddy. Julian never stopped wondering what had become of her.

She was somewhere in the UK, he knew that much. His constant nagging at Helena had finally forced Robert McLaughlan's address from her but that was as far as Julian could get. 'She went to England with her father,' was all Helena would tell him.

Both Julian and Harold wrote to Maddy but their letters were neither acknowledged nor returned. It saddened him to think that he would never see her again.

190

It was years later, when he was writing his first play and stripping himself bare in the process, that Julian realised he must have been jealous of Maddy. He'd been aware of feeling a touch envious of her and Alex, of course—who wouldn't wish for such an all-consuming love? But no, he eventually admitted, it was Maddy herself of whom he'd been jealous. Deep down he'd wanted Alex to love him like that.

Julian hated the insight his plays had given him, he hated his obsession for Alex—at times, he hated Alex for being the object of his obsession. Now, for the first time in years, Julian could feel the weight being lifted from him. With David in his life Alex could at long last be relegated to an emotional back seat. Julian intended to keep it that way. And to prove it, he decided his next play, for which he was already making notes, would be nothing whatsoever to do with Alex Rainford.

There was an impromptu round of applause following the read-through and Alex gave Julian a triumphant wink. He looked at the other people seated around the table: Susannah, David the new leading man, Harold Beauchamp, Rosie Lee, the two young bit-part and understudy actors, the stage director, the set designer, the costume designer and Julian himself. The applause was for Julian—or rather for his play. The casting was spot-on, of course, thought Alex smugly. They were the right actors for the right roles, they were talented and they had all performed the reading beautifully. But the play's the thing, he told himself, and Julian's play's bloody terrific.

'Terrific, Julian,' he said, standing up. 'Terrific

read, everyone. Bloody terrific.' Then Alex wished everyone good luck and left them to it as he'd told Julian he would.

'Nothing worse than an interfering producer,' he'd said. 'Don't you worry, I won't hang around.' Julian had been surprised and grateful. He'd been sure that Alex wouldn't be able to relinquish his hold on *I, Me and Us* and that his directorial interference could well lead to serious friction.

'We've got a great team, buddy,' Alex continued, 'and I've got to get those bums on seats, so I'll see you around.'

'Thanks Alex, I'll keep you posted.' And Julian didn't see Alex for nearly two weeks.

By the end of that first fortnight the 'limited twelve week season' was sold out. Alex had advertised the 'limited season' in case the show was a flop but he'd actually put a tentative booking on the theatre for a full six months and a further nine-month national tour was in the pipeline.

The new ads now read: *Extended by popular demand*. And that's even before the show's opened, Alex gloated, justifiably proud of himself. Such was the power of publicity. By Christ, the reviews had better be good.

The weekend before they were to start final dress rehearsals and previews Alex decided to throw a party.

'Just before production week, Alex?' Susannah was mildly horrified.

'On the Saturday, Sooz. Everyone's got Sunday to recover and we don't have to make it a massive crowd.'

Susannah finally capitulated, as long as it was a luncheon party, the numbers didn't exceed thirty and everyone was encouraged to leave before nightfall. It was exactly what Alex had had in mind, so he sighed heavily and pretended to give in.

Alex loved entertaining in their new five-bedroom mansion on the peninsula. And he particularly loved daytime entertaining so that everyone could admire the magnificent view over Pittwater from the landscaped garden or from the indoor swimming pool.

'What a wonderful host you are, dear boy,' Harold said, as he surveyed the lavish smorgasbord set out on the terrace.

'I had a good teacher, Harold.' Alex had made a study of Harold's impeccable entertaining style and now delighted in returning the old man's years of hospitality. Harold was warmed and flattered. He was fully aware that Alex loved to show off but then he was young, successful and wealthy, so why shouldn't he?

The years had not diminished Harold's love for Alex. And the more he saw how manipulative and self-obsessed Alex was, the more he forgave him. Licence must be granted to truly charismatic people, he believed. There were too few of them around; they should be encouraged. The world would be such a drab place without them.

'Try the glazed ham,' said Alex, carving a choice sliver, 'I get it from a great new deli in Crows Nest where they smoke their own.' He popped the piece of ham in Harold's mouth.

'Heaven,' Harold rolled his eyes ecstatically. 'Sheer heaven.'

'They've got the best range of imported cheeses, too. You should take a look.'

'I never shop on the north side, dear boy, I'm

an eastern suburbs lad born and bred. But you must get in some stock for me and I shall trust your judgement.'

It was strong praise, indeed, and Alex accepted the compliment for what it was. Harold never allowed anyone to purchase his food supplies; they were bound to get it wrong. Alex started then and there to make a mental shopping list.

'Isn't the ham divine? Would you carve some for me too, darling?' Susannah put an arm halfway around Harold's ample back and held her plate out to Alex.

'Further proof of your excellent cuisine, Alexei, it's such a relief to see this one eat something other than a quail egg at long last.'

'I had to,' Susannah smiled, 'I got sick of your nagging.' She leaned over Harold for the bearnaise sauce. 'Have you tried the fresh asparagus? Alex steamed it himself. Oh, there's Myra Nielson, trust her to be so late.' And Susannah sailed off to play hostess.

Alex watched as she took Myra's hand and kissed her on the cheek, then shook hands with Myra's companion, all the while balancing her plate of food gracefully and moving like a dancer. Everything Susannah did was graceful. Except in bed.

They'd been halfway through the first week of rehearsals when Susannah had brought her stage role home. She became sexually harsh, aggressive and masculine. Alex, complying to her every order, found it fascinating to lie, stand, kneel wherever she wanted and passively allow himself to be used. I'm her own flesh-and-blood dildo, he thought. It's as if the dick's hers, not mine.

Myra's companion was a tall woman in her mid-forties with red hair and a slightly hard face. Susannah gestured towards Alex, Myra smiled and waved, Alex waved back and the three women crossed the terrace.

'Hello, Alex, sorry I'm a little late. I don't think you've met Anita.'

She looks like a dyke, thought Alex as he shook hands with the woman. Her handshake was as strong as any man's and when Alex caught the look in Myra's eyes he knew he was right. So this was why Myra hadn't wanted to resume their affair . . . 'I think we'll give it a rest for a while, Alex,' she'd said. He hadn't bothered to ask why, presuming there was someone else in her life and, although his ego was piqued, he hadn't really cared. After all, Susannah was sexually active enough for any man.

'You look wonderful, Myra.' His smile was genuine. 'But then, you always do.' Alex no longer felt piqued. He hadn't lost, after all. If Myra chose another woman, then there was no competition and therefore no winner.

Myra read his smile and smiled back. It didn't bother her if Alex's ego chose to believe in a stalemate. She knew better. She had declared the contest over, therefore she was the winner. 'Thank you, Alex, I feel wonderful.'

Susannah finished her plate of ham and asparagus, took a bottle of Moët Vintage from one of the drinks waiters and circulated.

'Top up, boys?' She joined Julian and David who were standing in the far corner of the terrace admiring the yachts heading for Broken Bay and the open ocean beyond.

A bottle of champagne and twenty minutes later the three of them were still talking about the show. And they would have continued to do so if Susannah hadn't looked at her watch. 'I'd better circulate,' she said. Twenty minutes, she thought to herself, time's up. 'You two should mingle too, we're being shockingly in-house, we should all be talking about current affairs or something.' And with that she blew them a kiss and headed off for the most distant upstairs en suite.

'She's right, you know, we are being a bit exclusive,' Julian said. 'People are probably already talking.'

'Stuff them,' David replied. He was full of champagne, the joy of spring and his love for Julian. 'Stuff the lot of them.'

And Julian, who was in very much the same condition, felt a rush of emotion. Maybe he'd been wrong. Maybe they would last. He pulled himself together—someone had to practise discretion. 'Let's mingle,' he said.

Susannah finished brushing her teeth, gargled, checked her make-up and hair then flushed the toilet a second time, just to be sure. She sprayed a second round of Chanel about too, although she knew it wasn't necessary.

Susannah had it down to a fine art. She always excused herself from the table well within half an hour of eating. That way the bile hadn't had time to get to work and it wasn't really unpleasant at all. Not like vomiting, just a gentle little purge and she felt wonderful afterwards, purified, tummy muscles tight.

She always carried a miniature kit of toothbrush,

toothpaste, mouthspray and cologne, even in her evening bag, so that she could never be caught out. Discovering the perfect way to stay slim and avoid the nagging of people concerned about her diet had been a vast relief to Susannah. And there was the added pleasure of actually being able to enjoy the taste of food without the sickening knowledge that it was going to make her fat. The hideous feeling of nausea that used to accompany any attempt to eat normally was a thing of the past.

Of course she didn't abuse the privilege. She only purged herself several times a week after dinner parties or restaurant outings; the rest of the time she stuck to her rigid diet. It always amused her when she decided to pig out at a party.

'Where do you put it?' was the inevitable comment when she piled her plate high, 'You're such a tiny little thing.'

'To a wonderful company and a wonderful show.' Alex raised his glass in tribute. 'Thanks for all your hard work.' He nodded and a waiter appeared carrying a giant chocolate cake with *I, Me and Us* emblazoned across it in white icing. 'Here's to a magnificent opening night. May it be everything every one of us is hoping for, and more!'

It was. Thanks to the massive publicity campaign the world premiere of *I, Me and Us* was the glittering social event of the season. More importantly though, the critics were unanimous in their praise for two of the most exciting new talents in the Australian theatre, Alex Rainford, entrepreneur and Julian Oldfellow, playwright/director.

'Their collaboration resulted in the most

stimulating evening I have spent in the theatre in all of the twenty-five years I have been writing for this newspaper,' gushed Old Bill Foley. And nobody bothered pointing out that fifteen of those years had been spent covering rugby league matches, because everyone agreed with him.

'We did it, Julian.' Alex leaned back in his seat behind the massive desk in the production office and toasted Julian with his coffee cup. 'We bloody well did it. Congratulations.'

'To you too, Alex.' Julian returned the toast with his own coffee cup but his smile was a little fixed. He knew what was coming next and he wasn't looking forward to it. He had a feeling Alex's reaction to the decision he'd made wasn't going to be good.

It was nearly a week after opening night. Alex had called the meeting: 'Just the two of us, we need to decide where we're going.'

'So what's the plan of attack, do you reckon?' Alex put his coffee cup down and prepared for action. 'If I grab the rights to a pretty safe bet, some middle-of-the-road Broadway hit, do you think you could keep writing while you direct it?' When Julian didn't answer immediately he added, 'Of course I'd give you strong backup.' Julian still hesitated. 'We can't just sit around and wait while you finish your next play, Julian, we need to keep our names hot.'

Julian shifted uncomfortably in his chair.

'Well, for Christ's sake, you are writing another play, aren't you?' Alex snapped.

'Yes. Sure.'

'So, when will you have it finished, and can

you direct one play while you write another?' Alex repeated impatiently.

Julian took a deep breath, thinking he might as well get it over and done with. 'I want to go alone for a while, Alex.' The pause seemed interminable. 'Well not alone, of course, but with another producer.'

'Why?' Alex's face was completely unreadable.

'It's no big deal. Just for my next play, that's all. We can collaborate again after that.'

'Why?'

'I need a bit of space, I suppose. Sometimes I feel I'm too influenced by you.'

'But that influence has helped you write a great play. That influence has been creative, wouldn't you agree?'

Julian was beginning to feel a little unnerved.

'Wouldn't you agree, Julian?' Alex persisted.

'Yes, yes of course, it's just that . . .' How on earth could he offer a reasonable answer? Julian wondered. He only knew that he had to prove to himself that he could write without Alex. 'To be quite honest, Alex (Oh God, that sounded corny, and he wasn't being quite honest anyway), you're a pretty powerful person at times and I . . . well, I just want to discover myself a bit more, relate to other things about me without your influence affecting my reaction.' What a wimp he sounded.

Alex smiled patiently. 'That's a load of bullshit, Julian, you discovered yourself years ago. You're one person who knows himself exceedingly well. You always have—it's the first thing I admired about you.' He stood up. 'Want a drink? It's a bit early, but if we're going to bust up the partnership we should wish each other luck, don't you think?'

Julian nodded. Alex poured them both a Scotch and they clinked glasses.

'It's David you really want to get to know, isn't it? Cheers.' And he took a swig of Scotch. Julian stared at him, unable to speak. 'I'd give it about six months, a year at the outside. Go for your life, have a good time.' The smile was pure Alex. Charming and cheeky—and just a little dangerous. 'I'll book your next play for a year from now, shall I?'

Was he right? Julian wondered. Was it really that simple? And if it was, then surely to exchange Alex's influence in his life for David's and their mutual love was a good thing. So why did he feel such foreboding? 'How did you know about David?' was all he could say.

'Oh, come on now, buddy, you think you can hide anything from me?'

'How? Nobody knew. Nobody.'

The smile flickered for a moment. 'I'm not nobody, Julian.' Then it returned and with it a wealth of warmth and affection. 'I wish you every success and every happiness—you know that.'

Julian felt slightly ill.

ACT II

SCENE 4: 1980–1981

A child's squeal rose high in the early morning air and shattered itself amongst the columns of Sacre Coeur Cathedral. There was a second's pause then the child's voice broke the silence again. 'Yuk! What is it?'

A tiny, lone figure on the massive steps of the cathedral started picking at the glutinous mess in her hair. 'Yuk,' she said again.

'Cut,' a voice called. And from behind the arches sprang a dozen people, including hairdresser, make-up artist, cameraman, director and Madeleine Frances, who was first to examine her daughter's head.

'*Crotte de pigeon*,' she announced and everyone burst out laughing. Maddy looked up at the first of the pigeons settling themselves on their morning roosts to catch the early sun. 'A pigeon just pooed on your head, Jen,' she said and the laughter started afresh at the look of disgust on the little girl's face.

Maddy stifled her own smile and took the box of tissues from the make-up man. '*Ça va, Jean-Marc. Je vais le faire.*'

The director called a short break while Maddy sat Jenny down on the step, squatted beside her and started cleaning the mess out of her hair. 'Gee, talk about a lucky sign,' she said.

Jenny looked suspiciously at her mother.

'I'm not kidding,' Maddy insisted. 'Your first trip to Paris and a pigeon poos on your head from the top of Sacre Coeur Cathedral! Wow!'

Jenny continued to study her mother's face for any telltale sign of duplicity. 'That's lucky?'

'About as lucky as you can get,' Maddy said. And she meant it.

Jenny smiled back at her. 'Great!'

It was three days before Christmas and it was cold on the steps of Sacre Coeur. Cold and very beautiful. There had been rain during the night and the whole of Paris sparkled at their feet in the early morning sun. Maddy always loved the view of Paris from Montmartre.

Although this was her third French film—each one shot in Paris—it was the first time she'd been able to bring Jenny along and the director had even insisted on casting the child. It was a small, non-speaking role, Jenny having not one word of French at her command, but she was thrilled nevertheless.

Over the past several years Maddy had polished up her own convent-taught French to a quite passable degree. Not so her Italian. To her humiliation she'd been dubbed in the one and only Italian film she'd made. The director hadn't minded in the least—he'd expected it. From the outset, he'd booked his sound studios for an extra fortnight for that express purpose. But, always a perfectionist, Maddy had been cross that the three-week Italian crash course she put herself through when she found she had the role hadn't resulted in her total command of the language.

'OK, Jen, you're all cleaned up. Let's get this show on the road.'

The day's shoot at Sacre Coeur went smoothly— it was a happy unit and they were on schedule, so there was little pressure—and a wrap was called at four in the afternoon. Maddy wanted an early morning start with Jenny and she hoped everyone would understand when she begged out of the wrap party to be held later that night. They did and there were the customary fond hugs and exchanges of phone numbers which would never be followed up as Maddy said her goodbyes.

When she and Jenny got back to their tiny hotel two blocks from the Champs Elysees the fat lady was in the tiny foyer waiting for the tiny lift. '*Bonjour,*' she said. '*Bonjour,*' they replied and started running up the stairs to the fifth floor.

The first day they'd been there the fat lady had insisted they join her in the lift. It had taken them several minutes to get the cage doors of the lift closed around the sandwiched flesh and a further several minutes to concertina them open on the fifth floor.

The stairs were so tiny that they had to jog up in single file. They always jogged and they were always out of breath by the time they arrived, but it was all part of being in Paris and they loved it. And from their tiny room they could see the Arc de Triomphe.

'When I'm a famous actress I'm going to buy a little flat in Paris,' Jenny panted, leaning out of the window, 'and it's going to have a view of the Arc de Triomphe.'

'Good for you.' Maddy lay flat on her back on the double bed which virtually took up the whole room and gasped for breath.

They went to their favourite restaurant that night where Jenny had her usual frogs' legs in white wine sauce and half of Maddy's *escargots a la maison*.

'For a nearly-ten-year-old you have sophisticated and very expensive tastes,' Maddy said. 'You'd better hope you meet a millionaire somewhere along the line.'

'Why? I'm going to be a millionaire myself.'

'Quite right, dumb statement, and don't talk with your mouth full of snails.'

The following morning the tiny maid—all the staff in the hotel seemed to be tiny—arrived with their huge cups of steaming cafe au lait, croissants, bread rolls and jams at seven o'clock. By half-past eight they were off on their tour of Paris.

This may well be one of the happiest days of my life, Maddy decided, as she looked at Jenny skipping through the Tuileries Gardens. But then, she thought, so many of the happiest moments of my life these days relate to Jenny.

I haven't been a good mother, she mused, as she watched the child throwing bread to the clusters of pigeons fluttering at her feet. Too much ambition, too many rungs of the ladder to climb. And there still are, aren't there? she asked herself. Madeleine Frances has a long way to go yet, Maddy McLaughlan, so don't kid yourself you're going to change overnight. Strange how totally Jenny understands, though. Hell, Jenny understands me better than I do myself.

Already Jenny was determined to be an actor, just as her mother had been determined at the age of ten, but, probably through Maddy's example, Jenny seemed very aware of the sacrifices involved. It had even been Jenny's idea to delay their trip to Australia by twelve months. True, Maddy had given her the unspoken option. What a shit I am, she thought, hating herself as she told Jenny about the West End offer—I shouldn't have said a word. But then came the flood of relief at Jenny's reply: 'You can't knock back your first lead in the West End, Mum; we'll have to put the trip off.'

The following day Maddy had gone out and bought two first-class return Qantas air vouchers, which she planned to give to Jenny on April the 13th, her tenth birthday. At least the poor kid can look at them for a year, she thought, and she swore to herself that no matter what offer came up, they were off to Sydney in 1982. Jenny'll be eleven and I'll be, oh hell, Maddy groaned, thirty. Midlife crisis time, don't think about it.

Maddy rarely did think about age, but then she didn't have to. She still looked eighteen. At times she cursed her extraordinarily youthful appearance—when was she ever going to play the great classic roles?—but she was also fully aware that it was one of her main assets. Her gamine image, with her delicate bone structure and short cropped blonde hair, was particularly popular with the European film directors.

'Come on, Jen, I'm starving.'

Jenny finished feeding the pigeons and they walked through the gardens and sat on one of the park benches near The Louvre to eat their mid-morning crispy rolls with camembert cheese.

'Oh no!' Jenny exclaimed when she got up. 'I s'pose you'll tell me this is lucky too.' She pointed at the pigeon mess on the back of her jeans and Maddy burst out laughing.

'Well, why does it have to happen to me?' Jenny was very indignant. 'Why didn't it happen to you?'

'Because I look before I sit on a park bench, stupid.' Maddy stood up, still laughing. 'Come and we'll wash you down in the loo.'

This time though, Jenny wasn't going to be as easily humoured and she was still grumbling fifteen minutes later as she passed by the Venus de Milo, unimpressed. 'She's got no arms,' she said, rubbing the seat of her wet jeans, 'and I'm cold.'

Maddy looked at the strong little face. Jenny was angry. There was an irritable scowl in place of the customary direct gaze and even the sprinkling of freckles across her nose were flushed with annoyance. Strange how someone could have freckles in the middle of a European winter, Maddy thought. The true Aussie genes, I guess. Oh, hell, she really is mad at me, I shouldn't have laughed at her. I wonder what I can do to jolly her out of it?

Then they turned the corner into another gallery and there, on the far wall, was the Mona Lisa.

'Looks just like the postcards,' Jenny said sullenly. 'And it's not very big.'

'Go and look at it from over there,' Maddy suggested and Jenny walked reluctantly to the far wall, giving her wet backside an ostentatious rub on the way. She stood there for at least a minute. Then she walked to the opposite wall, then walked up close to the barriers around the painting, prowling from side to side as close as she could get to it. The guard seated by one of the gallery doors gave her a warning glance. Finally, she returned to her mother, excited, her eyes glowing. 'Mum, everywhere I go she's looking at me.' The derisive laughter and the wet backside were both forgotten.

At the end of the day the Mona Lisa was still the highlight. The ferry trip down the Seine, the market stalls along the embankment, even the coach trip out to Versailles and the guided tour of the palace paled into insignificance by comparison.

'How can they do that, Mum?' Jenny asked as she was tucked into bed. 'How can they paint a picture that follows you everywhere?'

'I don't know, Jen, I guess that's why it's a masterpiece. I'm sorry I laughed about the pigeon poo.'

'Oh, that's OK.' A big yawn. 'Gee, I wonder how they do it.'

'Rodney!' As Maddy walked out of the customs hall at Heathrow Airport the first person she saw was Rodney Baines.

'Roddie! Hi!' Jenny ran to him and he picked her up and spun her around.

'Hello, trouble,' he said, then, 'Oh, sorry,' as Jenny's sneaker clocked the woman beside him in the small of the back.

'You shouldn't have come out to meet us.' Maddy kissed him on the cheek as he put Jenny down and took their suitcases. 'Honestly, I didn't expect you to.'

'Didn't have anything better to do.' Rodney shrugged. 'I thought you might want to have a Christmas Eve lunch before you head off for Windsor.'

'We'd love to,' Maddy said. 'But let's go home and get some unpacking done first.'

An hour later they were trudging up the four very steep flights of stairs to Maddy's apartment in Great Titchfield Street.

The first thing Maddy had thought when the estate agent showed her the building two years before was 'Oh no! More stairs!' but, once she saw the apartment itself, she knew she'd be happy climbing a further four flights if this was at the top.

From then on, every time she opened the door to the cosy living room with its heavy wooden mantelpiece and large open fireplace, it made Maddy happy to think that this was hers. Today was no exception. 'Hello, home,' she said and threw herself gratefully into one of the monstrous but comfortable armchairs she'd bought at Shepherds Bush markets.

Although the living room was large, the two bedrooms, kitchen and bathroom which led off from the sides were tiny. Maddy didn't mind one bit. The whole place oozed with character and the narrow spiral staircase on the landing outside her door led to a communal rooftop which gave her spine-tingling views of the other rooftops and chimney pots of Central London.

'How did the movie go?' Rodney asked, slurping on his milkshake. They were seated in The Drugstore waiting for their hamburgers. They had made the mistake of letting Jenny choose the restaurant.

'But there are a hundred decent places within walking distance Jen, why Chelsea?'

'Because I like The Drugstore and you said I could choose.'

'And because she wants a ride in the Jag, of course,' Rodney said.

'Of course,' Maddy nodded. 'Ask a silly question . . .' Jenny adored driving around in Rodney's silver Jaguar. In summer he'd open the sun roof for her and in winter he'd turn the heater full on. Today there was an icy hint of snow in the air and Maddy had snuggled up cosily in the back seat watching the streets of London glide by.

'You're getting quite a name for yourself with these European chaps, aren't you?' Rodney said after Maddy had told him briefly about the shoot. 'That's wonderful.'

'All thanks to the magic we created, my darling.' Maddy raised her strawberry milkshake. 'Here's to *Androgyne*.'

Rodney was right. Maddy's popularity with European film-makers was a direct result of her performance in *Androgyne* which had rapidly developed a cult following amongst cinéma vérité fans. The films offered her were all of the modest-budget variety but they were, in the main, interesting and worthwhile and Maddy had become very popular in art cinema circles.

Of course Phil Pendlebury was still approached

209

with the stray enquiry about Maddy's interest in making pornographic films—such was the erotic power of *Androgyne*. But, thanks to the skilful direction of Viktor Hoff, the overall effect of *Androgyne* had remained artistic and it was hailed in elite circles as a lesson in good-taste erotica.

Maddy had certainly had her doubts as to its good taste during the filming. If it hadn't been for her faith in Viktor Hoff and the persuasive powers of Phil Pendlebury ('There *is* such a thing as a contract, lovie, you could well get blacklisted') she would have walked out.

Her misgivings revolved around Rodney Baines. And after the first week of filming, every other member of the cast and crew felt the same. It wasn't that anyone disliked him. In fact they all agreed that he was possibly the most pleasant man they'd ever met. And, because he was so affable, even the most censorious critic quickly forgave him his pornographic background. A man was entitled to earn a living whichever way he chose, after all, and here the poor fellow was trying his level best to become a legitimate actor; it was beholden upon his workmates to give him all the help they could. And they did. They gave him crash courses in movement, voice, acting, camera technique, all of which Rodney deeply appreciated. He was a keen pupil and his performance rapidly developed. The wooden quality disappeared and was replaced by a confidence and control he'd never had before.

Not so his penis. His penis was utterly uncontrollable and, despite his own anger and frustration, showed no sign of obeying any form of discipline whatsoever.

Viktor had decided to shoot the film in sequence wherever possible, so for the first week, when clothes remained on, Rodney's trouble with his penis wasn't evident. The second week, however, when they started on the nude scenes—and there were many—the problem quickly became evident.

'Cut!' Viktor yelled.

The moment Rodney had lowered his underpants his giant penis had sprung to the fore.

'Roddie, Roddie, no, no, *no*! You must control your erection,' barked Viktor in his broken English. 'No erection in soft-core, you understand?' He noticed Maddy's reaction and quickly added, 'A term only, my dear Madeleine, "artistic" is what we do here.'

Then he drew Rodney to one side and spelled the rules out as simply as he could. 'We have soft-core pornography licence, Roddie, and in soft-core, no hard cock, you understand? No real sex and no hard cock. Full frontal we can do, yes, but always floppy, you understand?'

'I understand. Sorry, Viktor.'

'Is OK. You do good job.' Viktor turned to the crew, waving his hands expansively. 'Everybody do good job. Madeleine, you are beautiful.' He blew her a kiss. 'Setting up for another take, please.'

'Cut!' The same thing happened. And it happened again and again and again.

'I'm sorry,' Rodney said each time, mortified. 'I really am awfully sorry.'

For years Rodney Baines' penis had been trained to leap to attention whenever he dropped his trousers and now it was impossible for it to remain flaccid when unveiled.

In shooting the first nude scene Viktor had

intended doing Rodney's shots before Maddy's so that she could keep her panties on. Not something he normally did but he was a kind man and he knew the girl must be nervous.

'Ice,' he demanded, refusing to give up. 'Bring me ice, much ice, in buckets.'

'I'm really sorry, Viktor, really I am. I feel awful.'

The ice arrived and Rodney obligingly plunged his penis into the bucket. Without risking frostbite it took several dunking sessions to have any effect whatsoever and, even then, they could rely on only a few minutes' working time before the penis once more rose to the occasion.

'Cut!' A tired sigh. 'Ice!'

Eventually Rodney's shots were completed and Viktor turned to Maddy, exhausted. 'We are ready for you now, Madeleine. No need for worry, we will be gentle.'

But there were problems with Maddy too. Although Rodney's wayward penis was firmly strapped into a set of jocks for Maddy's shots, every time she had to lower her own underpants and flicker a glance over his apparently naked groin, she burst out laughing.

'I'm sorry, I'm terribly sorry,' she said after the fifth take, the laughter turning to hiccups. 'I think I'm a bit hysterical.'

That morning Maddy had been nervous at the thought of acting in her first nude scene. Now all she could think of was the fact that she was in a soft-core porn film with a very nice man who couldn't control his penis. It was bizarre.

'All right.' Viktor's control was admirable. 'We finish for today. Tomorrow we push ourselves together and we work hard.'

'Plenty more ice in the morning,' he muttered to the first assistant who nodded and called a wrap for the day. Then they all went to the pub for a pint of ale.

When Maddy rang Phil Pendlebury that evening and told him what had happened he read her the riot act in no uncertain terms.

'Now you pull yourself together, my love. This is not a porn movie, this is a Viktor Hoff film, you got me?'

'Yes Phil, it's just—'

'Just nothing, lovie. It could be your big break and you can't afford to stuff it up. So you get yourself on that set tomorrow and you act up a storm.'

He was right, of course. OK, Maddy told herself, you're on. She knew immediately how she was going to go about it, and she knew immediately that it was going to be easy.

It was. During working hours, or more specifically during working hours which involved sex scenes, Rodney Baines simply became Alex Rainford.

Maddy had thought about Alex many, many times over the years. With Jenny a walking reminder it was difficult not to: the older the child grew the more she looked like him. And then there was 'Outback Force'. It had been a shock to turn on the television set and see Alex. The series had been quite popular in the UK and had only been dropped recently when Alex's character left the show.

Although she was still thankful for the fact that she'd escaped him, Maddy was grateful for the happy times she remembered. She knew she would never love as strongly as that again and she was indebted to Alex for the experience.

The one aspect of their relationship which Maddy had ceased to dwell upon, perhaps deliberately, was their lovemaking. After Jenny's birth Maddy had led a life of celibacy for three years. It hadn't been difficult. And the sexual salivating, the pawing and the groping that she constantly witnessed during her stints at Danny's Downstairs were a helpful deterrent. Then, for no apparent reason, she leapt into two unsatisfactory affairs lasting roughly six months apiece and several one-night stands that left her feeling unattractive. She supposed she must have been sexually frustrated without realising it. Anyway, with that out of the way, she put sex aside and concentrated fully on her career.

Now here she was in *Androgyne* playing a sexual nymphet, but she felt not an ounce of sexuality in her entire being. All she could do was laugh at the poor man with the unruly penis. Well, all that had to change. And Alex was the one who could change it.

That night Maddy lay in her bed and thought of Alex and their lovemaking. She thought of the first time which everyone had warned her would be hell. It wasn't. She thought of the time he'd surprised her as 'rough trade' and she'd begged him for it. She thought of the fast, furious fuck in the middle of the day at Watsons Bay. God, had she ever been that wanton? She thought of the touch of his hands and the feel of his body and slowly the ache between her legs began—the familiar ache that had seemed ever-present when she was with Alex and that she hadn't felt for years now. Maddy masturbated that night, refused to feel any convent-bred guilt, and turned up to work the next day still feeling horny and ready to go.

Her horniness was so communicative that it didn't make poor Rodney Baines' job any easier and, when it came to the sex simulation where they both had to be naked on the bed, embracing and caressing each other, his poor penis had been subjected to so many dunkings that it was blue with cold and felt like a damp, icy snake against her thigh. Even so, after several minutes contact, she would feel a rebellious tremor as it once again quivered its way to attention.

'Cut! Ice!'

'I'm sorry, I'm most awfully sorry.'

And Maddy would close her eyes, quell the gurgle of laughter which threatened and concentrate on the eroticism of the images from the previous night.

Not only did *Androgyne* serve as the career boost Phil Pendlebury had anticipated, it cemented the only two true friendships Maddy had made since she came to England. Previously at the end of each rep season or tour, she had remained in touch with one or two members of the cast for a while but gradually the contact petered out as she concentrated all her free time on Jenny. Not so with Rodney Baines and Viktor Hoff. They refused to let her drop them.

She didn't see Viktor for months on end but he would ring her regularly from whatever exotic film location he happened to be in at the time. The first two film offers she had were directly through Viktor's influence. 'Viktor Hoff suggested we test you,' she was told. 'He's very impressed with your work.' From then on, in every film crew with which she worked there would be at least one person who would say, 'You're a friend of Viktor Hoff's, aren't you?'

Like it or not, Viktor Hoff was laying claim to her friendship and there was little Maddy could do about it. She had to admit it was very flattering— Viktor was a talent snob and only claimed as friends people he considered hugely gifted.

Rodney Baines was a different kind of friend. He was the kind of girlfriend Maddy had never had. He was the kind of friend Julian Oldfellow had been.

Maddy often thought of Julian. And Harold. She had agonised over whether or not to reply to their letters. But they were both so close to Alex she didn't dare. She couldn't risk any possible contact with Alex until it was absolutely necessary. Until Jenny wanted to meet her father—and that might well be never, which was fine by Maddy.

Not that Maddy had ever tried to hide the truth from Jenny. She'd told the child that she'd had an affair with a fellow actor at NADA and that he hadn't wanted to marry her so she'd come to England with Grandpa. It was that simple. And Jenny accepted it without question, so far showing no interest whatsoever in her father. The truth was that the child's homelife with Alma and Robert in Windsor was so stable that she didn't want for any form of parental influence. Robert was her father and grandfather rolled into one, he doted on her and she could wrap him around her little finger; Alma was her grandmother, and Maddy . . . well, Maddy was everything: mother, sister, playmate, best friend.

And now Jenny had another father-figure in her

life. Rodney Baines. He adored them both. Dear old Rodney, Maddy now thought, as she watched him ordering extra nuts for Jenny's ice cream sundae. It was difficult to equate his patrician good looks and social ease with a porn star. Rodney was a gentleman, and one simply didn't equate a gentleman with pornography.

These days Rodney made two porn films a year and was paid a fortune for it. Without Viktor Hoff's influence, his one other foray into the world of legitimate cinema had failed miserably and he'd returned to the genre he knew best where the pressure upon him was minimal. He was relieved to be back on his home ground and the money kept him in the lifestyle to which he'd grown happily accustomed. He was deeply grateful to *Androgyne* though, because *Androgyne* had given him Maddy.

Rodney loved women but invariably his relationships with them were sexual. And sexuality, which to Rodney was very simple, seemed to complicate women. Complicate them to the point where the relationship soured. Maddy was a breakthrough. Maddy was the platonic relationship he'd never had, maybe the sister he'd never had, and Jenny was the daughter he would have loved to have had. Rodney couldn't do enough for them.

They exchanged Christmas presents over coffee. Rodney disappeared into the toilets to reappear parading the Pierre Cardin sweater Maddy had given him.

'Oh hell, I've been stupid,' he said as he sat to watch the girls opening their gifts.

'Why?' Maddy asked. The gifts were large bottles of scent: Joy for Maddy and Miss Dior for Jenny.

217

'That's why. I forgot. You probably bought a whole range of French stuff duty-free on your way in.'

'We certainly didn't, it's far too expensive; Jenny's been told she's too young. Anyway and we're saving for next year's holiday.'

'Fantastic!' Jenny jumped up and thrust her neck against Rodney's face. 'Smell that!' she insisted.

When Jenny told Rodney his present was breakable, he opened it very carefully. 'Bet you don't know what it is,' she said.

Rodney looked down at the ugly little statuette. 'Don't tell me, don't tell me . . .' A further second's pause. 'It's from a church, right?'

'Yes.'

'It's a replica of a gargoyle.'

'Oh.' Jenny was sure he wouldn't have known that.

'And it's from . . . um . . .'

'Guess, guess.'

'Um . . . Notre Dame?'

'Wrong!' Jenny squealed triumphantly. 'Sacre Coeur!' And Rodney and Maddy shared a smile.

'The real ones are huge and they're all different,' Jenny explained, turning the ugly bird-like figure around on the table, 'and they're put way up on the sides of the cathedral to frighten off the evil spirits.' The statue fascinated Jenny. 'And a pigeon pooed on me from right near this one.'

'I bet that means good luck,' Rodney said.

'Yes, it does,' Jenny nodded.

It was midafternoon when Rodney dropped them at Paddington Station. As usual Maddy refused to let him drive them to Windsor and as usual he didn't insist. He'd gathered very early in their friendship that Maddy kept her Windsor and London existences separate. Rodney supposed it was because of her father. Maddy had mentioned that he didn't approve of her career.

Actually Robert McLaughlan had mellowed considerably over the last few years. Maddy was sure it was due to Alma's influence. Alma had changed too. She was softer, a little more feminine, her back a little less ramrod straight.

The romantic in Maddy was sure they were lovers but for the life of her she couldn't catch them out. There was no physical contact between them, Alma still called Robert 'Mr McLaughlan' and she still appeared to sleep in the little basement bedroom. Well, whatever it was, it was working, Maddy thought—good luck to them and good on you, Alma.

It was a pleasant family Christmas—a white one, which never ceased to delight Maddy. It made sense of all the Christmas cards with snowmen, sleighs and white-tipped fir trees which exchanged hands every sweltering Australian December. The same blistering Decembers when people ate midday turkeys, hams, plum puddings and brandy sauces, then arranged to meet at the beach to swim or sleep it off.

On Boxing Day, as they all admired the snowman that Jenny had made and pelted each other with snowballs, Robert and Maddy McLaughlan were both aware that something fresh had been forged in their relationship. They didn't know what it was until New Year's Eve, two days before Maddy was to return to London.

Maybe it was the wine that loosened their

tongues but they suddenly found themselves talking as they'd never talked before. Even at their closest, when Maddy was a child, they'd never really talked. Robert had found it somehow dangerous and confronting. Now he had a desperate need to rectify things.

God only knows why, Maddy thought, much as she was enjoying their contact. Then she looked at Alma, sitting by the open fire playing Snap with Jenny and she had a feeling she did know.

Jenny was yawning and trying to stay awake till midnight. They had eaten one of Alma's excellent meals, accompanied by one of Robert's excellent reds, and they were drinking coffee and port waiting to toast in the New Year. Robert had apologised for his years of intractability and Maddy had apologised for her years of wayward behaviour and it was Robert who got to the basics.

'I'd like to think that you were proud of the name McLaughlan, Maddy,' he said. 'You and Jenny both.'

'Jenny's always been a McLaughlan, Dad.' She waited to see if that was all the reassurance her father was seeking but it wasn't, and she was glad. 'I never did really change it, you know. Madeleine Frances is only a stage name.' She grinned at him. 'If they ever take my passport or if I ever go to jail I'm still a McLaughlan.'

For the first time Robert was the one who initiated the hug. It was a brief one, as their hugs always had been, and he, as always, was the one to break contact first, but Maddy was grateful for the breakthrough it signalled.

Then Robert averted his face and reached for the port. 'Another one?'

Although *The Lady from Maxim's* didn't go into production until mid-January, Phil Pendlebury had arranged a week of rigorous dance classes for Maddy before the commencement of rehearsals.

'You want to be one up on them, love—"The Shrimp" is a hell of an energetic role so we got to get you good and fit and able to trot out a bloody great cancan.'

As usual Phil was right. The lady from Maxim's, otherwise known as 'The Shrimp', was a Parisian nightclub dancer with suspect morals who delighted in shocking the upper classes. One of the highlights of the play was her frenzied cancan during the Duchess's garden party in Act Two.

Maddy reported to Peg McSween's dance studios feeling more than her customary buzz of excitement at the prospect of starting a new job. This was the title role in a major West End production. Her first. And it was a classic French farce written by the master of them all, Georges Feydeau.

She could hardly believe it was only yesterday that she felt so terribly sad as she and Jenny said their goodbyes—it was going to be a long break this time: three months. Yet here she was delighting in the weeks of work ahead. God, she was mercurial.

'I'll miss you, Jen,' she'd said. 'I'll really miss you.' And she smiled as she remembered Jenny's answer. 'Not that much you won't, Mum. "The Shrimp" won't let you.' Then Jenny had yelled 'Chookas!' as she waved the train goodbye.

Robert and Alma were taking Jenny to the Isle of Man for the remainder of her school holidays. Another breakthrough, Maddy thought, Robert never holidayed. The five weeks of rehearsals would

221

be over and the show would be well and truly run in by the time Jenny and Maddy saw each other again during the next school holidays. Then she and Jen could be together for a whole three weeks, Maddy consoled herself. Jenny could watch from the wings the way she loved to and it would be her tenth birthday and Maddy could give her the Qantas flight vouchers and maybe feel as if she wasn't such a bad mother after all. And, of course, they were bound to chat on the phone endlessly each Sunday. They had agreed, though, because Maddy's schedule was a gruelling eight performances a week Monday to Saturday, that she would remain in London and rest on Sundays.

'Careful, careful, we don't want a hamstring injury now, do we?' Peg's soft Edinburgh burr was motherly, caring. 'We take it very gently, Madeleine.'

When people first met Peg they were invariably lulled into a false sense of security. 'We take it very gently twenty times in a row, dear.' Peg was a martinet. 'And we hold the position for twenty seconds each time. We don't push, we don't pull, we don't bounce, we just hold the position.'

And this was only the beginning of the warm-up! Maddy groaned inwardly. Everything ached. Everything had been aching for four days now. Mind you, she had to admit that by the end of the warm-up she was loose enough for the next work-out, and the fourth day was certainly less painful than the second and the third.

'They didn't tell me you'd had any dance background, dear. I'm delighted, it's a great help.' And Maddy blessed Norah Hogarth and NADA's dance classes all those years ago.

In the execution of the Act Two cancan Maddy was required to throw cartwheels and leap into a full split by way of finale. As her breathing improved, the cartwheels were fine, albeit exhausting following a full five minutes of cancan. The splits were another thing altogether and Peg finally decided it was time to give up.

'We'll cheat it, dear. Back knee bent, hurdle position, throw up the skirts, let out a scream and they'll never know the difference.' Thank goodness there were times when Peg could be kind, Maddy thought.

After the first week of rehearsals the cancan sequence was the least of Maddy's worries. She had broken through the pain barrier, was fitter than she'd been since her NADA days and she knew the sequence backwards. With the dance now conquered, she had to concentrate on the problem of translation.

'It's all very well to say play her vocally cockney and physically French, Ned,' she complained. 'But a coquette from the Place Pigalle and a Soho hooker don't translate the same way on stage. Maybe they do in real life but they certainly don't in the theatre.'

'I know, I know, Madeleine,' Ned agreed testily. 'It's a problem inherent in the translation. You're not unique: every English actress who's played the role in the last eighty years has had to cope with it.'

'So what do I do?' she wailed.

'How the hell do I know?' Ned screamed back at her. 'Play it in French! The audience won't understand a word of it, but play it in French!'

Ned Forsythe, the director, was a huge, hairy bear of a man: physically gentle, but with a tendency to roar when he lost his temper. He and Maddy had worked together before and, although they sometimes clashed, it was Ned who had insisted on casting Maddy as 'The Shrimp'.

'But it's the title role,' Bernard, the obtuse producer insisted. 'We need a name, like Veronica Chisolm—the public love her.'

Veronica Chisolm had starred in Bernard's last three productions and it was a well-known fact to everyone but his wife that they were having an affair. Whether they would still be having an affair if he discontinued casting Veronica was a case of conjecture and Bernard didn't want to take the risk.

Ned decided someone had to. The thought of directing the overtly British, handsome but horsey Veronica Chisolm as 'The Shrimp' was more than he could bear. Besides which, Veronica was forty if she was a day.

'I tell you what, Bernard, why don't we cast her as the wife? It's a wonderful part.'

'Good grief, no.' Bernard was horrified. 'Vonnie wouldn't accept anything but the leading female role. I mean, the wife's a "heavy" for God's sake; she should be played by a forty year old character actress.'

Exactly, Ned thought. 'Look, Bernard,' he said. 'Victoria was a wonderful Donna Lucia: no one has ever said "Brazil, where the nuts come from" quite like her. But *Charlie's Aunt* and *The Lady From Maxim's* require very different styles of performance and, believe me, "The Shrimp" is not her.' Bernard was shaking his head. 'We need someone petite,' Ned insisted, 'someone gamine.' Bernard was still shaking his head. 'Someone *else*, for God's sake!'

'Ned, I really think—'

224

'Or I walk!' Ned held his breath. This was the biggest production he'd been offered to date and he didn't want to lose the job. But the punt paid off.

'We'll audition her,' agreed Bernard. And Maddy did the rest.

It took the cast a little while to realise that Ned's yelling was not only harmless but quite therapeutic. For him anyway. 'I'm Aries,' he'd say dismissively, 'I need to get it off my chest.'

It was true that, once he'd erupted, he was as gentle as a lamb. Every now and then, though, Maddy decided not to let him get away with it and she screamed back at him. Afterwards she would smile sweetly and shrug, 'I'm Aries too.' It became a running gag.

The production was physically exhausting for each of the leading actors and, by the final curtain, they were all bathed in sweat, despite the midwinter temperatures. But it was rewarding and, after several previews, they were relatively sure they had a successful show. As relatively sure as they could be, of course.

'It's all in the hands of the critics now,' Ned announced after notes following the final preview.

'Pray, everyone. Pray,' Gerald O'Dougherty urged and they all laughed. Gerald was a talented and very popular leading man, of the lightweight, debonair variety. His faint Irish brogue lent colour to the comedy and farce roles in which he specialised.

'Home time,' Ned announced. 'Lots of rest and I'll see you at the warm-up tomorrow night, forty-five minutes before the half. For those who wish to attend,' he hastily added to the collection of elderly ladies who played the duchess's cronies in the all-important Act Two garden party scene. Ned prayed that opening night zeal would not tempt any of them to participate in the warm-up—it would probably kill them.

Maddy set off for the theatre a good three hours before the half the following day. She was far too restless to stay at home. It was a fifteen-minute walk and she enjoyed the icy chill in the air as she swung her arms briskly and exercised her diaphragm, drawing in deep draughts of breath to her lungs.

'Hands on ribcage, feel those diaphragms.' The image of Jonathan Thomas flashed briefly through her mind. Poor man. Don't think about it—look at the theatres. She was in Charing Cross Road now; it was getting dark and the neons were on. The titles of plays and the names of the stars and the writers blazed gaudily in the gathering dusk.

She turned the corner. There it was. In bright lights THE LADY FROM MAXIM'S. Her name wasn't above the title yet, but it was getting a lot closer. It said: *Gerald O'Dougherty in* . . . Then, underneath the title, . . . *with Madeleine Frances as 'The Shrimp'*.

Maddy was quite happy with that. There were wonderful stills in the street display boxes and the foyer, including two lifesize shots of her, mid cancan. She'd been trying desperately to act nonchalant for the whole week they'd been up but it was difficult. Maddy felt a thrill every time she saw the photos and her name in lights. The films she'd made paled into insignificance. This was what she'd aimed for.

What an age it seemed to have taken. But she'd made it. The title role. The West End. And here it was—her opening night. All she needed to do was prove she was good enough to stay.

The cue for the cancan was coming up. Maddy braced herself. Act One had been a breeze. Here came the test. The opening chords sounded. She was on.

She lifted up the skirt of the heavy velvet dress, grabbed a fistful of petticoats with each hand and bounded onstage with a gleeful shriek. Chin up, head back, chest out, the Lady from Maxim's strutted her stuff before the duchess's guests in their demure garden party ensembles complete with their parasols and picture hats.

The music became more frantic and the gathering more shocked as 'The Shrimp' exposed her fishnet-clad thighs and her lacy knickers for all to see. She took off her black satin garter and snapped it over the bald pate of a marquis; she cartwheeled through a group of society matrons; she flaunted her uplifted bosom in front of a group of youths.

By now the sweat was pouring down Maddy's face (fortunately the audience was too far away to notice) and, several wild minutes later, after three more cartwheels and a killing series of high kicks, came the finale.

She squealed, threw herself in the air, yards of red velvet and petticoats held aloft for one last glorious display of fishnet, satin and lace. Then there was the familiar crunch of the floor against her right knee, left leg extended in front as she cheated the splits.

There was a gasp of admiration. Peggy had been

right. No one knew it was a cheat and the bruise she'd worn on her right knee since the start of rehearsals was worth it.

The audience erupted into spontaneous applause. Maddy rose, sashayed over to the huge wicker garden seat centre stage, cocked a leg saucily over the arm and said, 'Cheer up, darling' to the duchess. The cancan was over—it was on with the play.

There was no reply. The old bitch is asleep—again! Maddy realised, aghast. The ancient character actress who played the duchess had fallen asleep through every dress rehearsal and two of the previews. But she couldn't have fallen asleep on the opening night! Dear God, not the opening night!

She had.

Maddy kicked the chair.

'Hhrm . . . oh . . . ah . . .'

'Cheer up, darling,' Maddy repeated as she saw recognition dawning in the rheumy eyes behind the inch-long false lashes. The painted mouth wreathed into a thousand smiles and there was a gay and girlish laugh. The duchess lived once more and on they went with the show.

There were a few other hiccups during the performance, as there always were on opening nights, but who cared? The audience was already rising to its feet as Gerald O'Dougherty took his curtain call with the cast members lined up on either side of him. But when he turned upstage to acknowledge 'The Shrimp' and Maddy cartwheeled over to join him, the entire house leapt to its feet.

When Gerald called a halt after nine curtain calls the applause was still thundering. 'Leave them wanting more,' he muttered to Maddy as he kissed her hand again, smiled dazzlingly at the audience and gave the signal for the last curtain to the stage manager.

Ned had suggested, very tentatively, that the final walkdown in the curtain call should go to Maddy and he'd been quite taken aback when Gerald agreed. 'Good grief, man, of course; she's the star of the show.' Unlike many highly successful actors, Gerald had no pretensions about star status. He certainly agreed it was good business that his name be publicised above Maddy's—his huge theatrical following put bums on seats, after all— but the star of the show was an altogether different matter. And the star of this show was Maddy. Ned hadn't worked with Gerald before and he was surprised and delighted by the man's generosity. He knew it was a rare quality in a West End star.

Gerald's insistence that he was a 'working actor' was genuine but he nevertheless exercised the power of his position in controlling the curtain calls. In full company calls, all actors were to take their bows from him and the number of calls were to be solely at his discretion. It wasn't ego; it was total professionalism. Gerald's timing was impeccable and, if there was one thing he couldn't stand, it was sloppy timing in others: whether in directors, in actors, or in lighting and sound cues—but, above all, in curtain calls.

'You were stunning, my darling, simply stunning.' He put his arm around her and kissed her and, as usual, the embrace lasted a little too long and the hand was a little too close to her breast to be ignored. Gerald had been trying to get her to bed since the first day of rehearsals.

'Thanks, Gerald,' Maddy said, sliding his hand down to her waist. 'Thanks for everything.' And she meant it. She was grateful not only for the generosity of the curtain call, but for the support his performance gave her. It was a joy to work with such an accomplished actor. 'You were pretty stunning yourself.' And, as the hand progressed back to her breast, she wriggled out of his embrace and headed for her dressing room. Amusing, talented and charming as he was, there was just a touch of the sleaze about Gerald. If only he could learn to take 'no' for an answer. But Gerald never could. Even though his success rate was barely fifty-fifty, he never accepted resistance as genuine. Gerald had been a debonair working roué for as long as he'd been a debonair working actor and the two had become entwined.

'Thanks, Jess,' Maddy heaved a sigh of relief as her dresser finished unlacing her boned corset. The period costumes were a real killer. The cancan would be a breeze if she didn't have to do it in a heavy velvet dress with petticoats that weighed a ton, a saucy little hat with lace that obscured her vision and the dreaded corset that restricted her breathing. Even though the corset was made of elasticised fabric to give her as much freedom as possible, it had to look strictly authentic for the Act One bedroom scene when she appeared in her underwear, and it had to keep her bosom fully uplifted throughout the play. It certainly worked. The mounds of her breasts were most attractively evident in the beautiful Edwardian gowns that had been designed for her. Yes, the corset was worth it, thought Maddy, but it was a bloody relief to get out of it.

There was a tap at the door. Jess opened it a fraction. 'She decent?' It was Ned.

'Decent enough for you,' Maddy called as she wrapped a towel around herself.

'Fan-bloody-tastic, sweetheart.' Ned swept her off her feet in a huge bear hug. She lost the towel and hugged him back naked except for her panties, thinking nothing of it—there was no modesty in the theatre.

Jess was poised ready to throw a robe over Maddy as soon as possible. There certainly *used* to be modesty in the theatre. Jess had been a dresser for forty-five of her sixty years and she didn't approve of the slack modern standards.

Despite his healthy heterosexuality and despite Maddy's highly desirable body, Ned barely noticed she was seminaked. He was too excited. 'Back in ten minutes,' he said as Jess threw the robe around Maddy and hastily closed it over the offending breasts. 'There's a mass of people waiting to congratulate you.' And he was gone.

The rest of the night was a whirl. A crowd of them went on to Joe Allen's, the actors' hangout in Covent Garden, for supper. Maddy was on a personal high, giddy with praise and champagne.

The next morning she awoke with a mild hangover and a hefty sense of reality. If the critics hadn't liked the show and if the word of mouth wasn't good, the night before had meant nothing.

As it turned out, the critics had some reservations about the translation and adaptation (exactly along the lines of Maddy's own reservations at the outset of rehearsals), but they voted the production a winner and were unanimous in their

231

praise of Maddy's performance. As to the word of mouth, within a week the bookings soared and, within a month, Bernard informed the company they were assured of a full year's run. *The Lady from Maxim's* was most certainly a hit.

It was the night Bernard made his announcement that Maddy met Douglas Mackie. He wasn't anything like she'd expected him to be, but then what had she expected anyway? She had no idea—she'd never been pursued by a real 'Stage-door Johnny' before.

Certainly, admirers gathered at the stage door after performances. On matinee days there were kids with autograph books and on Saturday nights there were the inevitable young men besotted by the corset, the breasts and the cheeky charm of 'The Shrimp'. But the huge bouquets of flowers that had arrived three times a week for the past month were another thing altogether, as was the enigmatic note that always accompanied them: *Congratulations on an excellent performance. I look forward to meeting you in the near future. Douglas Mackie.*

After the first half-dozen bouquets Maddy had to admit that she was intrigued, as was the rest of the cast.

'A pimply-faced adolescent with access to Daddy's credit card,' was Gerald's opinion.

'A sophisticated theatre-goer with a great knowledge of tradition,' was Meg's opinion. Margaret Ailwood played Gerald's religious zealot wife and, to those who knew her, it was a prime case of type-casting. Meg's obsession with theatre superstition and her insistence that the rules be adhered to had definitely reached fanatic proportions.

Meg changed her views about Douglas Mackie when the sixth bouquet was delivered. 'Quick, quick!' she gasped. 'Bring it outside.' Once in the side lane, she started ripping the white lilies out of the arrangement. 'Well, he certainly has no knowledge of theatre tradition,' she admitted. 'Lilies of the valley! Fancy sending lilies of the valley!'

'What's wrong with lilies of the valley?' Maddy asked, feeling very ignorant. She knew about not whistling in the dressing rooms and never quoting from *Macbeth*—they were both very bad luck indeed—but lilies of the valley? That was a new one to her.

'Death, dear.' Meg was obviously astonished that Maddy didn't know. 'Death to the show.'

'Oh.' Maddy felt duly chastened and immediately agreed that Bob the doorman be instructed to remove any lilies of the valley should they be present in future bouquets.

'I'll come with you, dear, to make sure he understands properly,' Meg insisted.

'And don't just put them in your rubbish bin, Bob,' she stressed when he nodded agreement. 'They're to go outside the theatre altogether. There are bins in the side alley.'

'Sure, Miss Ailwood, I'll see to it, don't you worry.' Bob was used to strange demands from actors, but Miss Ailwood wasn't a bad old stick, not up herself like some of the others.

Then there came the night, two weeks later, when the message on the card accompanying the bouquet read *I look forward to the opportunity of meeting you after the performance tonight. Douglas Mackie.* My God, Maddy thought, what'll I do?

She immediately rang Rodney who agreed to go to supper after the show.

'A Mr Mackie at the stage door for you,' the assistant stage manager said. 'Shall I show him up?'

The curtain had been down for exactly fifteen minutes. Just the right amount of time had been allowed for her to have showered, cleaned off her make-up and changed. Damn, Maddy thought, he obviously expects me to go out with him.

'No thanks,' she called back. 'I'll be down in a minute.' Hurry up, Rodney, for God's sake, hurry up.

'Miss Frances? Douglas Mackie. How do you do.'

'How do you do.' His handshake was firm—if anything, just a little too firm. 'Thank you for the flowers.'

Maddy couldn't think of anything else to say. Douglas Mackie was incredibly attractive. Or was he? She couldn't be sure. He wasn't conventionally handsome. Maddy was confused. There was something disturbing, something confronting about him. The only thing Maddy was sure about was that she was immediately and magnetically drawn to him.

'It's my pleasure,' Douglas Mackie was saying. And his voice, too, with its faint Scots burr, was attractive. 'I was quite overwhelmed by your performance and I wanted very much to meet you.'

Did he mean to send her up? Why did she get the feeling he was laughing at her? But then was he? Was that mockery in his eyes or was it genuine admiration?

'Sorry I'm late.' It was Rodney, out of breath.

'Awful trouble parking the car.' He noticed Douglas. 'Hi,' he said, offering his hand. 'Rodney Baines. We're just on our way out to supper.'

'Hello. Douglas Mackie. Of course you are.' Damn, Maddy thought. The twinkle was still there as Douglas turned back to her. 'I wondered whether, once I'd introduced myself, you might have supper with me? Maybe one evening next week?'

'Um . . . well . . .' Maddy floundered.

Rodney was about to 'save' her once more but fortunately Douglas interrupted. 'Why don't I just arrive on . . . say, Thursday . . . and you can decide then and there?'

'All right,' Maddy agreed hastily before Rodney could save her again. 'That'd be fine.'

'I thought you wanted rescuing,' Rodney hissed as they watched the stage door close behind Douglas.

'I changed my mind. Sorry. Come on, let's eat. I'm starving.'

Douglas arrived at exactly the same time, fifteen minutes after the curtain had come down, and sent a message that he was waiting for her at the stage door.

Maddy wondered momentarily about asking him to come up to her dressing room, but then dismissed the idea. It was far too personal. Pasted all around her mirror were photographs of Jenny together with telegrams and cards from well-wishers. On the bench, alongside her make-up, were mementos and good luck tokens. No, the inner sanctum was granted only to close friends and she didn't want him to get the wrong idea.

She had actually been regretting her hasty decision to go out with him. And of course Rodney hadn't helped.

'So he sent you a dozen bouquets of flowers—so what? You know nothing about the man. He could be an axe murderer, he could be—'

'All right, all right . . .'

'I think I should come with you.' Maddy stared him down. 'Well, I should follow you then. I'd keep out of sight.'

'Don't be ridiculous, Rodney. We're only going out for supper and I'll make sure it's somewhere very crowded.'

'What if—'

'And I'll make sure it's within walking distance so I don't have to get in his car.'

Rodney finally had to give up.

'Do you mind if we walk? I don't have a car,' Douglas said as Bob closed the stage door behind them.

'Oh. Sure.'

'Anywhere particular you want to go?'

'What about Joe Allen's at Covent Garden?'

'Fine,' Douglas shrugged. 'I don't know it; you'll have to show me the way.' But when they got there and saw that the place was seething with actors and the general after-show supper crowd, he said, 'Do you mind if we go somewhere else?'

Maddy wasn't given time to answer as he steered her down a side street. 'Great little place where we can talk. Quiet. Only a few blocks from here.'

It was a balmy late spring evening, with summer in the air, but he was walking briskly—a midwinter walk to keep out the cold, and it annoyed Maddy. She barely noticed where they were going—his insistent pressure on her arm forcing her into a semi-trot. Far from being frightened, she found she was becoming intensely irritated. After several minutes, she stopped abruptly and ripped her arm away from him.

'Do you think we could let up on the jogging? I'm wearing heels, you know.'

'I'm sorry.' Douglas smiled.

Damn it, she thought, there it was again. That humorous twinkle that could have been admiration or mockery. And again, whichever it was, it was bloody attractive.

'We're here now, anyway,' he said.

'Here' proved to be a small two-storey terrace house which had been converted to a Greek restaurant. Douglas waved a hello to the waiter who obviously knew him and led her through to one of the less crowded rooms out the back.

'Nice, isn't it?' Douglas said. 'Quiet. Good food, too. I hope you don't mind drinking out of coffee cups though, they're not licensed.' Maddy didn't have much option. A large complimentary mug of retsina was dumped in front of her, along with a basket of bread, a plate of Kalamata olives and the plastic menu. Maddy started to relax. It was her sort of place, after all—maybe tonight would be fun.

It . was. Douglas Mackie was the strangest mixture of everything she liked and disliked in a man, which left her delightfully confused.

'Mind if I order for us?' he asked and then went right ahead. Yes, Maddy thought, I *do* mind if you order for me, I loathe people ordering for me. But, as she watched him doing it, she felt totally unoffended. It wasn't arrogance; he was simply used to taking command.

Douglas's attention to the menu gave Maddy

time to study him a little more closely. No, he certainly wasn't handsome: his nose was too big and his jaw was too square. But his thatch of unruly hair was attractively greying, his deep brown eyes held that irresistible twinkle and his mouth . . .

'Do you like goat's cheese?'

'No, I hate it,' she answered. Hell, he'd nearly caught her out.

'Thought you might. It's an acquired taste.'

Now that *was* arrogant, Maddy thought, suddenly very irritated. 'May I have some more retsina, please. It's an acquired taste but I'm very fond of retsina.'

He smiled. 'Sorry.' And she knew he meant it. 'Baby calamari?'

'Love them.'

'Taramasalata?' She nodded. 'Dolmades?' She laughed. 'I love it all except goat's cheese. Keep ordering.'

The conversation was mainly about food until the first courses arrived. Then Maddy asked, 'You didn't really see the show all those times, did you?'

'What show?' Douglas shovelled a heap of taramasalata onto a piece of crusty white bread and popped it into his mouth.

'*The Lady from Maxim's.*'

'Oh.' He nodded and chewed vigorously for a couple of seconds. 'What about it?'

'You didn't really see it twelve times?'

'Good God, no. Why should I?'

A dolmade was halfway to Maddy's mouth but she stopped it right there. 'Because that's how many bouquets you sent. Bouquets with messages that read "Congratulations on a wonderful performance".'

'Oh. Yes.' Douglas seemed unperturbed. 'I put a weekly order in. The florist wrote those messages.'

Attraction was going right out the window. Maddy suddenly felt an icy chill.

'So how many times did you see the show?'

'Just the once.' Another shovel of taramasalata.

How can he keep eating? Maddy asked herself. But she maintained her control admirably. 'Why did you pretend you saw it so many times?' she queried, a steely edge to her voice.

'I didn't. I just sent the flowers.' Douglas seemed blissfully unaware of the danger signs.

'And why did you send the flowers?' Maddy's teeth were firmly clenched by now. She felt that she might scream at any moment.

'I had to go out of town on business for a few weeks and I wanted to make sure you'd know who I was when I came back and introduced myself.'

'I see.' She was confused again. His manner was so ingenuous she wasn't sure whether she was insulted or not.

'You probably get flowers from different admirers every night,' he continued, 'so I thought I'd better compete. I'm really not sure of the correct procedure—I don't go to the theatre much.'

'Why did you go this time? What attracted you?'

'Oh.' Douglas grinned. That was an easy one. 'Those lifesize pictures of you doing the cancan.' He shook his head in genuine admiration. 'Fantastic.'

'All that leg in fishnet tights and garters, you liked that did you?' Douglas nodded. 'Thought you were in for a girlie show perhaps?' The glint in Maddy's eye was now positively dangerous.

'Possibly. I didn't really know what to expect. But I must say I wasn't disappointed.'

'Well, I bloody well am.' Maddy rose from the table. 'If you don't know the difference between a Soho strip act and a Feydeau farce then I don't see much point in continuing the conversation.' It wasn't the perfect exit line, she thought, but it would have to do and she turned to leave.

His hand flashed out and she was seated again before she knew it. He hadn't hurt her, at least she didn't think so. Her wrist smarted a little bit. How the hell had he managed to do that? He hadn't even moved from his chair. Maddy's anger abated momentarily as she tried to figure it out.

'Stop taking yourself so seriously,' he said. Then, before she could protest further, 'You were wonderful. You fascinated and beguiled me. I'll come to the play twelve times if you want me to but I don't see the point. It's not the performance I want to get to know. It's you. If you'll let me.'

Maddy was at a loss for words. What on earth could she say in reply to that? Finally she laughed. 'I give up,' she said. 'Let's have another retsina.'

'Do you mind if I order a bottle of red?' he asked, topping up her glass. 'Retsina's a taste I've never quite acquired.'

Later that night Maddy found herself equally delighted and confused. Although sex on first dates normally went against her better judgement, it seemed the perfectly natural thing to go to bed with Douglas. Their attraction to each other had been eminently readable from the outset and she would have felt hypocritical and prudish if she'd said no. Well, that's what she told herself. The truth was, for the first time in years Maddy was aching for a man to touch her. Not just any man. This man.

And as she gave herself to him, she felt him respond in kind. As her desire grew, so did his. As her passion grew, so did his. And finally, as their cries and their sweat and their bodies mingled, they climaxed together in what seemed to Maddy a perfect culmination.

It shocked her. She had somehow assumed she would never experience all-consuming sex again. Not the way she had known it with Alex. Alex had played her to such perfection that surely sex could never be as good again, she'd told herself. Now she realised with a shock it could not only be 'as good', it could be better. It could be better when it wasn't a case of one person 'playing' another at all. It could be better when it was a case of responding, of giving and taking and, damn it, maybe loving.

Maddy looked at the face on the pillow beside her. Douglas was still gently caressing the small of her back but his eyes were closed and he was on the verge of sleep. Surely one couldn't fall in love this quickly, Maddy thought. Surely not. It was all so confusing.

A month later it was still all so confusing. She saw Douglas at least three times a week. He continued to delight and exasperate her with his combination of boyish charm and male chauvinism, but he avoided any intimate discussion, which meant she did too. The only time she ever felt she knew him was when they made love.

Whether their lovemaking was languid or frenzied, exploratory or explosive, Douglas always seemed vulnerable and Maddy often had to stifle her desire to tell him she loved him.

Afterwards, she was always glad she'd held back. Besides, she wasn't sure she loved him at all. How could you love someone you didn't know? It was just infatuation, she told herself impatiently. Hell, he never even asked her back to his place—it was always assumed they would go to her flat.

Then it occurred to Maddy that he might be married. Good God! A wave of horror swept over her. Why hadn't she thought of it before? That was it! He was married! Oh shit!

'Why don't we go to your place?' It was a Saturday night and they were walking up Charing Cross Road, heading automatically for Great Titchfield Street, when she blurted it out.

'Your place is nicer,' he answered.

'I don't care. Why don't we go there tonight? Now.'

'Go where?'

'Your place!' She was determined to find out the truth.

'It's a bit messy.' He shrugged. 'Some other night maybe.'

'No, tonight. I want to go there tonight.' She sounded like a petulant ten-year-old and she knew it.

His look was enigmatic: part amusement, part irritation, but finally he nodded. 'All right, come on.'

He hailed a cab. 'Hampstead,' he told the driver.

It was a basement flat. Douglas had been quite right—it was nowhere near as nice as her apartment.

Nonplussed, Maddy looked about the sparse, characterless room.

'I'm not married,' Douglas said, but she didn't answer. 'You thought I was married, didn't you? I'm not.'

'It's not messy. It's not messy at all.'

'Did you hear me, Madeleine? I'm not married. I never have been.'

'Why did you tell me it was messy?'

'What the hell does that matter?' He was becoming irritated.

'It matters because you lied. Why did you lie?'

'Because I didn't want you here, that's why,' he snapped. 'It's just a place where I live—it has nothing to do with us.'

Maddy continued to gaze around at the empty bookcase and mantelpiece, at the lone coffee cup on the bare table. A dinner table was at one end of the room and a lounge suite at the other. An open-plan living area, she thought, but nobody seems to live here. Weird. It made her uneasy.

'I think I'd like it better messy,' she said. 'Where's the kitchen?'

He led her through the arch in the dining area. The kitchen was the same, untouched.

'I eat out,' he explained as he took a bottle of Scotch and two glasses from a cupboard. 'Nightcap? Only Scotch I'm afraid,' and he started pouring without waiting for an answer. 'If I'd known you were coming I'd have laid on the Bollinger.'

For some strange reason Maddy started to feel guilty. Like an intruder. She'd barged into an area of this man's life he didn't want to share. But surely she had a right? They were sharing their bodies, after all, how intimate could one get?

Nevertheless she felt guilty. 'I'm sorry,' she said. 'I shouldn't have . . .'

'Sit down, Madeleine.' There was that edge to his voice again. That edge which seemed to demand obedience and she found herself seated at the kitchen table before she could analyse whether she was annoyed or not.

'I travel a lot on business and I don't like hotels, so I keep this flat as a London base. Does that suffice?' He continued in the same brusque tone. 'I care a great deal for you. Probably more than I have for any woman before and it's happened so fast I'm not sure what I'm supposed to do about it.'

'Nothing, Douglas,' Maddy interrupted. She felt as self-conscious and uncomfortable as he appeared to be and she was wishing she hadn't forced this confrontation.

But he cut her short. 'I'm thirty-five years old, I've never married, I've led a selfish life and I doubt whether I can change. In fact I doubt whether I want to change. But right now I know that I don't want to lose you, Madeleine, and I'm not sure how—'

'You won't,' she interrupted gently. 'I'm happy with things as they are, I don't want to change you, and my friends call me Maddy.'

Then they sat and talked and Maddy told him all about herself. She was Australian, her name wasn't Frances but McLaughlan, she had a ten year old daughter. 'Well, she will be soon. She's coming to stay with me for her school holidays. I can't wait for you to meet her.'

From the outset Maddy had been reticent about telling Douglas of Jenny, but now she was sure it was all right. She loved him, and despite the fact that he was too inhibited to tell her, she was sure he loved her too.

True to style, his reaction to the news of Jenny was enigmatic. 'Yes, I'll look forward to meeting her,' was all he said. But Maddy refused to let it worry her.

Then it was Douglas's turn. He came from Glasgow, he said. The tough part of town, not far from the Gorbals. 'About as tough as you get. Dad a boxer, two tough little brothers and Mum the toughest one of the lot of us,' he laughed. 'It was a good childhood.'

There wasn't much more detail Maddy managed to get out of him but she didn't try too hard. It would all happen in time, she told herself, as the familiarity grew between them.

That night in his spartan bedroom, as their bodies merged into one, Maddy clung to him and whispered, 'I love you'. And she meant it.

She woke to the smell of eggs and bacon and freshly brewed coffee.

She pulled on one of Douglas's T-shirts and joined him in the kitchen where he was transferring bacon from a frypan to a plate.

'Morning,' he said. 'I was going to surprise you.' He returned her kiss and put the bacon in the oven.

'You have.' She smiled. 'I thought you ate out.'

'Normally I do. But then normally I don't have visitors.' He deftly cracked two eggs into the sizzling pan and dropped the shells into the bin.

'I'm impressed,' she said.

'Hoped you might be. I'm quite good at the basic stuff.'

He was right. The breakfast was good. The coffee was good, the company was good, everything was good, Maddy thought as she chatted happily away.

Then suddenly everything went sour. She had just said, 'We'll have to have a birthday party for Jenny when she comes to London.' His reply was so casual that at first she thought she hadn't heard correctly.

'Won't be here, I'm afraid. I have to leave on Monday. I'll be away for two months.'

'Monday? You mean tomorrow?' She could hardly take it in.

He nodded. 'Bit of a bugger, isn't it, but business is business.'

'But . . .' Maddy stared back at him . . . 'last night . . . when I was talking about Jenny and you two meeting each other . . .' She stopped, confused.

'Yes?'

'Well . . . you didn't say anything . . . You didn't . . .'

'I didn't know till this morning.' His smile was charming. 'It is midday, you realise. I was on the phone for a good two hours before doing the shopping and cooking up a storm.' He stood to clear the table. 'It's only for a couple of months.'

She continued to stare at him in disbelief.

'Oh, come on, Madeleine,' he said a trifle impatiently as he took her plate. Then, 'Maddy . . .' He paused thoughtfully.

'Maddy, Madeleine . . . that's going to take some getting used to. I'm not sure if I don't actually prefer Madeleine.' The phone rang. 'See? That's been happening all morning.'

As he disappeared into the lounge room Maddy realised her day had just crashed down around her. It wasn't the fact that he had to go away for two months, disappointing as that was. It was his offhand attitude. What sort of game was he playing with her?

She was just getting over the hurt and starting to fume when Douglas returned.

'I have to go out, I'm afraid. I should only be an hour or two; do you want to hang around here or do you want to go home?'

Damn it, she thought angrily, he wasn't just offhand now, he was totally distracted. He wasn't even looking at her as he picked his keys up from the kitchen bench.

'I'll go home,' she snapped.

'Right. Want me to ring you a cab?' He was halfway through the arch.

She called after him. 'I can ring my own, thanks.'

'Fine, then, I'll see you at your place tonight.' And he was gone.

Maddy sat, sipped her coffee and fumed for a good ten minutes. How dare he! Then she forced herself to calm down and think through the situation. Just who was this man to whom she was giving herself? Just who was Douglas Mackie? And she determined to find out.

As Maddy rifled through cupboards and drawers she tried to push her guilt aside but she wasn't altogether successful. My God, was this really her? Was this really Maddy McLaughlan ransacking someone's personal belongings, invading their privacy like this?

So what? the enraged part of her responded. He was sleeping with her, letting her tell him she loved him—the least he could do was share a little

247

honesty. Besides, what personal belongings? What privacy? Each fresh invasion revealed nothing.

Douglas Mackie was a mystery. There were no letters addressed to him, no personal papers, no bills, no desk diaries. Maddy was about to give up when she found the leather suitcase under the bed.

It was of the small, overnight variety and had obviously seen a lot of use. Maddy squatted on the floor beside it, pushed the locks aside and the lid sprang open. Inside was an abundant proof of identity. But whose? Letters addressed to Donald McBride. A wallet with Mastercard, Diners Club and driver's licence, all in the name of Donald McBride. And, in the lid pocket of the suitcase, a passport: Donald McBride, born Edinburgh, December, 1945.

She willed herself to read the details without really taking in the photograph but, when she allowed her eyes to stray to the face on the left-hand side, she already knew who was going to be staring back at her. And she was right. It was Douglas Mackie.

Act III

1982–1985

ACT III

SCENE 1: 1982

Julian was preoccupied as he sat back in the uncomfortable cinema seat and waited for the lights to fade.

He was thinking of the other theatre, only a few blocks away, where people would be sitting watching his play. It was Wednesday, matinee day. He wondered how many people would be there. About two dozen, he thought gloomily. It was only three weeks into the season too—another nine whole weeks to go.

David had been quite right. It was better that he was here watching a movie than there dwelling on his own failure. And his second failure at that. The first play he'd written since his split with Alex had been just as ignominiously received. Not that the critics had roasted either of them—that might even have been preferable. Their unanimous opinion had been 'lacklustre' and, deep down, Julian had to agree with them.

In fact, life in general was somewhat lacklustre, he thought dismally. Although they never discussed it, both he and David were aware that their relationship was on the wane. And they both knew why. David couldn't live life openly as a homosexual. 'I guess I've been closet for too long, Jules,' he said jokingly, when he insisted they keep a low profile. 'It's not good for my career if people know,' was his further justification.

Bullshit, Julian thought. So long as it was kept from the press and the general public, it didn't matter one iota. The many actors who lived a life of openly admitted homosexuality were closely protected by an industry which looked after its own. As were the drug addicts, the alcoholics, the terminally ill and those who beat up on small dogs, he thought. You can't adjust to yourself, old buddy, and you're looking for an excuse. But he didn't say anything. 'Sure,' he agreed.

Within a year, the relationship had been thoroughly undermined by David's guilt. Added to the guilt of not being 'straight' had been the guilt of forcing Julian to live a lie. Julian understood, but then the more understanding Julian was, the more guilt David felt. It was a vicious circle and they both knew it.

Alex didn't help. Every time they saw him, and they saw him regularly at the theatre and various associated functions, he greeted them with a warmth normally reserved for lovers: 'Hello, you two!', invariably loud and invariably in the company of others. Then he'd flash a quick look to Julian, a quirky look which excluded David and which said, 'We share something special, don't we, Julian?'

Then, on the way home, it would start. 'You see, Julian, people know! It's not good for my career . . .' On and on, David painting himself in wimpy, unattractive colours and all because Alex had successfully goaded his guilt. Julian couldn't tell David that Alex was doing it deliberately. After all, what was he doing? And why? It was far too complex.

Yes, life's a bastard, Julian thought as the lights faded to black and the screen became a swirl of colour. And one of David's art films wasn't going to solve things.

David was a movie buff who subscribed to every film society and attended every film festival Sydney had to offer. Julian enjoyed one in ten of the films he was dragged along to and this wasn't going to be one of them, he thought as the title flashed up on the screen. But David was genuinely trying to take his mind off the matinee day at the theatre around the corner and Julian was grateful for that.

'You'll love it, Julian, honestly,' David had urged. 'I've seen it three times. *Androgyne* is one of the best cinéma vérité films ever made.'

Shit, muttered Julian as 'Rodney Baines and Madeleine Frances' appeared in tasteful print at the top left-hand corner of the screen. He sank deeper into the seat and let his mind wander.

Alex's production of *Hedda Gabler* opens next week, he thought, I wonder how it'll go? Julian hoped it would do well, mainly for the cast's sake. Alex had, of course, surrounded himself with his old faithfuls: Susannah playing Hedda, Harold as

Judge Brack and Rosie Lee as Mrs Elvsted.

Following two failed productions of new Australian plays, Alex had decided on a safer policy of well-known modern classics. Even so, he was only just scraping by. The critics accused him of egomania when he directed himself as Dr John in his own production of *Summer and Smoke*. And so they should, admitted Julian. Bloody stupid decision, even though he only did it to save on the budget. Susannah's superb Alma had rescued the production, though.

In fact Susannah proceeded to rescue all of Alex's productions as she went from strength to strength. She developed a healthy theatrical following and Alex, quickly recognising this, built his season entirely around her. He now kept himself well out of the acting and directing limelight, concentrating his energies on amassing huge publicity campaigns. He'd employed Roger Kingsley to direct *Hedda Gabler*, Roger only too willingly accepting a hefty cut in salary, as he'd long since been swept out of The Way In Theatre by the new young brooms.

The only production Susannah had been unable to rescue was *Cat on a Hot Tin Roof*. Her Maggie was criticised as being 'emaciated and lacking in ripe sensuality'. It was true, Susannah was looking anything but 'ripe' lately. She was being shockingly overworked, but then that was the way she wanted it, indeed, demanded it. After her roasting as Maggie she sailed through *Blythe Spirit* to rave reviews. Now, having played Tennessee Williams and Noel Coward, she was demanding Alex plunge her into the heavier stuff.

She'll be a superb Hedda, Julian decided as he

watched a screen full of figures in masks and period costumes swirling before him. But then she always was a superb actress, even in the old NADA days. She and Maddy were always the pick of the bunch.

Maddy! The youth on the screen lowered his mask and smiled invitingly up at the man in cavalier costume. My God, Julian thought, as the cavalier lowered his own mask and smiled back, that boy looks like Maddy.

He stopped thinking about Alex and Susannah and Hedda and concentrated on the film. David was right, it was a beautifully crafted piece.

When the youth proved to be a young woman Julian leant forward in his seat, which was no longer uncomfortable, and studied the face closely.

It *was* Maddy. It had to be. How long ago had the film been made? She looked incredibly young. Younger even than she had at NADA, but then the short, dark hair might account for that, and of course the lighting was superb.

'What's her name?' he whispered to David.

'Madeleine Frances. Isn't she dynamic?'

'How long ago was it made?'

'About five years.'

Julian sat captivated for the next ninety minutes. As soon as the lights came up, he plied David with questions.

'I don't know much about her,' David answered. 'I think *Androgyne* was her first film. Well, it was the first one I saw her in. She's done several others.' He shrugged. 'Variable quality, certainly none as good as *Androgyne* but she's always great.'

That night Julian rang Harold. 'What time are you rehearsing tomorrow, Harold?'

'Not till the evening, dear boy. Full technical-dress. Shudder, shudder! Why, what did you have in mind?'

'I want you to come to the movies with me in the afternoon. The Roma, downstairs.'

'But that's an art cinema! I'm thirty years too old for poignant films—they're tiring.'

'I think you'll like this one.'

'Oh Lord,' he grizzled, 'all those beautiful people wandering around wondering where they are and what they're doing there . . . Must I?'

'Yes, you must. I'll pick you up at two.'

'Good grief!' Harold exclaimed, sitting bolt upright. 'It's Maddy!'

'Ssshh,' said a male voice behind him. And a woman in front turned and glared.

'It is! It's Maddy!' he said again, ignoring them both.

After the movie they decided on their plan of attack and midnight found Julian waiting at the stage door for Harold as he left rehearsal.

'Alex will be out in a minute: you sure you don't want me to ask him back to supper too?'

'Harold, we agreed!' Julian couldn't hide his exasperation. 'We have to keep quiet about Maddy until we've spoken to her. She might not want any contact with Alex.'

'I know, I know we agreed.' Harold was obviously undecided. 'It's just that . . .'

As he tailed off Julian leapt in. ' "Just that" nothing. She had an abortion to the bloke and then disappeared without a trace. I think we can safely assume she doesn't want to know him, for God's sake.'

'Yes, yes,' Harold agreed peevishly, 'I know we mustn't involve him, for goodness sake, but I could have asked him along a little later, just for supper.' He looked hopefully at Julian. 'Maybe next week, after the show's opened? Maybe then the three of us could get together? What do you think?'

'Maybe.'

'It's a great shame you two have let such a wonderful friendship drift. Good grief, not to mention partnership. You had the world . . .'

'Yes, I know, Harold. It's only temporary, though, we both wanted to try a couple of solo flights, that's all.'

'So you'll come to supper with Alex next week?'

'Maybe.'

'You mustn't let love affairs destroy your friendships, you know—too many people do that. David's a lovely fellow, but one needs one's friends. I often feel that—'

'I'll come to supper with Alex next week, I promise.' Anything to shut him up, Julian thought. Harold was old now, with a tendency to nag and a tendency to forget that they'd had a conversation a dozen times before.

While Harold pottered around his kitchen Julian planted himself in the armchair by the phone and started dialling overseas directory assistance, pen and pencil at the ready.

Twenty minutes later he hung up the receiver and called to Harold. 'I'm ready. You want to come in while I start?'

'Coming, dear boy, coming,' Harold answered and made his entrance carrying a bottle of Pouilly Fuisse and two glasses on a silver tray. 'How sweet of you to bring my favourite,' he said, kissing the bottle before he started pouring. 'Everything's doing a quiet simmer so we can take as long as we like. To Maddy.' And they clinked glasses.

Julian had tried to persuade Harold to come back to his place and make the calls from there but he knew it was useless even as he suggested it. Harold could never pass up an opportunity to 'mother'. 'Oh no, dear boy, I prefer being in my own nest. Besides you must let me cook you a bit of supper.'

Julian put down his glass and checked his watch as he picked up the receiver again. 'Right,' he said, 'ten in the morning London time. Perfect. Enquiries didn't have a number for Pentameter Productions so—'

'Who're they?'

'The production company that made *Androgyne*. So we'll try Pinewood Studios first, that's where a lot of the interiors were shot.'

'How do you know all this?'

'I checked the credits when I watched the movie, of course.'

'Clever. Very clever.' Harold offered a small white dish. 'Have a cracked green olive.'

The *Androgyne* production company was no longer in existence as it turned out, but a helpful girl at Pinewood Studios put Julian onto a French/English production company. Another helpful girl supplied the information that, when Madeleine Frances had worked for them, her postal address had been care of a doctor in Windsor. 'A Dr Mac something or other. Don't know if they were on together or just sharing,' the girl said, enjoying the chat. 'Madeleine was always sort of private.'

So Maddy was still with her father. The address and phone number of Dr McLaughlan in Windsor were easy to find and of course it was the same address to which both Julian and Harold had previously written. Now, when Julian rang, a female voice answered.

'Yes?' Alma said.

Then followed a verbal game of hide and seek as Alma evaded every question Julian flung at her. The only definite information he ended up with was the fact that Miss McLaughlan no longer lived with her father but had moved to London. And Alma promised to pass on a message when next she saw Maddy.

'When will that be?' Julian asked.

'I really couldn't be sure,' Alma replied sharply. She found this young man's persistence suspect. The call was from Australia—he could well be Jenny's father and Alma knew how strongly Maddy wanted to avoid any contact with Jenny's father.

'I'll tell Miss McLaughlan you rang.' And she hung up.

Julian heaved an exasperated sigh as he put down the receiver. He was sure the woman wouldn't give Maddy the message.

For once Harold knew better than to jump in with advice. Telephones really were infuriating instruments and Harold loathed them. Always had. He clucked sympathetically and topped up their glasses.

Julian looked at the next number on his list. British Actors Equity. He was certain he'd be able to get hold of Maddy's agent via Equity, presuming she had an agent, of course, but he knew full well it was every agent's strict policy to withhold clients' addresses and phone numbers.

Sure enough. 'Sorry, old son, no can do, client details strictly confidential and all that.' Phil Pendlebury's voice was honestly apologetic. 'Tell you what, though. I'll be speaking to her some time today, I'll make sure she gets a message.'

'Thanks. Tell her Julian and Harold called.' Julian left both their phone numbers. 'Don't forget, will you? Please!'

'Don't you worry, son, she rings in every day.' Phil sensed the disappointment in Julian's voice and felt sorry for him. The call was from Australia—maybe it was Jenny's father, who could say? But agency policy was agency policy and it was none of his business, after all, and Maddy never spoke about the father of her child so . . . Yes, you keep your nose well out of it, Phil, he told himself.

Nevertheless he wanted to offer some reassurance, so he said, 'Tell you what I'll do. If she doesn't call today I'll go around to her place and slip a note under the door, she only lives a couple of blocks away, how does that grab you?'

'Thanks very much,' Julian said, 'I'd appreciate that.' The man at Actors Equity had told him that Pendlebury's office was in the West End. So Maddy was living in central London. Knowing where she was somehow gave him more hope. And he believed that Phil Pendlebury would give her his message. Things were looking up.

Julian wasn't sure why he felt such a strong urge to renew acquaintance with Maddy. Something to do with his disenchantment with Alex and his fading relationship with David, maybe. Perhaps something to do with the fact that those NADA days with Maddy and Alex were among the happiest days of his life. Whatever it was, now that he'd started his enquiries he was damned if he was going to give up.

As Phil Pendlebury replaced the receiver at his end he wondered whether he should have told the young man that Maddy was flying out to Australia with her daughter next week. No, he reminded himself, it was none of his business.

Julian had been wrong about Alma. Alma was always very reliable with messages. In fact, by the time Phil Pendlebury hung up, Maddy already knew of Julian's contact.

'I was a little evasive with him, Miss McLaughlan.' Alma always spoke louder into the phone and her Midlands accent was always more pronounced. 'After all, I wasn't sure who he might be.'

Alma wasn't fishing and Maddy knew it but she felt the need to reassure the woman. 'It's all right, Alma, he's not Jenny's father, just an old friend.'

'Oh dear, I do hope he wasn't insulted.'

'He wouldn't have been, I'm sure. Don't you worry, you did the right thing.'

Maddy received Julian's message with mixed feelings. She was deeply touched that both he and Harold thought of her as much as they obviously did. Should she contact them when she was in Sydney next week? Was Alex still very much a part of their lives? Yes, she told herself, he was bound to be. Oh hell, Maddy thought, life's so bloody complicated these days.

The main complication was, of course, Douglas

Mackie. Or was it Donald McBride? Or David McGuinness? Or a number of other aliases he admitted to assuming when she'd confronted him about the passport she'd discovered. My God, could that really have been a year ago?

'It *is* Douglas Mackie, actually,' he'd told her, and he was infuriatingly calm. 'But it doesn't really matter, does it, whether I'm Douglas, Donald or David? Take your choice, call me what you like.'

'Right. You're a bastard.' And she'd walked to the door of her apartment, opened it and waited for him to leave.

He didn't. 'Why?' he asked.

'Why?' She stared at him incredulously. 'For lying to me. For leading me on. For—'

'I didn't. I didn't lie to you and I didn't lead you on. My name is Douglas Mackie and I care very much for you.' She stared back at him as he continued, totally unperturbed. 'I sometimes need to assume a different identity for business purposes, Madeleine.' He held up his hand as he saw her about to interrupt. 'And don't ask me what business—it's not necessary that you know. Suffice it to say that not everyone leads a life as simple as yours.'

That was when Maddy exploded. 'Simple!' Not only was he a two-faced lying con man, he was a smug, pompous shit into the bargain. 'What the hell makes you think acting is *simple*! It's one of the hardest, most competitive professions one can—'

'I didn't say it was "easy".' There was a slight edge to his voice but he maintained his patience. 'I said it was "simple". Your job is simply to learn your part and arrive at the theatre on time. I grant you,' he admitted, 'after that it's a case of whether or not you have the talent . . .'

'And whether or not you can get the job in the first place,' Maddy muttered rebelliously. And, as she did, she was amazed that he'd managed so successfully to steer her away from the original argument.

'Exactly.' It was if he was awarding her points in a debate. 'A difficult job, certainly, but a "simple" one—one that doesn't require subterfuge and false identities.' He smiled winningly as he crossed to her. 'A job for single-minded, ambitious people with tunnel vision.'

He was being charmingly insulting, probably to distract her even further, but it gave Maddy momentary food for thought. He wasn't far wrong, was he? She lived, breathed, ate and drank the theatre and she always had.

'I respect you for it, Madeleine, and I don't want to change you.' He kissed her. 'Just as you don't want to change me, remember? I'm going now; we'll only talk around in circles if I don't. I'll see you in a couple of months.' He kissed her once more and then he was gone.

Maddy agonised for a day or two before she realised it was pointless. He was right. Piqued as her curiosity was, she knew she'd have to take him as she found him; he obviously wasn't going to tell her about himself. Her only other alternative was to finish the relationship and she didn't think she could do that.

As always, the theatre was a total distraction, and then there was Jenny. Jenny arrived in London for her holidays, they had a special birthday dinner and Maddy presented her with the return tickets to Sydney.

'First class! Wow!' Jenny's eyes were like saucers. 'Can we afford it, Mum?'

'Of course we can, darling.' Maddy crossed her legs, mimed a cigarette holder and blew imaginary smoke into the air. 'Your mother's a West End star, don't you know.'

'What happens if you have a big offer next April?' There was no condemnation in the child's voice, but there was doubt, and it was fearful.

Tears sprang instantly to Maddy's eyes and she looked down at the food that she'd long since finished eating and pretended to toy with another mouthful. 'Then I'll say no, won't I?'

'But if it was a really big offer, you wouldn't be able to.'

A sudden rush of anger quelled Maddy's tears as quickly as they'd risen. 'Oh yes I would, Jen. Believe me I would.' Douglas had been right when he'd accused her of tunnel vision, she thought, and she wondered briefly how many times Jenny must have suffered because of it. She took the girl's hands in her own. 'Nothing is going to stop us going to Sydney next April, I can promise you. Nothing!'

It was only a fortnight later that a huge bouquet of flowers arrived backstage at the theatre. The card read: *Congratulations on an excellent performance. I look forward to meeting you after the show.* And it was in the florist's handwriting.

'You could at least have written the card youself,' she said, as Bob the doorman showed Douglas into her dressing room.

'Didn't want to break the tradition, did I?' he said.

'It's been less than three weeks. What happened to the two months?'

Douglas shrugged. 'I couldn't stay away. Besides, I wanted to meet Jenny.'

Maddy looked to the sofa in the corner where Jenny sat quietly watching them. 'Jen, this is Douglas.'

'Hi. Mum's told me about you.'

Over the next twelve months Douglas continued to be unforthcoming about his work and his background and his regular 'business trips'. Maddy tried not to pry. She tried to 'take him as he was', but there was a basic mistrust inside her which left her unrelaxed and wary.

Douglas remained touchingly vulnerable in their lovemaking but wore his customary guard up at other times and to Maddy, who loved him deeply, it was very frustrating. They seemed to have reached an emotional stalemate.

Jenny was also confused by Douglas's nonchalance. She liked the way he treated her as an equal and an adult but she was confused when, for no apparent reason, he'd become distracted and pay her no attention at all. Or when he'd suddenly disappear for weeks on end without even saying goodbye.

It was very confusing for everyone, Maddy thought; much as she knew she would miss Douglas, she was looking forward to the trip to Sydney. Perhaps the distance, being home again, would give her the courage to end the relationship. She felt she should, if only she could find the strength.

And now, with less than a week to go, there was the contact from Julian and Harold. And with it the reminder of Alex. Yes, life was bloody complicated these days, Maddy thought.

Life wasn't complicated for Alex. It was frustrating, disappointing and downright unfulfilling.

Big changes were called for, he decided. He'd had enough of producing short seasons of established plays and praying that Susannah's theatre following would pull in sixty per cent houses. He wanted a brand-new smash hit that would run for a year, play to capacity houses, tour the capital cities and make him a fortune. It wasn't just the money he wanted, although the lifestyle he insisted on maintaining certainly required it. It was the stimulation and the power—above all the power.

But first he needed a play. He needed a bold playwright. He needed Julian Oldfellow. And he knew he'd get him. After all, Julian had taken his year off to spend time with his poofter friend, and that relationship was dying its death, according to Harold. 'I'll give it a year at the most,' Alex could remember himself saying. And he'd been right. Time to come back to the fold, Julian.

It didn't bother Alex at all that Julian's last two plays had flopped. He knew that in some strange way he himself was Julian's inspiration. And he knew for a fact that, as a duo, their work was dynamic. The thought that their relationship was sorely in need of repair also didn't bother Alex. One evening was all he needed. One evening with Julian would do the trick, and Harold had already extracted Julian's promise to come to supper next week after *Hedda* had opened.

Hedda. Oh God! Alex put all thoughts of Julian

aside. One thing at a time, he told himself. *Hedda Gabler* was in a mess. Tonight was their final dress rehearsal, they opened the next day—and Alex had big reasons to worry.

Until three days ago he had kept his customary distance from the company. But when he attended the first full dress rehearsal he decided it was time to interfere. The show wasn't good enough.

Alex cancelled the three scheduled public previews, called day and night dress rehearsals instead, and had endless rows with Roger Kingsley over the changes he wanted made.

'For God's sake, Roger, just shut up and do as you're told,' Alex finally snapped.

'I beg your pardon,' said Roger, looking down his nose with queenly indignation, 'but I am the director around here.'

'No you're not. You're sacked.'

'What?' Roger dropped the queenly act and stared back in disbelief.

'I said, you're sacked.'

'But I have a contract. You can't—'

'I can. You'll be paid out in full.'

Alex hadn't taken much notice of Susannah's complaints about Roger over the past several weeks. Susannah always had a whinge about a fellow actor, or a stage manager or a director when she was working. She was such a perfectionist herself that she overreacted to any imperfections in the work of others. Alex had long ago decided it was also her way of letting off steam.

Not this time. This time she'd been right. 'His blocking and general staging's up to shit, he's turning it into a Victorian melodrama and he's totally confused all of the cast except Harold and me about character relationships and balances. Honestly. You ask Harold.'

Alex had heard complaints along similar lines from Harold already. 'The man's doing his own personal rewrite of *Hedda Gabler*, dear boy. Nothing whatsoever to do with Mr Ibsen.'

Actors, Alex thought, God save me from them. 'He's just trying to put his personal stamp on the production, Harold. Give him a chance. God knows we accused him of playing it too safe for years at The Way In.'

'Well, he's revenging himself upon us now, I can tell you. He—'

'Can't stay, got a meeting with the party booking organisers. You want those bums on seats, don't you?'

If only he'd listened, Alex now thought as he tried to pick up the production pieces. And if only he hadn't given Roger so much power. The man's choice of music was funereal and his lighting was so dismal that even the stills photographs taken for front-of-house were morbid and boring and would have to be reshot. Why signal a tragedy from the beginning?

The biggest worry of the lot, however, was the set. Roger had changed the original design to suit his gloomy and Gothic version of the play. When the set designer argued that he would need the producer's permission for such a radical change, Roger waved the man aside with the assurance that Alex had granted him full authority in all artistic areas. On phoning Alex, the set designer had found this was indeed the case. 'Roger's the boss in that area, Steve, go for it.'

Alex groaned at the memory. It hadn't occurred

to him that Roger was designing a Gothic monster. A few minor set changes, he'd thought. Just another example of Roger wanting to put his personal stamp on things, he'd thought. But you *didn't* think, did you, Alex, he now told himself, you just didn't bloody think.

It was an expensive lesson. Now, three days after Alex had given Steve the order to return the set to its original design, Steve was insisting his team needed a further twenty-four hours to finish it.

Christ! We could all do with a further twenty-four hours, Alex cursed. He still hadn't found the music he wanted and he wasn't altogether happy with the new lighting design and, since his changes in blocking and his performance notes, the actors could all do with more rehearsal. How am I going to do it? he wondered. How the hell am I going to buy myself twenty-four hours? That very night, at the end of the dress rehearsal, the answer came to him.

'Yes, that is what you are looking forward to, isn't it, Mr Brack?' Susannah's voice rang out from behind the curtains of the drawing room alcove, centre stage. 'You, the only cock in the yard.'

There was a pause while the three actors on stage waited for the gunshot. The stills photographer zoomed in on the alcove to capture the discovery of Hedda's suicide.

There was no gunshot. A further pause. Still no gunshot. Damn, Harold thought, the props gun must have jammed.

Alex, sitting in the stalls with his notepad and pencil, was thinking exactly the same thing. He added to his list of notes that an ASM was to stand by in the wings with a second props gun in case of emergency. It should have been the duty of the stage manager to start with, he thought, irritated that Susannah had demanded she fire the gun herself.

Harold waited several seconds until the pause started to feel a little uncomfortable. Then he rose from the table and looked upstage to the drawing room alcove. In true tradition, the dress rehearsal was to be played as per performance and any mishaps had to be taken in the actors' stride. Besides, there were twenty people out front, friends and family of the front-of-house staff.

'Did you hear a sound, Tesman?' Harold asked, trying to stay in character. 'A strangled sort of sound?' And he crossed to the alcove curtains. The drawing room alcove was mocked up from several wardrobe racks draped with black tabs. It was the major part of the set currently under reconstruction by Steve and his gang.

'A strangled sound, Judge? Why yes, I believe I did.' Neville, the actor playing Tesman, picked up his cue admirably and joined Harold at the curtains.

'Madam Hedda, are you all right?' Harold called, praying that Susannah was able to find something to strangle herself with. Then he remembered. Of course, she had the sash of her gown. He gave a nod to Neville, a signal that they needed to buy more time for Susannah.

'Answer us, Hedda,' Neville called obligingly.

Harold waited two seconds. No answer from Hedda. Plenty of time for the sash around the throat. He drew aside the curtains.

Hedda's body was not sprawled upon the sofa, the gun by her side and the blood-stained cushion beneath her head as the stage directions dictated. Susannah was lying unconscious in a crumpled heap on the floor.

'Susannah!' Harold exclaimed as he knelt beside her. 'Alex! Quick! She's fainted.'

The stills photographer, poised to capture the discovery of Hedda's body, had clicked away the moment Harold drew the curtains. Now he guiltily stepped aside as Alex knelt beside his wife and lifted her head.

Susannah's face was deathly pale beneath the make-up and there were dark circles of fatigue under her eyes. She looked fragile and beautiful, her head resting on Alex's knee, her rich auburn hair splayed across his thigh.

It wasn't a deep faint and she was already stirring. Harold gestured to the ASM for a glass of water.

'What happened?' Susannah murmured.

'You fainted, darling,' Alex explained and, as he did, he knew with a surge of gratitude and relief that he'd found his way out.

'Oh God, how embarrassing.' She struggled to lift her head.

'No, no, don't try and get up.' Alex eased her head back onto his knee and gave a sharp nod to the photographer.

The photographer, incredulous, opened his mouth to speak but Alex's second nod and his gesture for silence were unmistakable.

Oh well, you're the boss, the photographer thought, as he surreptitiously raised his camera.

'Harold, you look after her,' Alex instructed

271

when he was sure that the photographer had taken at least three shots. 'I'm going to call an ambulance.' He got up and Harold immediately took his place.

'You'll do no such bloody thing, Alex,' Susannah snapped. 'There's nothing wrong with me—I'm tired, that's all.'

'All right, no ambulance, so long as you stay where you are,' Alex snapped back. 'I don't want you fainting again. We've got a show to open tomorrow.' When Susannah got tough the only way to handle her was to get tough back. 'But I'm calling a doctor in.'

'Oh, no you're not.'

'A doctor or an ambulance: take your choice.'

'All right, all right.' Susannah gave in gracelessly. 'So long as it's Les.'

Alex nodded agreement. 'Stay where you are till you get your breath back.' Then, as he left to make the phone call, he muttered to the photographer. 'Get some wide shots with the company too.' The other cast members and stage management crew were gathered around, Rosie Lee protectively preventing them from crowding Susannah.

When Alex returned several minutes later he was irritated to find Susannah comfortably settled on the sofa, but a nod from the photographer assured him that Susannah's collapse on the stage floor had been well and truly captured on film.

'Les is on his way,' Alex announced. 'Everyone can go home. I'll be in touch about rehearsal time tomorrow morning.'

Dr Les, as he was affectionately known in the industry, was a 'tame' medical practitioner who understood the problems that beset actors and treated and prescribed accordingly. He didn't do anything illegal but his methods were certainly unorthodox. He could be relied upon to administer a cortisone injection backstage between the opera company's matinee and evening show to enable an asthmatic singer to get through the night. Or a quick vitamin B shot for an actor suffering from fatigue. Minor fractures could be strapped and pain killers prescribed on the spot to enable performers to struggle through the show.

Unlike many practitioners, Dr Les understood the meaning of that old adage, 'the show must go on'. Actors were bloody stupid, he thought, but if they were prepared to stagger through performances in agony or in a state of near collapse, who was he to tell them to take two days off work and rest up? They wouldn't listen anyway, so he might as well be on call to make things easier for them.

'Pulse and blood pressure normal.' He lifted Susannah's eyelids and examined each eye. 'Have you been eating properly, Susannah?' he asked.

Susannah nodded and Dr Les looked at Alex for confirmation as he took the thermometer from her mouth.

'Yes, she has,' Alex agreed.

'I'm just tired, that's all,' Susannah insisted. 'A quick vitamin shot and I'll be fine.'

Dr Les read the thermometer. 'No temperature. Periods normal?'

'No, but they never are when I'm working.'

They discussed Susannah's irregular menstrual cycle and the fact that she was slightly anaemic. Dr Les told her she was suffering from fatigue and that she must remember to eat properly while she was working so hard.

'I know you performers,' he scolded. 'You're either dieting ridiculously or forgetting to eat altogether—bloody stupid the lot of you.' Then he gave her a Vitamin B shot, recommended a high-protein diet, left a supply of sleeping pills and departed with the instructions that she should rest up as much as possible before opening night.

'Christ, that shot hurt,' Susannah complained, rubbing her left buttock. 'What time's rehearsal tomorrow?'

'There isn't one,' Alex replied.

'What! You're joking.'

He shook his head. 'I'm calling a meeting for notes an hour before the half. No rehearsal.'

Nothing Susannah said could dissuade him. 'Trust me, Susannah, I know what I'm doing.'

'My God, I feel wonderful,' Susannah said to Alex when she woke the next day. He had given her a sleeping tablet the night before and she had slept soundly till three in the afternoon. 'I'm starving too.'

'Thought you might be. I've got the full works standing by: tomatoes, eggs, ham—I'll even make you a hollandaise sauce if you like.'

'Yum. I like.'

Alex waited until Susannah had eaten her eggs Benedict before dumping a pile of newspapers on the table in front of her. 'Now that you have your strength back, take a look at these. And don't be mad at me, Sooz, it was the only way out and I took it.'

Both morning and afternoon editions carried the story. It was front-page news in the morning editions: 'STAR COLLAPSES. GALA OPENING

CANCELLED'. The story was accompanied by pictures: Susannah's limp and crumpled body, her eyes closed, her face deathly pale against the black stagecloth floor; a close-up of Susannah and Alex, Susannah's face a delicate porcelain as Alex cradled her gently in his lap; a shot of the entire company circled around Susannah, Harold at her side smoothing the hair from her brow.

'God almighty, how did this happen?' Susannah exclaimed. 'And what the hell do they mean, "opening cancelled"?'

'Read on,' Alex answered.

The articles stated that Susannah had suffered a complete collapse due to nervous exhaustion and was medically unable to perform that night. A press reception had been held that morning by her producer/husband, Alex Rainford, who stated that naturally all tickets for the opening would be refunded or transferred and that he deeply regretted any inconvenience to patrons. He further announced that, against all medical advice, and indeed against his own advice, Miss Wright was insisting that the opening should take place tomorrow.

'The thought of disappointing her many followers for even twenty-four hours is so devastating to her,' Alex was quoted as saying, 'that she simply refuses to rest for any longer than a day.'

'What a load of horseshit!' It was difficult to tell whether Susannah was angry or not. She looked stunned more than anything.

'Exactly, but it's bought us twenty-four hours.'

'You held a press conference this morning?'

He nodded. 'And I rang all the critics and VIPs.' He picked up a pile of telegrams. 'These have arrived from the well-wishers.'

'What about the company? Everyone knows it's a pack of lies.'

'I've rung them all and said you had a relapse when you got home. All except Harold and Rosie, that is, I told them the truth.'

'What did they say?'

'Rosie said it was a disgraceful thing to do. Harold called me a fraud and pissed himself laughing. He said it was a pity we're not doing *La Dame Aux Camelias* because you'd get great reviews for the death scene.' Alex looked thoughtful. 'He's not wrong, actually,' he continued. 'The fact that you're soldiering on so bravely can only work in our favour with the critics.'

'Well, I agree with Rosie,' Susannah said disapprovingly. 'It's a disgraceful thing to do.' A slow smile spread across her face. 'But, by God, it's clever.'

As she embraced him, her lean body felt exciting. Or maybe it was his triumph over the odds that was exciting, Alex thought. Whatever it was, he wanted her.

'No you don't,' Susannah countered, backing off. 'I want to shower and clean my teeth and feel human first. I've been sleeping for over twelve hours.'

As she knelt beside the lavatory bowl, Susannah remembered Dr Les's comment: 'You performers, either dieting ridiculously or forgetting to eat altogether'. Well, she had been throwing up a lot lately which probably amounted to the same thing. Most days she threw up; sometimes even twice a day when social dinners or publicity luncheons required her to eat. She knew she should cut back on it. But not now. Not after eggs Benedict? The mere thought of allowing such a calorie-filled dish to digest started to make her feel physically ill. She'd eat an apple and a spoonful of cottage cheese later in the day, she promised herself. And then she'd stick to a low-calorie diet and only throw up when it was really necessary.

Half an hour later, when Susannah had rid herself of the eggs Benedict, scoured her teeth, showered, washed and conditioned her hair, the knob of the bathroom door rattled irritably. 'Susannah, I'm going to the theatre,' Alex called.

Susannah opened the door and stood before him naked, bedraggled and rather fetching. 'Oh. I thought you wanted to fool around.'

'Too late, sweetheart, you missed your chance.' Although Alex said it jokingly he was genuinely irritated. Not so much because Susannah had disappeared to the bathroom for half an hour but because she'd locked the door. She always locked the door these days and, for someone as sexually abandoned as she was, Alex found it annoyingly coy. When he'd challenged her about it a year or so ago, she'd countered with equal irritation.

'For God's sake, Alex, women like the bathroom to themselves from time to time. I mean, hell, I might have a period, I might be taking a crap, who knows.'

He didn't point out that such moments of personal hygiene had never been a matter of privacy in their early days. It was yet another sign of the growing distance between them.

'Steve's bumping the new set in tonight and I'm giving the cast notes at six-thirty.'

'I take it you don't want me to make a miraculous recovery and appear for notes.'

'No bloody way.'

Alex left and Susannah felt slightly piqued. She knew he'd been irritated, but what right did he have? Now she was faced with an interminable night alone—God knew what time Alex would be home.

She wandered around the house naked, looked at the view across the bay, then decided to have a sauna. That was a productive way to fill in an evening. A long sauna with the thermostat turned up could knock off a good kilo, provided she didn't replace the fluid loss for a couple of hours.

Susannah wrapped the heavy duty plastic garbage bags around her body and lay back on the wooden bench. She tried to switch her mind off to the peace that surrounded her: the ticking of the electric heating unit in the corner; the mild sizzle of the water she'd just thrown on the stones. But she couldn't switch off. Thoughts nibbled at her brain like mice at a piece of cheese.

Thoughts about her and Alex. They weren't really a couple any more. But then had they ever been?

Thoughts about her family. Daddy's health was worse than ever and Michael wasn't able to come down for her show. Susannah missed her brother dreadfully but now, with Mummy's health starting to fail, Michael was needed more than ever to dance attendance on their father.

As the heat took over and sweat trickled around her body, seeking an outlet from the garbage bags, Susannah thought of *Hedda Gabler*. Whenever her personal life seemed too much to contemplate, Susannah found escape in her work. Thank God

Alex had come to *Hedda*'s rescue, she thought. And thank God for his twenty-four hour plan. She breathed deeply, the hot air scorching her lungs, and smiled to herself. Good old Alex. What right did she have to berate him, or indeed herself, for anything lacking in their relationship? They fulfilled each other's careers perfectly, didn't they? And that was, after all, why they'd married in the first place.

She hoped Alex would remember to give Neville the notes from their discussion about the opening scene. The pace needed to be picked up and Neville needed to . . .

Of course Alex would remember, she told herself. Beads of sweat started to hit the tiles of the sauna floor and Susannah relaxed.

When Susannah finally stirred at ten, Alex had already been on the phone for nearly an hour and had a pot of tea brewing.

'Breakfast raring to go too,' he said proudly. 'You name it. Eggs Benedict?'

'No thanks, sweetheart,' Susannah said, remembering her promise to herself.

'Did you eat last night?' Alex asked.

'Oh damn! No, I forgot.' Of course! She'd meant to have her apple and cottage cheese, she reprimanded herself. But she'd been in the sauna until midnight by which time she was so exhausted she'd taken her tenth quick dip in the cold plunge pool and collapsed into bed. No wonder she'd slept so deeply and no wonder she now had a headache. Better drink some water, she told herself.

'That's naughty, Susannah. You heard what Les said. You're going to have something to eat right now. What can I get you?'

Susannah looked dutifully chastised. 'A green apple and some cottage cheese, please.' She caught his look and added hastily 'On rye bread.

'Why the special treatment?' she asked as she followed him into the kitchen.

'For my favourite leading lady nothing is too much trouble.'

It was true. Alex always cosseted her just before an opening night. He knew the strain she was under, Susannah thought gratefully. She wasn't unaware of his ulterior motive, of course, she knew he wanted to get the best possible performance out of her. They understood each other.

As Alex opened the refrigerator door Susannah kissed him deeply and pressed her groin against his, determined to make up for the night before.

But Alex's sexual response was lukewarm. 'Just wait till you see the set, Sooz,' he said eagerly as he broke away from the kiss. 'Steve's done a great job and now that they've got a whole extra day to dress it he reckons it'll look fantastic. New drapes to replace that dreary maroon shit.' He tossed her an apple and slammed the refrigerator door shut. 'And the bookings! Christ alive, the bookings!'

Far from being insulted by his dismissal of her sexual advances, Susannah found his enthusiasm exciting.

'The bookings have gone mad!' he continued. 'I've already told the theatre we're extending the season and we haven't even opened!'

'You're a genius, my darling.'

'What a pity we can't rig a scam like this for every opening night.'

They laughed together like delighted children but they both knew Alex wasn't really joking at all. Yes, we understand each other, Susannah thought.

They had to quell their frivolity during the full dress rehearsal Alex called for three-thirty that afternoon. Everyone in the company was so concerned about Susannah that she felt like a terrible fraud as she nodded bravely and said she was sure she'd be able to get through the evening performance.

'We'd better just do a walk-through dress then, hadn't we, Herr Direktor?' Harold asked with a cheeky glint in his eye.

'Only Susannah, thank you, Harold,' Alex answered warningly. 'I'll expect full-level performances from the rest of the company.'

Halfway through Act Two, Mavis from front-of-house crept up to Alex as he scribbled his notes by shielded torchlight in the stalls.

'Excuse me, Mr Rainford,' she whispered 'but Miss Wright's mother is on the phone. She's calling from the Gold Coast.'

'So what?' Alex hissed. 'I don't care if she's calling from the Arctic wastelands, she can't interrupt a dress rehearsal.'

'I'm fully aware of that, Mr Rainford,' Mavis replied stiffly. She was a stickler for theatrical form herself and, under normal circumstances, would never have approached him until after the rehearsal. 'But Mrs Wright has heard of her daughter's illness and is very distressed. I wondered what message you might like me to give her.'

Oh shit, Alex thought. The story couldn't have made the Queensland papers, surely—that was something he certainly hadn't contemplated. 'Of course, Mavis, I'm sorry.' He knew better than to get offside with Mavis; she was a valuable ally. 'Tell Mrs Wright that she mustn't worry. Susannah is fine and she'll ring during interval in fifteen minutes.'

'Very well.' As Mavis turned to go Alex hoped she caught his grateful smile in the dim torchlight.

'Hell,' Susannah said when Alex told her. 'That's all they need.' And she hurried off to her dressing room to ring her parents.

When Alex joined her twenty minutes later she was just hanging up the receiver and her face was glowing. 'Michael's on his way to Sydney,' she said. 'When he heard about the story in the papers he took off straight away.'

'That's amazing.'

'Yes, isn't he wonderful?'

But Alex was shaking his head in disbelief. 'That's amazing. The story made the Queensland papers—I don't believe it.'

'No, it didn't,' Susannah corrected him. 'A friend of Daddy's arrived from Sydney this afternoon and he rang to say he was sorry to hear the news. Daddy sent straight out for the Sydney papers and then rang Michael.'

'He'll probably be pissed off when he finds he's made the trip for nothing. Did you try to stop him?'

She nodded. 'Yes, I rang but Priscilla said he left an hour ago.' Susannah's eyes were shining with excitement. 'He'll be here just in time for the curtain. Oh Alex, he won't miss my opening night after all.' She threw her arms around him. 'And it's going to be a magnificent opening night, my darling!'

Who's she hugging? Alex wondered. Him or

me? He didn't mind. As always, the sibling relationship fascinated him. Susannah and Michael were always giggling and whispering together. More like lovers than brother and sister, Alex often thought. The undivided attention they paid to each other frequently excluded even their own spouses.

Alex didn't mind at all; he found it very interesting. Not so Priscilla, Michael's wife. On one of their early meetings, when Alex made a jocular remark about sibling flirtation Priscilla's attack had been ferocious.

'How dare you?' she hissed. 'What a disgusting thing to say!' There was a moment's silence while Alex remained staring at her, then she covered, primly. 'You television people might find that sort of comment funny but I think it's smutty and highly unnecessary.'

She'd sailed out of the room, grateful that no one else had witnessed her outburst while Michael and Susannah remained whispering in the corner, oblivious.

Alex wondered whether Priscilla's obvious jealousy was grounded on more than just their exclusion of her. I wonder if Susannah and Michael have been lovers? he thought. Maybe they still are.

As fascinating as the prospect was, Alex doubted it. Susannah and Michael's conspiracy obviously sprang from childhood. And childhood in the Wright family would have meant total father dominance aided and abetted by mother, leaving the children with just each other.

Whatever the cause and whatever the extent, the force of their love for each other was impossible to hide and, Alex decided, compelling to watch. And if Michael's impending arrival spurred

Susannah on to greater heights, all the better.

He kissed her, then spanked her bottom lightly. 'Freshen the make-up, interval's over.'

As he spoke there was a tap on the door and the ASM's voice. 'Stand by for Act Three, Miss Wright.'

Alex had finished giving the cast and stage management their notes and most of them had left the theatre to dine. Susannah, who never ate prior to a performance, was resting in her dressing room.

There was a tap on the production office door and Mavis appeared. 'A call for Miss Wright has come through on the box office phone, Mr Rainford.'

'That's all right, Mavis, you can have it put through to her dressing room. She's only resting.' Susannah never slept prior to a performance.

Mavis stepped inside the office and closed the door behind her mysteriously. 'I thought I'd better check with you before I did,' she said. 'We wouldn't want Miss Wright upset before the opening unless it was absolutely necessary, would we?'

'No, we certainly wouldn't.' Alex rose from his desk and smiled agreeably, glad that he hadn't alienated the woman with his previous irritation. In her colourless way she reminded him a little of his mother and, just like his mother, she had an underlying strength and tenacity which could be very useful if channelled in his direction.

'It's Westmead Hospital on the phone, you see,' Mavis continued. 'There's been some sort of accident involving a member of Miss Wright's family. They wouldn't tell me any more than that but I thought you might wish to speak to them.'

'Thank you, Mavis.' She handed him a piece of paper with the telephone number on it and left.

The way the sister at the hospital broke the news was quite brutal, Alex thought. A forced landing had gone wrong at Bankstown Airport. Michael had received extensive brain damage and was in a coma.

'Frankly, Mr Rainford, it would be advisable for your wife to get to the hospital as soon as possible; her brother doesn't have much time.'

'But . . . how did it happen?' Alex was confused, trying to buy time. 'He's an extremely experienced pilot.'

'Something to do with faulty landing equipment, I believe,' Sister Tresize replied busily. There was a slight trace of 'this isn't part of my job' in her voice and then she continued efficiently with the part that was. 'As your wife was the nearest of kin in Sydney I thought it best she be contacted first. Do you want the hospital to inform Mr Wright's—'

'No,' Alex said. His mind was in gear now. What a bastard it all was. These things did happen, of course, but what bloody awful timing. 'No, we'll tell his wife and his parents.'

'Very well.'

'Will he regain consciousness?' Alex asked hastily before Sister Tresize hung up.

'Oh no. I'm afraid that's quite impossible.'

Alex went straight around to the front-of-house office. Mavis seemed to be expecting him. She put aside the correspondence files she'd been working on and awaited his orders. Her face registered concern when he told her the news but she didn't utter a word.

'They say he won't regain consciousness for a very long time, if ever,' Alex finished. He neglected to add that they also said he could die at any moment.

'I see.' Mavis waited long enough to be sure Alex had nothing further to add. 'I take it you don't think we should say anything to Miss Wright until after the performance.'

'Well . . .' He left it hanging.

'I agree. We can't afford another cancelled opening.'

Alex had expected Mavis to take some convincing. My God, she's lethal, he realised, rather taken aback.

He was right. In her own domain Mavis was a force to be reckoned with. She'd been running the theatre's front of house for nearly twenty years. She'd seen producers, directors, playwrights and actors come and go, and not for one minute had she questioned or interfered with their artistic policies. But when it came to the box office, front of house and general staff management she expected equal consideration. The clockwork running of the theatre was totally her concern.

'It's only a matter of several hours, after all,' she continued, 'and if her brother is not going to regain consciousness during that time, I think we should delay the news.'

'Right.' Alex breathed an inward sigh of relief. 'If the hospital should ring again . . .'

'I'll have all calls transferred to me here and I'll keep you informed,' she nodded. Alex turned to go. 'That poor young man,' Mavis said, and there was genuine sympathy in her voice. Then she returned to her desk and picked up her correspondence files. The show must go on.

As Alex passed by the greenroom on the way to Susannah's dressing room he heard the early edition television news: '. . . *Bankstown Airport . . . steered the aircraft off the runway to avoid a group of maintenance workers.*'

'Evening, boys.' Alex nodded a greeting to the four stage hands who were eating pizza and watching the news on the greenroom set.

'. . . *the identity of the heroic young pilot has not yet been released pending notification of his family,*' the newsreader continued. There was a distant shot of an unidentifiable body being carried away on a stretcher by paramedics. '. . . *he remains in a critical condition.*'

Out of the corner of his eye Alex saw Susannah come out of her dressing room down the corridor. She started walking towards the greenroom.

He rushed to meet her. 'I thought you were resting,' he said and he embraced her.

'I wanted to take my mind off things,' she answered. 'I thought I might have a cup of tea with the boys and watch the news.'

'It's half over,' murmured Alex as he kissed her neck, 'and I know a much better way to take your mind off things.'

One minute later they were on the floor of Susannah's dressing room. They'd removed only the barest essentials of clothing. In the full-length mirror, Alex watched Susannah's silk dressing gown billowing about her as she opened her thighs to him.

She moaned as she lifted her pelvis and drew him into her and she continued to moan gently with each thrust. Alex, watching in the mirror, knew she was using him, knew she was luxuriating in the feel of him. It was a sexual massage, her way of relaxing, and the sight of her in the mirror and the awful secret of her brother combined to excite him to the point where he found himself fighting to preserve his control. Susannah's moans quickened and finally evaporated in a contented sigh of fulfilment. Not a moment too soon, thought Alex, as he let himself go with a strangled cry of relief.

'Now that's what I call unwinding,' Susannah said and she stretched languidly. 'Maybe we should include that in a regular opening night relaxation routine?'

'Suits me.' Alex grinned and zipped up his trousers. 'And now I'll get you that cup of tea.'

As Alex stepped out of the shower, he heard Susannah on the telephone. 'Yes, thank you. As soon as he gets in tell him his sister rang.'

Susannah opened the bathroom door. 'Michael hasn't arrived at the Hilton yet.'

'Well, maybe he's not staying at the Hilton this time.' Alex towelled himself vigorously.

'He always stays at the Hilton. Anyway, Priscilla rang and made a booking.'

'Do my back for me, will you, sweetheart?' Alex handed her the towel.

'He might have thought it was a bit of a rush trying to get to the hotel and then on to the theatre,' Susannah said thoughtfully as she dried Alex's back. 'Maybe he's decided to come straight from the airport.'

'Maybe.' Alex changed as quickly as he could. 'I'd better get out there and prepare to mingle,' he said. 'I can't come backstage at interval—we're laying on Dom in the manager's office for the VIPs. Not that you will need any favours bought from the critics, my darling.' He kissed her gently. 'Your Hedda is magnificent.' Then he kissed her again. 'Be wonderful and have fun.'

Susannah nodded gratefully and smiled. 'You too.' As he was about to close the door she added, 'You look great in your evening drag.'

It was the biggest, most glamorous, and most important opening night Alex had experienced since *I, Me and Us*. He was fully aware that the buzz in the air was due to the massive publicity, the sympathy for Susannah and the morbid curiosity about whether she'd be able to make it through the gruelling performance the day after her collapse. But it renewed his taste for the spectacular. Enough middle of the road, he vowed. His next show would be new, dangerous and exciting. It would be a Rainford/Oldfellow blockbuster. He couldn't wait for his meeting with Julian at Harold's next week.

'Excuse me, Mr Rainford.' Mavis smiled apologetically and Alex excused himself to the wealthy investor, signalling for the waiter to refill the man's glass. It was interval, the Dom was flowing freely and Acts One and Two had been splendid.

'Yes, Mavis.'

'I wouldn't interrupt if I didn't think it was absolutely essential, Mr Rainford, I hope you—'

'Yes, I realise that, Mavis.'

'The hospital rang during Act One to see where Miss Rainford was and I told them she would be there as soon as she possibly could.'

'Fine, that's fine,' he said encouragingly.

'But they rang again only a few minutes ago to say that they don't expect him to last long. Oh dear,' Mavis fretted, obviously riddled with guilt, 'we'll have to tell her, Mr Rainford.'

'No, we won't, Mavis.' He put a steadying hand on her arm.

'But . . .' Mavis left her objection hanging.

And then Alex said the words she wanted to hear. 'I'll take full responsibility.'

'Very well, Mr Rainford.'

As she left Alex made a beeline for Myra Nielson. Myra's starting to look her age just a little, he thought. Well, hell, who could blame her—she must be close to fifty by now. Still a good-looking woman, though, and more powerful than ever. He wondered whether he should renew their sexual acquaintance—that is, if she wanted to, if she wasn't sharing her favours exclusively with women these days.

'Myra, how nice to see you.' Alex was pleased to note that she was in the company of a young man.

'Alex! What a triumph. You must be very proud.' Three years off sixty, Myra was certainly not exclusive in the granting of her sexual favours. She was as rapacious as ever and, while her escort went in search of a waiter to refill her glass, she made an assignation with Alex for the following week. 'We have so much to catch up on, don't we?' Her smile said it all.

The performance continued as triumphantly as it had started. Susannah went from strength to strength, taking the rest of the cast with her as the play built towards its climax.

There was an audible gasp as the gunshot rang out. Neville, Harold and Rosie rushed to the alcove and Neville flung aside the curtains.

TESMAN

Shot herself! Shot herself in the temple!
Fancy that!

BRACK

Good God!—People don't do such things.

Several seconds of silence followed Harold's final line. Then the applause broke out. It was deafening.

Sections of the audience had already got to their feet during the curtain calls, but when Susannah walked down centre stage to join the cast, there was a complete standing ovation.

As the cries of 'Bravo' were at their loudest, Alex felt a hand on his arm and the familiar, 'Excuse me, Mr Rainford'.

He was standing at the back of the stalls near one of the exits and he silently followed her out into the foyer.

'They're on the telephone again,' Mavis whispered. 'They want to speak to either you or Miss Wright and they won't leave a message.' Her face was white with guilt. 'I think—' She couldn't complete the sentence.

Mavis was right. And Sister Tresize was more brutal than ever. 'Tell Miss Wright her brother died fifteen minutes ago, in case she's interested.' Sister Tresize was good at her job, but public relations wasn't her strong suit.

Alex instructed her not to move the body, and told her that Susannah would be there within half an hour. Then he mingled with the critics, investors and general well-wishers for ten minutes. Enough time for Susannah to take off her make-up and shower and change. She never accepted visitors to her dressing room, preferring to meet them in the greenroom or bar.

Susannah was ready and waiting for him when he went backstage. The moment he opened the dressing room door her mouth was upon his. The kiss was hungry, demanding. She barely noticed his passive response as she broke the embrace.

'I told you it'd be a wonderful opening night, darling. It was, wasn't it? It felt marvellous. Are they all raving about it?' Susannah babbled in her excitement.

'Oh yes, they're all gathered in the bar waiting for you.'

'Then what are we doing here?' She grabbed her evening bag.

'I don't think you'll want to see them when you hear the news,' Alex said.

'Where's Michael? Did he get here in time for the Act One curtain? What news?'

'It's about Michael, actually.' Alex took a deep breath. There really was only one way to say it. 'There's been a very bad accident, Susannah. Michael's plane crashed on landing.'

Alex had never seen blood drain from someone's face so quickly. One minute flushed pink with excitement, the next white as a ghost. Fascinating.

'He died half an hour ago.'

What followed was a nightmare. The dash to Westmead Hospital, the icy reception from Sister

Tresize and her staff, the hysterical telephone calls to Queensland. Only one thing remained clear in Susannah's mind: the sight of Michael's dead face upon the crisp, white hospital linen.

His head was covered when they arrived and Sister Tresize had to draw back the sheet. Why did they do that? Susannah wondered. I could have pretended he was asleep. Despair flooded through her whole being. Oh, dear God, just for a few seconds I could have pretended he was asleep. Michael certainly looked as though he was asleep. There wasn't a mark on him and his face was peaceful in repose. Tears coursed down Susannah's face as she stroked his cheek and gently kissed him on the lips. 'I love you, my darling.' She wasn't sure whether she whispered it or whether she thought it but it didn't matter.

Sister Tresize, standing a discreet distance away by the door, watched Susannah kiss her brother. For the first time in many years, she was shocked. The poor woman hadn't been told, she realised. She looked at the husband who seemed fascinated by the face upon the white sheet. Michael Wright had been in a coma for three hours before he died and the husband hadn't said anything.

Sister Tresize had seen many strange reactions to death in her twenty-five-year nursing career and she thought she'd inured herself to them all but the cool detachment of this man was something new. It was shocking.

Alex sensed the woman looking at him and glanced briefly in her direction. She certainly wasn't the waspish creature he'd expected. She was a handsome, healthy, buxom woman in her early forties, actually very attractive. But he returned to the more interesting spectacle of Susannah's bedside performance and her brother's dead face.

How beautiful he is in death, Alex marvelled. A boy's face flashed through his mind: Tim. Yes, Tim had also been beautiful in death. Not as beautiful as Michael, though. Michael's face was the face of a hero: manly, handsome, gallant. Alex felt a rush of affection for Michael. Michael had died a heroic death, the reports said. He'd knowingly risked his life to save others. Alex felt happy for him.

ACT III

SCENE 2: 1982

'You knew, didn't you?' They'd been home from the hospital for two hours and there'd been more lengthy phone calls to Queensland, namely to Susannah's mother who seemed the only one capable of maintaining a conversation. Both Priscilla and Franklin Wright had gone under.

'The hospital told Mummy that they rang the theatre hours before Michael died and that you said you'd ring the family.' Susannah was no longer hysterical. She'd had several hefty Scotches, the sedative Alex had given her twenty minutes before was starting to take effect, and he'd finally persuaded her to lie down. For the moment her grief was numb. But it would be back tomorrow, and the next day, and the day after that. She felt exhausted.

'I wondered why that woman was so cold when we got to the hospital. How long had you known?'

Alex looked at her sympathetically but he didn't reply.

'How many hours, Alex? Did you know when we were fucking on the dressing room floor?'

He nodded.

'Oh my God!' She didn't have enough strength left in her to feel rage but the tears threatened to come again.

Alex knelt beside her. He didn't attempt to touch her but his face was close to hers. 'Listen to me, Susannah. They said he would never regain consciousness. He wouldn't have known whether you were there or not. You had an opening night. You had a thousand people waiting to see you. What was I supposed to do?'

Susannah's eyes, now barely able to focus, looked at him.

'I hoped he wouldn't die before you could get there,' Alex continued, 'I really did.'

A glimmer in Susannah's eyes told him that he'd made contact.

'What else could I do, Susannah? What else could I do?'

As Susannah's mind slipped into unconsciousness she was aware of only one thing that truly appalled her. She understood! She understood so well that if the situation had been reversed she knew she would have done the same thing herself. She was appalled at the callous attitude of the theatre, she was appalled that 'the show must go on', and she was appalled that the next night would see her up on that stage. The only sensation that remained as she passed out was one of utter self-loathing.

Michael's heroic death made headlines the next day, as did Susannah's heroic insistence she perform.

'No, I'm not being particularly brave,' she was quoted as saying. 'Performing *Hedda Gabler* is the only thing that's keeping me going.'

It was perhaps the one completely true statement she'd made to the press in a very long time, Susannah thought listlessly. But then she'd lost sight of what was real and what wasn't long before. Michael was probably the only thing that had ever been real in her life. He was certainly the only person who had ever known the real her, Susannah was convinced of that.

Alex stood quietly and supportively by his wife's side during the brief press interviews he allowed. He was quick to whisk her away when he sensed she'd had enough and he didn't participate in the interviews himself. What was the point, after all? Susannah was far more effective left on her own.

Her Hedda was not quite the same, Alex thought, after seeing the next few performances, and it probably never would be. It was technically flawless but there was a spark missing which was hardly surprising. Not that it really mattered. No one else noticed and the entire season was booked out.

Alex was wrong. Someone else had noticed. Maddy had noticed.

Maddy hadn't seen Susannah since NADA, twelve years before. Enough time for changes, certainly, but not this drastic, she thought. Where was the vivacious Susannah Wright? The craftsmanship of the actress onstage was undeniable but where was the electricity and charm which had always been Susannah's trademark? And she looked so ill! Susannah had always been thin, but now she was positively emaciated. The make-up didn't disguise the dark rings under her eyes and even her glorious titian hair had lost its lustre. Her recent family trauma couldn't be solely responsible for such a change, surely.

Maddy was fully aware of the turn of events. She and Jenny had arrived in Sydney the day after Michael's death. She'd read about the accident in the press and her mother, still an avid devotee of the theatre, had told her of Susannah's previous troubles—her collapse and the cancellation of the original opening night. Poor Susannah, Maddy thought. She would have got in touch if Susannah hadn't been married to Alex. Any contact with Alex was unthinkable.

Despite her dread of bumping into Alex, Maddy hadn't been able to resist coming to the show. She was keen to see not only the faces from her past, but Susannah's performance of Hedda. *Hedda Gabler* was a role Maddy had always longed to play.

Strange, she thought. Susannah and I were constant rivals at drama school and now here she is, not only playing Hedda but married to Alex. Maddy felt no envy. Far from it. She felt an overwhelming pity for Susannah and a flood of relief at her own escape. Suddenly she wished Douglas was with her.

Maddy hadn't dared tell Jenny she was going to the theatre. 'Going to see some old friends,' was what she'd said, which wasn't really a lie. But she'd had to promise to take Jenny out the next day.

'The movies or the theatre?' Maddy had asked. Silly question.

'The theatre, of course.' Jenny didn't care which theatre. Maybe we'll go to Julian's play, Maddy thought.

As she sat back and watched Susannah and Harold and Rosie Lee, Maddy found herself overwhelmed by a bittersweet nostalgia. Those wonderful days seemed so long ago.

Dear Harold. He was looking old now. Well, he'd have to be in his mid to late seventies. He was still a marvellous actor. Much as she longed to see them, Maddy hadn't yet made up her mind as to whether or not she would contact Julian and Harold. She decided not to think about it until after she'd seen Julian's play and she spent most of the interval casting furtive glances around the foyer from behind a potted palm. Alex was nowhere to be seen, thank goodness.

As soon as the performance was over Maddy ducked out of the main entrance and into the chilly night air. She felt quite safe, as the stage door was around the other side of the block. But nevertheless she kept in the shadows until she saw a vacant taxi approaching.

She stepped out to hail it and collided with a man who had just crossed the street and was hurrying past the theatre entrance.

'Oh,' she gasped, 'I'm terribly—' She looked at him for only the briefest moment before dropping her eyes in the pretence of fumbling with her handbag.

It was Alex. 'That's all right.' He flashed her an automatic smile and continued walking.

Maddy didn't dare look up until she'd seated herself in the taxi. Then, from the safety of the shadows, she turned just in time to see him round the corner of the block on his way to the stage door.

For one split-second Alex had looked directly into her eyes. And he hadn't recognised her.

'Kirribilli, please.' Maddy closed the taxi door and leaned back, aware that her pulse was racing. His smile, although a token courtesy to a stranger in the street, had been pure Rainford. Dazzling, magnetic. And she was shaken by the effect it had had on her.

'Good show tonight?' Alex accepted the glass of port Harold offered him. When he was performing Harold never drank during the day but he always kept a bottle of port in his dressing room and allowed himself two medicinal nips. One before the show and one during interval. 'Essential for the voice,' he insisted.

'Oh yes, excellent,' he replied as he cold-creamed his face. 'Packed house, good audience. Where were you? You're usually in on a Friday.'

'Had to chat up a prospective investor,' Alex answered. 'Now hurry it up. Julian'll be waiting for us.'

'Don't rush me. He has a key to the flat, he can let himself in. I don't like to be rushed.' But Harold was loving it. His darling boy was bossing him around, and he was about to cook supper for his two dear boys and to reunite them in their friendship. He rather hoped Alex felt a twinge of jealousy at the fact that Julian had a key to the flat.

Alex hadn't even heard Harold. His mind was on Myra. He hadn't been lying when he'd said he had to chat up a prospective investor. After they'd made love he and Myra had talked avidly about joining forces in another venture. She'd been fascinated to hear that Alex was planning to produce Julian's next play.

'He doesn't know it yet,' Alex grinned, 'but he will by the end of the evening. We're having supper together.'

Myra smiled back. One couldn't help but admire Alex's cocky confidence. And he was as attractive as ever—possibly more so. The cheeky laughter lines which used to disappear as the smile faded now remained there. They had become character grooves, and gave his face an added strength. How old would he be? she wondered. Thirty-one? Thirty-two? Yes, he was aging magnificently.

As for sex, it was the same battle royal between them. From the moment they entered the bedroom it was obvious that both had decided to take the first game. Neither had won; it had been a draw. But Myra had only just managed to stay the pace. My God, this is exhausting, she thought, as they galloped towards their mutual climax. I can't make a regular habit of this—I'm too old.

She'd never contemplated herself feeling 'too old' for anything. Certainly nothing sexual. But over the last few years Myra had realised that concessions did have to be made. The lighting certainly had to be softer, mirrors had to be strategically placed to cover flattering angles and, most important of all, there was to be no riding on top unless it was in the dark.

Myra remembered with vivid clarity the large,

black lacquered, glass-topped coffee table and the young man stretched out on it. She was astride him and riding home when she caught sight of herself in the table's surface. She had three chins and looked seventy. It was a terrible shock. The biggest shock of all was the face of the twenty-six-year-old looking back at her. My God, he's seeing that, she realised, and it put her completely off her stride. She never rode on top again.

Maybe she really was getting old, Myra thought, as she decided with a certain sense of relief, that Alex should be yet another sexual concession. She'd made it through the final round tonight. While the scores were even, she could withdraw from the Rainford-Nielson sexual stakes.

Besides, Alex had far more to offer than sex. Myra couldn't wait to work on another production with him.

Alex was thinking along exactly the same lines. He was thrilled that Myra wanted to be in on the deal. It practically guaranteed him investment from the private quarter. And of course it was the added carrot to dangle in front of Julian.

To keep in favour he was even prepared to concede a draw in round one of the sexual battle: as he sensed Myra starting to tire, he timed himself perfectly. It was a small price to pay.

'Myra Nielson's really hot on the idea, Julian.'

'What idea? There isn't even a script.' They had finished Harold's excellent supper and were sipping the last of the red wine and nibbling at the huge wedge of Brie Harold had placed in the centre of the table.

'But there will be, won't there?' Alex leaned

forward enthusiastically. 'There will be a script. There's something in your mind already, isn't there?'

Damn it, how can he read me so well? Julian felt a flash of annoyance. Alex was quite right. Despite the fact that he'd tried to distance himself, Julian had found Alex to be yet again a source of inspiration. As thrilling as his idea was, though, he was fighting to resist it, fighting to resist Alex's encouragement.

Alex read the irritation in Julian's eyes and chastised himself. There's something going on in that head, don't let him know that you know or he'll close up. 'And with Myra behind us we're laughing.' Keep it general, he warned himself. 'Not only are we in front with the private investors but the press too. She's more powerful than ever, Julian. Just think . . .'

As Alex started to paint the mammoth production he had in mind—the theatres he'd book, the promotion campaigns he'd mount, the prime tour circuit he'd plan—the beginnings of a play germinated in Julian's mind.

It had started from the moment he'd arrived at Harold's flat. He hadn't wanted to come. David had moved out two days ago and he'd been depressed ever since. Somehow, unreasonable as it might be, he blamed Alex for the split and as a result he'd been determined to keep his distance tonight. He didn't want to get drawn into chats about old times with him; he was there purely as a favour to Harold.

'I was sorry to hear about Susannah's brother,' he said. 'She must have been tremendously upset.' Well, that part was easy; he had been genuinely moved and had written Susannah an extremely touching letter.

'She was. She loved your letter. Thanks.'

Harold looked up from the salad he was tossing. 'She's still an absolute mess, poor dear. Thank God she's got me and Rosie to look after her.'

Julian nodded sympathetically. 'And after being so terribly ill herself.'

'Oh, that part was staged.' Julian looked confused and Alex glared at Harold who continued with gay abandon. 'Didn't you know? Alex built that up to epic proportions in order to buy an extra twenty-four hours. The press loved it.' Harold didn't draw breath as he turned to Alex. ' "Fie, fie, unknit that threat'ning unkind brow"—we don't keep secrets from Julian.' He finished tossing the salad and tipped some bread rolls into a wicker basket. 'The terrible thing is, the press loved the news of poor Michael's death even more. One of you boys open the Henschke please.' Harold took the bread and salad to the table. 'The show could run for a year.'

Julian felt a slight but familiar tingle at the back of his spine as he looked at Alex.

'It's ghastly, isn't it,' Harold continued, 'to think that the more macabre the publicity, the greater effect it has.'

Alex sensed Julian's interest and the irritation he'd felt towards Harold disappeared immediately, along with the original idea of playing for respect and understanding as Susannah's stalwart husband.

'Poor Susannah,' he said as he started opening the wine. 'She didn't know. All through the performance she didn't know.' And Julian sat enthralled as Alex told the story, clinically and

304

without embellishment, of Michael's death.

Once again, the power Alex had over people riveted Julian and, hard as he tried to ignore it, his fascination grew as the evening progressed.

There were frivolous moments, mainly provided by Harold who was basking in the company of his two favourite young men and delighting in the fact that he had successfully forged their reunion. But, ironically, it was one of Harold's theatrical anecdotes which finally ignited the spark in Julian.

It was one of his Noel Coward stories and Julian had heard it before. The one where an irritating person accosted Coward in the street and accused him of being a fairy.

' "A fairy!" he said . . .' Harold pursed his lips, put one hand on his hip and, with the other, flourished an imaginary umbrella. He tapped Julian on the shoulder with his 'wand'. ' "Then vanish!" ' And he sat down with a hearty laugh.

Vanish. The word hung magically in the air for Julian. That's what Alex did to people, he thought. Alex made people vanish.

All those years ago at NADA Jonathan Thomas had vanished. Then Maddy's baby had vanished. Perhaps Alex hadn't meant Maddy herself to go but it would probably only have been a matter of time before she became a hindrance. He certainly hadn't missed her for long.

Now Michael Wright had vanished. And there appeared to be no reason for his disappearance other than it served Alex's purpose.

And of course David had vanished. Julian refused to admit that it would probably have happened without Alex's influence. Alex had said that the affair would last no more than a year. That was the distance he'd allowed them and that was the distance they'd lasted. No more, no less. Just like the others, David had been willed out of existence.

What a wonderful character for a play, Julian thought, as the idea grew chillingly in his mind. A conjurer. A man who willed people to disappear. Sometimes they died, sometimes they just went away. But, whatever the turn of events, they simply ceased to exist in the conjurer's sphere.

Julian knew there was no turning back. The play was there.

Harold had been well and truly infected with Alex's excitement at the prospect of another joint venture. 'Another *I, Me and Us*,' he exclaimed. 'That'd set them all on their ears!'

'No. Bigger than *I, Me and Us*, Harold. Much bigger. An international hit—one that'll sell to the West End.'

Julian was staring fixedly at the table. He could see the bare stage. Two small boys. Brothers. That was the beginning. One of them wants to be an only child like his best friend down the street who gets twice as many presents as he does. He dares his brother to do something. Something dangerous. The brother accepts the dare and is killed. It is the first successful vanishing act.

'Some more Brie?' Harold had noticed Julian staring at the cheese.

'No.' Julian rose to his feet. 'No thank you, Harold. I'm sorry, but I won't stay for coffee. It was a great supper. Thanks.'

As he walked to the door, Alex called after him. 'Shall we meet next week?' When Julian shook his head, Alex smiled benignly. 'That's all right, you do the writing. I'll work on the rest.'

'Give me three weeks.' Julian opened the front door. 'Three weeks and I'll have your first draft.' And he closed the door behind him.

The moment Julian had gone, Alex jumped up and hugged Harold. 'Did you hear that, Harold? I'll have my play in three weeks. In three weeks!'

And Harold was very happy for his darling boy. He was very happy for both his darling boys as he went off to the kitchen to fetch the coffee and brandy.

Alex didn't get home until three o'clock in the morning. Apart from a sleepy grunt of acknowledgement Susannah didn't notice. But then Susannah didn't notice anything lately.

Alex tried to be kind to her. Tried to help her through her period of mourning, but to no avail. She seemed to prefer him keeping out of her way. The only time she showed any animation was when she was on stage. Any topic Alex brought up for conversation was met with a listless shrug of indifference and even the prospect of another play with Julian failed to arouse her interest. She never left the house and she refused all invitations.

Alex was actually glad when she knocked back Harold's invitation to supper. It would be easier for him to work on Julian. But he was annoyed when she steadfastly refused to join him at the ski chalet on Sunday.

'It's just the break you need, Susannah. You need to get out of Sydney for a couple of days. The Claytons are coming up early Sunday morning and we'll be back in time for you to rest before the Monday performance.'

There was the usual shrug of indifference. 'I

can't stand the Claytons. I can't stand any of that trendy après-ski set.'

'Then I'll stay in town and we'll go up together on the Sunday, for Christ's sake.' But he couldn't budge her. Finally, he gave up in disgust. 'Bugger it, what's the point!' And he left for Thredbo first thing Saturday morning. The reports of early falls were excellent, it was the first weekend of the season and he was damned if he was going to miss out on the break he'd planned for weeks.

Hell, other entrepreneurs had their boats or their racehorses or their bloody polo ponies—all he asked was his several weekends at the snow during the winter months.

Alex's love of skiing and the chalet life in general had been a major expense over the past several years. It was only recently that he'd curbed his European trips and settled for the local resorts. Not for much longer, though, he decided. Next year it'll be Europe again. Switzerland or Austria? Hell, why not be different? Maybe Scotland this time. And maybe I'll take Julian with me.

Alex spent the afternoon on the slopes of Crackenback and was ensconced in the chalet bar at around seven-thirty pm.

At eight o'clock he excused himself from the pretty twenty-three-year-old with the promise in her eyes. He took himself off to the restaurant to dine alone. The Claytons were very wealthy, very reliable investors. The Claytons were also star-fuckers who worshipped Susannah and Alex and dined out on the intimate friendship they maintained with the dynamic duo of the theatre. The last thing Alex needed when the Claytons arrived tomorrow was a snow-bunny on his arm.

'Not much of a house for a Saturday night,' Jenny commented as she looked critically around the auditorium.

'Yes. Sad, isn't it?' Maddy answered, keeping a wary eye out for anyone she might know, particularly Julian.

'Maybe it's not much of a play,' Jenny said with all the ruthlessness of an eleven-year-old.

'Jen!' Maddy couldn't help smiling but she defended Julian just the same. 'I told you, I know the playwright.'

'Doesn't mean it's a good play though, does it?'

'No, it doesn't. You're right. But let's reserve our judgement till we've seen it, shall we?'

'OK.'

'I like it,' Jenny said at interval. 'Well, so far I like it.'

'Yes,' Maddy agreed. 'It has its moments.'

'Can I get to meet him?'

'Who?' But Maddy knew who she meant.

'The playwright.'

'I told you, Jen, he's not here. I've been looking.'

'But you could ring him—the theatre would know where he is. We could meet him tomorrow.'

'All right, all right. Now do you want to go to the loo? There's another five minutes.' Jenny shook her head. 'Then let's go back for Act Two.'

It wasn't the first time Jenny had asked about people from her mother's past. Ever since they'd arrived in Sydney the requests had been continual.

Relatives had been an easy answer for the first

week but now Helena and her family and Todd Hall and his weren't enough. Not that Helena and Todd hadn't been highly successful. They had. Maddy had been delighted with the instantly established rapport. Helena refused to be called 'grandma', 'gran' or 'nanna' but she loved the role and, while her grandmother act was at times a little cloying, Jenny didn't mind. In fact the child seemed to realise unconsciously that Helena needed to play roles in order to justify her existence.

Helena hadn't changed much. Another harbourside home—Kirribilli this time. Another successful professional man—cardiologist this time. And another commitment to the role of society hostess and tireless charity worker.

'Only Variety Club and handicapped children these days,' she insisted. 'Oh, Maddy darling, I've changed radically—my whole life has changed radically. When I think how I frittered away my energies on meaningless charities when I could have devoted myself to my kiddies.'

The antique grandfather clock which had been in Todd's family for generations struck five.

'Oh, is that the time? Check there's plenty of ice and lift out the Glenfiddich will you, dear? Toddy'll be home in a minute.' And Helena started clearing up the endless mailing list she'd been working on for the Variety Club's Black and White Ball.

'Todd of Todd Hall' was a very nice man— a protestant version of Robert, really. A little less stitched-up but reserved nevertheless with a penchant for a well-ordered life and a pretty and supportive wife. Helena fitted the bill perfectly and they were very happy together. When they saw the sandy-haired little girl with the strong face, the direct grey-blue eyes and the even temperament, they quickly became doting grandparents.

Nevertheless, Helena was thrown when Jenny posed the question out of the blue. 'Did you know my father?'

While Helena fumbled for the answer, Maddy dived in. 'No, she didn't, really. Like I told you, he was a student at NADA and we weren't together for very long.'

'I was asking Helena, Mum.' Jenny wasn't being rude, Maddy realised, just her usual disconcertingly direct self. And she did, after all, deserve an answer. They all looked at Helena.

'Well . . .' Helena could barely remember Alex. 'He was very attractive, and . . . well . . .' It was no use. 'Your mother's quite right. I hardly knew him.'

Jenny turned to her mother. 'Is he here in Sydney? Are we going to see him?'

It was Maddy's turn to be thrown. 'I hadn't planned on it. Do you want to?'

Jenny shrugged. But it wasn't a diffident shrug. She was watching Maddy closely, realising that her mother had been unsettled by the question.

'Why the sudden interest?,' Maddy asked. 'You didn't seem to care one way or another when we were in England.'

'That's because we were in England.'

'Oh.'

'Would *you* like to see him, Mum?' The eyes didn't waver; they demanded to be met head-on.

Maddy did just that. 'No,' she said.

'Fair enough.'

Why did Maddy feel such a chill at the prospect

311

of seeing Alex? And what right did she have to deny the child a meeting with her father? She felt riddled with guilt. 'Maybe when you're a bit older, what do you think?'

Jenny had read her mother's guilt. 'Mum,' she said, 'I don't mind.' And then she smiled. 'Really!' And Maddy knew she was off the hook.

Jenny's queries about the past continued, though. She particularly wanted to hear about NADA and the people Maddy knew there. And now she wanted to meet Julian.

During the second act of the play Maddy's mind kept weighing heavily on whether or not she should seek Julian out and introduce him to her daughter. How close was he with Alex these days? Could she trust him with the secret of Jenny? Maddy was still pondering her decision at the end of the performance as they walked out of the auditorium into the foyer.

'I didn't like the second act as much as the first.' Jenny chatted away, oblivious to the fact that her mother wasn't really listening.

'Maddy?' A tall bony man with lank hair that fell across his brow was waiting for them beside the foyer door.

Maddy froze for a moment before she realised with a sense of relief that her decision had been made for her. Julian's eyes had flickered to Jenny and, when they returned to meet her own, there was a query in them. She nodded slightly. Julian now knew and she was glad.

'Julian! How lovely to see you.' And it was. She hugged him, forcing back the tears. 'This is my daughter, Jenny.'

312

Julian had called in to the theatre at interval. He hadn't intended to stay for the second act. Then he'd seen Maddy. She was looking about a little nervously as if she didn't want to be noticed. But surely by coming to the theatre she was hoping to make contact. Why the mystery? Why didn't she want to initiate the contact herself?

Then he'd looked at the child with her and he knew. The child was Alex Rainford's. He could tell not only by her physical appearance but, as he watched her in animated discussion with her mother, the girl's intensity—her very mannerisms— were Alex's.

He'd watched as Maddy gestured towards the women's toilets. He saw Jenny shake her head and then he watched as they returned to the auditorium. He followed, positioning himself in one of the many empty seats up the back and then he studied them as the lights started to fade. Maddy had changed. With her cropped blonde hair and her slim body she looked as young as ever but she'd matured. There was a womanliness about her now and it suited her.

Julian had slipped out into the foyer just before the curtain and waited for them, hoping that he was right about Maddy's desire to make contact. Why bring the child to the theatre if she hadn't been hoping subconsciously he'd be there? Now, as he hugged her, he knew he'd been right.

'Jen. This is Julian Oldfellow, the playwright.'

'Oh, great!' Jenny beamed. 'I was trying to nag Mum into letting me meet you.'

'What a good idea. She's been avoiding me altogether too much. How about lunch tomorrow? My place at Bondi?'

'Bondi Beach?'

Julian nodded.

'Wow! I've never been to Bondi Beach.'

Julian looked questioningly at Maddy, who laughed. 'All right! I can't take you both on.'

'I suppose a coffee now is out of the question?' Julian asked.

Maddy nodded firmly. 'It's past Jenny's bed-time.' But she accepted Julian's offer of a lift home.

As Jenny sat in the back seat and unwound the window to get a better view of the harbour lights, Julian murmured to Maddy, 'Can I ask Harold tomorrow, or would you rather I didn't?'

Maddy hesitated, then shook her head. 'Let's keep it just between ourselves for the moment, Julian. We'll talk about it tomorrow. I need your advice.' Julian nodded and Maddy called over to the rear seat. 'Stick your head back in the car, Jen.' They were crossing the Harbour Bridge now and Jenny was leaning out of the window to watch the arch of lights zooming by overhead. She pretended not to hear.

'I said now,' Maddy demanded. 'And close the window, it's cold.'

'Nag, nag, nag,' Jenny muttered. Julian and Maddy shared a smile.

Julian picked them up the next morning, telling them to bring some warm clothing for a walk along the beach.

There was the bite of winter in the air but the sky was blue and the air was clear when they arrived at Bondi. A steady stream of long white breakers rolled invitingly to the shore.

314

'Good day for the surfies,' Julian said. 'Look at them, the idiots. It'd be freezing out there.' At least two dozen wetsuit-clad surfboard riders were braving the waves, much to Jenny's delight.

Not long ago David would have been one of them, Julian thought, with a rush of nostalgia. Then he shook off the feeling. Don't be maudlin, he reprimanded himself—it's not healthy.

After dumping their gear at Julian's they walked for miles, Jenny skipping on ahead, indefatigable. So's Maddy, Julian thought, already aware of tomorrow's cramp in his calf muscles.

'Sure you don't want to call it a day?' he suggested for the fifth time and Maddy once again smiled as she shook her head.

'Not just yet.' She laughed at Julian's painful grimace. 'You're getting positively middle-aged, Julian. Just to the cemetery, I promise. Then we can sit and talk while Jenny explores. She loves cemeteries.'

They crested the hill and saw Waverley Cemetery ahead of them. Maddy sought a choice park bench where they could look back along the headlands to the view of Bondi in the distance and Jenny started her exploration of the headstones.

Julian sank gratefully onto the bench and, after regaining his breath, sat back, ignored the view and looked demandingly at her. 'Right. You want to dive straight in or do you need me to break the ice?'

Maddy shook her head gently, took a deep breath and plunged in. She told him about the doctor and the faked abortion; she told him about the rift with her father and her seedy life in London while she tried to carve a career for herself; she

315

told him about *Androgyne* and the start of her success. She spared no details and pulled no punches and the telling was a salve to her. For the past twelve years there'd been no one to whom she could bare it all.

Julian listened patiently, offering a smile of encouragement here and there. He laughed uproariously at the story of *Androgyne* and Rodney Baines.

'Stop it, Julian,' Maddy admonished, although she was grinning broadly herself. 'He's a lovely man and a very, very dear friend.'

'I'm delighted to hear it, Maddy. You could obviously do with one over there, it sounds like a bloody uphill battle.' But he kept chortling nevertheless. 'The dick that defies an ice bucket— I'll never be able to watch that film seriously again.' He dabbed at his eyes, the chill in the air and the tears of mirth were making them sting. 'I can't wait to tell Harold.'

Maddy's smile faded. 'I'm not sure if you should, Julian.'

'Why not? It's the sort of story he adores. Besides, he was mad about the film. Said it had shades of *Les Enfants du Paradis* about it; "just a tad short of a masterpiece", he said.' Julian noticed Maddy's sombre look and decided to joke her out of it. 'Mind you, he said he'd have liked a touch more vulgarity. "A touch more *La Grande Bouffe*," was what he said. He said,' and Julian struck a pose, ' "I feel cheated if I don't get any repulsive eating or furious fornicating scenes. The Europeans do all that salivating and slobbering so well".'

Julian burst out laughing at his excellent imitation of Harold. 'He didn't mean it, of course, he so loves playing the cantankerous old actor these days. He spends most of his afternoons lolling around eating chocolates and reading the *Bulletin*, *Time* and *Life* magazines because he says when you're fat and over seventy sex is out the window, so what else is there?' Julian grinned and shrugged. 'Just another aspect of the jaded aging actor image he likes to present—I don't think sex was ever that important to Harold, anyway.'

Maddy was still looking serious so Julian stopped camping it up. 'What's the matter, Maddy? What's worrying you?'

'I don't want Alex to know about Jenny.'

'I agree with you,' Julian nodded. 'And you can rely on me not to tell him.'

'But could I rely on Harold?'

Julian didn't answer.

'Are they as close as they used to be?' Maddy asked.

He nodded. 'As far as Harold's concerned, possibly even more so. He worships Alex.' Julian breathed a regretful sigh. 'You're right. Even if Harold swore on the Bible, you wouldn't be able to trust him, not in anything relating to Alex. A night of camaraderie, a good bottle or two of red under the belt, his love for Alex overshadowing everything . . .' Julian shrugged '. . . he wouldn't be able to resist reuniting you two and your beautiful child. He'd do it with the best of motives, of course, but . . .' Julian shrugged again.

Maddy nodded and they both turned to watch Jenny as she ran up the grassy slope towards them.

'How's it going, darling?' Maddy asked when the child arrived panting beside them.

'There are lots of children buried here,' Jenny said.

'Well, I guess there would be, it's a fairly big cemetery.'

'There's a Celia Dora who was twelve and a Thomas William who was thirteen and they were both born in 1886, and there's a six month old baby called William Norman with the most beautiful headstone: a white lamb with "Suffer little children to come unto me" written under it. It's right over the other side; do you want to come and have a look?'

'No thanks, sweetheart.' Maddy flashed a smile at Julian. 'I think we'd better preserve our strength for the walk back.'

'Do we have to go now?' Jenny looked disappointed.

'No, lunch'll keep,' Julian interrupted. Then he assured Maddy, 'I'm happy just sitting here. Really!' he insisted when she looked doubtful. 'And there's a lot more talking to be done. Believe me!'

'Off you go, Jen,' Maddy said. 'Take your time.

'I don't know why she's so interested in cemeteries,' she mused to Julian as Jenny skipped happily down the slope. 'She's not at all morbid and yet she seems to have this fascination with death. Weird.'

The two of them watched the child weaving her way through the tombstones.

'It's shocking of me, isn't it?' Maddy said eventually. It wasn't a question and Julian waited for her to continue. 'I don't have any right keeping the child from meeting her father.'

'Does she want to?'

Maddy nodded. 'Not obsessively though. I've told her I'll introduce them when she's a bit older.'

'I'd leave it till she's a *lot* older, if I were you.'

Maddy glanced at Julian, surprised. There was an uncharacteristic bitterness in his voice.

He didn't look at her for several moments while he made his decision and when he finally turned towards her it was with great urgency. 'Don't ever let her meet him, Maddy. If you can possibly help it, don't ever let him into her life.'

It took Julian a long time to tell Maddy everything he knew of Alex. He told as much of his story as objectively as he could, starting with Alex's childhood and the death of Tim. At the end of that segment he decided it was time to leave. It was a gruesome enough story without the headstones of little Celia Dora, Thomas William and William Norman looking on. Besides, the wind had sprung up and it was way past lunchtime.

After they had eaten, they settled Jenny in the study happily poring over Julian's endless array of books. Over coffee, Julian embarked upon the Jonathan Thomas saga.

He told it succinctly without embellishment but Maddy's face reflected her growing horror as she realised how Alex had used the erotic photographs. The photographs, which she had thought were such a personal and precious thing between the two of them, had also been the final straw for poor, sad, guilt-ridden Jonathan Thomas. She was sickened by the thought.

Julian ploughed on remorselessly and it was only when he had finished telling her about Michael Wright's death that he started losing control.

'I'm writing a play about it all, Maddy.' He was trying to keep it light but his voice was strained. '*The Conjurer*—good title, don't you think? About

319

a man who wills people to disappear from his life. And they do. Just like that.' Julian's control suddenly went out the window as he leaned forward in his chair, knuckles tightening around his coffee mug. 'That's what Alex does, Maddy, don't you realise? Alex makes people disappear.'

Julian stopped. He rose abruptly and crossed to the living room window where he remained staring out at the vine-covered patio. 'He repels me,' he admitted. 'But I can't seem to write without him. He knows it too. I think he's known it since that Friday night in the pub when he told me about his brother's death.'

Poor Julian, he's torturing himself, Maddy thought, as she listened to him recount his attempt to break free of Alex's influence, the failure of his next plays and now the ironic rebirth of his inspiration during Harold's supper party.

'Alex again, you see.' Julian was indeed tortured but he was never one for prolonged self-dramatisation. 'Jesus,' he said, turning to her with a wry grin, 'if Alex remains my muse I might well corner the market on black plays. Who knows, maybe I should be grateful.'

Maddy joined him at the window and together they looked out at the patio.

It was Julian who broke the silence. 'So, you see, you mustn't feel guilty about keeping Jenny away from him.'

'I know,' Maddy said. And she did know. She knew that Alex had revelled in the power he had had over her. Now he was obviously gloating in the power he had over Julian. Surely he would relish even more the power he would have over his own adoring flesh and blood. And Jenny would adore him, Maddy realised. Alex would make sure of that.

Maddy saw Julian regularly over the next three weeks before she and Jenny returned to England. Each meeting drew them even closer together. Sometimes they talked voraciously, sometimes they walked quietly along the beach at Bondi watching Jenny chase the waves, and sometimes they read through the latest pages of *The Conjurer*.

'Straight off the press,' Julian would say. 'First draft only—so don't be too cruel.'

'It's great,' Maddy would say after each read and each time she meant it.

'Well, it's only first draft,' Julian repeated, secretly thrilled and in total agreement, 'but yes, it's coming on quite well, isn't it?'

Then it was time for Maddy and Jenny to leave. Maddy insisted that family farewells take place at Kirribilli. She was aware that Helena's reluctance was a gesture only. It was a surgery day for Todd, after all, and the Black and White Ball was only a week away. There was so much to be done.

Julian took them to the airport. 'Why can't lovers be this close?' he asked and he held her to him. Then, as they both felt the prickle of tears, he wailed, 'Oh God, do I really have to turn straight?'

Maddy giggled. 'It wouldn't solve anything if you did.'

'Of course not.' Julian hugged her again. 'I hope he's right for you, Maddy.'

They'd talked a lot about Douglas Mackie. He hadn't rung once during Maddy's month-long holiday in Sydney. It had strengthened her resolve. Good, she thought. I'll get back to London and call it a day.

Then, twenty-four hours before she was due to fly home, the phone rang. It was Douglas. 'Sorry I couldn't call you. I was out of town on business.'

'What business?' she wanted to ask. Don't they have a telephone, these business associates?

'I've missed you,' he said. 'Very much.' That bloody Scots burr, Maddy cursed, going weak at the knees, thrilling to the sound of his voice. I bet he's laying it on thick deliberately, the shit. 'I'll be at the airport,' he said, and hung up.

'Yes, I hope he's right for me too, Julian,' Maddy said and she turned to go.

Jenny waved furiously but Maddy didn't look back as she walked into the customs lounge.

ACT III

SCENE 3: 1982–1984

Douglas Mackie wasn't at the airport. But Rodney Baines was.

'I know you told me not to bother,' he said. 'Douglas was picking you up and all that. But, face it, he's let you down more often than not in the past, hasn't he?' Rodney looked around meaningfully. He didn't approve of Douglas. Or rather he didn't approve of the way Douglas constantly deserted Maddy. He could see the hurt in her face so he didn't push the issue. 'Besides,' he added, 'I've missed you and I couldn't wait to see you.'

'Thanks, Rodney. You're a darling, and I've missed you too.' Bugger Douglas, she thought yet again.

The drive from Heathrow to London was magical. Late spring was always Maddy's favourite time of the year in England. Late spring and early autumn. It's good to be back, she thought.

Jenny was enjoying the drive too. Rodney had opened the sun roof for her and she had both back windows down.

'I love this car—this is my favourite car,' she declared. 'Sydney's a great place, Roddie, you'd love it.' And from then on she didn't stop.

As soon as they reached the outskirts of London, Jenny spent most of the time with her head out of the window, despite Maddy's admonitions.

'I love London,' she said. 'And now I love Sydney too. I don't know which one I love best.' Maddy knew exactly how she felt.

'Open the fridge, Jen,' Rodney said.

Maddy turned to the back seat and watched as Jenny opened the Jag's new, custom-made refrigerator. 'Oh, very fancy,' she said, and Jenny nodded agreement.

'Yes, I thought so,' Rodney smiled. There was a bottle of champagne and three icy cold glasses inside. 'Welcome home.'

'She's a big girl now,' he insisted as Maddy threw him a querying glance about the third glass. 'Eleven, for heaven's sake; she has to start experiencing the good life sooner or later.' He nodded at the bottle. 'Start opening. We'll have a quick cruise around.'

'She can have a quarter of a glass, then, no more,' Maddy agreed. Jenny shrieked with delight and they spent the next twenty minutes sipping champagne as they drove around the streets of London looking at their favourite views.

'You're setting a very bad example,' Maddy whispered to Rodney who was holding his glass out to her as they drove past Westminster Abbey.

'Yes, wonderful, isn't it?' he nodded. Then to Jenny. 'Did you know that the Houses of Parliament and Westminster Abbey are made from totally different coloured stone, Jen? Gold and dove-grey. Difficult to tell when they're all black with muck like this but you'll be able to see one day soon when they finish cleaning them up.'

He grinned as Maddy handed his glass back. 'I give up,' she muttered but she was deeply grateful to Rodney. It was taking her mind off Douglas Mackie.

Not for long. No sooner had they struggled up the stairs to Maddy's flat than the front door buzzer rang. 'Flowers for Miss MacLaughlan,' came the voice through the intercom system.

'Douglas, I'll bet,' said Rodney.

Of course he was right. There was a note with the flowers: *Sorry about the airport. Unavoidable. See you around eleven. Love, Douglas.* It was in the florist's handwriting and Maddy knew that he'd rung from 'out of town' and arranged for the flowers to be delivered an hour or so after her arrival home from the airport.

Douglas turned up shortly before midnight. By ten past twelve they were in bed clinging to each other and the rest of the world didn't exist.

So much for her good intentions, Maddy thought when she awoke the following morning and looked at Douglas sleeping beside her. So much for putting an end to the relationship and getting her life in order. She gazed at the face, so boyish in sleep, and knew that she loved him more than she'd ever thought possible.

What the hell, she decided. Douglas stirred. She kissed him and they made love again.

For the next year or so Maddy resigned herself to Douglas's disappearing acts and to the bizarre relationship she had with him. He insisted on keeping his flat, although when he was in London he invariably stayed at her apartment. He never once suggested they should live together and as a matter of pride Maddy resolved that she wouldn't either.

She decided instead to surrender herself to the love they had for one another and, fortunately, her career was galloping along at such a rate that she really didn't have time to contemplate any alternative anyway.

Jenny was twelve, going on thirteen, and happy at boarding school. Maddy had completed a very successful season of *Rashomon* for the 1983 Edinburgh Festival—Viktor Hoff directing her in the second stage production of his career.

'The Americans, poof . . .' Viktor had declared, as he made a rudely dismissive gesture, '. . . they do not want that I should crack their film market. Scared of the Hoff magic they are. European theatre, she is far more exciting.'

Indeed, his first production for the Black Theatre of Prague had been hugely innovative and a runaway success. 'Now I give Japan to Scotland,' he announced, 'with my little Aussie in the lead.'

It was a typical Viktor Hoff triumph. *Rashomon* was an American adaptation of an ancient Japanese legend and Viktor's production boasted an

Australian, a Scot and a Japanese playing the three leads. Against all odds, it worked—so much so that the production transferred to London.

While technical rehearsals for the London production were under way things began to go wrong with Douglas and Maddy.

It all started with the flour canister. When Maddy thought about it later the only remarkable thing may have been that she hadn't made the discovery earlier. Although not really. She'd stayed at Douglas's flat less than a dozen times in the three years they'd been together and never for any extended period. This time she was there for a whole weekend while her apartment was getting its long overdue paint job.

It was Sunday. Monday afternoon would see the final technical dress rehearsal for *Rashomon* and then the hard slog would begin. Douglas had another 'out of town' month coming up too, so Maddy decided to surprise him with a home-cooked seafood meal. At the Billingsgate Fish Markets she decided on the dover sole—one of his favourites: pan fried, lightly sprinkled with flour to make it go crispy on the outside. Finding the flour was the trouble. On the rare occasions they stayed at Douglas's it was dinner out or takeaway and he always cooked breakfast himself.

She found the flour canister oddly situated behind the rarely used spare saucepans. There was no flour in it. But there was a gun. A Heckler and Koch 9mm semi-automatic. Also in the canister was a full magazine. All ready to go. The gun looked shiny and lethal and well cared for. Maddy had never had anything to do with guns and she was shocked. But she wasn't surprised. Apprehensive, perhaps, but not surprised.

Douglas didn't appear shocked, surprised or apprehensive when she confronted him with it. He appeared disappointed. And weary—as though he really couldn't be bothered offering an explanation.

'I'm one of the good guys, Madeleine.' She kept staring at him. 'Honestly. You'll have to take my word for it.'

'One of what sort of "good guys"?'

'Call it military, if you like—that's my training.'

And Maddy had to be satisfied with that. She believed him. It pleased her to think that he wasn't tied up in some way with the underworld, a thought that had crossed her mind many a time during his mysterious disappearances. But she worried at the necessity of his carrying a gun.

'It's only a precaution,' he assured her. And again she had to be satisfied.

'So what am I supposed to do?' she wailed over the phone to Julian.

Julian was her lifeline; they took turns in ringing each other weekly. The bills were huge but it was worth it to both of them. Maddy didn't dare discuss Douglas with either Rodney or Viktor. Neither approved of the affair, both were overprotective and both had the same answer: 'Leave the man—he's not worth it.'

Other women had girlfriends they could share such things with, Maddy mused. The only girlfriend she had was Jenny, and one could hardly discuss one's lover with a twelve-year-old.

The weekly telephone link was equally as important

to Julian. *The Conjurer* had been every inch the success he had hoped it would be and now, six months after its Australian world premiere, he and Alex were fielding the first of a series of nibbles by British producers. But exciting and successful as his life had once more become, Julian's only true confidante was Maddy.

'You know what Alex said when he read the opening scene? The scene where the little boy deliberately dares his older brother to do something that he knows will kill him? He said, "It wasn't like that".' Maddy could practically feel Julian's shudder down the telephone wire. 'It was weird, Maddy, really weird. He was very cool, very calm: "It wasn't like that". And then he went on reading the play and when he'd finished he said it was possibly the best play he'd ever read.'

And now, six months after the Australian success, there was talk of *The Conjurer* coming to the UK.

'Another six months and I'll probably be in London. I can meet your man in the flesh,' Julian said. 'I'm sure I'll be able to give you better advice then. You know, when I can get the actual "vibes", all that sort of thing.'

'So what am I supposed to do in the meantime? He disappears for months on end and now I find he's got a gun! What am I supposed to do?'

'Be a good little gangster's moll and shut up about it.' (Julian didn't altogether believe the military story.)

'Oh, for God's sake, Julian . . .'

'Maddy,' he interrupted. 'You love the bloke, don't you?'

There was a pause on the end of the line, a

pause which spoke volumes to Julian. 'Exactly. So you may have picked a dud, but you'll just have to stick it out, won't you? I mean, you can try and talk yourself out of love with him but it doesn't really work that way, does it?'

'Get off the phone, Julian,' said Maddy in mock exasperation.

'Well, it doesn't, does it? Or so I'm told.'

'I said, get off the phone, Julian.'

'Speak to you next week, see you in six months,' he chanted and then he hung up.

Maddy laughed. A dose of Julian always did her good.

Things became complicated after the discovery of the gun. Maddy worried more when Douglas was away and Douglas became more secretive, possibly in an attempt to stop her worrying. It was a vicious circle and Maddy was definitely feeling the strain. Then the ghastly night of Jenny's thirteenth birthday pushed her close to breaking point.

It had promised to be such a lovely evening. Jenny was home from boarding school for the holidays. She and Douglas were going to go to Maddy's show and then the three of them were going out to supper.

Jenny hadn't yet seen *Rashomon* and she was very excited about it. She loved watching her mother work. She positively glowed with pride; every time she sat out front, she felt like turning around and announcing to the rest of the audience, 'That's my mother up there'. She told Maddy so. 'It's not just because you're my mother, though,' she warned, 'it's because you're very good. If you handed in a rotten performance I wouldn't feel the same way.'

330

'I should hope not,' Maddy said. It was true—Jenny's critical faculties were not to be sneered at. She'd spent her life surrounded by the theatre and Maddy valued her criticism. 'Do you want to come in and watch me make up? It's a two-hour job.' Jenny nodded. Try and stop her!

At five-thirty Jenny pulled up a chair, leaned on Maddy's dressing table and studied every step over the full two hours, fascinated. It was indeed an elaborate process. Viktor had called in two make-up experts to advise Maddy in the early days of the production. A special effects expert taught her how to get a hooded eyelid effect with latex and a Japanese expert drew up a chart for her and instructed her in the full classical Japanese make-up.

'Wow,' Jenny breathed, very impressed as Maddy rose, pressed her palms together and bowed. '*Kon-ban-wa*,' she said in a light breathless voice, her tiny bright red Cupid's-bow mouth barely moving, her eyes lowered.

'Wow!' Jenny said again.

'Wait till you see it with the kimono.'

As Maddy started undoing her robe there was a tap at the door.

Jenny took the large bouquet of flowers from the assistant stage manager and was surprised when she read the accompanying envelope. 'Hey, they're for me!' she said, taking out the card.

'Flowers for the birthday girl,' Maddy smiled. How sweet of Douglas, she thought.

'"Sorry, can't get there in time for the show. Meet you backstage afterwards. Happy birthday, Love, Douglas,"' Jenny read out.

Maddy didn't feel the customary mixture of

worry, hurt and disappointment. She felt angry. She didn't even bother looking at the note; she knew it would be in the florist's handwriting. She felt consumed with anger. How dare he! Letting her down was one thing. But this was Jenny's birthday! How dare he!

'Hey, Mum, calm down. It's no big deal.' It was strange to see her mother's eyes flashing behind the hooded lids and the flush of anger rising beneath the white makeup. 'Really. I don't mind.' And Jenny didn't. It was the show she wanted to see—it didn't matter who was sitting next to her.

Maddy slipped out of her robe. It might not matter to you, Jen, she thought, but it sure as hell matters to me. 'Give me a hand with the kimono,' she said.

Jenny was enthralled by *Rashomon*. Ten minutes into the play when the exquisite little Japanese lady arrived riding side-saddle on the white pony she forgot that this was her mother. She even forgot the stories Maddy had told her over the phone of the early previews in Edinburgh when the horse had shit during its brief stage appearance.

'Twice he did it,' Maddy had said and Jenny had found it hysterically funny. 'Oh, but that's nowhere near as bad as the peeing,' Maddy insisted. 'He did it during a dress rehearsal. He pee-ed. Do you know how long it takes a horse to pee? All over the stage it was, everywhere.' Jenny could barely hold on to the phone she was laughing so hard at this stage.

'It's not funny, Jen,' Maddy insisted, loving the sound of her daughter's helpless laughter. 'I tell you, I had to do the rape scene rolling all over the stage in horse pee.' There was a long wait before Jenny had calmed down enough for Maddy to continue. 'The wrangler says it was only nerves, the poor little thing,' she said eventually. 'He says that it won't happen again. Now they give him a big workout each afternoon before they bring him into the theatre so he's more tired than anything. We get on very well. He's really sweet; his name's Andy Hardy.'

He wasn't Andy Hardy to Jenny. Not now. Even though she'd called him that when she'd patted him backstage. Now he was the pony carrying the wife of a Samurai warrior through the forest to Kyoto a thousand years ago.

At the end of Act One the lights dimmed and only a spotlight remained on the face of the Japanese wife as she appealed to the magistrate. Then, just as the spotlight went to black, and before the audience had time to applaud, the strangest thing happened. There was a faint whirring sound, the heavy iron safety curtain started to descend and the actor playing the magistrate stepped downstage and addressed the audience.

'Ladies and gentlemen, may I have your attention please?' The front-of-house lights came up and he waited a moment for the murmurs of surprise to die down. 'The management requests that everyone leave the theatre as quickly and as quietly as possible, please.' He raised his voice as the first cries of consternation signalled the possibility of a panic. 'A call has been received which is most likely a hoax but the police would like to search the auditorium.'

The rest of the actor's words urging people to look after the small children and the elderly were wasted as members of the audience leapt from their seats and raced for the exits. It was pandemonium.

Jenny was sitting in one of the special house seats the management reserved for VIPs, about eight rows back in the stalls, and was fortunately by the right-hand centre aisle. The moment the safety curtain had started its descent she felt her wrist grabbed and the stage director whispered in her ear, 'Jenny, come with me'.

She barely heard the actor's voice making the announcement as she was whisked down the aisle and through the prompt side door to backstage.

Maddy was waiting for her. She had her robe on over her costume and she was tying a scarf around her head. 'Come on, Jen,' she said. 'Nothing to be frightened about. We'll go to the pub next door and have a lemonade.'

'What's going on?' Jenny asked as they settled themselves into a corner of the bar and sipped their lemonades.

'A bomb threat,' Maddy said. 'Bound to be a hoax. They're happening quite a lot lately.'

'A bomb threat. Who by?'

Maddy shrugged. 'You tell me. The IRA, the PLO—any number of organisations that specialise in terrorism.'

'How do you know it's a hoax?'

'We get them all the time.'

'But how do you know?' Jenny demanded. 'How do you really *know*!'

'Hell, I don't, Jen, but . . . well, we're not a government body, are we? I mean, we're not the BBC. And there were no VIPs in the house, were there? The Queen wasn't out front, was she? And the play doesn't make any political statements—

it's a thousand year old Japanese legend, for God's sake. It has to be a hoax.'

'The people in the audience didn't think it was a hoax.'

'No. That's why the bastards do it, to scare people. It's a horrible business, isn't it?' Maddy downed her lemonade. 'Try not to let it spoil your birthday though. They'll call us back in soon and we can get on with Act Two. Do you want another lemonade?'

Jenny nodded and looked around the bar. 'I must say you all look pretty stupid,' she grinned.

Like Maddy, most of the cast had become a little blasé about the recent bomb hoaxes and, like Maddy, they'd headed for the bar. While the anxious public hung back in the streets watching the police activities, nine actors in various forms of ancient Japanese costume and make-up lounged around over their beers, brandies and lemonades.

Maddy looked at herself in the mirror behind the bar, the white face, the black wig barely covered by the scarf and the peculiar shape of her dressing robe with the heavy kimono underneath. 'Yes,' she laughed, 'we look bloody ridiculous, don't we?'

But they were not called back in and they didn't get on with Act Two. This time the audience had been right. It had been no hoax. The bomb threat was real and no one was allowed back inside the theatre.

As she sat in the back seat of the cab with Jenny, Maddy's chest was tight with fear, her face bloodless under the white make-up. The voice of the front-of-house manager was still ringing in her ears. 'They found it under the step by one of the aisle seats. Right hand, centre block of H row.'

The seats in the centre block of H row were always reserved by the management as house seats. And Jenny had been sitting on the right-hand aisle.

Fortunately Jenny had no idea that the bomb had been discovered beside her seat. She didn't even know which row she had been in.

Now Maddy tried desperately to cover her jangling nerves as she waited for Douglas to come home. She kept herself busy changing and taking off her make-up, avoiding Jenny's discerning gaze and talking all the while.

'Well, that was some way to spend a thirteenth birthday, wasn't it? You can dine out on that one.' She tossed a handful of tissues into the bathroom wastepaper bin, turned on the tap and started filling up the washbasin. My God, I look terrible, she thought, as she caught sight of her tight face and frightened eyes in the mirror.

'I wonder if geisha girls look as bad as this when they take their make-up off,' she said, trying to smile.

After three washes with the liquid cleanser she put out her hand. 'Towel.' Jenny handed her the towel. 'Do you still want to go to supper or shall we rustle something up here?' She poured some astringent onto a make-up remover pad and started dabbing at her face. 'Hey, we could get takeaway. What do you reckon? Really pig out on all the favourites.'

'You're very nervy, Mum,' Jenny finally said. 'Don't worry. It's all over. Nothing happened.'

That was it. Maddy dropped all pretences. She hugged the child to her so hard that it hurt. 'Oh,

Jenny,' she sobbed. 'Oh, Jenny, baby, baby, baby.'

Jenny stroked her mother's hair comfortingly. Poor Mum, she thought, she's really in a bad way.

When Douglas arrived twenty minutes later Maddy was pretty much recovered. 'It was just shock,' she told Jenny. 'I needed a howl—it's good therapy.' Which was true.

Douglas had been told of the bomb when he arrived at the theatre and he was duly sympathetic. 'So you didn't even get to see the whole show? What a bummer. Still, it'll make a great story for your mates at school.'

'Yes, that's what Mum said.'

Maddy felt unreasonably irritated. Douglas was doing exactly as she'd done herself, underplaying the situation for Jenny's sake, but what right did he have? He hadn't been there—he didn't know where the bomb had been found. Hell, if he'd turned up as he'd promised it might have been his bloody seat!

Oh no. Suddenly Maddy felt ill. Surely it couldn't be possible . . . It couldn't have been meant for Douglas. If a bomb went off it didn't get just one person anyway, did it; a quarter of the theatre would probably have been wiped out. If someone wanted to kill Douglas, surely they wouldn't do it that way? Would they?

The takeaway arrived. Maddy pretended to eat.

But it often did happen that way, didn't it? Terrorists didn't care how many they killed if the person they were after was important enough. So how important was Douglas? He'd said military. What military? Who? Why?

Maddy's brain was screaming. And still she pretended to eat and join in the chat which was mostly about the play.

Finally it was time for Jenny to go to bed and, alone with Douglas, Maddy was able to drop the pretence. She got straight to the point. 'The bomb was found beside Maddy's seat,' she said.

'Oh.' Douglas's reaction said nothing.

'It could have been meant for you, couldn't it?' She felt her self-control disappearing as he remained silent. 'Well, couldn't it!' She wanted to scream but didn't dare let Jenny hear so it came out a venomous hiss.

For the first time Douglas seemed to register how genuinely upset Maddy was. 'I'm sorry,' he said, 'I didn't realise . . .'

Maddy pulled away from him. 'Answer me, Douglas. Was it meant for you?'

He shook his head. 'No.'

Maddy waited for more but nothing appeared to be forthcoming. 'Oh, Jesus, what am I supposed to do? What's going on?'

'Now listen to me, Madeleine.' Douglas pulled her to him. 'Whichever organisation it was, they were not after me, do you understand? You're worrying yourself into a frenzy at the thought that Jenny could have been killed but I'm sure you'll find the morning news reports will say it was a hoax.'

'A hoax? But they found—'

'I'm sure the bomb would never have gone off.'

'Then why?'

'Call it a publicity campaign—a public awareness exercise. They want to make people realise how easily they can do such things.'

Maddy sat back in the sofa, exhausted. She didn't know what to think any more. Her mind was numb.

As it turned out, Douglas was quite right. The following morning it was reported that the IRA had claimed responsibility for the mock bomb planted amongst the theatre's seats normally reserved for VIPs. Furthermore, the bomb had been planted during a capacity performance. That such a threat could be carried out so easily was positive proof of the efficiency of their organisation.

Relieved as Maddy was that Jenny's life had never been in danger, her misgivings were not entirely eased. She couldn't persuade herself that Douglas wasn't in some indirect way connected with the bomb threat. It was too coincidental. And it was one thing for him to place himself in danger, but Jenny . . .

Douglas was aware of her tension. 'Do you want me to go?' he asked several days later. He'd taken Jenny to see *Rashomon*, then the three of them had had their belated birthday supper afterwards. Now he and Maddy were lying in each other's arms. She didn't answer.

'I know how worried you've been,' he continued. 'Do you want me to go?'

It was agony for Maddy. She couldn't bear the thought of losing him. But then Jenny . . . As she clung to him she felt him harden against her thigh. Oh Christ, this wasn't the right time to ask.

'No, I don't want you to go,' she said, and kissed him, her mouth opening hungrily.

Maddy managed to persuade herself not to feel too guilty about her decision. Jenny would be back at school in a week and well out of harm's way. If, indeed, there was any harm. She was probably overreacting anyway, she told herself.

Then, several days after Jenny left, there was an exciting turn of events which completely distracted Maddy.

Viktor Hoff was offered a chance to direct for the National Theatre.

'Moliere's *Misanthrope*, Madeleine,' he crowed, 'and you are to be my Celimene.' Viktor was justifiably thrilled with the offer. It meant that after only one stage production in England, he'd been accepted by the Establishment.

'I shall give them pure Moliere, such a classical production like which they never have seen.'

'But maybe they're offering you the production because they want something avant-garde, Viktor,' Maddy pointed out. 'With your reputation they're probably expecting you to set it in Manila in the 1980s or something.'

'No, it will be seventeenth-century Paris— powdered wigs and silk breeches, Moliere will be pleased. Of course,' he added with a cheeky grin, 'I don't straight away tell the National that I direct it half in English and half in French. Moliere will be even more pleased, yes?'

Maddy laughed. 'I can't wait.'

'I can't wait, Julian,' she said over the phone that night. 'It's four months before we go into production and Viktor's working on the original French and two of his favourite translations and he's going to direct it so that it can be played in front of either English or French audiences. God only knows if it'll work, of course, but it's certainly bold.'

'Wonderful. I'll look forward to seeing it.'

'You're joking. Really? You're coming to London?'

'In December. We had offers from two West End managements for *The Conjurer* and we're going to sound them out for future business but we're actually accepting the '85 Chichester Festival. It's a safer way of going about it rather than heading straight for London. If the show goes well it'll transfer anyway, and if it flops then hopefully the whole world won't know about it.'

Maddy was thrilled. She longed to see Julian. 'Six months away, though—it seems an age.'

'It's tomorrow, Maddy, believe me.'

'How's everything else going?' she asked. He seemed a bit down.

'Oh fine, fine.'

Things weren't really fine, Julian thought as he hung up. Normally he would confide all to Maddy but what was there to confide? By rights he should be ecstatically happy. He had a hit play about to be launched internationally and investors were queueing up to fund the new play he was writing for Alex. That was what wasn't fine, of course. He was writing the play for Alex.

'Author! Author!' the audience had yelled after the opening night performance of *The Conjurer* and Alex had literally pushed Julian down the aisle towards the stage. When he'd taken his three self-conscious bows and walked offstage Alex was waiting for him in the wings. 'Welcome back, Julian,' he said as he hugged him very close.

And now Julian was writing his next play for Alex. And probably the next one after this, he thought. And the next, and the next. He was back in Alex's pocket and Alex knew it.

'What's the next play going to be about, Julian?' he'd asked.

'Oh, about a modern day Faustus,' Julian had answered off the top of his head, 'except my character sells his soul to his friend instead of the devil.'

Alex laughed. 'How pertinent. Make it a comedy.'

And Julian had. These days he did everything Alex asked, he thought gloomily, feeling very manipulated. But then if it was success he was after . . . Hell, he'd even agreed to holiday with Alex in Europe before their business meetings in England at the end of the year.

'The Austrian Alps, Julian, you've never been there, have you?' Alex enthused. 'And after Chichester we'll go to Scotland. I believe there's a great resort at Aviemore. I've never skiied in Scotland, have you?'

'You know bloody well I haven't, Alex. I had a day's lessons at Thredbo ten years ago and I wasn't very good at it.'

'I'll teach you. You'll love it.'

'Well, I suppose I can always hire a toboggan instead.'

Harold was thrilled that his boys were reunited. 'To friendship,' he toasted, raising his gin and lime.

As the three of them clinked glasses Julian looked at Alex. The eyes smiled back at him with genuine affection and Julian wondered why he felt such foreboding.

'We need more limes, dear boy,' Harold said to Alex. 'Only three left in the box.' Alex still did Harold's shopping for him: the more exotic items that Harold couldn't get from the corner deli half a block away.

'That box was full a week ago, Harold,' Alex said, cutting up one of the three remaining limes. 'You've been nudging the gin a bit, haven't you?'

'I eat limes with crayfish too,' Harold said defensively. 'And oysters.'

'Rubbish. You're an old soak.'

Alex's love for Harold was his one true redeeming feature, Julian thought. Harold could be very difficult to take at times; lately he'd been ill and he was a terrible invalid.

The truth was that Harold had never ceased to amuse Alex. Harold himself knew it and he was always at his wittiest in Alex's company. Even his whingeing took on an extra colour when Alex was around.

'Stoicism is not a characteristic I admire,' he pronounced, although secretly he did. 'The only pleasure to be reaped from pain is in letting everybody know that you have it.'

Harold's health had deteriorated rapidly over the past year but he refused to see a doctor. 'What for?' he'd say in reply to Julian's nagging. 'There's no cure for mortality. I turn eighty next year.' He'd stopped lying about his age at seventy-five. Now he boasted about it.

'Four score years it shall be before I shuffle off this mortal coil. And over sixty of them spent treading the boards. Not to be sneered at, dear boy, not to be sneered at.'

It was because of his illness that Harold refused the role Julian had written for him in *The Conjurer*.

'But it's a gem of a part,' Alex insisted. 'Pure Beauchamp. It's only in Act One; you wouldn't have to stay for the curtain, so you'd be home by interval.'

'My favourite sort of role, my dear Alexei, I admit. And I'm deeply grateful for the opportunity but I intend to take this year out.' Harold ignored Alex's attempt to interrupt. 'I'll allow my arm to be twisted for the odd well-paid film cameo but theatre is banned for '84, I'm afraid.' And he refused to budge.

'So much for loyalty,' Alex complained to Julian. 'Harold knocks us back and Susannah accepts another offer.' It was only a token whinge at Harold, but Alex was genuinely annoyed with Susannah. She was moody, she was sullen and now she was letting him down.

'A nine-month tour!' he exclaimed. 'Why?'

'It'll be fun,' she said. 'It's a frothy piece and the change'll do me good. Besides, I'm looking forward to getting away from Sydney for a while.'

Susannah and Alex didn't bother hiding the rift in their relationship. Not that they had screaming rows—it might have been healthier if they had— and publicly their image remained the same but, to those close to them like Julian and Harold, it was obvious that the marriage was over.

Susannah had discovered not long after her brother's death that Alex had been unfaithful to her. A slighted rival actress had been only too happy to boast of her own one-night stand with Alex, and she'd been even happier to hint at the unsubstantiated rumour of his long-term affair with Myra Nielson.

Although she hadn't suspected Alex of infidelity Susannah believed the actress. But she wasn't destroyed by the knowledge. Nothing could destroy her now. The worst had happened. Michael was dead. And she'd survived. Alex hadn't really meant anything to her, anyway, Susannah decided, just as she hadn't really meant anything to him. They had been of use to each other, that was all.

Michael was the only one she'd ever loved and, without him, there was nothing but work. Susannah maintained her pride in her work but, outside of the theatre, there was not one thing that interested her, least of all herself. Her erratic eating habits worsened as her self-esteem hit an all-time low. Left to her own devices while Alex worked with Julian on the script or wooed investors in ski chalets, Susannah binged and purged relentlessly. On her way home from the theatre, having starved herself all day, she would lust after forbidden food. Not just one pie but three, and chips, and a Chiko roll. These were never enough and she'd search the pantry cupboards for biscuits and cakes, and the freezer for ice cream until finally, clasping her distended stomach in both hands, she'd weave her way to the bathroom, disgusted, and vomit the lot.

She knew that it was wrong. She'd heard it diagnosed as bulimia nervosa and discussed as an illness but she didn't believe she was ill. Before she binged she would persuade herself that if she wanted to eat, why not go the whole hog? And each time she purged herself and was lean once more she felt as if she'd done a penance.

No matter how Susannah justified her behaviour though, there was always the odd time when she looked in the bathroom mirror. The time, just before she knelt by the lavatory bowl, when she thought of the goose in *Mondo Cane*. She'd seen the film when she was a child and she'd never

345

forgotten the goose. Its webbed feet nailed to the floor, unable to exercise, it was force-fed through a funnel until its liver enlarged, ruptured and the animal died. Susannah had never eaten goose liver pate since.

On those odd occasions when she looked in the mirror and saw the goose, Susannah knew she was in a real mess. And it was the morning after one of those moments of insight that she picked up the phone and accepted the nine-month tour of *My Fat Friend*.

She could have laughed out loud at the choice of play. It was about a girl with an eating problem who goes from very fat to very thin. And a comedy at that! But then maybe it was the play itself which had signalled her. Whatever it was, it would get her away from Alex who was totally unsympathetic to her depression, and it would get her out of Sydney. Whether it would get her away from herself remained to be seen.

Susannah didn't keep in contact with Alex during the *Fat Friend* tour and, with the excitement of *The Conjurer* production and the success of the Sydney season, he barely noticed her absence. By the time he and Julian were entering negotiations for the UK production he had, in true Rainford fashion, virtually forgotten she existed. It therefore came as a surprise, but no great disappointment, when Susannah phoned him from Adelaide to say the tour had been so successful that the management had extended the season to include six-week runs in Perth, Hobart and New Zealand. There was a month's break before the new leg of the tour and she was going to holiday in Bali. She would be away from Sydney for another six months at least.

'Have a nice holiday,' Alex said. He was pleased when she hung up and he could get back to the first rough draft of *Friend Faustus* that Julian had given him.

Julian had handed it over with his usual self-deprecating request to 'be kind', as it was a rough draft only, but as usual it had the masterly Oldfellow touch and Alex, although only halfway through it, already loved it. Others mightn't, he conceded: the comedy was very black and sometimes sick, but it was hysterically funny. Hell, Alex thought, if he could inspire Julian to this degree after the lengthy falling out they'd had, what couldn't he do during their trip to Europe together? Alex couldn't wait.

Several days before their departure for Europe, Alex finally heard from Susannah again. 'Hi, it's me,' said the voice at the end of the phone. 'We close in Auckland this Saturday and I'm flying back on Tuesday. We have to talk.'

'I won't be here,' Alex answered. 'Julian and I leave next week. We're holidaying in Europe before pre-production meetings for *The Conjurer* in Chichester.'

There was a pause. 'Congratulations.' Then a longer pause. 'Have a nice trip. We'll talk when you get back.'

Alex hung up and didn't give the conversation or Susannah another thought.

Only one thing marred the excitement of the impending trip for both Alex and Julian. Harold had been diagnosed with cancer. After finally being persuaded to seek medical advice, if only to alleviate the pain, he'd been told that he had a year, possibly two, left.

'If he'd come to us earlier it might have been operable,' the doctor complained to Alex and Julian, who were acting as nearest of kin. 'But, given his age, I'm loath to recommend surgery now.'

Strangely enough, now that Harold had something really big to whinge about he didn't bother. His new medication kept the pain at bay and, after the initial shock, the thought of death didn't seem too disturbing to him.

'After seventy it's something you tend to live with,' he confided to Julian. 'And according to the doctor I shall well and truly make my four score years. I should have been most unhappy if I hadn't. Now you two go off and have a wonderful time in Europe and don't worry about me. I shall be here when you get back, I promise.'

Despite the unease he felt at having Alex for a travelling companion, Julian was very excited about the trip. He was a thirty-six year old writer, after all, he scolded himself, and he should have seen much more of the world than he had.

Although a seasoned traveller, Alex was even more excited. Or he certainly seemed to be. During the flight he flirted with the flight attendants and talked endlessly to Julian about the wonderful places they'd go and the things they'd do.

Gradually Julian's unease dissolved and, by the time they landed in Zurich, he felt as warmed and charmed by Alex as he had when they'd first met nearly fifteen years ago.

They hired a car in Zurich and travelled to Innsbruck where Alex had planned a weekend's skiing. Julian found the drive through the picturesque villages nestling in the splendour of the Swiss-Austrian alps as breathtaking as Alex had promised it would be.

To his surprise, Julian's first day's skiing lesson also proved to be as much fun as Alex had said it would be. All arms and legs, he spent most of his time flat on his back or with his face in the snow and the two of them giggled like schoolboys.

'I admit you're not a natural,' Alex said over rum-laced coffees by the open fire that night. 'But you'll be fine with a couple more days' instruction.'

'Hardly fair on you, though. Tomorrow I'll sign up with one of the pros,' Julian insisted. 'Then you can be left on your own to tackle the slopes.'

'I was hoping you'd say that,' Alex grinned.

Julian laughed. He was loving it all. However transient their present camaraderie might prove to be, Alex was the perfect travelling companion. And their holiday had only just begun. Still to come was a full ten-day sightseeing drive around the border areas. Then a drive to Munich and the flight to London. London and Maddy, Julian thought. What a perfect holiday.

Maddy had been thrilled to hear from Julian a week before he left for Europe. They hadn't been in touch with each other for over a month. The weekly phone calls had become a thing of the past as Julian worked round the clock on the final draft of *Friend Faustus* and Maddy prepared for the opening night of *The Misanthrope*.

'Oh, Julian, what perfect timing! We start previews next week and we open in a fortnight. The show'll be well run-in by the time you get to London, although God knows what you'll think of it. Honestly, I don't know myself—I've lost all objectivity, with the shitfights that have been going on between Viktor and the National.'

Julian smiled as he realised this wasn't going to be the quick phone call he'd intended, just to announce his impending arrival. Maddy needed to talk. He put that night's *Faustus* workload on mental hold and settled back in the armchair with his coffee.

'What shitfights? Tell me.'

'Well . . .!' And off Maddy went. The members of the National Theatre Board had gone off their collective heads when they'd discovered Viktor was rehearsing the play half in French and half in English. Viktor had gone off *his* head when the Board had insisted that they were an English theatre company, their audiences were English and the play had to be performed in English.

'Doesn't sound altogether unfair, does it?' Julian said.

'Perhaps not. But Viktor's used to total control. Being ordered around by a committee sent him absolutely insane. He walked out twice and then, when they were talking about appointing a new director, he walked back in. He couldn't believe they'd do the production without him—there was no way he was going to let them.'

Julian laughed. 'So who gave in in the end?'

'They made a compromise that actually might work. About a quarter of the play is performed in French. When the characters lose their tempers or whisper bitchy asides they break into French and, if the meaning's obscured, the line is repeated in English.

'It's really quite effective,' she rattled on

excitedly. 'The French has become a sort of exclamation mark. Anyway, it's given the production authenticity if nothing else. But it's also added half an hour to the show, so maybe it's just going to be plain boring. I really can't tell. I've never worked so hard or been so confused in my life.'

'Or so stimulated, by the sounds of it.'

'Yes, well, that's Viktor,' Maddy sighed in exasperation. 'I love him, but . . . Oh, darling, I can't tell you how good it is to have someone to talk to. Jen's with me for the school holidays, of course, but I think I've already bored her witless.'

'What about Douglas? Isn't that what lovers are for?' Julian tried to keep the note of concern out of his voice.

'Oh.' There was a pause as Maddy drew breath for the first time. 'Douglas is still away.'

'But when I spoke to you over a month ago you were expecting him back in a couple of days.'

'Yes, he came back. But only for a minute. And now he's gone away again.'

Julian smiled. When Maddy got the sulks she sounded like a ten-year-old. 'All right, I can tell you don't want to talk about it.'

'Not right now,' Maddy admitted. 'Can we talk about it when I see you over here?'

'Of course we can,' promised Julian. 'Now I have to hang up or you'll never see me over there. I've promised myself I'm not going to get on the plane until I've finished the new play.'

'Oh no!' Maddy sounded mortified. 'Julian, I'm sorry, I've talked about myself non-stop. How's it going? Tell me, tell me.'

'When I see you over there,' Julian laughed. 'Goodbye, my darling.'

'But . . .'

'Goodbye.'

Maddy hadn't wanted to talk about Douglas because she wasn't sure there was anything to talk about. She wasn't even sure if she was ever going to see him again.

The customary flowers had preceded his last return and their reunion had been as thrilling as it always was. For both of them. They luxuriated in each other's bodies and, when they were sated, there was the simple joy of being together.

'I never know how much I miss you until we're together again,' Douglas said. And Maddy felt exactly the same way.

Except for one thing. Her guilt about Jenny. The questions the bomb threat had raised were still there and Maddy still didn't have the answers. She couldn't convince herself that it was right for her daughter to live in the same space as a man who carried a gun and whose life was possibly under threat. And Jenny was due home for the school holidays shortly after Douglas's return.

Douglas read her ambivalence and, as he did, he felt his own surge of guilt. She shouldn't have her guard up, he thought, she should be thrilled at the prospect of her daughter coming home.

He made an instant decision. 'Pity I won't be here. I have to leave on Saturday.'

'But you only just got back.'

'I know. I'm sorry.' Something in his voice said he didn't want to talk about it.

'How long will you be this time?' Maddy asked on the day he was to leave. 'Do you know?'

'No I don't. Quite a while, I should think.'

There was something unspoken between them and Maddy was confused. Should she say to him, 'I know you're going because of my daughter'? She was sure he was. Perhaps he was waiting for her to say, 'Don't go because of Jenny', but she couldn't.

Finally it was Douglas who said it—more or less. 'I understand how you feel,' was actually what he said. Then he kissed her goodbye. 'Give my love to Jenny.' And, before she could answer, he left.

Oh no, Maddy thought miserably. What was that supposed to mean? Is he coming back or isn't he?

Over a month later, the day before Julian was due to arrive in London, she still hadn't heard a word from Douglas.

'I can't wait to see Julian tomorrow.' Jenny topped up her glass of orange juice. 'Can we go to his play at Chichester when it opens?'

'I don't see why not. You'll be back at school by then but we can pop down one weekend.'

Julian had rung from Munich the previous day to tell Maddy of his arrival details.

'Oh great,' Maddy had said. 'Sunday. I can meet you at the airport.'

'Don't be ridiculous, Maddy,' Julian said somewhat testily, 'Alex'll be with me.'

'Oh. Of course. Sorry, I forgot. Are you all right? You sound funny.'

'I'm fine,' he said, but his voice was strained. 'I'll tell you all about it on Sunday.'

It was Saturday night. Maddy and Jenny had just arrived home from the theatre. Jenny had seen *The*

Misanthrope for the second time and was still slightly reserved in her opinion.

'It's much better than the preview I saw,' she said. 'I'm glad they cut a bit more of it out, it was awfully long. And I'm still not sure about all that French.'

You're not the only one, Maddy thought. The press had been good. They'd called it 'an innovative production', and the houses weren't bad, but the advance bookings were another thing altogether and Maddy suspected that word had got out that the play was a little long and a little esoteric.

Viktor was happy, though; he felt he'd made his point. His production had been critically acclaimed, which meant the National's reputation had not been sullied, and he was presently nagging the board to arrange an exchange production with the Comedie Francaise in Paris. It looked as though he was going to pull it off too. 'And then, Madeleine, my darling,' he confided, 'we do Moliere three-quarter in the French and one quarter only in the English. Perfect, eh!'

Another whole new production, Maddy thought wearily—and it would be at breakneck speed, of course. Viktor was a darling but he was so exhausting to work with.

'Hey Jen, you'd better check your nachos,' Maddy reminded her. As Jenny raced off into the kitchen, Maddy turned on the television set to get the late news headlines. 'Don't serve up too much for me, and go easy on the chilli sauce,' she called.

There'd been a matinee that afternoon and Maddy hadn't read the papers but everyone had been talking about the bomb blast in Northern Ireland. The opening news headlines gave it full coverage. 'Late this afternoon, in Armagh, Northern Ireland, a bomb killed eighteen people and seriously injured thirty-two,' the announcer stated. 'Our Northern Ireland correspondent has the details.'

The reporter was standing in the streets of Armagh at the scene of the crime and obviously not long after the bomb had exploded. The air was still smouldering and he had to virtually yell to get above the screams and general confusion in the background.

This was the devastation that had been wreaked by the explosion of a one-thousand pound bomb, he said, and the IRA had claimed responsibility. The reporter talked about the massive damage and loss of life, and then the camera followed him as he walked through the streets among the crowd. Then the reporter said, 'Now let's talk to some local people who've been witness to this shocking event.'

And there he was. The first person the reporter spoke to. Douglas Mackie. But was it? For a brief second his face had been clearly caught by the camera then he'd turned away. He was a frustrating subject for the cameraman and the reporter as he kept gesturing to the streets and the buildings and it was impossible to cover him.

Maddy couldn't catch the name he gave and, as the reporter attempted to thrust the microphone at him, the man continued gesticulating and saying over and over again, 'A terrible thing, what a terrible thing it is.' The accent was pure Belfast.

Seconds later the reporter decided to give up on him. 'That was local resident Daniel McSwiney who was witness to today's tragedy and it is indeed a terrible thing. Excuse me, miss . . .'

The reporter turned to the next person in the crowd but Maddy didn't see who it was. She didn't see the television at all as she stared blindly at the screen.

All she saw was Douglas's face in that split-second before he'd turned away. It had looked grimy, unshaved. What had he been wearing? She racked her brains to remember, but it had all happened so fast. Surely it had been peasant clothing of some description. He hadn't really looked like Douglas and yet she knew it was him. And that Irish brogue had been so authentic. What had happened to the Scots burr? It hadn't sounded like Douglas's voice, but she knew it was.

And, last of all, the name. Daniel McSwiney. The passport she'd found flashed through her mind. The name Donald McBride opposite his picture. Then the admission to the other aliases he'd assumed: 'Does it matter whether I'm Douglas Mackie, Donald McBride or David McGuinness?' he'd asked. And now it was Daniel McSwiney.

Yes, Maddy thought, sickened by the knowledge, it had been Douglas all right.

ACT III

SCENE 4: 1984–1985

Julian pretended to be asleep through the entire flight from Munich to Heathrow. But he could hear Alex flirting with the attractive young woman seated across the aisle. She was obviously falling for it too.

As far as Alex was concerned it appeared nothing had happened. He'd forgotten Berchtesgaden completely. But Julian hadn't. He would never forget Berchtesgaden.

The drive around the Austrian, Swiss and Italian border country had been magnificent. And so companionable that, as they wound their way up the mountain to Berchtesgaden, any doubts that Julian had about travelling with Alex had well and truly disappeared.

How could he have allowed himself to be lulled into such a false sense of security? Julian wondered, wishing that the drone of the plane's engines would send him off to sleep so that he could escape the turmoil in his brain. Alex had been playing with him all the time—just as a cat allows a captive mouse a taste of freedom before it pounces again.

'You'll love Berchtesgaden, Julian,' Alex enthused. 'Very pretty, very tranquil. I always drive up here after a skiing trip—a sort of pilgrimage before I have to go back home.'

Alex was right. Berchtesgaden was very pretty: a little snow-covered village high in the Alps, a stream, a bridge, a town square. But it was not all that much different from many of the other alpine villages they'd passed through, Julian thought. And then he saw the statue. A stone statue, by the fountain, in the middle of the square. It was beautiful.

It was a woman, lifesize, lowering a bucket into the well, with a small child by her side, tugging at her skirts. All of her weight was on the ball of one foot as she concentrated on the bucket and the well. But there was no way she would falter. She was perfectly balanced. And she was strong. Strong, capable and womanly. Julian wandered around her, admiring from every angle. He felt the folds of the stone skirt where the infant had such a fierce hold, he felt the smoothness of her strong forearms and examined the delicate touch on the earth of the foot which wasn't bearing the weight. What a wonderful mixture of strength and delicacy, he thought, and he sought out Alex so that they could admire it together.

Alex's attention was equally captured. He was

leaning over the railing staring up at the side of the mountain high above. Several other tourists were at the same spot, staring up at the same mountainside, some with binoculars.

'Hitler's winter weekender,' Alex explained as Julian joined him. 'Interesting, isn't it?'

Of course, Julian remembered, that was why Berchtesgaden had a familiar ring about it. It was the village closest to the Berghof, Hitler's eyrie. He looked up at the dwelling carved high into the side of the neighbouring mountain. Then he looked back at Alex.

'Interesting man,' Alex murmured. 'Very complex.' He turned to Julian. 'Fascinating, too, don't you think?'

Julian had the feeling he was being led into something and he didn't like it. 'Perhaps,' he said glibly, 'if you find evil fascinating.'

'Oh, don't evade me, Julian,' Alex snapped irritably. 'Everyone finds evil fascinating. Are you ready to go?'

Julian followed him to the car.

'I'll drive,' Alex said.

'You sure?' asked Julian. 'It's my turn—you drove up.'

'I know these roads. Besides, I feel like driving.'

'Fine by me.' Julian vastly preferred sightseeing from the passenger's side.

Alex put the key in the ignition but he didn't start the engine straight away. 'I'm sorry I barked at you,' he said softly, staring through the windscreen at the drifts of snow. 'But you've been evading me for a long time now and it annoys me sometimes.'

Julian didn't like the turn of conversation. He

wished Alex would start the car so they could turn the heater on—it was freezing.

But Alex didn't. 'You know me better than anyone ever has or ever will, Julian. You know me inside out; I'm there in all your plays—and yet you evade me. The real me.' Alex turned to him and smiled charmingly. 'I feel a little used at times.'

All right, Julian thought, it was time to meet him head on. 'No, you don't, Alex. You love it. You deliberately tease and confuse to keep yourself interesting. And that's fine by me, so long as I find you a source of inspiration. In the meantime, I do not have to personally connect with your brain, which at times, quite frankly, I find warped. I don't even have to like you.'

Alex laughed loudly. 'That's true. You don't have to like Hitler to find him interesting.'

'All right, so evil's interesting, I admit that. Now can you turn the heating on? It's bloody freezing.'

Alex turned the ignition on and waited a few minutes for the engine to warm up. 'Actually, it's not the evil I find so fascinating about Hitler, it's the death. If it weren't for death, life would be an awful bore, wouldn't it? I can't understand this preoccupation with immortality. I can think of nothing more hideous.'

Julian leaned over and turned the heater on.

'That'll take a few more minutes,' Alex said. 'There's so much death you can experience while you're living, isn't there? I suppose that's why kids pull the wings off flies. I mean, you see the death process all around you: old people dying, car accidents, illnesses. The next interesting step would be to *inflict* death wouldn't it? Ah, that's better,' he said as the heat started to pervade the car. 'Time to go.'

As they started down the mountain, Alex glanced at Julian. 'Do you fear death?'

'No, I don't think so,' Julian answered and an image flashed through his mind. An image of a cat toying with a mouse.

'Nor do I.' Alex pressed down hard on the accelerator. 'Let's test it, shall we?'

'What the fuck are you doing, Alex!' Julian screamed, as the speedometer climbed steadily and the tyres started to squeal as they slewed around the hairpin bends in the narrow mountain road.

'Testing,' Alex said calmly. 'Just testing.'

There was nothing Julian could do. If he tried to wrest the steering wheel from Alex the car would most certainly go over the steep cliff. One glance at Alex's face, the manic gleam in his eye, the twist to his lip, and Julian knew that pleading would do no good. That was what Alex wanted.

Julian planted his feet firmly in front of him, put his hands on the dashboard and waited for the impact. For what seemed like an eternity, landscape flashed by, tyres screamed and the car skidded from one side of the narrow, twisting road to the other.

It wasn't until they were almost at the bottom that Alex slowed down. 'Well done, Julian,' he said with unsettling calmness, still negotiating the car around the bends. They rounded a corner and a tourist bus appeared twenty metres ahead of them. 'Oh, look—a bus,' Alex smiled. 'Weren't we lucky?'

They drove in silence for a long time until finally Julian turned to Alex and said, 'I think perhaps you're insane, Alex.'

'Oh, I doubt it.' Alex shook his head. 'Of course

I haven't been examined for about twenty-five years, but the tests were negative when I was eight and I don't see why things should have changed since then. Do you?' He smiled disarmingly.

Julian refused to answer and stared out of the window instead.

When Alex realised Julian wasn't going to communicate he continued. 'I think you should write a drama next, Julian.

'The black comedies are very good, very clever, but you've proved you can do that. After we make *Friend Faustus* the huge success I know it's going to be, I think you should write a drama—maybe a tragedy. About a man obsessed with death.'

The road was deserted except for an ancient Fiat just ahead but Alex checked the rear-vision mirrors, switched on the indicator, overtook the car, switched on the other indicator and pulled in ahead. He was driving with exaggerated care now and it was irritating Julian.

'That's it,' Alex went on. 'A man obsessed with death. But he wants to take his obsession a step further. He wants to inflict a death. How does he go about it?' Alex started to become enthused about the idea. 'Maybe he accomplishes the perfect murder himself or maybe he manipulates someone else to do it. What do you think?'

Julian turned and looked at him.

'Well, what do you think?' Alex repeated. 'Everyone's obsessed with death in one way or another, Julian. It would have broad appeal.'

Is Alex serious? Julian wondered. 'Maybe there's a play there,' he said, 'I'll think about it.' As he stared out of the window, a chill of fear ran down his spine. Did Alex seriously want him to write the perfect murder for him? And why? Was there someone Alex wanted to kill?

And now Julian's brain refused to be lulled by the drone of the aeroplane engines. Berchtesgaden, the drive down the mountain and Alex's conversation kept churning around in his mind.

Try as he might, he couldn't rid himself of the theme. A man obsessed with death creates the perfect murder scenario: he manipulates another to commit the crime simply so that he can watch a death for which he himself was responsible. Just a power game. No motive. Very difficult to trace.

Stop it, Julian, stop it, he told himself. You don't want to write this play. But the ideas kept coming, and coming, and coming. And Julian knew he couldn't wait to put pen to paper and make notes. But I won't write the play, he promised himself. A few notes, that's all. A few notes for future reference.

'I don't believe it!' Maddy's eyes were wide with amazement as Julian finished recounting the story of Berchtesgaden.

'No exaggeration, I promise. It's a miracle we weren't killed.'

'He's mad. He must be.' She shook her head in disbelief.

'I don't know,' Julian said. 'I really don't know.'

It was Sunday night and they'd long finished eating the meal Maddy had prepared, followed by Jenny's rather sludgy trifle.

They'd sent Jenny to bed at eleven-thirty and by midnight Maddy had been brought up to date on recent events. But there was one thing Julian hadn't mentioned. His idea for another play. He felt strangely guilty about the two hours of notes he'd made in his London hotel room immediately after they'd booked in. They're only notes, he told himself, but he still felt guilty.

'Well, I think he's mad,' Maddy continued. 'People don't do things like that unless they're mad. And it's all the more reason to keep Jenny well away from him.'

Julian and Maddy talked till four in the morning. Maddy told him all about Douglas and the bomb in Armagh and the television news broadcast.

'Do you think he's IRA?' she asked.

'It does look that way, doesn't it?' Julian wished he could say no—it was obvious Maddy was torturing herself. 'Oh, Christ, Maddy, I don't know, I really don't.'

The following night Alex insisted he and Julian go to the theatre together.

'Here you are,' he said, dumping the entertainments section of the newspaper on the bar in front of Julian. They'd just returned from their third and final business meeting for the day. 'I had a good study of what's on around town, so make your choice and we'll toss a coin.'

Julian had anticipated such a suggestion and had his reply at the ready. 'But we're off to Chichester tomorrow. We'd cover more ground if we went to different shows and compared notes afterwards.' (Maddy had booked him in to see *The Misanthrope* that night with Jenny who was quite happy to see the production for the third time.)

'That's not very companionable of you, Julian.'

Alex looked genuinely disappointed. 'I tell you what. If you really want to check out what's on in London, why don't we come back here for a few days after Scotland?' He seemed very pleased with his suggestion. 'Yes, that's the best idea,' he said as he picked up the newspaper.

Julian was momentarily stunned. Did Alex still expect him to go to Scotland? To journey into the arctic highlands with a madman who'd tried to kill him? He couldn't believe it.

'I tell you my choice for tonight,' Alex continued, shoving the paper at him. 'The National's production of *The Misanthrope*. It's supposed to be really original. Just the sort of thing you love—what do you say?'

What did he say? Julian's mind raced. What the hell did he say? 'How do you know it's really original?' he asked, buying time.

'I went for a wander while you were partying it up with your pals last night.' It was a slight dig. Alex had been put out when Julian had insisted upon going their separate ways. 'But it's our first night in London,' he'd said.

'Friends of the family, Alex, I can't get out of it,' Julian had insisted.

Alex continued, 'I spent a good hour and a half doing the rounds of the West End and *The Misanthrope* looked far and away the most interesting. They've got blow-ups of the full reviews in the foyer—not just excerpts—and that's always a good sign. Some of it's played in the original French and it's directed by Viktor Hoff.'

Julian was genuinely surprised. 'I didn't know you were into Viktor Hoff's work.'

Alex nodded. 'The couple of movies of his I've

seen have been great. Really bizarre. I never did see *Androgyne*, that's supposed to have been his best. Did you?'

'*Androgyne*?' Julian looked closely at Alex. This wasn't a game, was it? It didn't appear to be, but with Alex it was so often difficult to tell. 'Yes, I've seen *Androgyne*; it was on in Sydney a couple of years ago.'

'I know. I wanted Harold to go with me but he wouldn't. "Cinéma vérité is too exhausting, dear boy", all of that rubbish. And I never got around to going on my own.'

Good old Harold, thought Julian with a rush of affection. It must have been difficult for him to keep his mouth shut but he'd done it.

Alex signalled to the barman for another round of drinks. 'So, what do you say we check out Hoff's prowess in the theatre?'

Julian studied the newspaper. 'Let's have a look at what else is on.'

'*The Misanthrope* is the best choice, Julian, believe me.'

'What happened to tossing a coin?' Julian was racking his brain for a way out.

'Oh, I didn't really mean that,' Alex gave a glib wave of his hand. 'I knew you'd want to go to the National.'

'Well, you knew wrong,' Julian said petulantly. 'I want to go somewhere else.'

'All right, all right,' said Alex, gesturing dismissively. He was fed up by now. 'You go somewhere else, I'll go to the National and we'll compare bloody notes.' He turned to pay the barman for the fresh drinks.

'Forget it, we'll go to *The Misanthrope*. Shall

I ring and book now?' Julian stood up and searched his pockets for some change.

Alex looked at him, surprised. 'Why the sudden change of heart?'

'No change of heart—I really would like to see *The Misanthrope*.' Julian shrugged. Mustn't arouse suspicion, he told himself. 'I just don't like being bossed around.'

'Rubbish, you love it,' Alex grinned.

'Back in a minute.' Julian headed for the telephone in the foyer.

'Oh my God,' Maddy said, aghast. 'Couldn't you stop him?'

'No way. I tried, believe me.'

'What'll we do?'

'Nothing we can do, except arrange for the seats to be towards the back and hope that he doesn't recognise you with the wig and period make-up.'

A series of images flashed through Maddy's brain. Sydney. King Street. Night time. A collision with a man on the footpath as she hailed a cab. Yes, it might work. Alex hadn't recognised her then, had he?

'Right,' she agreed. 'Thank goodness for the warning. At least I can keep Jenny out of the way.'

'Rotten seats,' Alex grumbled. 'The house is only half full—why did they put us back here?'

'Don't ask me,' Julian answered, crossing his fingers as the lights started to fade. Then she appeared and he breathed a sigh of relief. It was difficult even for him to discern Maddy beneath the crinoline, the powdered wig and the heavy make-up. The affected voice too, and the rapid bouts of

French added to the disguise. There was no way Alex would pick her.

Then why was he straining forward for a closer look every time she appeared on stage? Julian asked himself, not daring to glance at Alex. And if he'd recognised her, why wasn't he saying anything?

As the lights came up at interval Julian leaned back in his seat and tried to sound casual. 'Well, what do you think?'

'The woman playing Celimene's fantastic, isn't she? What's her name?'

Julian's mind raced. If he feigned ignorance Alex might buy a programme. A programme with a studio portrait and a biography on Maddy. Alex only ever bought a programme when he needed to know someone's name. 'Programme's are a rip-off,' he maintained. 'A tidy little sideline that goes straight into the producer's pocket. I should know.'

'Madeleine Frances,' Julian answered.

Alex frowned. He'd heard the name before somewhere.

'Viktor Hoff's had a crush on her for years,' Julian continued. 'She played the lead in *Androgyne*.'

'Ah, right,' Alex said. 'Knew I'd heard the name.'

'She doesn't seem to do much film any more. She's pretty big in the theatre though. Come on, I'm dying for a beer.'

'Let's go backstage and meet her after the show,' Alex suggested as he stood up and followed Julian out of the auditorium.

'Why?' Hell, Julian thought, I'd better warn Maddy not to waste time taking her make-up off.

'Oh, come on now. If you rack your brains hard enough surely you can guess why.'

Julian stopped so abruptly that Alex nearly crashed into him at the exit doors. 'No, Alex, I can't.' His heart was pounding at an alarming rate. It was cat and mouse time again, he told himself. Alex had known all along.

'Shit, Julian. She's the horniest woman I've seen in years.'

'Oh.' Julian tried to laugh. 'Silly me. You stay here, I'll get the beers.'

Julian elbowed his way through to the bar and waited his turn. 'Thank you,' he said to the young woman who handed him the drinks. Then he whispered, 'I wonder if you could arrange a message to be sent backstage to Miss Frances during Act Two.'

'Sure.'

'Don't bother.' Alex was right beside him. 'I've already done it. Here I'll take those.'

Julian automatically handed the beers over, paid the girl and joined Alex who'd backed away from the bar crowd. 'You've done what?'

'Sent one of my cards backstage, of course, gave it to the front-of-house manager.'

'Oh.'

'Well, I wouldn't get very far with her if she thought I was just another fan, would I?'

'Good thinking.' Julian smiled and relaxed. He knew Alex's cards. They were top quality, very impressive with *Alex Rainford, Producer* in embossed lettering. He started to breathe easily.

After the performance Julian didn't have to work hard at delay tactics.

'Well, of course we must give the woman time

to get her make-up off, Julian,' Alex agreed. 'Very rude not to.' Then he wandered out to peruse the foyer display which included, to Julian's horror, a portrait of Maddy.

Julian stared at the photograph, trying to convince himself that it didn't look anything like the Maddy of NADA days. But to Julian it did. Certainly the hair was cropped short, the face more angular and sophisticated, but to Julian it was still Maddy.

To his amazement, Alex gave the photo only a cursory glance. 'She looks better in the wig; I don't like the short hair,' he said, and then strolled around the foyer looking at the portraits of the other actors.

Julian knew then that Alex had completely and utterly forgotten Maddy. It was as if she had never been a part of his life at all.

Alex was disappointed when the stage doorman told him Madeleine Frances had already left the theatre.

'Did she get my card?' he asked.

'Yes, Mr Rainford. And she left her apologies, but she had a prior engagement.'

'Not to worry,' Alex shrugged. 'We might chase her up when we come back from Scotland, Julian, what do you think?'

'We'? . . 'Scotland'? is what Julian thought, and then he decided to dismiss it. He'd face that one after Chichester. There'd been enough pressure on him for one night.

'I've booked the tickets to Edinburgh,' Alex said, 'and I've arranged a hire car so we can drive from

370

there.' Julian stared at him in horror. 'I think we should spend a couple of days in Edinburgh though, don't you? What a magnificent city.'

It was four days later. The meetings in Chichester had gone very smoothly. The managing director had introduced them to the woman who was to direct *The Conjurer*, they'd met the set and costume designer and everyone seemed to be in accord as to the style of production.

There was one jarring moment when Alex tried to chat up the director only to find that she was a confirmed lesbian. Well, it was jarring to her, and to Julian who was present at the time, but Alex was bemused more than anything.

'Fascinating woman,' he said later. 'I would never have picked her.'

'So, what do you think, Julian?' Alex now urged. 'A few days in Edinburgh?'

'You're not really serious, are you?'

'About what?' Alex asked innocently.

'Skiing in Aviemore.'

'Of course.' Alex looked completely bewildered. 'That was always our plan.'

'Oh, for Christ's sake, Alex!' Julian exploded. 'Stop playing games. That was before you tried to bloody kill me!'

'Oh.' Alex looked enlightened—or he pretended to; Julian had long since given up trying to tell the difference. 'I wasn't trying to kill you.'

'Well, yourself then,' Julian answered sullenly. 'How the hell do I know?'

'I wasn't trying to kill myself either. It was just a test, that's all, just a test.'

'Well, it was a bloody stupid test and I think you're a bloody madman and I'm not bloody going.'

Julian realised he wasn't sounding very sensible but Alex always did that to him.

'Are you chicken?'

'Of course I'm not chicken!'

There was a long pause while Alex waited for Julian to regain his composure, then he continued calmly, 'Did you have a nice time in Innsbruck, Julian? Before we left for Berchtesgaden,' he added hastily as he caught the look in Julian's eye.

'Yes, of course I did,' Julian snapped.

'Then let's repeat that in Aviemore,' Alex said persuasively, 'and we can spend a few days en route in Edinburgh, you can visit the castle, we can go to the theatre . . .'

Edinburgh was somewhere Julian desperately wanted to go. Perhaps he'd stay there and Alex could go on to Aviemore alone, he thought.

But Alex didn't go on to Aviemore alone. By the time they were due to leave Edinburgh they were having such a good time that Julian saw little reason to alter their arrangements.

It was a pretty little chalet and they settled in comfortably from the moment they arrived. Perhaps it was because there weren't many snow-bunnies around, or perhaps it was because he was trying to make amends (Julian couldn't work out which) but Alex was extremely attentive and considerate and, once again, excellent company.

'That's very good, Julian. Really.' Alex watched like a proud parent as Julian showed him the progress he'd made. He'd been taking skiing lessons for three days in a row now and the improvement was considerable.

'You should have a go at the higher slopes,' Alex urged. 'Do you want to come up with me tomorrow?'

'You're joking!' Julian protested. 'I'm not ready.'

'Yes, you are.'

'How do you know?'

'Well, I don't, do I?' Alex answered with a touch of impatience. 'No one knows until they try, do they? There has to be a first time for everything.' Julian continued to look doubtful. 'Hell, Julian,' Alex goaded, 'we're only here for another three days. If you chicken out for too long we'll be on our way home and you'll never know if you could have done it.'

Julian felt a flash of anger. How dare Alex suggest he was 'chickening out'? Just because he wasn't the natural athlete that Alex was and had to tackle things with a little more caution . . .

'Anyway, don't take my word for it,' Alex backed off, smiling amiably, aware that he may have gone a little too far. 'Ask your ski instructor.'

Julian did. Hans said yes. 'Sure, why not?' was his laconic reply. 'Start from the middle station— don't go up to the top—and keep a watch on the weather.' He shrugged. 'You can only fall down, can't you?'

Apart from the fact that his name was Hans and that he was German and had a suntan, Hans was everything one didn't expect a ski instructor to be. He was ugly, nearly fifty, had a potbelly and was short on charm.

There was a blizzard warning the following day and the top station was closed.

'Hans said to watch out for the weather,' Julian commented a touch nervously as they waited for the chairlift. 'Perhaps we should leave it till tomorrow?' He was rather wishing he hadn't let himself be talked into this. Maybe Alex was right, maybe he was chicken. Hell, what was wrong with that? He'd never professed to being the athletic type.

'If you leave it till tomorrow you might never get a go at it,' Alex replied. 'Once these blizzards set in the slopes can be closed to skiers for days.'

There were only two more people in front of them now, it would be their turn for the chairlift any second.

'And if the weather was any real problem, they wouldn't be operating the lifts, would they?' Alex reasoned. 'Make up your mind Julian, it's now or never.' Alex swung himself into the chair and Julian found himself clumsily following suit, nearly dropping one of his stocks in the process. There was no backing out now, he thought glumly.

'Well done.' Alex gave one of his proud parent smiles.

There weren't as many people as usual out on the slopes that morning and those who were appeared very experienced to Julian as he watched them swooping down the mountainside. If this is the middle station I'd hate to be at the top, he thought, and he looked longingly at the chalet, so tiny, way below.

'Blizzard warning,' the voice announced through the loudspeaker. 'All chairlifts and cable cars up the mountain will cease operation as of this moment. All skiers are to make their way to the chalet immediately. Thank you.'

Julian looked around. The other skiers had gone. Only he and Alex remained.

'Shit, Alex.'

But Alex appeared to take no notice of the announcement whatsoever. 'No worries, you'll be fine. You ready?' Julian gave a sick nod. 'Right. Off we go!' Alex dug his poles into the snow and took off.

Julian stared after Alex, waiting for him to stop so that he could make his own haphazard way down the mountain, safe in the knowledge that Alex was watching protectively.

But Alex didn't stop. Well maybe he did, but there was no way Julian could tell. A minute after Alex had left him, the air turned white and Julian could see no further than several metres. A minute after that he could see no further than one metre and a minute after that he was totally blind in a world of white.

He skiied a few metres down the steep slope, then fell over and picked himself up. A few more metres, then over he went again. And again. And again. Each time he fell over he heard Hans' words: 'Well, you can only fall down, can't you?' But he had to fall over in the right direction. Somewhere down the bottom of this mountain was the chalet.

As the blizzard whirled about him, Julian knew that the chances of his falling all the way down the mountainside through this blinding white and landing right at the doors of the chalet were a thousand to one. But he tried not to think about that. He tried not to think about anything except keeping on going.

Each time he fell he told himself not to panic. And each time he picked himself up out of the snow it seemed to work. It was only when he lost his goggles that he lost control. That was when the panic set in. He groped about desperately on his hands and knees as the driving snow knifed its way into his eyes. It was useless. He struggled to his feet. And then, to his horror, he realised that he'd lost one of his stocks. While he was groping for the goggles he'd slipped his hand through the leather loop.

Julian's heart pumped wildly and he began to whimper. Stop it, Julian, stop it, he told himself. You mustn't lose control. The stock must be just to your left. Kneel down. Don't crawl around, stay perfectly still. He dropped to his knees and carefully felt about to his left. When his hand touched the rod of cold metal his whimpers turned to sobs and he clutched it to his chest gratefully. Then he sat back on his heels and, for several seconds, he wept with relief.

When he finally stood up his panic had gone. There was no time for panic. He had to keep on going.

So he skiied and fell and struggled to his feet. And skiied and fell and struggled to his feet again. Get up, he told himself when every aching muscle told him to stay there. Get up, he told himself, when his body told him to curl into a ball.

On and on. The mountainside was endless. He must have passed the chalet ages ago. He felt as though he were falling down a huge abyss.

Then, through the painful cracks that were his eyes, a colour other than white appeared. A hazy yellow. And, as he fell forward, his elbow hit something hard. Something other than snow. It was a step. And there were voices. And then there were other hazy, yellow glows. People with torches, the light of the chalet behind them. He had actually fallen down the mountainside and into the back porch of the chalet.

Did I say it was a thousand to one chance? Julian asked himself. Try ten thousand. Hundreds of thousands. A million to one chance. And he wanted to laugh.

They thawed him out, and fed him soup. The doctor announced that no serious damage had been done, although he stated gravely that 'another half hour and it might have been a different matter altogether'. All the while, Julian looked through the sea of faces at Alex. Alex, who was so concerned.

'Hell, Julian, what happened? I thought you were right behind me.' Julian didn't say anything. 'And when I looked back, you weren't there.' Still Julian said nothing. 'Christ, you were lucky.'

It was only later, when they were alone, that Julian asked sharply, 'Why didn't you look back?'

'I did. I told you. I thought you were right behind me, but when I looked, you weren't there. You waited too long before taking off, Julian. You should have left straight after me.'

'Why the fuck didn't you wait for me then?' Julian could feel himself shaking with rage.

'Wait for you?' Alex held up his hands in innocent outrage. 'Are you joking? There was a bloody blizzard!'

Julian could take no more. 'You bastard! You fucking bastard!' he screamed hysterically. 'You do want to kill me, don't you? You want to rig my

377

death and then you want to watch me die—that's what you want, isn't it, you sick fucking bastard!'

Alex looked astonished. He'd never seen Julian so angry. 'Good God, Julian, why should I want to kill you when you write such wonderful plays for me? I just want to be your source of inspiration, that's all.'

An image flashed through Julian's mind: an image of himself, terror-stricken, whimpering and crawling about in the raging blizzard. And then he hit Alex. He hit him as hard as he could.

The blow didn't make much of a connection. Alex saw it coming, went with it and fell back onto the sofa. He was surprised that Julian should resort to violence. To the best of Alex's knowledge Julian had never hit anyone in his life.

Julian hadn't. And the action startled him out of his hysteria. He stared down at Alex who looked back, surprised but unruffled.

'I don't need your sick mind for my inspiration, Alex,' Julian hissed. 'So from now on, you lay off me. You understand? You play your macabre games with someone else.' He stormed off to the bar to get drunk.

The blizzard raged solidly for two days. On the third day it abated enough for rescuers to find the corpses of three mountain climbers.

Julian and Alex watched as the bodies were carried by on stretchers. Julian turned away to avoid Alex's fascination. He knew that Alex was imagining the frozen blue-white faces in the body bags.

On the fourth day the blizzard cleared enough for Alex and Julian to drive back to Edinburgh. They returned the hire car and flew to Heathrow.

Julian had changed his ticket to connect with a flight to Sydney the same day.

'But I thought we were going to spend a few days seeing the shows in London,' Alex grumbled.

'You can if you like,' Julian said. 'It's Christmas in two weeks and I'm going to spend it with the family in Wagga.'

'But you loathe Wagga,' said Alex incredulously. 'You don't even like your family that much.'

At that moment Julian felt a great love for his family. He ached for the familiar sanity of Gwen's afternoon teas, Norman's beer with the news on telly and Wendy's raucous twins. He was going home, he insisted.

'Oh all right,' Alex gave in with bad grace. 'We'll go home.'

Julian was relieved in one way that Alex decided to come with him. It would save any hassle for Maddy, although Alex appeared to have forgotten completely his desire to chase up Madeleine Frances.

Maddy was confused by Julian's telegram: *Heading straight home. Will ring from Sydney.* She hoped nothing was wrong.

Julian couldn't bring himself to ring her from London. Maddy would know by the sound of his voice that something was wrong and he wasn't up to telling her the story. By the time he rang from Wagga he'd be able to say, 'I was pretending I could ski and got lost in a blizzard'. Perhaps, from the secure suburbia of his childhood home, he'd believe it himself.

Maddy spent Christmas Day and Boxing Day morning at Windsor. Then it was back to London

379

on Wednesday afternoon in time for the evening performance.

She had left Jenny with Robert and Alma, promising to return on Sunday. But she didn't.

Douglas came back on Saturday.

Maddy walked into her dressing room after the matinee to find him waiting there for her. She was so surprised that all she could think of saying was, 'How come Sam let you in?' Sam the doorman never let anyone beyond the stage door before checking with the actors—let alone into the dressing rooms.

'I slipped through,' Douglas explained. 'No one noticed.' Maddy knew this was a lie. No one 'slipped through' the stage door when Sam was on duty. But she let it pass.

'So what do you want?' she asked coldly, the anger starting to set in.

There was a tap at the door. In the instant before it opened, Douglas gave a quick shake of his head to Maddy and stepped behind the corner screen.

The mild, bespectacled face of Maria, Maddy's nineteen year old, sixteen stone dresser, peered through the door. 'Ready for me, Miss Frances?'

'Give me ten minutes, Maria. I need to make an urgent phone call.'

'Sorry about the drama,' Douglas said when Maria had gone, 'but I can't let anyone know I'm here.'

'I'm not surprised. In fact I'm amazed you had the audacity to come back to London at all.'

He seemed a little taken aback at her vehemence. 'I'm sorry I was away so long without contacting you, but I had my reasons. I—'

'I know your reasons, Douglas. Or Daniel, or whatever your bloody name is this time.' The control she'd been fighting to maintain was rapidly disappearing and she knew it but she didn't care. 'And which funny voice are we using today, Scots or bog-Irish? I thought *I* was the actor in this relationship.'

'Oh. You saw the Armagh broadcast.' Douglas nodded as though that explained everything. 'I didn't think you would. Or rather I didn't think you'd recognise me if you saw it.'

Maddy stared back at him, momentarily speechless. How could he be so cool?

'Well, you have to admit, the accent was spot-on,' he continued. 'And I must have had a touch of charisma to make such an impression in just a few seconds.'

Maddy's outrage was genuine. 'I don't find this at all funny. We're talking about the IRA, for God's sake. We're talking about a terrorist bomb, we're talking about—'

'I know, I know,' Douglas interrupted. 'I also know how that newscast must have appeared to you, Madeleine, but you're wrong.' She tried to interject but he continued. 'I mustn't stay here any longer. If I'm seen it could be dangerous. For you more than me. Could you meet me later—at a safe place where I can explain everything?'

She wanted to believe him. She so wanted to believe him. Maddy nodded before she could question her motives. She wanted to be alone with him. She wanted to feel his mouth on hers. She wanted to feel his hands on her body. Oh God, she must be insane, she told herself.

Douglas crossed to the telephone and dialled a number. 'Has a Mr Coburn checked in yet?' he asked. 'Yes, thank you, put me through.' There was a slight pause. 'Everything cleared? Good.' He checked his watch. 'Make it 1800 hours.'

He hung up and turned to Maddy. 'The Grafton Hotel, Tottenham Court Road. I'll meet you at five to six—that gives you half an hour. Wait by the third floor lifts. If I don't acknowledge you, you mustn't acknowledge me, understand?' She nodded.

He opened the door a fraction and glanced down the corridor. It was empty. When he looked back at her he smiled for the first time. 'Don't wear the wig, it's a bit conspicuous. Besides, I prefer the real thing.'

Maddy caught sight of herself in the mirror— the crinoline, the powdered face, the beauty spots and the fully-coiffured, white wig. She had completely forgotten she was in costume. But she was too worried to smile at her incongruous appearance.

'I've missed you,' Douglas said and kissed her lightly. 'Now give me two minutes, then come and distract the doorman. Talk to him from the side door, not from the check-in window.' Another glance down the corridor and he was gone.

Maddy took off her wig, quickly brushed her hair and followed exactly two minutes later. Right outside the door she bumped into the dresser. Had Maria seen Douglas? she wondered briefly. 'Are you ready, Miss Frances?' The bovine face was unruffled. No, she couldn't have seen him.

'Just one more minute, Maria—I have to give a message to Sam.' Maddy dashed off down the corridor before Maria could offer to deliver the message for her.

There was no sign of Douglas. She circled around the front window of Sam's office which faced the stage door and called to him through the side door. 'Sam, do you have a moment?'

Sam took his head out of the sports pages and jumped to his feet. 'Of course, Miss Frances.'

'I was wondering . . .' She lowered her voice confidentially so that he would join her at the door, which of course he did. 'I was wondering . . .' Good grief, what was she wondering?

'What, Miss Frances?' Sam whispered back, flattered that she should confide in him.

'I was wondering whether anyone might have been asking for me. A man.' She looked demure, girlish, hopeful—everything that might appear alluring.

'Yes, Miss Frances. About quarter of an hour ago. He asked what dressing room you were in. I said I'd ring through and tell you he was here but he didn't want me to. Went on about how much he admired you—I thought he was just another fan.'

'Oh.' Maddy was puzzled. Douglas had said he'd slipped by unseen. 'What did he look like?'

'Late twenties, stocky, short dark hair.'

So Douglas had an accomplice. Behind Sam's head, she saw a tall shadow slip silently out through the stage door. 'Yes, that sounds like him, thank you, Sam.'

'I'm sorry, Miss Frances, I didn't know . . .'

'It's perfectly all right,' she reassured Sam. 'He's shy; he's probably waiting for me outside.' And Maddy ran back to her dressing room.

Barely five minutes later, when she dashed out the stage door in her street clothes with her make-up scrubbed off, Sam felt a little concerned. He hoped he hadn't messed things up for Miss Frances and her young lover.

Maddy arrived at the Grafton Hotel ten minutes before six. It was a small, attractive Georgian building not very far from her flat. She strolled about the downstairs bar and restaurant, looking at the cocktail lists and menu and, four minutes later, went to the foyer and pressed the lift button.

At exactly five to six she stepped out of the lift on the third floor and waited for Douglas. Twice the lift stopped on the way up, but Douglas was not in it. The third time it stopped, at precisely one minute to six, and Douglas appeared. A young woman was with him. He didn't even look in Maddy's direction, so she pushed the other lift button and pretended she was waiting to go down. She tried to tell herself the situation was becoming as ridiculous as a B-grade spy movie, but her pulse was racing and the palms of her hands were sticky.

Douglas studied the room number signs for a moment and, as soon as the young woman took the right corridor, he took the left. Maddy heard a key turning in the lock as the young woman let herself into a room several doors down from the lift and, a second after the door closed, Douglas was at her side.

'Hi,' he said.

Maddy didn't answer as she saw one of the other doors open further down the corridor and a man step out. She expected Douglas to turn aside and ignore her, but he didn't. He watched the man.

The man was in his late twenties, average height, well built, with short, dark hair. He and Douglas looked at each other for a split second. The accomplice, Maddy thought.

The man rubbed the right side of his nose with

his right index finger, then walked past them to the staircase beside the lift and started jogging down, the easy jog of a person in training.

Douglas took Maddy's arm and led her to the room. They went inside and he locked the door after them.

It was a nice room, tastefully furnished, with large windows overlooking the bustle of Tottenham Court Road.

'Well,' said Maddy, turning to him, 'where do we—' She didn't get any further. His arms were around her and he was kissing her. Deeply, longingly. And she was kissing him back. But it was wrong, Maddy knew. It was wrong.

'No,' she said, and it took every ounce of willpower to break away. 'This isn't where we start. I need answers, Douglas. I need answers now.'

'Yes, I suppose that's fair enough,' he replied. 'Drink?'

Maddy nodded. 'Just a tonic water thanks.'

As he opened the refrigerator door she noticed for the first time how tired he looked. She watched silently as he poured himself a large Scotch, added ice cubes to her tonic water then crossed to her, handed her the drink and clinked their glasses together.

'I've missed you so very, very much,' he said.

Maddy didn't dare answer. They looked at each other and Maddy had to fight the urge to embrace him, to put his head on her breast and stroke his hair. 'You look very tired,' was all she said.

He nodded, downed the Scotch in one gulp and indicated for her to sit down. 'Answers,' he said.

She sat quietly on the bed and waited.

'My name is Douglas Mackie. I am thirty-nine

years old and I was born in Glasgow. I've never lied to you, Madeleine.' Tired as he looked, it was obvious Douglas couldn't relax. He paced about the room—keeping away from the window, Maddy noticed.

'There's a wealth of things I haven't told you about myself, but I've never lied.' He poured himself another Scotch. 'I'm in the army—Major, Special Air Service Regiment.' He took a sip of the drink and turned to look at her. 'I know there have been times when you thought I was involved with criminals or the IRA or God knows what, but it was actually safer for both of us to let you believe that.'

He waited for her to say something but she didn't so he continued. 'The 22 SAS is the covert operations arm of the SASR. Our briefs are top secret and our missions are always carried out undercover. Our identities need to be protected for our own safety and the safety of our families and friends.'

Maddy was about to say something, but this time he stopped her. 'Jenny has never been in danger because of me, I swear. The dummy bomb in the theatre was a crazy coincidence—it had nothing to do with me or my work with the SAS. There was never any danger as long as my identity was unknown.' He finished the Scotch and put down the glass.

'And now it isn't?' Maddy asked quietly.

He shrugged. 'We can't be sure, but it's quite possible the newscast in Armagh may have blown my cover. At least that's what my superiors think.' He took a deep breath. 'So they're posting me to Hong Kong for a year. A cushy desk job while the heat dies down. Then they'll put me out in the field again with a new ID if necessary.'

Maddy couldn't take it all in. 'When do you leave?'

'Tomorrow morning. In the meantime I'm to see or contact no one. Especially you.'

'Why especially me?'

'You're the only person I've seen on a regular basis for the past four years. The army would therefore assume that you are the person of major importance to me and therefore the person most likely to pose a security threat to them. And they're right on both counts.'

What a strange way to tell somebody that you love them, Maddy thought vaguely.

'They've posted a marker to be with me at all times. He booked this hotel room and he sticks by my side all the way to Hong Kong.'

'A marker?' Maddy asked. 'The man who came out of this room?' She rubbed the right side of her nostril with her right index finger.

Douglas nodded. 'That's the all-clear sign. He'd checked the room out for me.'

'Surely he doesn't approve of this,' Maddy said.

Douglas allowed himself a slight smile. 'Oh, Col's pretty understanding. We've worked together a lot—he knows I'd do the same for him. As a matter of fact, the big brass probably know I'm going to try to see you one last time but they also know if Col and I are looking after each other we'll be careful.'

One last time. The words had an awful ring of finality about them. 'Hong Kong for a whole year,' she said. 'That's a hell of a long time.'

Douglas sat on the bed beside her. 'It's a hell of a place. Fancy joining me there?'

Maddy stared at him, amazed. It was the last thing she'd expected. 'Are you joking?' she asked.

'No. But I'm probably wishing. I certainly don't expect you to say yes.'

Maddy was confused. She was still trying to comprehend all he'd told her, and now he'd landed her with an instant decision which would affect her whole life.

Instinctively she started backing off. 'Well, there's Jenny,' she said. 'What about Jenny?' (Jenny was safely in boarding school and could easily come to Hong Kong for holidays. In fact she'd love it.) 'And there's my . . . life here.' (Why had she guiltily stopped herself from saying 'my career'?) 'I mean, Dad and Alma and my flat, and . . .' (Dad and Alma were a world unto themselves; her flat was just a flat.) The excuses petered out lamely.

'I know, Madeleine, I know.' He kissed her gently, then held her to him. 'Don't feel guilty because your work is so important to you. It's part of you, it's part of what I fell in love with.' He smiled. 'With you it's the theatre, with me it's the army. We're very alike.'

He had never once told her he loved her. Maddy felt like screaming, 'I'll go to Hong Kong with you, I'll go anywhere in the world with you'. But she didn't. She kissed him instead. And the kiss wasn't so gentle this time. Suddenly they were making love. Fiercely, passionately. And just as suddenly, it was over and they clung hard to each other, their bodies shuddering from the impact.

'A whole year,' Maddy murmured when they'd got their breath back and lay staring up at the ceiling.

'Probably a lot longer,' he said. 'I don't know

where they'll send me after Hong Kong.' He leaned up onto his elbow and looked at her. 'That's why I asked you to join me.'

There was something awful and final in the air and she waited for Douglas to tell her. He stroked her hair as he did.

'I think we should assume that it's over, Madeleine.'

Even though she'd known what he was going to say, a sick feeling engulfed her.

'I refuse to leave the army,' he continued, 'and you refuse to leave the theatre.' She tried to interrupt but he wouldn't let her. 'No, no listen to me. If you came to Hong Kong, it wouldn't work and you know it. I don't want to change you, Madeleine, just as you don't want to change me . . .'

'Oh hell.' He slumped on to his back and stared up at the ceiling again. 'I don't know what else to say. Maybe time will change us. Maybe one day I'll want to leave the army, maybe one day you'll want to leave the theatre—I don't know, I really don't.'

'I don't know either,' Maddy said as she put her head on his shoulder.

A minute later she sat bolt upright. 'Christ alive, what's the time?'

Douglas laughed and it was such a healthy sound. 'It's fifteen minutes before the half, don't worry you'll make it. Why don't you stay sweaty?' he called as she leapt naked for the shower.

'Phone for a taxi,' she yelled back.

Five minutes later she kissed him goodbye and said, 'I'll come back here straight after the show.'

'No.'

'What?' She looked at him, puzzled.

'I'm leaving in five minutes myself. I arranged this room just for us, now. The army has a safe house lined up and . . .' He shrugged. 'It's better this way.'

'So this is it?' No, it's too sudden, something inside her was saying. I want to stay up all night and talk. I want to watch the dawn together and cry when you leave.

'Yes, this is it. Now hurry up, you'll be late for the half.' And he bundled her out into the hall.

She turned back but the door was already closed.

As she hurried through the foyer she saw Col 'the marker' in the cocktail bar. He was seated near the door reading a newspaper, but she knew he saw her.

As she climbed into the taxi she looked up at the third storey window. No one was there.

That was it then. It had all happened so quickly.

She was five minutes late for the half. She busied herself with her make-up and wig preparation. She held her breath for Maria to tighten the laces of her stays. She climbed into her crinoline. And all the while she kept her mind blank. There was no room for distraction; she had a performance before her. Douglas had been right. It was better this way. She felt the same at interval. And after the curtain call. And in her dressing room as she washed her make-up off. Even in the cab ride home she looked at the river as they crossed Waterloo Bridge and she looked at the people as they drove through the West End and her mind remained numb.

But when she opened the door to her flat she opened the floodgates. There was nothing left to distract her. All she could think of was Douglas and the thought that she would never see him again and she was utterly miserable.

After a restless night she awoke feeling exactly the same way. She wished it wasn't Sunday, she wished she had to go to the theatre.

Try as she might Maddy couldn't talk herself out of her despair. She told herself that, in the four years of their relationship, Douglas had been away from her as often as he'd been by her side and she'd survived quite happily in his absence. But it didn't work. This time it was different and she knew it. And Jenny would know it too. She wouldn't be able to hide her misery from her daughter.

She was grateful when Alma answered the phone. 'No, I don't need to speak to her,' Maddy said, 'just tell her something's come up. Take her for a picnic to Windsor Castle, she always likes that.'

Maddy spent three hours walking around Regent's Park. It was a damp, cold day. She fed the ducks and the walk did her good but the sight of so many couples hugging each other to keep warm didn't.

She'd been home about an hour when the door opened and Jenny barged in.

'What's going on?' she demanded. She looked closely at her mother's face. 'You've been crying.'

'What on earth are you doing here?' Maddy tried to evade the scrutiny by tidying up the weekend newspapers which had been strewn all over the flat since Saturday morning.

'I bet it's Douglas, isn't it?' Jenny demanded. 'He's come back, hasn't he? What's happened?'

'You're supposed to be having a picnic at Windsor Castle,' Maddy said weakly.

'Mum, do you know what the bloody temperature is out there?'

'Don't swear,' Maddy replied automatically.

'Alma knew there was something wrong the moment you suggested it. And I'm too old for picnics at Windsor Castle, anyway.'

Maddy stopped feigning distraction and stared at her. 'You love picnics at Windsor Castle.'

'Only because it means it's Sunday and you're not at the theatre and I can be with you! Windsor Castle bores me witless and the weather's usually ratshit!'

Maddy forgot the reprimand and continued staring at her daughter.

'Mum,' Jenny said gently, her smile verging on maternal, 'I'm not a baby any more, I'm nearly fourteen. Now come on, tell me, what's he done?'

Maddy burst into tears. 'He's gone. And I love him. And I don't think I ever knew how much.'

Jenny cuddled her and Maddy wondered when her daughter had grown so tall. 'And I'm sorry I'm such a bloody rotten mother,' she sobbed.

'Don't swear.'

ACT IV

1990–1992

ACT IV

SCENE 1: 1990–1991

Harold Beauchamp was dying. Finally. Four years after they told him he would.

'Well, I certainly milked that curtain call, didn't I?' he joked to Alex when he was hospitalised for the final time.

Harold was ready to go. Bouts of chemotherapy had kept the cancer at bay but finally the treatments had ceased to be effective. Drugs which had previously dulled the pain were no longer strong enough and Harold was actually relieved when they hospitalised him for the end. He floated in and out of a drug-induced state. During his moments of lucidity, he was not only at peace with himself but obviously finding the whole process rather interesting and very flattering.

He regularly received visitors in his private room and such occasions were an opportunity for him to give a starring performance to the many people who flocked to see him. He loved them for it. Even when he wasn't fully conscious, when he was only vaguely aware of their presence on the other side of the blur that surrounded him, he was grateful. Actors, directors, writers and others he'd worked with over the years trooped in.

The press was already carrying stories of his illness and tributes to his long and impressive career. His death would make page one and the obituaries were bound to be plentiful and highly complimentary. Alex and Julian religiously cut out the articles, brought them to the hospital and read them to him. And it was Alex and Julian who spread the word that Harold welcomed visitors.

One of the most cheering aspects of the whole business, Harold decided, was that it was bringing his boys back together. If his death could serve to reunite such a beautiful friendship, then it was well worthwhile.

The rift between Julian and Alex had not been repaired. Certainly not as far as Julian was concerned. As far as Julian was concerned it never could be. He told himself, however, to be sensible and not allow it to jeopardise his career. It would be foolish to ignore the fact that he and Alex were a highly successful theatrical partnership. He allowed Alex to produce his next two plays, although he refused to direct them himself. A playwright could keep a far greater distance from the producer than a director was able to.

Both plays were black comedies and both plays were satisfactorily successful. They weren't the hit that his first play had been, though, and Julian was aware that he should vary his style.

There was always his drama, of course. The one about a man obsessed with death. The one that had resulted from the events at Berchtesgaden and Aviemore. Hard as he'd tried to ignore the play, Julian had been compelled to write it. And the experience had been cathartic. When he'd finished, he felt eased, happier that he could now see things from a clearer perspective.

He convinced himself that he'd overdramatised the events. Alex was a selfish shit and a twisted one at that. But Alex hadn't wanted to kill him. And how could he ever have thought Alex had an ulterior motive in wanting him to write the perfect murder? Alex didn't want to kill anyone, for God's sake—he just wanted a good hefty drama. And, because his rather warped mind was obsessed with death, that was the theme he wanted. Simple.

So why did Julian balk at giving Alex the play? Why? It was good. In Julian's opinion quite possibly the best thing he'd ever written.

But there was something vaguely evil about the play. Julian knew it. That was why he couldn't bring himself to show it to Alex. And the Machiavellian leading role was so clearly based upon Alex himself. It didn't seem right to feed Alex's obsession with death or to encourage his predilection for manipulating people.

However cloudy Julian's motives, he decided to hang onto the play. For a while at least.

And for some strange reason Alex didn't nag him about it as Julian had thought he would. In fact, ever since Julian's outburst in Aviemore, Alex had kept his distance to a certain degree and treated

Julian with a healthier amount of respect. He still dropped the odd hint and made passing remarks about the play, though. Particularly following Myra Nielson's average review of one of Julian's comedies: 'The polished wit we have come to expect from a Julian Oldfellow comedy was certainly evident but it is to be wondered whether perhaps Mr Oldfellow isn't becoming a touch complacent, whether perhaps he shouldn't vary his style a little.'

'You see, Julian, the critics want something different too. A drama would really do the trick,' Alex hinted slyly, 'what do you reckon?'

But the suggestions were no stronger than that and, when Julian shrugged disinterestedly, Alex dropped the subject. He never made any direct reference to the play he had suggested at Berchtesgaden.

And now Harold's impending death was far too time-consuming for Alex to contemplate undertaking any new venture. Although he was busy negotiating a London deal for *Friend Faustus*, policing the current Sydney revival of *I, Me and Us* and casting the forthcoming tour of Julian's latest play, Alex spent every moment he could at the hospital.

One Wednesday morning, in the waiting room, he bumped into Susannah. He hadn't seen her in nearly four years. Not since she'd remarried and moved to Los Angeles. She was in Australia to spend Christmas with her parents, she said, and she'd come to pay her last respects to Harold.

Susannah hadn't married her *My Fat Friend* co-star. She'd only lived with him. In fact she was already living with him when Alex returned from his trip overseas with Julian.

'I told you we needed to talk, Alex,' was all she'd said and Alex had been quite taken aback. He'd mainly been taken aback at Susannah's choice. Courtenay Frame was such a 'big girl's blouse'! A good actor certainly, very stylish, but soft and squishy and definitely considered a closet gay. Alex supposed the man couldn't be gay if Susannah was shacked up with him, but nevertheless her choice of successor rankled.

Six months later, a dashing American commercial airline pilot went to a Sydney Theatre Company production of *Pygmalion* and fell in love with Susannah's Eliza. His ardour was such that Susannah immediately became infatuated with the pilot and, just as immediately, disenchanted with Courtenay. Alex felt much better about that. He actually wished her well when she moved to Los Angeles to marry the pilot and he sent the couple a very expensive wedding present.

It was a surprise, therefore, to see her looking so drab. She'd put on weight, he thought. Not that she was fat—far from it. But she was 'average'. The acute angles which had made her face so dramatic were no longer there. The long neck, the wide, bony shoulders, everything that had made Susannah the aesthetically interesting, high-bred creature she'd once been had gone. She looked 'average': averagely attractive, averagely intelligent, averagely stylish. And there was something else missing, something she'd lost. What was it? Alex wondered. Yes, he decided, that was it. It was her intensity.

'I'm sorry about Harold, Alex,' she said. 'You two were always so close. You must be very sad.'

Alex dismissed her sympathies with a wave of his hand.

'How are you, Susannah? You look so different.'

'I'm happy,' she answered. And, as she smiled, her face positively glowed. 'I am so happy, Alex! I have two babies, did you know that? Both girls.'

Five minutes later Alex was so bored that he excused himself. Susannah had become less than average, he decided. Susannah had become ordinary.

Strangely enough, the day Susannah visited Harold turned out to be the same day Maddy chose to make her visit, although their paths didn't cross at the hospital.

Maddy and Jenny were holidaying in Sydney, spending Christmas with Helena and Todd.

Maddy didn't agonise too much about whether or not she should make her presence known to Harold, despite Julian's warnings.

'He might unintentionally let something drop to Alex,' Julian had told her. 'He's semiconscious a lot of the time lately and he's always mumbling about the past.'

'Too bad if he does say something,' Maddy replied. 'I want to see him, I really do. As long as Alex doesn't find out about Jenny, who cares what he says?'

She meant it. Over the last few years Alex had seemed to pose less and less of a threat to her. Perhaps because he was less of a threat to Jenny. Jenny was now nineteen. One more year of her acting course at the Royal Academy of Dramatic Art and she'd be out in the big, bad world all on her own.

Jenny, about to graduate from London's RADA! It seemed incredible to Maddy. It seemed only yesterday she herself was topping the first year at Sydney's NADA.

However, as adult as Jenny might be, and as diminished as the threat of Alex had become, Maddy was still strongly convinced that they shouldn't meet. Not unless Jenny professed a desire to know her father. And, caught up in her studies as Jenny was, any interest in that area seemed to have disappeared altogether.

No, Maddy decided, seeing Harold didn't pose any real threat at all, especially if she arranged her visit for a time when there was no possibility of her bumping into Alex.

Julian worked it out for her. 'Harold receives visitors twice a day,' he explained. 'Midmorning and late afternoon. Alex is normally there at both sessions but this Wednesday he's going to a matinee of the new Davison play at The Wharf so you're quite safe.'

They got to the hospital early. Fortunately no other visitors had yet arrived. Julian made Maddy stay in the waiting room while he checked out Harold's condition. He so wanted her to see the old man on one of his good days.

'Julian! Dear boy.' Yes. It was one of Harold's good days. He was propped up in his bed, prepared and eager for his visitors. A gaudily decorated Christmas tree stood in the corner of his private ward. Harold had insisted on it. He was determined to last until Christmas. That was his goal.

'I have a special visitor for you, Harold.' A moment later, Julian ushered Maddy in.

'Hello, Harold,' she said, smiling warmly.

Although she'd prepared herself, Maddy was shocked by his appearance. She'd expected an old man, of course; Harold was now eighty-five. And she knew he was dying so she'd expected a sick, frail man. But the man in the bed was unrecognisable to her. This couldn't be Harold. He was tiny. And Harold had always been so huge. People didn't shrink that much when they were dying, surely.

As the eyes in the old man's wizened skull stared blankly back at her they seemed to cloud over. Oh no, Julian thought, he's going under. 'Do you know who this is, Harold?' he prompted.

Very slowly Harold nodded. 'Oh yes,' he said, 'yes, I know who this is.' The voice was quieter, more gentle, certainly, but it was just as thrilling to Maddy as it had always been. It was Harold's voice. He opened his frail arms wide and smiled. And, as the cloudiness left his eyes and his mind came back to her from out of the past, he was the Harold of old. 'Maddy! My darling girl.'

She sat on the bed and he held her to him while the tears rolled down her cheeks. For such a fragile creature his embrace was fierce.

Maddy was angry with herself. She hadn't meant to cry. 'I'm sorry, Harold,' she sobbed. 'I really am. It's just that it's been so long since I saw you and . . .' Oh hell, she was only making things worse.

'It doesn't matter, my dear,' Harold told her, soothingly, as if she were a child. 'I'm having the most wonderful time. Now, tell me, how do you stay so young? You must be all of thirty.'

Maddy laughed. The tears dried up quickly and Harold didn't seem so tiny any more. 'I'm thirty-eight, Harold.' She longed to say 'and I have a

402

nineteen year old daughter' but knew she daren't.

'Good heavens above! You look as young as you did when I saw you last. I thought I was tripping when you walked in. The drugs do that to me a lot lately.' He gave a chesty laugh which turned into an extended wheeze but, when Maddy looked to Julian, he shrugged. If it doesn't bother Harold, we don't worry about it, he signalled back.

And it certainly didn't worry Harold. 'Oh dear, oh dear, oh dear,' he gasped when he'd finished wheezing. 'What a wonderful surprise, Julian, I do so thank you. Why isn't Alex here to share this moment?'

When Julian reminded Harold that Alex was at a matinee that afternoon, Harold waved the news aside impatiently. 'Oh yes, and a Davison play at that! He should be here to share such an occasion.'

Maddy looked beseechingly at Julian, who explained, as simply as possible, that Maddy would rather Alex didn't know she was in Sydney.

'Why?' Harold demanded.

'Because she would, that's why!' Julian said rather brutally and he signalled Maddy not to interrupt. Harold was threatening to become difficult and Julian knew that when Harold became difficult the only way to treat him was like a naughty child. 'She leads a different life altogether now and the last thing she needs is a blast from the past— and certainly not a blast like Alex.'

'All right, all right,' Harold replied peevishly.

'Do you promise not to say anything?'

Harold's look to Julian was sullen. Then he turned to Maddy. 'Is that what you really want?'

'Yes, Harold,' Maddy nodded. 'I'd rather you didn't say anything.'

'Very well.' Harold seemed satisfied with that. 'I shan't.'

Harold kept his promise for five days. But on Christmas Eve, as his mind wandered through the maze of yesterdays, he blurted it out. Alex was seated beside the bed at the time, holding the old man's hand. Harold had been semiconscious for most of the day and the few other visitors had long since gone.

The doctors had told Alex that it was likely Harold would never regain consciousness and that he could die at any moment so Alex had been studying him intently, determined to witness the actual instant of death. He was startled when Harold's eyes sprang wide open.

'She came to see me yesterday.'

'Oh yes? Who?'

The eyes started to sag again. 'So beautiful. Still so beautiful.'

'Who?'

The eyes were closed now. 'Maddy. Your Maddy.'

'That's nice.' Maddy, Alex thought. The old man was remembering Maddy in his flights of fancy. Alex could barely recollect what she looked like himself. He could remember the photos he took of her, though. My God, they were horny, he thought. I wonder whatever happened to them? Chucked out with all the rest of the junk when he moved in with Susannah, he supposed. Alex never kept memorabilia.

'And Julian,' Harold continued. 'So over-protective. Selfish, I thought.' There was a peevish note to his rambling. 'Selfish to keep you two apart. Selfish to keep secrets.'

'Julian?' Alex stopped concentrating on the imminent death and focused on what Harold was saying. 'Julian brought Maddy to see you?'

'Yes, yes, yes.' The eyes remained closed and the brow furrowed irritably. 'Secrets, silly secrets.' Harold became incomprehensible as he once again lapsed into semiconsciousness.

Alex leaned forward to study him closely. Any minute now, he told himself. But, while he watched, a question lurked in the back of his mind. Why on earth would Julian want to keep Maddy a secret? Why was he being so 'overprotective'? Why was he swearing a dying man to secrecy?

Alex stored up the knowledge as 'useful information' and concentrated his full attention on Harold's breathing. It had become very shallow.

Once again it was a shock when the old man's eyes sprang open. For a moment Harold seemed to hold his breath as he concentrated very hard.

'What day is it?' he asked finally.

Alex hesitated for only a fraction of a second. 'It's Christmas Day, Harold.'

The eyes remained open and they were bright and clear. 'Christmas Day . . .'

'Yes,' Alex lied, 'you made it.'

Harold breathed a sigh of contentment. He was wide awake now. 'It's been a good life. And you're here with me at the end of it, Alex. That makes me very happy.'

Alex nodded, riveted. There was such joy in the old man. Such a surge of energy, right before the moment of death. It was fascinating.

If Harold had had the strength he would have thrown back his head and given a huge, boisterous bellow of laughter. Alex was so readable! But it didn't matter at all to Harold that Alex was waiting to witness his very last breath. In fact it was wonderful, it was joyful. He had remained fascinating to Alex until the very end.

Harold racked his brains to think of the perfect line for his departure. He had it. ' "To die would be a very great adventure",' he said. 'I always wanted to play Peter Pan so that I could say that line. But they only let girls play Peter Pan. "To die would be a very great adventure." ' He said it again and the words rolled off his tongue as he savoured every syllable.

Magnificent, he thought. Surely his finest performance. And he closed his eyes to capture in his mind the look of pure admiration on Alex's face. 'Mr Barrie was quite right,' he said as he drifted off to sleep.

Alex didn't have to wait too long. An hour later Harold stopped breathing.

The funeral was the day after Boxing Day but Maddy didn't go. Not because she wanted to avoid Alex. There would be so many people there she was sure she could have sat up the back unnoticed. She didn't go because she was on a plane back to London to start rehearsals for *Woman in Mind* the following day.

She sent some flowers: yellow roses. Harold's favourites. And she rang Julian from the airport, just before he left for the funeral. 'I wanted to let you know I'll be thinking of you,' she said. 'Of you and Harold and . . . everything.'

'Yes,' Julian answered. 'It's the end of an era, isn't it? Did you see Whitlam's obituary in this morning's *Herald*?'

'Yes, she did him proud, didn't she? He would have loved that.'

Maddy took a sleeping pill during the flight. It was something she rarely did, but she felt a bit miserable. Empty somehow. And more than a little lonely. Jenny had offered to curtail her holiday and come back to England with her mother but Maddy had thought that wasn't quite fair on the girl. She so loved her visits to Australia.

Maddy and Jenny had taken to spending each second Christmas in Sydney and Jenny adored the bizarre alternation. Snowmen, log fires and traditional hot turkey dinners at Windsor with Robert and Alma one year. Then the following year, beaches, sunbaking, oysters, seafood and cold meat platters on the Sydney harbourside patio with Helena and Todd.

Dear Jen, thought Maddy as she accepted the cushion and blanket the flight attendant offered her. She was such a pillar of strength and such a good friend. Maddy had become very reliant on her company, particularly over the last two years since Jenny had moved into the flat full-time.

'This beats boarding school, Mum, I can tell you,' she'd say time and time again as she messed about in the kitchen or sprawled out on the sofa with a stack of the weekend newspapers.

'You weren't unhappy at boarding school, were you?' Maddy asked guiltily. 'You never said—'

'Stop getting paranoid. Of course I wasn't, I had a great time. This just beats it, that's all.' The tone in Jenny's voice brooked the end of the discussion and Maddy felt she would never know whether or not her daughter was lying to protect her.

The plane hit a pocket of turbulence and Maddy was jolted out of the sleep she'd been drifting towards. She mustn't become too dependent on Jenny's company, she warned herself as she settled down again. There'd be lonely days ahead when Jenny graduated from RADA and went out on her own. Lonely days like those following Douglas's departure when work didn't seem as fulfilling as it once was, when the theatre lost some of its magic.

She'd often wondered, over the past five years, whether she should have accepted Douglas's offer and gone to Hong Kong. Too late now, of course. But she was still wondering as the sleeping pill took over.

Rehearsals for the new production were so consuming that Maddy didn't actually have time to miss Jenny too much. Her role in Ayckbourn's black comedy of a woman having a nervous breakdown was exhausting to say the least. The play reminded her a lot of Julian's style of writing and she told him so over the phone.

'It's about as black as you can get, but hysterically funny at the same time. Just like your plays.'

Julian accepted the comment as the compliment it was intended to be, but he felt slightly goaded at the same time. 'Well, I just might surprise you, my darling. I've written a drama, totally different style, which Alex is going to produce.'

There. He'd said it. Maddy was the first person he'd told and it somehow clinched in his mind the reluctant agreement he'd made with Alex.

It had been the day of Harold's funeral that Julian

had changed his mind. Not long after the service, as a matter of fact.

He and Alex had bought a bottle of Scotch and gone down to Double Bay. Neither of them wanted to go to the wake immediately. It was bound to be a raucous affair, which Harold would have loved, with the majority of the theatrical profession in attendance. It was being held at Kinselas, a trendy actors' nightclub. Harold's idea. 'Very apt, dear boy, very apt,' he'd chuckled. Kinselas was a converted funeral parlour.

They looked out at Sydney Harbour, the same view they'd looked at so many times from Harold's flat, and it was a full five minutes before either of them spoke.

'He's left his flat to the Actors Benevolent Fund, did you know that?' Alex asked.

'No, I didn't.' Julian took a swig from the bottle and handed it over. 'Good on him.'

'Yes.'

It was true. A week before he died Harold had said, 'You don't mind, do you, my dear Alexei? I'd leave it to you if I felt you needed it. To you and Julian. But you're both very well off.'

'Of course I don't mind, Harold,' Alex had replied, and he'd meant it. So long as he could live the lifestyle he liked, superfluous wealth and possessions were of little importance to him. 'He died magnificently.' Alex continued to stare out across the bay. 'Magnificent, he was. Bloody magnificent.'

They stood in silence for several minutes. Finally Alex said, 'You've written my drama, haven't you?' It was only then he turned to Julian. 'Why not stop mucking around and give it to me?'

The shock tactic succeeded. Julian's guilty reaction was eminently readable and he was at a loss for words.

'Why don't you want to give it to me?' Alex asked.

Julian shrugged. He knew there was no point in denying he'd written the play. 'Because I don't think you're the right person to have it,' he answered lamely.

'Why not?'

What could he say? Julian wondered. Could he say, 'Because the play is evil and the play is you and if the two combine something terrible will happen'? That was what he felt, but how could he say it? He decided that no explanation whatsoever was the best way out. 'I'm not giving you the play, Alex,' he said firmly. 'I'm never giving you the play. You'll just have to accept that.' Julian took the bottle back, swigged and waited for the argument.

None was forthcoming. Good, thought Julian. Alex had accepted the finality of his decision.

'You ready for the wake?' he asked Alex as he handed back the bottle.

'Yep.' Alex took a brief swig himself. 'Just one more question,' he said as they turned to go. 'Why don't you want me to see Maddy?' Julian stopped, frozen in his tracks. 'We were very close all those years ago, Julian. It broke my heart when she left. And now you want to keep us apart. I can't think why you'd want to do that.'

Bingo, Alex thought as he read all the signs. Julian is genuinely shocked that I know Maddy's back. And he's scared as hell that I might try and see her. Very interesting. Why?

The reason for Julian's consternation was certainly of interest to Alex, but it was of no great value so he didn't pursue it. 'Don't look so upset.' He put a comradely arm around Julian's shoulder. 'I won't see Maddy if you really don't want me to. And I won't even ask the reasons why. Just give me the play—that's all I'm after. Simple.'

Julian pulled away from the embrace and started striding angrily up the hill. It was blackmail, of course. Sheer blackmail. And of course he had no option but to accept the offer. Accept it and pray that Alex had such little interest in Maddy that he would honour the agreement.

Confident that he'd won, Alex followed, wondering again what the mystery was. Had Julian turned straight? Was he having an affair with Maddy? No, that was laughable. Maddy was in a relationship, perhaps, and Julian was afraid the relationship might be threatened if Alex came back into her life?

Yes, that was far more believable. And certainly far more exciting. It might be fun to see Maddy again after all these years, Alex thought. Not that he would dare seek her out, of course, until the play was well and truly into production.

'There's no point in being annoyed Julian, the most sensible—'

'Shut up!' Julian's face was a mask of anger and he strode on ahead. 'You'll get your play.'

When Jenny phoned her mother to say she'd be coming home a few days later than planned Maddy had to force the good humour a little.

'No, darling, of course I don't mind. (She did mind, she'd been a bit down lately and she'd been

411

relying on Jenny's return to give her a boost.) But you said you had such a lot to do before the start of the new term. Getting your books and . . .' (Careful Maddy, you're sounding like a nag.) 'Oh, well, who cares so long as you're having fun.'

'Mum!' Jenny was exasperated. Her mother was so predictable! 'Don't you want to know why?'

'Oh. Of course I do. (Bugger it, she'd been thinking of herself as usual. And, as usual, Jenny had caught her out.) 'I'm sorry, darling, I didn't mean . . .'

'I think I'm in love.'

Out it all came. His name was Paul, he was twenty-five years old, he was a recently qualified doctor of medicine and he was serving his first year's internship at St Vincent's Hospital. (Maddy breathed a sigh of relief that he wasn't an actor.)

'We met the day after you left. At a charity dinner. His mother's on the Variety Club Committee and she and Helena are great mates.'

'Oh, that's nice.' (Trendy socialite posing as philanthropist, Maddy thought.)

'No, Mum, you've got it all wrong. She's a terrific woman.'

'I didn't say a word.'

'You didn't have to.'

Damn, Jenny never let her get away with a trick.

'It's only for a few extra days,' Jenny continued. 'He wants us to spend New Year's Eve together.'

'That's fine, darling, but what about flights? The Gulf crisis—'

'I've already checked out the flights. I'm booked on Qantas via the States, not going anywhere near the Middle East. It'll be quite safe. Now, are you sure you don't mind?'

'Of course not.' What difference would it make if she did? Maddy thought. Once Jenny had decided on something, that was it. It was a quality which Maddy had learned to respect in her daughter, although on occasions it irked her. And it was a quality which she knew would take Jenny far. She was a strong and determined young woman. Not so very different from herself at that age, Maddy thought as she recalled her own resistance to her father and her determination to do everything on her own. And Jenny, like herself, had experienced a solitary childhood.

The recognition of this fact often precipitated a rush of guilt. And every rush of guilt brought about a sudden and equal rush of motherly concern which Jenny always saw through.

'You're fussing again, Mum. You don't need to. Get off your guilt trip.'

For a while Maddy worried that Jenny's teenage toughness might augur a 'hard' streak in the girl. The years from fifteen to seventeen were certainly difficult ones and the culmination came on Jenny's seventeenth birthday.

Maddy had allowed her to drink too much champagne, they'd started talking about sex and suddenly Jenny admitted that she had lost her virginity over six months ago.

'But you didn't say anything.' Maddy was deeply shocked. 'You always promised you'd tell me.'

'It was no big deal,' Jenny shrugged. 'Just a touch up in the back of his car.' She poured the last drops from the bottle into her glass. 'A touch up that got a bit out of hand, that's all.' She didn't know why she was playing it so tough. She only knew that she wanted to shock her mother. For once she didn't want to salve Maddy's guilt, she wanted to rub her nose in it. To say, 'Where were you for half of my childhood?' She also knew that the room was starting to spin and she was close to throwing up.

'Oh, Jen.' Maddy put her arm around her.

Jenny started to pull away. Then, all of a sudden, she gave in, dropped her head on her mother's shoulder and sobbed.

'I'm sorry, I'm just drunk, that's all.'

'Yes, I know,' Maddy said gently, stroking Jenny's hair.

'I didn't mean to get at you.'

'Yes, you did, and I deserve it. You're allowed to have a dig every now and then.'

'Oh, shit!'

'No, I mean it,' Maddy declared, 'I'm not playing martyr, you deserve—'

'I'm going to throw up.'

Things were much better after that night.

Jenny's flight from Sydney arrived on Saturday. There were no rehearsals and Maddy was able to meet her at the airport. As soon as she saw her daughter she recognised the change. Yes, she's in love, all right, thought Maddy.

Jenny had always been a good-looking girl. A little above average height, with a well-proportioned body and excellent bearing, the impression she gave was that of a fine, strong filly. Now, as the grey-blue eyes picked out Maddy from the crowd and, as Jenny tossed her sandy hair back over her shoulders and walked towards her mother, Maddy realised with a shock that her daughter's sexuality was virtually palpable. Heads turned to watch her with varying degrees of lust, envy and admiration. Oh yes, Maddy thought, she's certainly been sowing her wild oats.

For the following week it was 'Paul this', 'Paul that', and the phone rang at all hours. Then came the excited announcement that he would be in England the following month for a fortnight's holiday.

'He can't stand it any longer,' Jenny declared dramatically. 'He simply has to see me. Great, eh?'

'I suppose I'd better shift out so you can have the flat to yourselves,' Maddy said.

'No, your show'll be running by then,' Jenny smiled. 'Eight performances a week should give us time enough.'

How exhausting, Maddy thought. But then, everything was exhausting to her lately. Her role in *Woman in Mind*, which opened in a week, was exhausting. The winter was exhausting. It seemed to be a particularly bitter one and she resented getting out of bed in the morning for rehearsals. It was a pity. Normally she loved the rehearsal period of a play.

She didn't know why she was so jaded. Maybe she was getting old. She'd be thirty-nine in a minute. Hell, so close to forty. Maybe it was being in the company of such fervent young passion. Yes, that was it: she was probably jealous.

Then, on Friday, as she left rehearsals, it all changed.

He was standing on the opposite side of the street and, although there were plenty of other people about, he was the first thing that caught her eye as she stepped out onto the pavement. He was watching the stage door so intently that he literally willed her to look in his direction.

She darted several glances about to see if anyone else was looking and she wondered wildly what she was supposed to do. Their clandestine meeting over five years before had been so beset with cloak and dagger rules . . .

Rule number one. He was staring at her, but he wasn't acknowledging her. 'If I don't acknowledge you, don't acknowledge me.' Hell! What was the 'all clear' sign? Right index finger, right side of nose. Maybe she should do that. She did. She rubbed her nose frantically. And she watched as Douglas burst out laughing.

He crossed the street and he was still laughing as he picked her up and crushed her to him.

'You're hurting me,' she said breathlessly. 'And what's so bloody funny? Didn't I do it right?'

'Yes, you did it right,' he answered as he put her down. 'You overacted a bit, that's all.'

'Well, why didn't you acknowledge me? You said, "If I don't—".'

'I just wanted to watch you for a couple of seconds, that's all. Have you missed me? Are you with someone else? Can we go to your place and talk?'

'Yes, no, yes,' Maddy said and kissed him.

Talk they did. When Jenny arrived home an hour and a half later, Maddy and Douglas hadn't even scratched the surface. The questions tumbled out, the answers remained half finished. They both wanted to talk and ask about everything that had happened over the past five years, all the while taking pleasure in the knowledge that soon they would be exploring each other's bodies in the same feverish way.

'Douglas!'

'Hi, Jenny. Long time.' Douglas was so struck by the sexuality of the girl that it didn't seem right to say any of the usual trite comments like, 'Haven't you grown up?' or 'What happened to the little girl I knew?'

'Yes, five years,' Jenny answered. 'Hi, Mum, how was the tech?'

'Hell, as usual.' Maddy heaved a theatrical sigh but she wasn't joking. The first full technical run of a play was always torturous.

Douglas looked admiringly at the two women. It was difficult to believe that Maddy was Jenny's mother—they were so different in looks. But, although Jenny didn't have the delicate bones and fine features of her mother, there was certainly one thing they had in common. They were both extremely sensual-looking women. For the first time, Douglas wondered briefly about Jenny's father. He must have been a bit of a looker too, he supposed.

'How long are you in town this time?' Jenny asked and there was no mistaking the icy tone.

'Jen!'

Douglas had registered the dig. He'd registered the cool reception from the moment Jenny had entered the room. He shrugged at Maddy to show he understood. The girl was obviously being protective of her mother.

'Sorry. Just asking.' Jenny picked up the ice bucket. 'Shall I get a refill?'

'Yes,' said Maddy quickly. 'I'll give you a hand.'

As they disappeared into the kitchen, Douglas got up and inspected the view from the window at the far end of the lounge to allow them to talk about him at ease.

'Don't behave like a bitch,' Maddy hissed. 'Don't spoil things.'

'I'm sorry, Mum. I'm really sorry.' Jenny could have kicked herself. Why did she do it? As soon as she'd arrived home, one look at her mother's radiant face should have told her to back off. But no, she had to come out with the smartarse comments. So what if the man was going to fuck up her mother's life, walking in and out when he pleased? He sure as hell made her happy when he walked in, didn't he? And the couple of actors Maddy had tried it on with over the last several years—out of sheer desperation, Jenny could only suppose—had been dead losses.

'I'm glad he's back.' Jenny cracked a fresh tray of ice cubes into the bucket. 'I thought I might go and see Grandpa and Alma for the weekend.' She grinned and gave a lascivious wink.

'That's very thoughtful,' Maddy didn't acknowledge the wink, 'but I don't know if he's staying.'

'Well, we'll soon find out.' Before Maddy could stop her, Jenny picked up the ice bucket and disappeared into the lounge.

'You staying the weekend, Douglas?' she asked as she put some ice cubes into his glass and handed him the bottle of Scotch. Any malice had gone and the grey-blue eyes twinkled with humour.

'Oh. Well . . .' Douglas looked in confusion at Maddy who was standing in the kitchen doorway. 'I don't know, I . . .' Maddy smiled and nodded. 'Yes, I'd certainly like to,' he said.

'Good.' Jenny tipped some ice cubes into her mother's glass. 'That saves me having to get a babysitter for Mum.'

Later that night, after they'd made love, Douglas held Maddy to him so closely that she could scarcely breathe.

'What is it?' she asked. 'What's the matter?'

'I love you, Madeleine,' he said.

She savoured the words for several minutes. 'How long can you stay?'

'The weekend. Just the weekend.'

'Where do you—'

'Sssh.' He drew her to him again. 'Tomorrow. I'll tell you all about it tomorrow.'

Jenny had already left when they woke up. The note read, *Coming back Monday morning, have fun, Love, Jen. P.S. Am taking Alma to Windsor Castle for picnic Sunday.*

'No bacon and eggs,' Douglas said in mock horror as he explored the refrigerator.

'Try getting a teenage girl to eat bacon and eggs,' Maddy answered.

Ten minutes later he was back with the supplies and half an hour later they were eating not only bacon and eggs but sausages, fried tomatoes and mushrooms.

'The full catastrophe,' Maddy said with relish as she speared an egg yolk. 'I haven't had a breakfast like this for five years.'

'Nor have I.'

After breakfast they went for a long walk in Regent's Park. As they stood watching the ducks on the lake, they cuddled close to keep out the cold and Maddy thought of those other couples she'd watched so enviously the day after Douglas had left. Same park, same lake. She wondered if some of the ducks were the same. And she wondered whether she'd be back here in a few days' time, depressed all over again.

She took a deep breath. 'It's tomorrow, Douglas. You said you'd tell me all about it tomorrow. Where are you off to after the weekend? What's happening?'

'You warm enough?' he asked. She nodded and he led her to a park bench. Once they were seated, he said, 'I'm off to the Gulf after the weekend. There's going to be a war.'

Maddy stared back at him. 'But the deadline isn't until the fifteenth. Hussein's got nearly a whole week to get his troops out of Kuwait.' Douglas didn't say anything. 'Nobody believes he's going to take on the whole US army.' Still Douglas said nothing. 'He wouldn't, surely.'

'We believe he would. We believe he's about to take on the entire forces of the United Nations.'

Maddy was horrified.

'He's a madman,' Douglas continued, 'and he's prepared to risk a bloodbath.'

'But . . .' Maddy didn't know what to say. 'My God.' She looked out over the lake again and, when she finally spoke, it was with an edge of desperation. 'But surely you don't have to go in there until the actual invasion?' Surely she could buy a few more days with him, she was really saying: surely the longer he could delay going, the greater the possibility the war might not eventuate at all. Time, I have to buy time, she thought wildly.

Douglas read her desperation and smiled. 'I've

already been there,' he said. 'You know the mob I work for, you know the way we function. We've been on covert operations in the Gulf for the past fortnight.' He put his arm around her shoulders and drew her to him. 'They've given me these few days in London to tie up the loose ends, then it's back to Saudi Arabia until the invasion and then . . .' He gave a sigh of resignation. 'Then, my darling, who knows? Who the hell knows!'

The strangest mixture of emotions engulfed Maddy. She felt frightened, she felt confused and, above all, she felt angry. Had he come back into her life for a brief weekend before going off to get killed? Better he'd never returned at all, if that was the case. She knew it was fear dictating her anger but she didn't care. She didn't care if she was being selfish. It wasn't fair of him to die. Not now. Not when she was willing to accept freely any conditions he offered. She'd give up the theatre for him, she'd move to Hong Kong. Anything. She'd do anything.

She pulled away from his embrace. 'You could resign,' she said. 'You could leave the army.'

'No, I couldn't.'

'Why the hell not?' she demanded. 'You've given them your whole life. You're forty-five years old—surely they'd let you resign.'

'Forty-four,' Douglas corrected. 'And yes, they'd let me resign, but I couldn't possibly do it.'

'Why?' Maddy's anger was edging towards hysteria. 'Give me one good reason why. You don't owe them anything . . .'

'Oh, yes I do!' he countered. 'Maybe not the army, but my men . . . I owe my men.'

'What!' She was close to tears now. 'What do

you owe them? Some sort of bloody macho wartime camaraderie? Well, fuck that!'

'Let's walk.' Douglas stood and took her hand but she pulled away from him. 'Come on now.' He bent down and lifted her to her feet. 'You're getting yourself all worked up and that's silly. Let's walk.'

He put his arm around her and they walked beside the lake.

'I'm sorry,' she said while she fumbled for a tissue.

But he didn't seem to hear her. 'Let me tell you a story,' he said. They walked silently for several seconds and then he began. 'Do you remember when I first met you?'

The reply came, muffled through the tissues. '*The Lady from Maxim's*.'

'That's right. You were cancan-ing your way into the hearts of London theatregoers and Britain was at war with Argentina.'

Maddy felt her face flush and she looked away. She supposed she deserved it but it was a bit below the belt.

Douglas stopped and turned her to him. 'No, Madeleine, that wasn't a dig. I wasn't making fun of you. At the time, I was between operations in the Falklands and *The Lady from Maxim's* was just what I needed.' He grinned. 'It was one hell of a cancan, I can tell you.'

Maddy smiled back weakly.

'That's better,' he said. 'Now stop personalising and pay attention.' Arm in arm, they walked on.

'I thought I was pretty well toughened up when I went to the Falklands,' he said. 'I'd seen a lot of death, seen people killed en masse, killed people myself. I knew what was expected of me, and so did my men.'

'We were a good unit. I remember a covert night operation on Pebble Island: thirty Pacara aircraft destroyed in the one raid; minimum injuries sustained.' He shook his head in admiration. 'Good men.'

He stopped and watched two swans gliding across the water towards them. 'I'd seen a lot of heroism before I went to the Falklands and I thought I knew all about that too. Courage can be so contagious I've actually seen men compete to save each other. And it's not "macho wartime camaraderie". No, don't look away—that wasn't a dig either.'

The swans had arrived at the water's edge. Douglas watched them as they were rapidly joined by a host of ducks. And as he watched, Maddy realised that he wasn't really seeing them at all.

'We were on a mission. Just myself and six of the men. They were flying us to Argentina in a Sea King and we were hit. The chopper was badly damaged and the pilot made a crash landing in the Atlantic, just off the coast. He handled it well: we landed OK, but we couldn't open the doors in the hold. The only exit was through the cockpit windows.

'It was chaos. Cargo and netting and debris were everywhere, and the hold started to fill with water. It was freezing. But the men kept their heads. After the pilot, the copilot and the load-master got out, the rest of us hung on to the nearest solid object and, according to who was nearest to the cockpit, we waited our turn. We knew we only had a couple of minutes, of course. When those things fill with water they sink like a stone.

'I was third in line, with four behind me, and

the tail of the chopper was already sinking. When I was halfway into the cockpit, the whole thing lurched and the tail pointed straight to the bottom of the ocean. I was waist-deep in water, and I knew that the hold was flooded and that any second we'd go down. I tried to pull myself up into the cockpit but my leg was caught in the cargo netting and I realised there was no way I was going to get free. I thought, "Oh Christ, here we go".'

Maddy had been watching him without saying a word and she was startled when he suddenly turned to her. 'Strangest thing, you know. In that instant, all I could think of was the men behind me—they were going to die. They were already drowning in the hold below and any second I would be too. We were all going to die together and it seemed right somehow. I accepted it.

'And then I felt a hand on my leg. It explored the rope that had me trapped and then it disappeared. It was back a second later with a knife and it started to cut me free. Just the one hand it was, not two. The other hand must have had a purchase on something solid to gain the traction needed to saw the ropes.' He shrugged. 'Either that or the man was physically trapped beneath the debris, I don't know.'

Douglas paused and looked out across the lake. 'Then he tapped my leg. I can still feel it. Very methodically, three times, he tapped my leg. He was saying "You can go now".'

It was several moments before Douglas turned back to Maddy. 'I got out and the chopper went down like a ton of bricks. I'll never know which of the four men it was.

'For a long time after that I felt guilty to be

alive,' he said. 'Christ, it's cold.' He put an arm around her again. 'Let's go home.' Maddy still didn't dare say anything and they walked in silence for a minute or so.

'I don't feel guilty any more,' he said as they arrived at the park gates. 'But you can see why I owe, can't you, Madeleine? You can see why I have to go to the Gulf.'

Maddy nodded. 'Yes.'

When they got home they had a hot shower together and they made love. Very tenderly.

Afterwards Douglas said, 'If I get through this war OK, and I certainly intend to, I'm going to leave the army. Would you fancy settling down with me?'

'Is that a proposal?'

'I suppose it is.'

'You'd leave the army?'

'Well you won't leave the theatre, will you? I don't have much choice.'

'I might if you asked me.'

He smiled. 'Let's worry about who gives in when the time comes. But I take it that's a yes?'

'I suppose it is.'

Two days later he left.

Maddy followed the war avidly. And it was a very easy war to follow. 'The first television war', it gave birth to many famous quotes from the unaffected, uninformed and generally disinterested sector: 'What's happened with the war?' 'I don't know, I didn't watch TV last night'. 'Anything good on the telly?' 'No, just the war'.

It was over in less than two months. But Douglas

didn't come back. Enquiries proved that he wasn't on any casualty list but, despite the fact that Maddy, distraught, repeatedly made a nuisance of herself at Whitehall, that was the only news of him the army would release.

One Sunday night six months later, the front door buzzer sounded and a voice with a distinctive Cockney accent announced 'Colin Coburn here.' Who the hell's Colin Coburn? Maddy wondered, but she didn't have time to ask. The voice said, 'I have a message from Douglas Mackie', and her heart lurched.

Maddy opened the door to a stocky, dark-haired man in his mid-thirties and, although she hadn't seen him in over five years, she recognised him immediately. 'The marker,' she said.

Col smiled. 'That's right. The name's Colin Coburn.' They shook hands. 'I'm not supposed to be here, but the major wanted you to know that he was all right.

'You OK?' he asked as Maddy sank into a chair.

'Yes, fine,' she answered. 'I'm fine.' She felt lightheaded with relief. Although she'd resolutely refused to believe the worst, she'd been desperately worried.

He explained that Douglas was one of several SASR officers remaining in Northern Iraq to serve as military advisers to the Kurds. 'All covert, of course,' said Col. 'Nobody's supposed to know that, so keep it under your hat.'

Colin wasn't able to tell her any more. Douglas wasn't sure when he'd be back.

But it was enough for Maddy. Douglas was safe.

Life was very full for both Maddy and Jenny. Maddy was doing another film for Viktor Hoff which, as usual, was an exhausting experience. Jenny had just graduated from RADA.

Like her mother, Jenny had been an excellent student and she graduated with flying colours. A highly reputable agent signed her up, and her career appeared about to take off.

So why, Maddy wondered, was she so set upon getting engaged to Paul? It was a disastrous idea—but, of course, she didn't dare say so to Jenny.

'You're very young, darling,' she said tentatively. 'And you haven't even known him a year. Don't you think you should wait?'

'Why?'

Maddy heaved a sigh. She knew Jenny was going to be cantankerous. 'Because you're very young . . .'

'I'm twenty.'

'And you've only known him for ten months.'

'Don't you like him?'

'Yes, yes, I do.' Maddy backed off. I give up, she thought. Anything I say is only going to push her in the opposite direction. Christ, she's twenty years old, if she wants to stifle herself, let her. But she worried nevertheless.

Maddy had liked Paul when she'd met him. There was nothing to dislike. He was a very pleasant, very middle class, very nice young man, and he was obviously besotted with Jenny. That was the problem, Maddy thought. Paul was besotted with Jenny, and Jenny was besotted with sex.

Maddy could see herself in Jenny. She could see the girl revelling in her new-found sexuality just as Maddy herself had been unleashed by Alex and the passion they'd shared. Jenny was delighting

427

in her discovery, and there was certainly nothing wrong with that, but engagement? Marriage? No, Maddy thought, it wouldn't be fair: the person who would suffer would be Paul. But of course she couldn't say anything.

As it was, Jenny sensed her mother's disapproval and a further argument followed when Jenny insisted on spending the whole of her Christmas break in Sydney.

'Just a week with Grandpa and Alma in Windsor,' Maddy suggested. 'It's their turn, after all. And then you can go to Sydney.'

But Jenny had made her decision. She was in love, she was irritated with Maddy for not being totally in favour of an engagement, she was going to Sydney, and that was that.

Maddy gave up and concentrated on her film. It was a German/Swiss/Belgian production being shot half in French and half in German—a typical Viktor Hoff project. Viktor had never broken into the American film market, but the more bizarre areas of the European cinema continued to hold him in high regard.

There were only five more days of studio interiors to be shot in Munich following the two-week production break over Christmas. Like the rest of the cast and crew, Maddy returned to work very relaxed after the holiday break. She'd had a lovely time in Windsor with Robert and Alma— log fires and snowball fights made her feel like a child again.

Three days into the shoot the phone rang at six o'clock in the morning in her Munich hotel room. It was Jenny. 'Mum, don't be mad, please. But

I'm staying in Sydney. Well, for six months anyway . . .'

'You've done it.' Maddy heaved an exasperated sigh. 'You and Paul have gone and got engaged—'

'No. Well . . . he wants to and I was going to and . . . but no, it's not that.'

Maddy felt a jolt of alarm. 'You're not going to run off and get married or anything are you?'

'Don't be crazy, Mum. You and I might have our fights, for God's sake, but I want you at my wedding!'

'Then I hope you've told your agent that you're opting out,' Maddy said irritably. 'They'll be lining up tests and auditions and interviews for the new season and it's not very professional—'

'Mum, I've landed a job!' Jenny could hardly contain her excitement. 'A terrific job! Everyone in Sydney's been after it. It's the female lead and it's going to be the biggest production ever to come out of Australia.'

Oh, yes, Maddy thought, they all say that. 'What is it?' she asked, trying to sound enthusiastic.

'It's Julian Oldfellow's latest play. Just imagine, Mum! Imagine me being in one of *Julian's* plays! It's called *Centre Stage* and it's going to be an international success, just like his other plays, and it's being produced by the same bloke—Alex Rainford. He's also playing the lead—we'll be working opposite each other. I've met him, Mum. He's dynamic!'

ACT IV

SCENE 2: 1991–1992

From the moment Alex first read *Centre Stage* he
became obsessed with the play.

> A SPOTLIGHT ON A MAN STANDING
> ALONE, CENTRE STAGE. IT IS EDWIN.
> HE ADDRESSES THE AUDIENCE.
>
> #### EDWIN
>
> I watched a man die in the street once.
> It was a heart attack I think. I was
> about eight years old at the time. He
> was just a man. Just a man in the
> street. I didn't know him. But watching
> him die was the most intimate experience
> I've ever shared with another human
> being.

I was the last person he saw, the last
person he made contact with and, as I
watched his eyes glaze over, I felt
deeply grateful. It was an extraordinary
gift to share with a stranger.

EDWIN WALKS DOWNSTAGE

That was how it started. I've been
searching all my life for someone with
whom I could repeat that intimate
experience. And I've finally found her.
Tonight's the night.

THE STAGE LIGHTS UP. WE ARE IN
EDWIN'S HOME. HE SMILES AT THE
AUDIENCE.

And I wanted to share it with you.

HE TURNS UPSTAGE AS KATERINA
APPEARS.

My darling!

SHE RUNS TO HIM AND THEY
EMBRACE.

Throughout the play Edwin maintains his one-
to-one relationship with the audience. He shares
with them his manipulation of Katerina to the point
where she is willing to present him with the ultimate
gift. Her death.

Alex was spellbound. He remembered Tim's
ultimate gift—the gift of his death—and he realised
that it *was* the most intimate experience he'd shared
with a person. He thought of the sexual power he'd

had over women and he thrilled at the notion of a woman giving him her life.

'I want to play Edwin,' he announced to Julian as soon as he'd read *Centre Stage*. And when Julian stared back at him, aghast, Alex added, 'What better casting could there be? Edwin's me and we both know it.'

'But you're producing the thing, for God's sake,' Julian objected. 'You can't produce it and play the lead as well.'

'I don't intend to,' Alex countered smoothly. 'I've already spoken to Alain King and he's more than interested in co-producing.'

Julian had strong misgivings but Alex overrode them. 'Sure, it's a long time since I acted, but it's what I'm trained to do . . . and if I don't come up with the goods you and Alain can feel free to sack me. Just think of the press! A Julian Oldfellow play, coproduced by Alain King and starring Alex Rainford.'

'All right,' Julian reluctantly agreed. 'We'll see how you go.'

Alex was so elated by the prospect that he didn't point out Julian's limited contractual rights, which didn't include right of veto over casting. 'Thank you, Julian,' he said with just the right degree of humility.

After reading *Centre Stage* Alain King was as excited as Alex about its potential.

'The mistress should be much younger, though,' he insisted during an early production meeting. 'She should be a virgin when they meet, so that he initiates her sexually. That explains his power over her.'

'I'm not sure,' Julian demurred. 'The way they flirt with death during their sex acts is something they share. It's a dangerous game they play. His idea, certainly, but they both play it. It's more believable that way.'

'No, no,' Alain insisted. 'Edwin is far more obsessed with death than he is with sex—the sex is incidental to him. But if Katerina is a recently aroused young girl then, to her, the death games are purely an extension of the sex act, something extra she can give her lover at the peak of their passion.'

'I agree,' Alex said. 'It's a much more powerful statement that way.'

'Besides,' Alain added. 'Older man, young girl at the height of her sexuality . . . big seller.'

Oh yes, Julian thought with disgust, if you had your way, Katerina would be a thirteen-year-old. (Everyone in the business knew of Alain's penchant for youth.)

Nevertheless, Julian eventually agreed that a young actress was a good idea.

'Someone the public hasn't seen—a new face,' enthused Alain. 'We'll create a new star.' He was running hot.

Before they could start auditioning they had to decide on the director. 'I think we should get a woman,' Alex suggested. He wasn't quite sure why—maybe he thought he'd have more power over a woman, or maybe it was to appease the feminist lobby group—but the others didn't disagree with him and they unanimously decided on Naomi Wheatley.

Naomi was a safe choice. She was strong, efficient, experienced and respected within the industry. But she wasn't exactly innovative. She relied upon others for her inspiration which suited Alain and Alex down to the ground. Not that they'd be able to walk all over her, of course. They'd have to be diplomatic in their manipulation. After all, she'd been one of the early female directors who'd fought for her place in a male-dominated arena and, if crossed, she could be a formidable foe. But Alain and Alex had decided in private discussion that they could handle her.

Julian, who wasn't privy to the private discussion, was also pleased with the choice. A less stable, overemotional director would have spelt disaster and he felt a lot happier once Naomi was appointed.

Pre-production went smoothly. Julian wrote a new draft of the play, the theatre was booked and the premiere production of *Centre Stage* was all set for 1992.

Early in the year, while Naomi, Alex and Julian discussed casting and screened photographs and biographies of hundreds of actors, Alain disappeared from sight. He was determined to line up a network deal for the sale of the televised opening night performance. 'Olivier did it with the National Theatre season,' he explained. 'The precedent has been created. Televised stage productions can work. So long as the viewers know that it's a filmed stage performance and not a movie, they love it!' Alain was excited. This was so much more invigorating than grinding out television series. 'And we'll be the first to do it *live*!' he exclaimed.

Everyone agreed that if anyone could pull off the deal it would be Alain.

Then came the auditions. The four supporting roles in *Centre Stage* proved relatively easy to cast, mainly because they had the pick of the crop. Every major actor in the country was lining up for the opportunity to appear in the latest Oldfellow play co-produced by Rainford and King and starring none other than Alex Rainford himself.

A week into auditions Norman Oldfellow had a stroke. Julian left for Wagga Wagga to be by his mother's side.

He was happy to leave all the casting to Alain, Alex and Naomi. However he insisted that the elusive Katerina must be an actress they all agreed upon.

It wasn't easy. A week after the four principals had been cast, the leading lady was still to be found.

Each day they sifted through the photographs and biographies of the hopefuls they'd tested and each day they disagreed. 'Not sexy enough,' Alex would say. 'Too old,' from Alain. 'Too fragile,' from Naomi.

Auditions were extended by a week and, on the fourth day of the third week, they found her.

She was strong, young and full of life. And when she'd finished her reading, they all agreed in hushed tones that she was sexy.

'Too good to be true,' Naomi muttered. 'Let's see how she takes direction.'

'Act One, Scene Three, dear,' she called in her big, bass, smoker's voice, and the girl on stage started flicking through the script. 'Page twenty-three. We'll run through the confrontation between Edwin and Katerina.' Naomi nodded to Alex. 'If you wouldn't mind, Alex.'

Alex walked up onto the stage and accepted the script from Ian, the stage manager who'd been reading opposite the girl. As he turned to page twenty-three, he gave her an encouraging wink. 'You're doing a great job.' She smiled back at him gratefully.

Naomi worked them hard for a full hour. She was impressed. The girl was not only attractive and sensual, she was intelligent and she took direction well. It wasn't surprising, Naomi thought. Her biog stated that she was one of RADA's recent top graduates.

Alain, too, was impressed. Not only by the girl's talent but by the chemistry between her and Alex. Christ, he thought, if they're this hot together on the first reading, what sort of electricity are we going to get after a month's rehearsal? And they looked so strangely alike! Probably just the similar colouring but it was very effective.

Alex is bound to screw her, Alain thought. The lucky bastard. But he thought it without any ill will. Alex Rainford was the only person for whom Alain had ever felt admiration and respect. And that was only because Alex reminded him of himself. Go for it, he thought. Good on you. And he sat back and watched the girl with undisguised lust.

To Alex the girl was more than a talented RADA graduate, more than an object of lust, more than the answer to their prayers for a perfect Katerina. She was fascinating!

'That's fine. Thank you both,' Naomi bellowed once more from the stalls. 'Now, if you wouldn't mind joining us . . . yes, you too, dear,' she added as the girl hesitated.

Alain thought there was little point in seeing the other three hopeful Katerinas waiting in the theatre foyer for their turn to read. 'Let's call a halt and I'll take us all out to lunch,' he suggested to Naomi as he watched the girl leave the stage. But Naomi insisted that they could hardly send the poor kids home.

Alain didn't see why not but he decided it wouldn't be politic to cross Naomi so early in the production.

'I tell you what, Alex,' Naomi suggested as he and the girl joined them, 'why don't you take . . . um . . . Imogen, isn't it?' Naomi automatically consulted her auditionee list. 'Why don't you take Imogen out for a cup of coffee and tell her about the play. Alain and I will tie up the loose ends here.' (Shit, Alain thought.) 'And then we'll all have a bite of lunch together. Oh,' she added, turning to the girl, 'that is, if you're available.'

'Does that mean I've got the part?' the girl asked.

'It certainly does, dear.' Naomi beamed at her.

In the coffee lounge next door Alex leaned forward and gave the girl his full attention.

'Imogen . . . what?'

'McLaughlan. Imogen McLaughlan. My friends call me Jenny.'

'I like Imogen better.'

'Yes, so does my agent. She thinks it's a good stage name. It's from *Cymbeline*. Mum was doing a production of it at drama school when she got pregnant.'

'Really.' Alex wasn't particularly interested in Imogen's mother. 'What do you think of *Centre Stage*?'

'Well, they didn't give me a script, so I haven't read the whole play, only the scenes we did at the audition—but I think they're stunning.'

It was an hour and a half before the others joined them but Jenny and Alex didn't notice. They drank three cappuccinos apiece and didn't stop talking the whole time.

Alex told her that Julian had based the play upon him. He was interested to hear that Jenny had already met Julian—'on holiday from England, he's a friend of my mother's'—but he was far more interested to hear that Jenny had always had an inexplicable fascination for cemeteries.

'Ever since I was tiny,' she admitted. 'Mum used to worry—I think she saw it as a bit morbid in one so young.'

'How could she know?' Alex remarked dismissively. 'Most parents don't, do they? My obsession with death started at a very early age too.'

Jenny listened, riveted, her eyes never leaving his face, as he talked about his early childhood and his brother, Tim, who'd died as the result of some terrible shooting accident. She had never thought of herself as having an obsession with death (despite her curious interest in graves) but she was deeply flattered to think that this charismatic man should assume she did. Within a short time, Jenny was starting to find death a very interesting subject indeed.

She was starting to think that maybe she *did* have an obsession with death but didn't know it, when a voice said, 'Sorry to be so long'. It was Naomi and a very disgruntled looking Alain King.

The moment Alain walked into the coffee lounge and saw the two heads close together, he felt irritated. The rapt expression on the girl's face as she drank in Alex's every word with wonderment verged on the pornographic. He's doing everything but fuck her in a public place, Alain thought. Well, just don't fuck the show, mate. But he knew he was only envious. Alex could land them every time, the lucky bastard.

Alain couldn't have been further from the truth. Sex was the last thing on Alex's mind. Certainly, the girl was desirable and certainly one day he would have her. But when he did, it would be total. He would have full power over her and she would do anything for him. Just imagine! She too was obsessed with death! And she had been since she was a little girl. It was all meant to be. They had so much to share. There was plenty of time though.

He smiled up at Naomi and Alain. 'Where are we going to eat? I'm starving.'

Late that night Jenny rang her mother in Munich. She was bewildered by Maddy's reaction to her news.

'Oh my God!' gasped Maddy. Then there was a long silence.

'Are you still there, Mum?' They must have been cut off, Jenny thought.

Then, finally, 'What did Julian say? I'm surprised he hasn't rung me.' Her mother's voice sounded very strange.

'He wasn't there. His father's ill they said and he's gone to the country.' More silence.

'Hey, don't be mad, Mum. I didn't get the job just so that I could stay in Sydney with Paul, honestly!' Jenny realised with a guilty start that she hadn't once thought of Paul and that she hadn't even rung to tell him the news. 'It's the best break I could get. Alex says they've sold the television rights. They're going to send in a camera crew for the last week of rehearsals and they'll plot the whole thing so that they can shoot the opening night like a televised stage play. Isn't that incredible?

'And the play's bound to sell to the UK, like the rest of Julian's plays.' There was no stopping Jenny now. 'And Alex says that this time they're not going to just sell the rights to the play, they're going to take the whole Australian production to London. Isn't that brilliant! He says—'

'Darling, I finish filming in a few days,' Maddy interrupted. 'I'm going to come to Sydney. Shall we leave the rest of the talk till then?'

'Oh.' Jenny felt instantly deflated. Whatever had happened to 'Well done, Jen', 'Congratulations, darling', 'I'm proud of you'? 'All right,' she said coldly. 'Let me know when you're arriving and I'll try and meet you.'

Maddy was fully aware of Jenny's reaction. 'Congratulations, darling,' she said, 'I'm proud of you.' But it was too late and, after Jenny had hung up, she didn't have time to worry about it. She didn't have time to think about anything, which was probably merciful because, deep inside, there was a voice saying, 'You're a bad mother, you're a rotten mother, this is all your fault, if you hadn't kept him a secret, if you'd let them meet, if . . . if . . . if . . .'

But there was no time. She booked her flight to Sydney. Then she rang the production office and told them that she was leaving the day after the shoot. She was reminded that she was on hold for a further fortnight in case reshoots were required and, when she said she was sorry she couldn't be there, she was told she could be sued. She said sorry but she still couldn't be there.

She rang Viktor Hoff who said he'd look after the production office. Then she rang Phil Pendlebury who said he'd cancel the BBC radio series of poetry readings he'd accepted for next month. Then she rang Rodney Baines and told him not to meet her at Heathrow because she was going to Sydney instead.

She told each of them that it was 'family problems', no more, but each of them heard the strain in her voice and each of them worried.

The only person she couldn't get hold of was Julian. She tried him at Bondi Beach in case he'd left a forwarding number but he hadn't turned his answering machine on.

She vaguely remembered that his parents lived in Wagga Wagga. Or was it Woy Woy? It was one of those peculiar Australian names that people found so colourful. After thirty minutes of frustrated conversations with directory enquiries, she finally got through. When she did, she was told that Julian was at his father's funeral. It was his sister Wendy who told her. Wendy was at the family home preparing for the wake. 'They'll be back soon. Would you like Julian to ring you?'

'No,' Maddy said. Julian's sister sounded nice. 'Just tell him I'm very sorry to hear the news. I really am.'

It had been a distressing time for Julian. For a full fortnight he'd watched his father's slow struggle to recuperate from his stroke. It was a brave fight. Norman would never be well again but he had made it home from the hospital, and he was going to live. With the help of Wendy and a nurse employed to visit daily, he was as comfortable as could be expected and Gwen was able to cope.

Everyone agreed that it was safe for Julian to return to Sydney. Then came the second stroke and it was a massive one. Mercifully, Noman died but it was a cruel blow to his wife who had just prepared herself for a lifetime of devotion to her invalid husband. Widowhood came as a far greater shock to Gwen than the prospect of a lifetime of nursing.

Julian had rung Naomi who'd been duly sympathetic and told him not to bother about being late back. 'We may even have to delay the start of rehearsals,' she had said. 'We still can't find our Katerina.'

Then, just before he left for the funeral, an excited phone call had come from Alex. They'd found her. Imogen someone. They were all thrilled. She was perfect. Julian mustn't worry. He was going to love her.

Julian didn't worry. He knew that the girl would have to be good if the three of them were in unanimous agreement. Besides, he was emotionally drained and couldn't think about anything except helping his mother who was threatening to go to pieces at any moment. He was grateful for Wendy's daily support. But of course Wendy had a family of her own—she couldn't take on the whole burden.

'You'll have to start the blocking without me,' he said to Alex. 'Tell Naomi I'll be back on the third day of rehearsals. She should have the basic blocking done by then and we can concentrate on any rewrites after that.'

The first morning's read-through went smoothly enough. Alex and Imogen worked well together. Even though they were reading off the printed page, the sparks were there. The other four actors were also well cast, and there appeared to be no problems with the costume and set designers, both of whom had done their homework.

It was in the afternoon that the first hint of trouble arose—not that Naomi thought anything of it at the time. When they started blocking the moves of the play, Alex argued with her over every one of his stage directions.

'But Edwin wouldn't sit there,' he insisted. 'No, Edwin wouldn't cross to the window on that line.'

Alex was obviously one of those actors who wouldn't take direction, Naomi thought with mild exasperation. Oh well, not to worry, she'd worked with many of them before. She just let them have their way. But it was frustrating, nevertheless. Naomi had done a lot of work on the blocking and it meant she would have to alter many of the other characters' key moves to accommodate Alex.

The second day of blocking was just the same. He fought her every inch of the way and, by the end of rehearsal, Naomi was tired. But she was still determined not to let it worry her. They now had the whole play roughly blocked, she told herself, Julian would be here tomorrow and she'd have an ally. Not only the actor's closest friend but the writer of the bloody play, for God's sake! That should help.

Julian arrived late at the shabby rehearsal studios above the theatre. Naomi had delayed the start of the day's work so that everyone could meet him, but after half an hour she gave up and called a start to rehearsals. Naomi was a stickler for schedules and she intended to have the first three scenes fully worked before lunch.

An hour later she and Alex were still arguing about the opening speech and Naomi was praying for Julian to arrive. They weren't going to cover any ground this way.

'I tell you what, Alex, why don't we take it again from the top. Do it your own way for now and . . .'

It was at that moment that Julian entered through the side door. He was instantly aware of the friction in the air and equally aware that no one had noticed him. He stood watching quietly.

'Do it my own way?' Alex interrupted, not belligerently, but in utter amazement. 'But don't you understand, there is only one way! It's not *my* way. It's Edwin's way. There's only one way.'

'All right, Alex, all right,' Naomi agreed wearily. 'Let's do it Edwin's way and carry through to Katerina's entrance, shall we?' Bloody wanker, she thought. 'Let's see what happens after that.'

Julian was surprised. He'd never seen Alex behave so indulgently in rehearsal. He had always been helpful to directors—so long as the directors themselves weren't indulgent, which Naomi certainly wasn't. Her suggestions on the important opening speech were reasonable, technically efficient in their blocking and nonintrusive to Alex's interpretation of the character. Yet Alex was refusing even to consider them. Surprising.

Alex took his time over Edwin's opening speech to the audience. He played the whole thing directly at Naomi, obviously intent upon convincing her that his interpretation was the only one. Or was he? Studying the performance, Julian got the feeling that Naomi had ceased to be Naomi as far as Alex was concerned; she had become some faceless observer with whom Edwin felt compelled to share his passion and his power.

'I've finally found her,' Alex said as Edwin. 'Tonight's the night . . . And I wanted to share it with you.' He turned upstage. 'Darling!' he called.

Jenny walked on to the stage. Julian's gasp was so loud he was surprised heads didn't turn in his direction. After the initial shock he tried to persuade himself that it wasn't Jenny at all, just some freakish look-alike. But it didn't work. This was certainly Jenny.

What was going on? he asked himself. When had father and daughter met? Why hadn't Maddy told him? What had happened to the 'Imogen' everyone had been so excited about? Julian was totally confused. Alex and Jenny couldn't play the lovers Edwin and Katerina! There was something obscene about the mere thought.

Then, as Julian watched them, he realised that they had no idea of their true relationship. They couldn't, surely. They wouldn't be able to act the way they were if they did. The two of them together were mesmeric. A feeling of horror crept over Julian as he realised the effect that Alex was already having on the girl. It was the same effect that he'd had on Maddy over twenty years ago.

Over twenty years ago Julian had watched Alex exercise his power to such a degree that Maddy would have done anything he wanted. It was one of the principal observations upon which this very play was based. And now Alex was exercising the same power over Maddy's daughter. *His* daughter.

EDWIN

Photos, Kat.

EDWIN RUNS HIS FOREFINGER
GENTLY DOWN HER OPEN—
NECKED SHIRT AND BETWEEN HER
BREASTS.

Photos to tease me. And we take them
in public places. You'd like to do that
for me, wouldn't you?

The night in the Taylor Square hotel when Alex
had told him about Jonathan Thomas and the photos
was as clear in Julian's mind as if it had been
yesterday. And naturally, the photos had gone into
the play.

He watched as Alex gently ran his finger down
Jenny's T-shirt between her breasts. Even though
they were working with scripts in hand, Alex was
observing every necessary gesture to its fullest. In
fact, he referred to the script so rarely that it was
obvious he already knew it backwards.

No, this can't happen, Julian thought, as he
saw Jenny's reaction to the touch of Alex's hand.
This can't happen. The play can't take over.

Normally, in the early days of rehearsal when
actors went into a clinch and tried desperately to
see around each other's scripts and keep their
reading glasses from clashing, Julian found it funny.
Now, as Alex and Jenny started into the clinch,
it wasn't funny at all. It was ominous.

'Hi, everyone.' Julian stepped out from the doorway
and tried to look as though nothing was wrong.

Alex's flash of irritation at being interrupted
was quickly replaced by genuine relief when he saw
who it was. 'Julian! About time.'

'Julian.' Naomi kissed him on the cheek. 'I'm

sorry about your father. Did the flowers from the company arrive OK?'

'Yes, thanks. It was very kind of everyone.' Julian could read relief on Naomi's face too and he knew he was definitely going to be the ham in the sandwich with these two. But that was the least of his worries at the moment.

'This is Imogen. I believe you know her mother,' Alex said.

A quick glance at the two of them and Julian knew he'd been right—they had no idea.

'Hello, Jenny.' He embraced her warmly. 'Where did the "Imogen" come from?'

'It's always been there. I just didn't have an agent before.' Jenny smiled. 'It's still Jenny to friends, except for Alex who seems stuck on Imogen.' Julian wanted to recoil from the special look they shared.

'How's your mother? Does she know about your getting the role?'

'Yes,' Jenny nodded. 'She's arriving tomorrow morning. She didn't seem all that thrilled for me but then we've been having so many clashes lately it's hard to tell.' She sighed.

'Give me the flight details when we break and I'll go out and meet her.'

'Oh, terrific! Mum'd love that.'

'Let's call a fifteen-minute break now, shall we?' Naomi suggested and she nodded to the assistant stage manager to line up coffee.

Julian was halfway through being introduced to the stage manager and two of the other actors whom he hadn't met, but that didn't stop Alex from dragging him to one side out of earshot. Naomi knew full well that Alex was going to complain about her and hope to get Julian on side but she didn't worry unduly. Let him get it off his chest, she thought. Then she'd have a talk with Julian herself and they could sort out a strategy. Naomi was a very reasonable woman and she just wanted to run a well-ordered ship.

'She doesn't understand Edwin,' Alex muttered intensely. 'She has to leave me alone; I have to be free to do this my way. His way. Edwin's way.'

'I'll have a word with her.' Julian turned aside to accept the coffee offered him by the assistant stage manager.

'Don't you see that—' Alex pulled him back and the coffee spilt all over Julian's bare forearm and down the front of his short-sleeved shirt. 'Sorry,' Alex said.

The coffee scalded him and Julian's arm was smarting as he mopped at himself with his handkerchief but Alex didn't seem to notice. 'Don't you see that you and I are the only ones who truly know Edwin? She has to back off.'

'I said I'll have a word with her and I will, Alex,' Julian answered firmly. 'Now let me talk to the other actors.' As he left Alex brooding in the corner of the room it occurred to Julian yet again that Alex was mad.

Later, when they broke for lunch, Julian said as much to Naomi. He said it in a light-hearted fashion but he meant it. 'There's a touch of madness in the man, my darling, and he's going through an identity crisis with Edwin. He's not sure whether it's him or the bloke I wrote.'

'Well, you're not wrong there,' Naomi smiled.

'No, I'm not.' Julian dropped the banter. 'A

lot of this play is biographical, a lot of it's drawn from my personal knowledge of Alex which spans over twenty years and . . .' Julian shrugged helplessly, 'he thinks he knows this character better than anyone. Including me. And he's probably right.'

'So what do I do?' Naomi threw up her hands in frustration.

'You leave him alone. You let him run with it.'

Naomi looked doubtful; it could make for a very uneven production in her opinion.

'This play's about a megalomaniac,' Julian continued as he read her misgivings, 'and we've got a megalomaniac playing the central role. Why don't we let him go for a while? We can always cut him back if it gets out of hand.' Julian wasn't too sure about the last bit but it seemed the right thing to say.

At least it convinced Naomi. 'Right,' she agreed. 'I'll give it a go.'

Ten o'clock the following morning found Julian waiting for Maddy outside the customs hall at the international airport.

She saw him immediately and marched straight up to him. 'Does Jenny know about Alex yet?'

Julian shook his head. 'No, she doesn't.'

'Then what the hell's going on? How did it happen?' Her eyes blazed with anger. 'Why didn't you do something?'

'I didn't know,' Julian protested. 'Not until yesterday. I swear. If I'd known I would have stopped it.'

She continued to glare balefully at him.

He picked up her suitcases. 'Come on,' he said wearily. 'It's a long walk. I'm right over the other side of the carpark and it's bloody hot outside.'

'I'm sorry.' Maddy was instantly contrite. Julian had to put down the suitcases while she hugged him. He hugged her back. 'I was sorry to hear about your father,' she whispered in his ear. 'Are you all right?'

'Yes.' He nodded and picked up the suitcases again.

'Can we go to your place and talk?' Maddy asked.

'Sure. Your mother might be upset though. Jenny said she was expecting you to come straight home from the airport. She was going to come and meet you herself apparently.'

'No, she wasn't. She only said that after you offered to pick me up.'

'How do you know?'

'It's a pretty good guess,' Maddy laughed. 'I know Helena. Come on, let's go to Bondi. I'm dying to look at the ocean.'

Maddy jogged back up the beach and threw herself down on her towel. God, that water was good! And the sun! And the waves! She still loved bodysurfing.

And she loved Bondi, she thought, as she looked around at the deep bay with its rocky headlands and yellow-white sand. Bondi reminded her of NADA and her first taste of true freedom—NADA and Alex and Julian and those wonderful days.

Suddenly she realised that thinking about Alex had ceased to frighten her. The knowledge that Alex and Jenny were about to meet each other as father and daughter was no longer the daunting prospect it had once been. It was simply something she should have seen to years ago.

For the first time in a week Maddy felt strong. She was here now, here with Jenny and able to protect her. And Julian was standing by to help.

She watched him jog up the beach to join her. He hadn't really changed much, she thought. The lanky hair was starting to grey and there was a lack-of-exercise thickening about the waist but the image was the same. Gawky. All bones.

Yes, she thought, between the two of them they'd manage. And Alex couldn't be all bad, surely. After the shock, he and Jenny might even delight in the discovery of each other.

When she said as much to Julian he corrected her on both counts. 'Sure, he's not all bad, Maddy, but I'll tell you something that might be a lot worse. He's mad. It's quite possible he always has been. And I don't think for one minute that either of them will delight in the discovery of their relationship.'

Maddy's new-found strength and her hopes for a simple solution disappeared entirely as she listened to Julian.

He painted the picture as black as he saw it, sparing her nothing. He started with the play, its subject matter and its principal characters. Maddy was horrified. She'd had no idea the roles in *Centre Stage* were so sexually entwined.

'Well, you'll have to recast the girl's part,' she said. 'Jenny can't do it, that's obvious.'

'No, it's not,' Julian countered and, before Maddy could interject, he spelt it out for her. 'Face it, you're already having trouble with your daughter. Just what do you think her reaction will be if you cheat her of the biggest opportunity of her career?

'Because that's what it will be,' he continued, holding up a hand to stop Maddy from interrupting. 'London managements are already vying for the production on the strength of my other plays, Alain's sold the television deal and it looks as if the UK wants to be in on that too. It's a first, I tell you. And, disturbing as the play might be, it's far and away the most powerful thing I've ever written.'

'All right, all right.' Maddy's confusion was making her irritable. 'So she keeps the role. We tell her and Alex everything and they continue as they are. They're actors, for God's sake. Father and daughter teams have played love scenes before. What's wrong with that?'

Julian answered immediately. 'I agree Alex should be told. And he should be asked to hold back and stop encouraging the girl's infatuation. But I'm not sure about Jenny—I don't think for one minute she'd be able to perform this role if she knew that he was her father.'

Beyond that, Julian was unable to convey his misgivings. 'Read the script tonight,' he said finally. 'I think my worry is that the play could take over.' He squinted out at the ocean. The sun was beginning to give him a headache; he rarely spent time on the beach in midsummer. 'I may be dramatising the whole situation, Maddy,' he said. 'They may be infatuated with each other merely as actors— I know that happens. But I'm worried. And I don't know what the right plan of action is.'

They agreed, however, that Alex must be told as soon as possible.

'I'll arrange lunch tomorrow,' Julian offered.

'One o'clock, by the minotaur at Hyde Park Fountain?'

When Maddy arrived home, Helena was waiting impatiently.

'I was beginning to worry, darling,' she said with a furrowed brow.

Maddy got straight to the point. 'Did Jenny tell you she was going to audition for this part?'

'Oh yes, dear,' Helena gushed, 'and we were so thrilled when she got it.'

'And did she tell you all about the production?'

'Well, of course she did.' Helena was bewildered and a little offended by Maddy's belligerence. 'It's a wonderful opportunity for her. It's a Rainford/Oldfellow collaboration. We're all very excited.'

'And who the hell do you think Rainford and Oldfellow are?'

Oh dear, Helena thought, this cross-examining was becoming most unpleasant. 'I do still keep abreast of the theatre, Maddy—they're the most successful entrepreneur and playwright partnership—'

'That's right. Alex Rainford and Julian Oldfellow.'

'Yes. Alex Rainford and . . .' Realisation started to dawn. 'Oh my goodness. Not *your* Alex?'

'Yes, mother, if you want to put it that way, *my* Alex and my dearest friend Julian.'

'Well, I certainly never knew your friend Julian's surname,' Helena said, totally justified on that score. 'But . . . that means Alex is Jenny's . . .'

'Precisely.'

Helena started to apologise, although she wasn't quite sure what for. Maddy let her off the hook.

'Forget it. It doesn't matter. But for the moment Jenny mustn't know. Promise me that you won't say a word. Not even to Todd.'

'I promise, darling. I do. I promise.'

'I mean it! Not one word!' And Maddy went upstairs to her bedroom to read the script. What was the point in being angry with her mother? Helena had never had the capacity to think of anyone or anything other than herself and her impact on the social scene.

An hour and a half later Maddy put the script to one side, lay back on the bed and stared at the ceiling.

That blissful moment on Bondi Beach flashed through her mind. The moment when she'd looked at the waves, watched Julian jogging towards her and thought that everything might end up being simple. Oh, how she wished it could be.

The play was magnificent. There was no way she could rob Jenny of this role—or the ability to perform it to her best. And Maddy certainly agreed with Julian that it would be impossible for Jenny to do that if she knew that Alex was her father.

Not that there were heavily sexual scenes in the play—there weren't. It was all innuendo. There wasn't even any heavy kissing; their lips barely touched. But the girl must be sexually besotted with the man. She must be his slave. To the man, of course, she was nothing but a willing player in his game of death.

In the acting process it was necessary, therefore, for Jenny to have a certain infatuation for the actor playing opposite her. It wasn't necessary for the man though. And once he'd been told, surely it would be simple for Alex to keep control of the situation? Maddy couldn't help feeling that maybe Julian *had* been dramatising things; perhaps he had been confusing the acting process with reality.

Maddy was in a state of utter confusion. Several pages into the play she'd recognised that the characters were based upon herself and Alex and she was fascinated to read about the power Alex had had over her. She hadn't realised it herself all those years ago—not until she'd been faced with the abortion. She was equally fascinated to think that Julian had been observing it and writing about it all the while.

She wasn't offended by his use of the past. It was his right and the play was a wonderful observation. But Julian's thought that Alex was perhaps practising the same power games on the infatuated daughter of that original union . . . well, surely that was just a playwright's fanciful notion? Maybe it would be Julian's next play . . .

Maddy knew that ever since the episode at Berchtesgaden Julian had been convinced there was a madness in Alex. A madness and an obsession with death. Maddy herself had never been aware of that side of Alex: her recollection of him was of a dangerously charismatic man who had power over women, power over people in general. But, as for this obsession with death . . . could it perhaps be Julian's? Julian had always been obsessed with Alex. He'd admitted that all of his successful plays had, in one way or another, been inspired by Alex.

Stop it, she told herself, she must think rationally. The one that mattered was Jenny, a talented young actor on the threshold of her career.

Maddy couldn't help but recall her own early

years in London. Hands clutching at her backside as she carted around steins of lager in the Bier Keller, the stale smell of 'champagne' and the gloom of 'Danny's Downstairs'. This role could save Jenny all that. *Centre Stage* could push her five years up the ladder; she could skip all the crap in between.

As the images of the early years flickered through Maddy's mind, she drifted off into a jet-lagged sleep.

Jenny arrived home early the next morning full of apologies.

Maddy was up at seven, having slept most of the previous afternoon. She was halfway through her second cup of coffee on the terrace when a voice rang out behind her.

'Mum! I'm sorry!, I'm sorry, sorry, sorry, sorry, sorry.'

Maddy only just had time to put her coffee cup down before she was engulfed in a fierce hug.

'A few of us went out for drinks after rehearsals and we talked for hours. And then Paul joined us and then I went back to his place and then suddenly it was really late and . . . Hell, I didn't mean to stay out on your first night in town.'

Under normal circumstances Maddy probably would have been a little hurt, but these were not normal circumstances. It was a huge relief to think that Jenny had gone back to her young boyfriend's place for a night of lovemaking.

'It's all right, darling. I was so jet-lagged that I slept most of the time anyway. Now do you have a moment to talk to me before you go to rehearsal? I'm dying to hear about everything.'

'Yes, I'm not called till ten-thirty.'

And talk Jenny did. All about the play, the production, her role, the cast, the director, and Alex Rainford. She talked a lot about Alex Rainford.

'It's wonderful working opposite him, Mum. He's riveting.'

Strangely enough, the more Jenny talked about Alex, the more Maddy felt herself relax. Jenny was talking as an actor.

'He's living the role and he's bringing so much out of me that the response between us is electric. It's unbelievably exciting!'

Maddy knew exactly how she felt. Foolish as it may have sounded to others, there probably wasn't an actor around who hadn't felt that at least once in their career. Mind you, Maddy hoped the director was strict enough not to allow such 'electric response' to become indulgent. Nothing worse than wanky actors, she thought, but she didn't prick Jenny's bubble by saying it.

'You're damn lucky to experience that in your first job, Jen,' she said encouragingly. 'It's unusual.'

'Yes I know,' Jenny effused. 'And it's all because of Alex. I can't wait for you to meet him.'

Maddy took a breath. It was now or never. 'I have met him.' She tried to keep her smile relaxed. 'We went to drama school together.'

Jenny skidded to a halt. 'You're joking! Why didn't you say anything?'

'You didn't let me get a word in.'

'No, I mean, why didn't you ever tell me?'

'Oh darling, it was years ago. I haven't seen him since I was your age.' She didn't want Jenny to guess the truth and she knew she was taking a risk—but she also knew it was a risk she had to take. There must be as little deception as possible so that, when Jenny was finally told, the impact wouldn't be so devastating.

'I'm actually having lunch with him today,' she continued, 'but he doesn't know it. Julian's rigging it as a surprise, so don't say anything, whatever you do.'

'Fantastic!' Maddy needn't have worried. Jenny was so preoccupied with the play that the identity of her father was the last thing on her mind. 'That's fantastic!'

Maddy arrived at Hyde Park feeling distinctly nervous. She distracted herself by walking about the fountain inspecting the statues before taking up her position beside the minotaur.

She had always loved Hyde Park fountain and the minotaur was her favourite statue. She was so busy studying the rivulets of water winding their way between the muscles of the massive, bronze back that Julian's voice came as a surprise.

'Well, here we are.'

They stepped out from the other side of the minotaur and, with a shock, Maddy found herself staring into the steel-blue eyes of Alex.

He held her gaze for a moment, equally startled, and then the eyes crinkled at the corners. 'So, this is the surprise, Julian.' He was smiling broadly now. 'It's Madeleine Frances, isn't it?' He held out his hand.

Maddy's nervousness disappeared in a flash. He didn't even remember who she was! She laughed out loud. 'Yes, Alex, it's Madeleine Frances.' All her worrying about the impact of their meeting now seemed ludicrous. He didn't remember who she was. She wondered briefly if she'd ever meant anything to him at all.

'Good God, I don't believe it!' Alex's mouth dropped and he stared at her in amazement, his hand still outstretched. 'It's Maddy, isn't it?' He finally dropped his hand and peered at her closely. 'Is it Maddy?'

Maddy nodded, still grinning. Why did she feel such a peculiar sense of freedom? she wondered.

'Right. I'll leave you to it.' Julian turned to leave, feeling very superfluous, but Alex didn't notice. He was still staring at Maddy.

'Thanks, Julian,' Maddy said. When he'd left she turned to Alex. 'Are you mad keen to eat, or would you rather find a patch of grass and talk?' she asked.

'I'd rather do whatever you want to do,' he said, not taking his eyes off her for an instant.

Oh no, Alex, don't you dare! She put on her best school mistress voice. 'Patch of grass and talk it is, then.' As she led the way she could still feel his eyes on her. He was as charismatic as ever, possibly more so, but the knowledge that he hadn't even remembered her gave her strength.

When they were seated on the grass he took her hand. 'You look wonderful, Maddy.' And she did, Alex thought, her delicate bones framed by the cropped hair, and the laughter lines that had formed as soon as she smiled at him . . . She looked even better than he remembered. A scene from *Centre Stage* came into his mind: *Photos, Kat. Photos to tease me. And we take them in public places.* Those photos, Alex thought. Those photos all those years ago. 'You look really wonderful,' he repeated.

Maddy withdrew her hand. The delicate way she'd intended to broach the subject was no longer possible. Alex was finding her fascinating and that was very dangerous. She had to be brutal.

'I have some news that's going to shock you, Alex and it's about Jenny.' She felt strangely calm.

'Jenny?' He had no idea who she was talking about.

'The girl playing Katerina in *Centre Stage*.'

'Oh. Imogen. Yes.' Imogen was most certainly fascinating, but Alex didn't want to talk about her now. He didn't like to mix the objects of his fascination. One at a time. One at a time.

'She's my daughter.'

Alex's eyes widened. How amazing, and how interesting. Suddenly talking about Imogen was all he wanted to do—imagine the two of them being mother and daughter. Now that was extremely fascinating . . .

'And yours.'

Alex looked at her uncomprehendingly.

'She's *our* daughter, Alex, yours and mine.' Alex shook his head in disbelief while Maddy ploughed on. 'That abortion you thought I had when we were at NADA—I didn't have it. I went to England and I had the baby instead.'

'Imogen?'

'Yes.' Now that she knew the fatal attraction had been arrested, Maddy was quite enjoying being brutal. 'You probably don't remember, but it was final term and we were doing a production of *Cymbeline* at the time. You were playing Cymbeline, Susannah was playing the Queen and I was playing Imogen.' She shrugged. 'So Imogen it was. Jenny for short.'

Alex couldn't care less how the name had come about. He'd stopped listening to Maddy. Imogen.

460

His daughter. It opened up a whole new world. The opening speech of *Centre Stage* flashed through his mind: *It was the most intimate experience I've ever shared with another human being . . . I've been searching all my life for someone with whom I could repeat that intimate experience . . . I've finally found her . . .*

Had he truly found her? Imogen. His daughter. And she shared his obsession with death. It was amazing.

'Alex?' Maddy leaned forward to get his attention. He was staring intently at the grass and he was obviously miles away. 'Alex, I'm sorry to shock you, but I couldn't think of a gentler way.'

'Oh that's all right.' Alex looked up and smiled at her, very fondly. 'It's a bit of a shock, yes, something I hadn't expected, but she's a lovely girl and you must be very proud of her and . . .' He waited for Maddy to take over. He wasn't sure what she wanted him to do. He only knew that he wanted to go home and think about Imogen. Why was the image of Tim flashing into his brain every few seconds like a neon light? Was there a link between Tim and Imogen? He wanted to go away and think about it.

'She mustn't know, Alex,' Maddy urged. 'Not until after the production.'

Maddy caught his attention with that one. 'That's a good idea. Yes, that's a very good idea,' he said thoughtfully.

'Julian and I both think she wouldn't be able to handle the role if she knew.'

'I agree.' He nodded sympathetically. 'I don't think she would either.'

'Can you cope with keeping it a secret until

the production finishes?' Maddy couldn't believe how easy it was.

'Yes, I can do that.' Alex smiled again.

'There's one other thing,' Maddy said hesitantly. 'Julian has this idea that Jenny might be just a touch . . . infatuated with you. Personally I don't agree with him,' she added hastily. 'It's the "actors' love affair" syndrome, as far as I can see but . . . well, that can get out of hand, can't it, particularly with the young ones, and . . .' Maddy felt a little nonplussed by the way Alex was looking at her. What the hell, she'd have to spell it out. 'Julian and I just thought that now you know about your relationship, you might discourage any infatuation on her side, that's all.'

'Does Julian think I've been encouraging it?' Alex asked coldly. Christ alive, he thought, even the writer doesn't understand Edwin. Edwin doesn't care about sex, he merely uses the girl's obsession with it to gain power over her.

'No,' Maddy assured him, 'no, of course not,' knowing full well that Julian certainly did think that Alex was encouraging it, 'but she's very young and . . .'

'Maddy, I will look after Jenny, I promise you.' Alex's face was a picture of fatherly concern. 'I'm sure you and Julian are overreacting. She has a boyfriend and she's very happy with him . . .' Maddy was starting to feel a little embarrassed . . . 'but I promise you that if I feel that she's having any improper feelings towards me I will discourage them.' The eyes crinkled again, very engagingly.

Maddy couldn't help but laugh. 'All right, so I'm playing mother hen, but I'm speaking from

462

experience; you can have quite an effect on a girl, you know that?'

'It's good to hear,' he grinned. 'Come on, I have to get back to rehearsal.' He helped her to her feet and they walked to the fountain. When he kissed her on the cheek his eyes held a fondness Maddy had never seen before. 'I'm proud she's our daughter, she's a fine girl.'

Maddy felt an overwhelming sense of relief as she watched him go. Everything was going to be all right.

That night Alex had the first of his dreams.

There was the chook. Two chooks. The chook they'd killed and the chook that got away and headed for the river. And there was Agatha. Agatha who was bigger. But had he wanted to kill Agatha because she was bigger or because she was family? They used to feed Agatha snails by hand.

And there was Tim. He hadn't wanted to kill Tim, surely? But then, in the dream, Alex could see the lifeblood seep from his brother's body and, in the dream, he knew that little Lexie wanted to be responsible. Little Lexie wanted the power to be his. The only power Lexie had been granted was to watch the death, not to cause it.

Over the next few weeks of rehearsals the dreams became more vivid and more confused. Little Lexie's desire to be the instigator of the death became stronger and stronger. Tim became Jenny. And somewhere in the background there was Edwin. Or was it Alex himself? It was difficult to be sure— the images were rapidly becoming one and the same.

Alex always awoke with the same feeling. The feeling that the play was wrong, that Julian had messed it up. Edwin didn't want to accept the girl's self-sacrifice. He wanted to kill. And the girl should be his daughter as well as his mistress. She should be his own flesh and blood because Edwin knew that the true thrill of the kill lay in that fact. Edwin wanted to share the death of his own flesh and blood with his observer. It was his ultimate gift to his audience.

Alex was aware that he couldn't entirely rewrite the script and that if he suggested any such notion Julian would dismiss it, but he knew that by altering his interpretation, he could greatly change the general context of the play.

He insisted that Edwin would not call Katerina Kat but Katie, the diminutive used by her parents and family. 'His feelings towards her are more paternal than anything,' he urged. 'She's the one obsessed with sex, not him. His obsession is with death. Besides,' he added as he saw Julian's doubtful expression, 'if I play him as fatherly, it could add a whole new dimension to the play.'

Julian was at a loss as to Alex's motives. He was sure that Alex wouldn't jeopardise his performance to protect Jenny. It was out of character for him to act selflessly.

When Alex had come back from his meeting with Maddy he'd simply said to Julian, 'You've known all the time, have you?'

'No,' Julian had answered. 'I found out nine or ten years ago.'

Alex never brought up the subject again with Julian. And now here he was wanting to alter his performance entirely on the strength of his recent knowledge. Why?

Alex made his suggestion in the company of Naomi

464

so Julian was unable to express his misgivings.

And for once Naomi was on Alex's side. 'I think we should give it a try. It can't hurt to have a look at what Alex has in mind.'

After a run of the play, they were all in agreement. The element of evil that was added by Alex's new interpretation was amazingly effective.

The only person left unhappy and confused was Jenny. She could see the effectiveness of the performance but she was upset by the change in Alex's attitude to her offstage. He no longer called her Imogen, but Jenny, just like everyone else. And he treated her with the same happy familiarity as he did everyone else. The special feeling between them had gone.

She said as much to her mother and of course Maddy came up with the obvious answer. 'But you told me that Alex had decided to play it in a more fatherly way, darling. He's allowing the role to carry over into his daily life. A lot of actors do it, you know that.'

Maddy was greatly relieved. Jenny's disappointment proved that Julian had been right—there had been an element of infatuation. And Alex was countering it beautifully. It was very caring of him and it would certainly be a great help when they came to break the news to Jenny. Maddy felt deeply grateful. And very guilty. Could she have misjudged him all these years?

The obvious explanation wasn't of much use to Jenny. It didn't stop her fantasies. It didn't stop Alex's image appearing in her mind every time Paul made love to her. It didn't stop the fact that, several times, during her moment of ecstasy, she'd had to clench her teeth to stop herself calling out his name.

There was still a fortnight of rehearsals to go when Maddy received the call from an apologetic Viktor Hoff. They were demanding her return to Europe the following week for four days of reshooting and he couldn't get her off the hook.

'The producer-bitch, she tell me,' he said over the phone, 'she tell me that if she don't sue you, then she sue me. Rather you, my darling. I'm broke. Come back.'

Maddy didn't mind. She was happy with the way things were going in Sydney. Her only stipulation was that she must be clear to return in time for the opening night of *Centre Stage*.

To Maddy's astonishment, Rodney was waiting for her at Heathrow Airport. There was nothing unusual about that—Rodney was always waiting for her at airports—except that this time she hadn't even told him she was arriving, let alone what flight she would be on.

'How did you know?' she asked.

'Phil told me.' Phil Pendlebury acted as far more than an agent for Maddy, particularly when she was away. Her answering machine was automatically switched through to his office, he handled her bills and banking and personal enquiries and, despite her insistence, he refused to take any more than his customary ten per cent. He didn't know why.

'I suppose you've spoken to Douglas,' Rodney asked as he opened the car door for her.

The world stopped. 'No. Why?'

'Oh, Phil said that he rang last week wanting to know where you were. Phil gave him all the details and, when he offered to get in touch with you,

Douglas said he'd do it himself.' Rodney read the confusion on Maddy's face and added, 'I don't know why you don't give up on him and marry me instead.'

He was only half joking and they both knew it. 'I don't know why I don't either,' she smiled. 'You're a much better bet.'

It was true that Rodney was quite a catch. He'd given up pornography eight years ago and the production company he'd formed from his earnings had become extremely successful. He was earning a fortune making corporate videos and spending it all making environmentally-conscious documentaries.

Maddy called Phil Pendlebury as soon as she got home but he had no further news of Douglas.

'Sorry, sweetheart, but he didn't give me any details. I told him you were in Sydney and he said he was going to contact you direct.'

Maddy phoned Helena daily but they hadn't heard from him. Perhaps he was simply going to turn up—that would be just like Douglas. Maddy couldn't wait to get back in case he did. Besides, she longed for the Australian sunshine. The damp cold of London was depressing her and the weather in Munich for the four days she was there was even worse.

She spent her last night with Robert and Alma and finally she was aboard a Qantas jet headed for Sydney.

It was the opening night of *Centre Stage* the day after she landed. And Douglas might arrive at any moment. Maddy was very excited.

ACT IV

SCENE 3: 1992

Alain King was thrilled when he saw the first full
dress rehearsal of *Centre Stage*. It was the most
powerful play, the most powerful production and
the most powerful performance he had ever
witnessed.

The stage belonged to Alex. The girl was
excellent, definitely destined for a fine career in
the theatre, but Alex was compelling. The engaging
intimacy with which he wooed his audience was
hugely seductive. So seductive that they forgot he
was evil. The death of the girl at the end of the
play was a chilling shock.

After the rehearsal Alain looked at the cameras
set up in strategic positions around the theatre and
felt very proud of himself. He'd pulled off one of

the most successful television deals in the history of the industry. *Centre Stage* would go to air live nationally; the UK had already bought the rights, and, after a performance like this, it was an easy bet to assume there'd be a bid for the world rights as well.

He gave Alex time to change and then went backstage to the dressing rooms to congratulate him before the members of the cast were called for notes. Alain was proud of his protege. He'd always considered Alex the only actor worthy of his friendship. We're alike, he told himself yet again. The man knows what he wants and he goes out and gets it. He's a winner.

Alex was gratified by Alain's approval but he was distracted. He'd been distracted a lot lately. Everyone had noticed. They'd put it down to approaching-opening-night nerves and were mostly sympathetic. Alain, who hadn't been around for rehearsals, was a little taken aback at the aloof reception he received. But because it was Alex, he didn't dismiss it as 'actor-wanking'.

'You want to get a good night's sleep, Alex,' he said. 'You look as if you could do with it.'

Alex wasn't sleeping well. The familiar characters of his dreams took over as soon as he closed his eyes. He liked them and welcomed them as old friends but they left him drained, and lately they merged so into his daily life that sometimes he had trouble telling his waking and sleeping hours apart.

During the first dress rehearsal he even experienced moments of confusion when he could have sworn he was in his own dream . . . and that he and Edwin were one.

Several weeks earlier, Alex had insisted on no public previews and, though she'd been doubtful at the time, Naomi was now glad that she and Julian had agreed. It would have meant a lot more pressure and Alex was already looking exhausted.

They'd had a hard time convincing Alain, though. 'He doesn't want to perform before a live audience until the televised opening night,' Naomi had explained. 'It's not customary, I know,' Julian added as Alain scowled his disapproval, 'but I think in this case it's advisable. Alex is carrying the show and we have to do what's best for him.'

It was only after Alain had seen the first dress rehearsal that he agreed. Unconditionally. 'Give him what he wants.'

By the end of the week and a half of technical runs, dress rehearsals and camera run-throughs everybody was in a state of fatigue and Naomi called a clear day prior to opening night. 'Everyone to sleep during the day, please,' she announced. 'Full dress in the evening, then that's it. Nothing till opening night.'

For Jenny the day off before the opening meant she could go to the airport and meet her mother. She was glad. She'd missed Maddy and she needed someone to talk to, someone close.

She wouldn't be able to confide everything to Maddy, of course, but her mother invariably found a way to cheer her up when she was down and Jenny needed cheering up.

She saw Maddy in the crowd and waved.

'Jen! How wonderful! Why aren't you rehearsing?'

470

Jenny hugged her mother fiercely. 'They've given us the day off. There's a dress tonight.'

As they wheeled the luggage trolley to the car park, Maddy picked up on Jenny's mood. 'You're a bit subdued, darling. Is everything all right?'

'I broke up with Paul,' Jenny answered, then quickly added, 'My decision, so I've no right to whinge, but I guess it's made me feel a bit down.'

'Why did you break up? Do you want to tell me?'

This was the part Jenny couldn't confide. How could she admit to the shameful way she'd used one man's body while she mentally made love to another?

Jenny hadn't realised she'd been doing it until a month before. She'd known that Alex was often in her mind when she and Paul made love but she'd presumed that she loved Paul nevertheless.

Then, when Alex's manner towards her changed so drastically, when the sexual chemistry between them disappeared, she gradually realised that she hadn't been making love to Paul at all. And one night she was shocked to discover that Paul actually repulsed her. He repulsed her because he wasn't Alex. Jenny felt ashamed.

She couldn't tell that to Maddy. She couldn't tell that to anyone. 'It's nothing really, Mum. We just broke up, that's all.' Then she added with self-loathing, 'Personally I think I'm a bit of a shit and that he's too good for me.'

It was obvious Jenny didn't want to talk about it and that she was feeling guilty so Maddy didn't say anything for a few minutes. Then they arrived at the car which put a further stop to the conversation until they'd loaded the luggage and driven out of the carpark.

'Well, do you know what I think?' Maddy asked finally. She didn't wait for an answer. 'I think you're a very lucky girl who has no right to feel sorry for herself.'

Jenny looked at her, a little surprised.

'At the risk of sounding tough,' Maddy continued, 'you don't have time to be sorry for Paul. He's a twenty-six year old man—he'll get over you. And you have the biggest night of your life ahead of you, a night that every young actor dreams of! You don't have time to be indulgent.'

It was the right advice and Jenny knew it. And she knew her mother meant exactly what she said. Maddy hadn't achieved her success without developing the ability to do battle and she expected the same of her daughter.

'You're wrong, Mum, he's a twenty-seven year old man. And you're right, I *am* being indulgent and I don't have time to worry about him. And I'm so glad you're back in time for the opening.' Jenny felt better already. Roll on tomorrow night, she thought, with growing excitement.

The final dress rehearsal that evening was a bit of a shambles. Mainly because of Alex. He kept fluffing his words and forgetting his lines and he was irritable when the stage manager tried to prompt him. 'I know, I know, don't tell me,' he snapped.

Towards the end of the play Alex became completely lost. 'No, no, it doesn't go like that!' he yelled when the stage manager once more gave him a line.

'That'll do, we'll leave it for now,' Naomi called. There was only Alex's final speech to go. She couldn't get any more out of him and she knew it. 'Fifteen minutes to change then meet in the stalls for notes please.'

Naomi refused to let herself worry. Alex had never forgotten his summation speech before. He was just suffering typical pre-opening nerves. It would have been far more of a worry, she thought, if the end of the play had technical problems. The effect of the symbolic imagery was crucial to the final impact.

As Edwin addressed the audience, lights came up on a silk screen upstage and Katerina's silhouette appeared behind it, larger than life. She slowly disrobed during the speech and, when he joined her at the end, she was prepared for her death. Then Edwin stepped behind the screen and everything went to black except for the one spotlight behind the two giant silhouettes. Katerina, naked, with her head flung back and her arms outstretched, accepted him into her embrace, and as she did a scream of agony-ecstasy rang out. Blackout!

The staging, the lighting, the sound effects— all were crucial. But they had worked like clockwork in each of the previous dress rehearsals so Naomi was prepared to leave them for tonight. Anything to keep Alex happy; there was no point in pushing him further.

She gave only fifteen minutes of notes, mainly relating to technical aspects of the production, after which she said encouragingly, 'You know what they say: "bad dress rehearsal, good show". After tonight's effort, I'd say that means we have a smash hit.'

She smiled as she said it and everyone laughed, grateful for the banter. But they were all aware that Alex hadn't laughed. He hadn't even appeared to hear the comment. He was away in another world somewhere. Hell, I hope he comes back in time for the opening night, Julian thought. He'd never seen Alex so preoccupied.

He said as much when he cornered him at the stage door. 'Are you all right?' Julian asked. 'There's nothing wrong, is there?'

He was relieved to be met with one of Alex's most charming smiles. 'I'm sorry about tonight, Julian, I really am. My mind wasn't on the job.' He put his arm around Julian's shoulder and gave him a comradely squeeze. 'Don't you worry, though. Naomi's quite right: bad dress, good show. I'll be in top form tomorrow, I promise.'

'Of course you will.' Julian smiled back gratefully. 'You'll be dynamic.' And he left the theatre feeling positive and excited. The next night was going to be very important to a lot of people.

Alex arrived at the theatre over two hours before the half-hour call. He sat in his dressing room and looked at himself in the mirror for a long time. He heard Jenny arrive an hour later and he waited thirty minutes before going to her dressing room and tapping lightly on the door.

'Oh, Alex, I didn't know you were here already. Come in.' She was in a satin robe and her face was scrubbed clean ready to be made up. She looked very young.

'I thought I'd wish you good luck.' He smiled and closed the door behind him.

'Thanks,' Jenny said gratefully. 'You too. Chookas, as Mum would say.'

He stepped up to her, very close, and put his

hands on her shoulders. The satin was cool to touch and he could feel the heat of her body beneath the fabric.

'You're very good in this role,' he murmured.

His eyes were locked into hers and Jenny's heart was pounding wildly.

'We've drifted apart a little during rehearsals,' he said. 'My fault. I needed to distance myself for the part, you understand?'

Jenny nodded. She scarcely dared to breathe.

'But I want you to know,' he continued tenderly, 'that I care about you.' His eyes travelled to her mouth as he drew her close to him. 'I care about you very, very much, Imogen.' And he kissed her fully, sensually, his hands exploring the satin of her back.

As he walked back to his dressing room, Alex wiped his mouth with the back of his hand. He could still taste the fresh warmth of her lips and tongue. It wasn't right, he knew that. She was his daughter. He hadn't wanted to kiss her, but it had been necessary. He'd been fully aware that he'd distanced her sexually. But he'd also been aware that he could get her back at any time and in a matter of seconds. He needed the full sensuality of her performance tonight.

In his dressing room Alex sat down and slowly started applying his make-up. Jenny ceased to exist as he watched Edwin gradually materialise in the mirror before him.

Naomi had forbidden Julian and Alain to go backstage before or during the performance. She'd kept well away herself apart from a brief visit beforehand to wish the performers all the best and an even briefer visit at interval to say 'going great'.

Julian had readily agreed that it was poor form to hound the actors at such a crucial time but the two of them practically had to tie Alain down. Particularly at interval.

'I want to see Alex. It's going brilliantly. He's fucking fantastic! What's wrong with telling him that?' He wouldn't take no for an answer.

Finally the only way Julian could stop him was to warn him that the difficult part was yet to come and that Alex had stuffed up badly in the final dress rehearsal.

'Oh.' Alain's excitement was momentarily arrested. 'Well, he'd better not fuck up now. There's a lot of people watching this out in television land.'

The audience was as spellbound during Act Two as they had been during Act One. Alex had them eating out of his hand.

There was several seconds' blackout before the final scene. Alex and Jenny stood in the wings while the stagehands wheeled the giant silk screen on stage.

Jenny was still doing up the buttons of her blouse after her dash to the dressing room to don her body stocking and change of costume. She was flushed with excitement. She knew she'd been good. And Alex had been brilliant. They'd worked together as one. She was very aware of his presence beside her. She thought of their encounter in her dressing room. She remembered his mouth on hers and she longed for him to touch her again.

'There's something I want you to know, Jenny,' Alex whispered.

She turned to him eagerly, expectantly, her shadowed face so young in the mild glow of the backstage working light.

'I'm your father,' Alex said.

There was a moment's confusion in Jenny's mind. Alex was getting his role mixed up with reality, she thought.

Then he continued. 'That production of *Cymbeline* your mother was in at drama school, remember? The production in which she played Imogen?'

Jenny looked back at him, unable to move.

His face was bland, expressionless. 'I played Cymbeline,' he said.

Edwin's spotlight came up and Alex walked out onstage leaving Jenny staring after him. She knew it was the truth.

She could hear Alex starting on the final speech but her mind was numb. Jenny was on automatic pilot as she walked into her position behind the screen.

EDWIN
She'll be here at any moment. And she's quite prepared. She knows what she must do and she will do it willingly. With love.

THE STAGE LIGHTS NARROW TO A SPOT WHICH REMAINS ON EDWIN. BACKLIGHTING COMES UP ON THE UPSTAGE CENTRE SCREEN TO REVEAL THE SILHOUETTE OF KATERINA. EDWIN SMILES HAPPILY AT THE AUDIENCE.

EDWIN
Here she is. Katie. My Katie.

Jenny remained oblivious of her actions and everything around her as she slowly, mechanically, undid the buttons of her blouse. Vaguely she heard the words of Edwin's final speech. *'Death is the ultimate gift a human being has to give,'* Alex was saying. But all Jenny could think was, 'He's my father! Alex Rainford is my father!'

Then she was jolted back to reality as she heard the words *'There's been a change of plan'*. What was Alex saying? That wasn't in the script. He must have dried and he was buying time.

Jenny automatically slowed down her disrobing as she waited for him to get back on track. She'd think about Alex later, she told herself, she must concentrate on the performance for now.

'You see, I wasn't really honest,' Alex was saying to the audience. 'There was a death I saw when I was just a boy, but it wasn't a man in the street.'

In the audience, Naomi and Julian sat bolt upright. 'What the hell's he doing?' Naomi whispered. But Julian didn't answer.

'It was my brother Tim,' Alex continued, 'and he died for me. The ultimate human gift.'

He really has gone insane, thought Julian, horrified, as he rose from his seat. 'I'm going backstage,' he hissed to Naomi. 'I'll tell them to bring the curtain down.'

Alex started to walk slowly towards the screen. In the prompt corner the stage director was hissing through his headphones to the lighting operator: 'Keep the spotlight on him. Christ only knows what he's up to, but keep the fucking spotlight on him.'

Jenny had finished disrobing and her naked silhouette was frozen: head back, arms outstretched. She didn't know what else to do.

'It was the most intimate experience I've ever shared with another human being,' Alex said.

'He's gone back to the beginning of the play,' the ASM whispered to the stage director as he stood by ready to bring down the curtain.

'I know and they're loving it. Don't do a thing,' the stage director hissed back.

Alex stopped upstage, beside the screen. He turned to face the audience, savouring the moment. He'd been pleased with his rewrite. He'd spent a lot of time constructing it as he'd stared into his dressing room mirror.

> There was a death I saw
> When I was just a boy,
> But it wasn't a man in the street.
> It was my brother Tim
> And he died for me.
> The ultimate human gift.

But what came after that? 'It was the most intimate experience I've ever shared . . .' Yes, he'd said that. What next?

Well, of course, he had to tell them, didn't he? Yes, that was it.

'Tonight I'm going to share that experience with another,' he said and he stepped behind the silk screen.

For a second, Alex's giant silhouette appeared on the screen as he grasped Jenny's wrist. Then they both stepped out onto the stage.

'I'd like you to meet her. This is my daughter, Katie.'

Exposed, and in her flesh-coloured body stocking, Jenny appeared to the audience as a naked, fragile sacrifice. She was terrified. Behind the screen she'd felt trapped and confused but her main worry had been how they were going to finish the play without the audience knowing that the leading actor had gone off his trolley. Now, as she looked into Alex's eyes, she knew she was looking into the demented eyes of a madman.

'Don't worry, Katie.' Alex gestured to the audience. 'They're our friends. They're going to share our ultimate gift. Come along, let's sit and talk.' His grasp on her wrist was vicelike and Jenny was forced to follow him to the bed downstage near the prompt corner.

In the audience, Maddy had been watching, a little bewildered. She'd read the play only the once but surely this wasn't the original end? Very effective nevertheless, she thought. They must have changed it during rehearsal.

But when Alex pulled Jenny out from behind the screen, Maddy knew in an instant that the girl was terrified. Something was definitely wrong. She left the auditorium as quickly as she could, hurrying through the foyer and out into the street towards the stage door in the back lane.

Alain wasn't at all confused. He had never fully read the script, he hadn't felt it necessary. And, even though he'd seen an early dress rehearsal, he wasn't really aware of the change of text. Bloody magnificent, he was thinking. He was a little surprised, though, when Alex sat the girl on the bed and pulled a gun out from beneath his jacket. Alain certainly hadn't remembered a gun in the dress rehearsal. It was a good touch, though.

Alex was furious that he'd been forced to take out the gun earlier than he'd intended. The whole sequence, including the revelation of the gun, was supposed to be performed as a ritual, not a stick-em-up farce. He was angry, very very angry and his head was starting to hurt. He knew he had to make himself calm down. He must do things properly.

It was Julian who had forced the gun. Alex had seen him arrive in the wings as he led Jenny to the bed. His immediate concern was that Julian might be a little offended by his rewriting of the play. No, he told himself, as soon as Julian sees what happens at the end he'll know that I'm right.

But Julian didn't stand and watch. He crossed behind the set to reappear beside the stage manager in the prompt corner and Alex was horrified to see him issue an order for the curtain to be brought down.

That was when he pulled out the gun. 'Bring that curtain down and you're dead,' he hissed at the stage manager. His head started to ache as soon as he said it. It was wrong. It wasn't meant to go like that.

Julian was standing in the wings only a metre or so away and Alex appealed to him. 'Don't spoil it, Julian,' he whispered. 'The play hasn't finished yet. Wait for the end.'

Julian was frozen, staring in horror at the gun. Suddenly he looked across the stage to the opposite side of the wings. Alex followed his eyeline and saw that Maddy had arrived and was standing there, also staring at the gun.

Alex started to relax. Good. They were all here. All the special people. His gift would be for them too.

For the first time, the audience started to get a little restless and Alain began to curse the actors up on stage. Don't fuck up now, you wankers, he silently urged. Get on with it!

Naomi had left to find out why the hell Julian hadn't brought the curtain down.

Alex was the only one who knew what was going on. The ache in his head had gone as swiftly as it had arrived.

He could see them all. The audience. The television cameras which signalled all those people in their cosy homes. And of course, watching silently in the wings, the stage management crew, the director, and, on either side of him, Julian and Maddy.

Julian, who loved him and knew him so well. Julian, who had written his life for him.

And Maddy. How had he ever forgotten Maddy? She was so beautiful. And she'd given him the most precious possession in the world. She'd given him his daughter. His Katie. His own flesh and blood. Just as Tim had been. Only closer, closer than Tim. Katie was part of him.

He looked down at her beside him. She was staring back, trembling, not daring to move.

'Yes, we must treasure this moment, Katie,' he said, and he was concerned when her eyes flickered with fear. 'Oh no, no, you mustn't be frightened.'

He stroked her hair with the hand that held the gun. The cold metal of the muzzle caressed her temple. Jenny whimpered with terror.

'Yes, soon, my darling, soon,' Alex promised soothingly.

The image of Tim flashed through his mind. Tim's body. A river of red seeping towards the door.

482

Then Jonathan Thomas. Jonathan lying in a crimson bath. Yes. Blood. There would be lots of blood. They'd like that. Alex slowly rose from the bed and crossed to centre stage.

Although she was released from his grip, Jenny couldn't move. She watched Alex, mesmerised, like a rabbit in a spotlight.

Julian had also remained as still as possible, aware that any movement of his could push Alex over the edge. Now that Jenny was freed, though, should he risk trying to reason with him, or even try to wrestle the gun from him? Julian didn't know what to do.

'I share with you all the ultimate gift,' Alex said to the audience. And he smiled, first at Maddy, then Julian, then at Jenny.

'Watch, Katie. Watch closely,' he commanded as he turned to Jenny and raised the gun. She stared down the barrel, unable to move. 'This gift is for you, Katie, my darling daughter.'

Then Alex shot himself. Through the temple. Just as he'd planned.

After several seconds of horrified silence, the entire audience rose to its feet. The theatre resounded with cries of 'Bravo!' 'Author! author!'

EPILOGUE

The Network Five News Department picked up the scoop of the year. Footage of Alex Rainford's death went to air at eleven o'clock and the viewers of *Centre Stage* who hadn't switched channels or gone to bed discovered that the cries of 'Bravo!' and 'Author! Author!' were shortlived.

For several minutes after it had happened, the opening night audience had no idea that Alex had shot himself. With the exception of the horrified onlookers in the wings, everyone was stirred and impressed by the powerful finale of the play.

A theatre critic in row B thought the special effects employed when the leading character suicided were unnecessarily graphic for a play that had been so cleverly symbolic throughout, but those further back in the audience didn't see anything specific. They heard the report of the gun, saw the actor slump to the stage and, as he lay twitching, they rose to their feet applauding and cheering.

Some members of the audience seated near the prompt side exit heard a cameraman say 'Oh, sweet Jesus!' very loudly. Then they watched, annoyed, as he muttered frantically into his headset.

In the live transmission van set up outside the stage door, the director punched the network button. 'Go to commercial break,' he ordered. 'There's a cock-up here. Roll the credits over that last wide shot. And tell the news department to stand by.' Then he sent the command through to the cameramen. 'Keep rolling. And get in close.'

He stared at the monitor screens with their close-ups of Alex. 'Christ,' he said. The eyes were open, the smile was triumphant and a river of red channelled its way across the stage. Seconds later the curtain came down and Alex's image was blocked from the cameras.

The director pressed a button and barked an order to the cameraman backstage operating the hand-held. 'Over to you, Ned. Get in close.'

The door to the van was flung open and Alain stood there. 'What the hell's going on?' he demanded. 'The wimp on camera three said you'd punched back to the station. We want to cover the audience! We've got a standing ovation here!'

'We've got something a damn sight bigger than a standing ovation,' the director answered. 'Look at this.'

'Holy shit!' After the initial shock, Alain's reaction was one of anger. You bastard, he thought. You bastard, Rainford. You've stuffed up a hit

production. Advance bookings all but sold out . . .
UK rights bought up . . . Then it occurred to him
that a television special culminating in the actual
death, on screen, of the leading actor, would be
worth a fortune.

And the rights belong to me, thought Alain.
Well, to me and Julian. The production deal had
always been a three-way split. Alex, Julian and
Alain. So with Alex gone, that left two.

'Get on to the news department,' he said to
the director.

'I already have.'

It'll cost them a fortune, Alain thought smugly.
And he made sure it did.

Lurking in his mind was one other strange
reaction. Alain felt caught out, embarrassed. How
could he ever have thought that Alex and he
were alike? Alex Rainford was a loser. Alain hoped
he hadn't boasted to too many people about the
affinity he'd felt with Alex. It could be very
embarrassing.

As it turned out, apart from the news bulletins,
Alain didn't make a fortune from the rest of the
deal. Julian made sure of that. He refused to allow
the rights to a special called 'Death of an Actor'
which Alain wanted to make from the televised
production of *Centre Stage* and, when the case ended
up in court, Julian won.

After the court case, Julian decided to give up
writing for a year or two. 'Directing's so much
easier,' he said to Maddy. But they both knew it
would be quite a while before Julian would once
more put pen to paper.

Together they did everything they could to help

Jenny through the aftereffects of that ghastly night.

It took a while but, six months later, Jenny was acting again. She accepted a role in a production at the Sydney Opera House. The production was to be directed by Julian Oldfellow.

'So what if we are being nepotistic?' Julian said to Maddy. 'She's one of the best there is and if she'd auditioned for the part I'd have given it to her anyway.'

They agreed that it was the perfect role to get Jenny started again. Not too demanding, but showy enough to gain attention and pick up good reviews.

Jenny seemed content in Sydney so Maddy decided that was where they would stay. She found them a very attractive flat with fewer stairs than any flat she'd ever had and then she accepted the lead in an ABC miniseries.

Douglas was always at the back of her mind, though, and sometimes she wondered whether she should go back to London. No, she thought. Jenny needs me. He'll just have to come and find me.

She remembered with horror Jenny's catatonic state after the shooting. Then the lethargy that followed and the long weeks she and Julian spent trying to break through to the girl.

When Maddy tried to explain why she'd never told her about her father, Jenny just answered with a lacklustre shrug. 'Well, why would you want to tell me about him? He was mad.'

'But I didn't know that,' Maddy insisted. 'Julian knew. He told me several times over the past couple of years but I didn't really believe him. I suppose I put it down to his playwright's sense of drama.'

She tried to explain the tremendous power Alex

had always had over people. 'Once someone gained his interest, he wasn't content until he'd become the focal point of their lives.' And she thought of Harold, Julian, herself—Alex had exercised his power over all of them. She wondered how many more there were.

'I worried that he'd exercise that power over you too, Jen,' she said.

Gradually, Maddy broke through. After several weeks, the walls Jenny had built around herself slowly began to crumble.

The pressure of her guilt had been unbearable. Alex lived in her mind. She couldn't forget the initial electricity between the two of them, her fantasies about him as she made love to Paul and, most vivid of all, the kiss in her dressing room on opening night. Alex could have had her on the floor then and there. He could have had her at any time. Her own father!

One night she told her mother the truth. Maddy's relief at the breakthrough was tempered by the hideous prospect that Alex may have seduced his own daughter.

'He didn't, did he?' she asked. 'He didn't . . .'

'No.' Jenny shook her head. Unshed tears started to burn her eyes. 'But I wanted him to. I wanted him to, Mum.' Then she burst out sobbing, loud, healthy sobs, and Maddy wrapped her arms around her and held her close.

'I've been feeling so guilty!' she sobbed. 'I thought it was me! I thought—'

'Sssh, it's all right.' Maddy rocked her like a baby. 'It wasn't you. You were reacting to him exactly the way he wanted you to react.'

It was only then that Maddy started to breathe

freely. It would take time she knew, but they were finally on the road to recovery.

Late one Saturday afternoon Maddy was wandering along the Opera House forecourt, enjoying the Harbour view. She'd been to a matinee of Jenny's play and they'd had a coffee together in the greenroom afterwards. It was the fourth time Maddy had seen the show but she enjoyed playing proud mother. She felt a little intrusive, though, when the younger members of the cast decided to eat in the canteen before the evening show.

'No, no thanks, I'm really not hungry,' she said in reply to their invitation to join them. She was. She was starving.

I'll go home and cook a couple of chops, she told herself. 'I'd better get home and study some lines,' she said to Jenny as she kissed her goodbye. She smiled as she watched the young actors walk off to the canteen, talking nineteen to the dozen about the show, Jenny the loudest of them all.

Maddy went outside, leaned against the railings and looked at the harbour and the ferries and the early evening yachts for a full ten minutes. This play was the best possible form of therapy for Jenny, she thought. There were still the nightmares—there probably always would be—but Jenny had recovered. She was even talking about moving into a flat with one of the other girls in the cast. Maddy would miss her dreadfully, but it was a healthy sign and she was pleased. As she watched the yachts sail under the Harbour Bridge, she wondered idly whether she should get a smaller flat when Jenny moved out or whether she should go back to London.

Maddy gave a shiver—it was getting chilly. As she turned to go, she became aware of a man standing close by, staring at her, and she suddenly had the feeling that he'd been there for quite a while.

Without glancing in his direction, she walked briskly towards Circular Quay. Dusk was gathering and her car was parked in one of the dark alleys there. She hoped he wouldn't follow her.

He did. She quickened her pace. He quickened his. Damn. She'd better tell him to piss off while she was still in the relatively crowded, brightly lit Opera House walkway.

She stopped and turned. And then she just stared.

'I was wondering how long it'd take,' he said.

'Douglas!'

They kissed for a very long time, oblivious to the stares of the passers-by.

'Your place or mine?' he asked when they finally drew breath. Maddy laughed. 'I suppose you're staying in some nameless, faceless middle-of-the-road hotel . . .'

He nodded.

'My place,' she said.

As they walked along the embankment towards the Quay, Douglas put his hand into his breast pocket. 'I have a present for you.' He guided her to the nearest light by the embankment railing. 'And I want to give it to you now. No waiting.'

Maddy was surprised when he drew out an envelope. 'Oh,' she said, 'I thought it was going to be a ring.'

He gestured dismissively. 'No, no, plenty of time for that. This is far more important. Open it.'

Maddy did. And she stared at the contents in disbelief.

'My army discharge papers. I figured if you wouldn't come to me I'd have to come to you.'

Maddy felt a little frightened. 'Is this what you really want?'

'Bit late now, isn't it?' he said jokingly.

'But if it isn't—'

'It's what I want, Madeleine,' he interrupted. 'It's what I really want!' And he kissed her.

'Sydney or London?' he asked as they started walking to the car. 'Where do you want to live?'

'Wherever you want—I don't care.' Maddy knew she was grinning like an idiot but she couldn't stop.

'Let's try Sydney. I've never lived here before.'

'Fine,' she said happily, taking his arm.

'You'll probably get sick of me when I'm around all the time,' he warned. 'There'll be no mystery left.'

Maddy shook her head firmly. 'Oh no I won't.'

'Actually I will have to go away for the odd short trip, so you'll have a rest from me now and then.'

Maddy looked at him sharply.

'Don't worry,' he added reassuringly. 'Pure retirement stuff. A bit of private consultancy work here and there. Is this yours?'

They had arrived at Maddy's car and she fumbled in her handbag.

Douglas automatically held his hand out for the keys. 'Where are we headed?'

'Elizabeth Bay.'

He looked at her blankly as he opened the passenger door.

'That way.' She pointed to the right. 'I'll direct

you,' she said, as she climbed in thinking, 'The same Douglas, bossy as ever'.

Douglas closed the door after her and crossed to the driver's side. He paused for a second, looked at the nondescript cream Holden pulled up in the main street beside the laneway with its engine running, and rubbed the right side of his nose with his right index finger.

Then he got into the car and they drove off. The cream Holden followed.

Judy Nunn
The Glitter Game

THE GLITTER OF MONEY . . .
THE GLITTER OF POWER . . .
THE GLITTER OF STARDOM . . .

TELEVISION . . . THE SEDUCTIVE WORLD
WHERE EVERYONE PLAYS
THE GLITTER GAME.

The greatest smash-hit series ever created. The hottest female star in a cutthroat world where careers are made or destroyed with a word in the right ear . . . or a night in the right bed.

Only the ruthless make it to the top. And they will stop at nothing to stay there. Not even murder.

'Home and Away' star Judy Nunn's first adult novel is a delicious exposé of the high-voltage world of television, a scandalous behind-the-scenes look at *The Glitter Game* and what goes on when the cameras stop rolling.

'. . . a steamy novel that strips bare the sexy secrets of the soap business.'
People, UK

Jennifer Bacia
Shadows of Power

From the doorway the girl stared boldly at the man
who sat naked on the blue silk cover of the bed.
She could handle this one. She knew his tastes
were . . . exotic, but she wasn't afraid. And she had
been assured that her co-operation would
be amply rewarded.

Prostitution . . . organised crime . . . media
corruption . . . *Shadows of Power* is a compelling tale of
one woman's driving ambition and all-consuming
passion.

Sexually abused by her father and raised by her Irish
landlady—later discovered to be the owner of Sydney's
most notorious brothel—Lenore Hamlyn is determined
to escape her sordid past.

Defiant and determined, she emerges from her working-
class background to become the charismatic and
calculating Anthea James—Australia's most powerful
and highly-paid media personality.

Driven by her dream of achieving freedom for all
women, Anthea James has her sights set on gaining the
ultimate in political power.

But out of Anthea's past emerges the only man she has
ever loved, who now has the power to destroy her . . .

Jennifer Bacia
Angel of Honour

IN A WORLD OF PASSION, POWER AND REVENGE,
THE PRICE OF FREEDOM IS SOMETIMES THE
ULTIMATE SACRIFICE . . .

Her mother was a legendary screen goddess.
Her father was the President.

Wild, beautiful, passionate, she rebels against her
convent upbringing to pursue secret desires and
forbidden pleasures.

Rejecting the land of her birth for fame and fortune in
Europe, she loses herself in the decadent high society of
Paris and London . . . until a single, shattering event
changes her life for ever.

Her name is Noella de Bartez.

Angel of Honour is her story—the electrifying tale of her
rise to power, of the men who loved her, and the one
who betrayed her . . .

Jennifer Bacia
Whisper from the Gods

WAS THE PRESIDENT
OF THE UNITED STATES A MURDERER?

When Elizabeth Eden, screen goddess and sex symbol, is found dead at thirty-three, the official verdict is suicide.

Just a few short weeks later, President Tom Madigan, charismatic leader of America's golden age, is killed by an assassin's bullet.

Now, more than twenty years later, Robert Madigan, the President's only son, is making his bid for the White House. Victory seems assured . . . until the announcement that a blockbuster movie is to be made about the life—and death—of Elizabeth Eden.

Tess Jordan, one of the most powerful women in Hollywood, has fought her way to the top from the dangerous streets of New York. She is determined to tell the true story of Elizabeth Eden's corruption by the studio system. But other people are just as determined to stop the movie from being made.

As Tess probes deeper into the nest of lies and deception, she discovers that someone is prepared to kill—and kill again—to ensure that the explosive secrets of the past remain buried forever.

Di Morrissey
Heart of the Dreaming

At twenty-one Queenie Hanlon has the world at her feet.

Startlingly beautiful, wealthy and intelligent, she is the only daughter of Tingulla Station, the famed outback property in the wilds of western Queensland . . . and the lover of handsome bushman, TR Hamilton.

At twenty-two her life lies in ruins. A series of disasters has robbed her of everything she has ever loved. Everything except Tingulla—her ancestral home and her spirit's Dreaming place.

Now she's about to lose that too . . .

A sweeping saga of thwarted love and heroic struggle, of a brother's treachery and one man's enduring passion, *Heart of the Dreaming* is the exciting and triumphant story of one woman's remarkable courage and her determination to take on the world and win.